A DRAGON AT THE GATE

BOOK THREE OF THE NEW AENEID CYCLE

MICHAEL G. MUNZ

RED MUSE PRESS

Red Muse Press
Seattle, WA 2016

Cover Design by Amalia Chitulescu

*This is a work of fiction. Names, characters, places, brands, media,
and incidents are either the product of the author's imagination or
are used fictitiously. Any resemblance to similarly named places or
to persons living or deceased is unintentional.*

Print ISBN: 978-0-9977622-0-4

Library of Congress Control Number: 2016947280

ACKNOWLEDGEMENTS

To mention everyone who played some part in *A Dragon at the Gate*'s lengthy gestation process would take far too long. That said, I must recognize the following: my beta-readers Brian, Cain, Gareth, Joe, Sher, and Tom; my Twitter followers near and wide, who are always there to provide excellent moral support (or at least terrible jokes); the whole gang at the Super Awesome Geek Show, especially the always-enthusiastic Christina and John; David Taylor once again, who let me steal his name this time; all of my fellow former-Booktropians, thank you for your knowledge, camaraderie, support, and cider-bacon.

As always, thank you to the fans who've been waiting so patiently to find out how it all ends.

Lastly, this being the third book, I must mention my great, great, great(?) uncle Michael Flynn who, as I understand, had the claim to fame of being onboard the U.S.S. Maine when it exploded in 1898. He had a great name, which I obviously could not resist borrowing.

For my supportive and awesome sister Julie.

I

"THOSE ARE SIRENS."

"Aye," Caitlin said. "Ambulance, I'd wager. Horizon is right across from a hospital, ducks."

Felix shook his head. "Wrong kind of sirens. And my memory's not so bad that I don't know where Horizon is. I also remember that it's on the fifth through tenth floors of the Aria Building and that I once dropped my cheeseburger riding the elevator."

Michael searched the taxi's passenger side mirror for the source of the sirens. "Why were you eating a cheeseburger in an elevator?"

"Why wasn't there bacon on it? That's a better question."

Michael grinned despite their problems. His memory troubles aside, Felix was, at least, still Felix. Only a few days had passed since the experience on the Moon that linked Felix's memory implant to Gideon's memory. Though the procedure appeared to have saved Gideon, after a period of unconsciousness Felix had woken completely unable to remember the previous two hours, and with holes in his recollection of the time before that.

The sirens, whatever their source, were growing nearer.

"How often do you get that implant checked?" Michael asked.

"Every few months," Felix said, "unless there's a problem like this."

"He had his last one perhaps a week and a half ago," Caitlin added.

"No I didn't, I—" Felix stopped. "Oh."

In the back seat, beside Felix, Caitlin sighed. "Bollocks, I wish we'd been able to find Ondrea."

Michael nodded. They'd hoped to find Gideon's sister on Sunrise Station upon their return to Earth orbit, but Ondrea had vanished. "She probably bugged out with the rest of the Marquand group."

"Horizon's better anyway," said Felix. "They did the work originally. Ondrea just used the data."

"To bring Gideon back from the dead," Caitlin added.

"You don't have to keep checking what I remember, Caitlin."

"Aye, Felix, I do."

Michael nodded. "And if she didn't, I would."

It wasn't like Michael could do anything else. He wasn't a scientist. The sum of Gideon's memories made Gideon the man he was. If Felix's implant failed and somehow took Felix's own memories with it, what would happen to the friend that Michael knew?

"We're nearly there," Felix said. "They'll fix this, don't worry."

No one spoke. Michael wondered if Caitlin sensed the same lack of conviction in her boyfriend's voice that he did.

Moments later, the taxi pulled up to the curb in front of the Aria Building. Thirty stories of blue steel and glass towered above a dais of concrete, landscaped with shrubs and sapling maples whose wilt spoke of better days. Sure enough, Northgate's Corporate Mercy Hospital sat across the street in the Aria's shadow.

They were out of the taxi in moments. "Go," Michael told Caitlin and Felix as he stopped to pay the driver. "I'll catch up."

The two nodded and then trotted up the sidewalk that stretched along the landscaped section, toward the stairs that led up to the building's entrance. It was the same direction from which the sirens were approaching.

They did sound different from ambulance sirens.

Michael finished paying the driver, turned to follow his friends, and then realized the reason for the difference. A silver convertible tore around the street corner ahead. Tires screeched and metal slammed into metal as two other cars swerved out of its way, only to collide with each other instead. Gunfire exploded from an assault rifle braced on the convertible's driver's side door. Bullets shattered windows and pedestrians alike. In the convertible's wake followed the flashing blue and violet lights of two red and black CPMC response cruisers.

With CPMC involved, the convertible's driver had likely gone full-bore CP: an explosion of irrational, psychopathic violence, borne of cybernetic overload that would not stop until he burned himself out or CPMC put him down.

Cybernetic Psychoses Monitoring and Control: that was their job. Michael had witnessed a CPMC response team's ruthless efficiency once before. They would stop the driver, yes, but would it be fast enough? Michael yelled a warning to Caitlin and Felix and dashed toward them into danger.

Caitlin dragged Felix into the cover of the landscaped section just off the sidewalk. The two hunkered down with a few others against the concrete wall between them and the steps of the Aria Building. Michael's shoes pounded the pavement as he closed the distance. A handful of the corporate freelancers guarding the building—contracted Aegis Security, by their uniforms—had already dashed out of its front doors to take up positions atop the stairs.

The convertible plunged down the street, only moments away. The driver fired another burst from the rifle into an oncoming car and then swerved left to avoid another. Tires squealed and people scattered as the convertible launched up the Aria Building's front steps. It got halfway to the doors before screeching to a metal-mangling stop against the steel railing that ran up the center. An airbag burst into the driver's face, and augmented arms ripped it to shreds a moment later. The driver's eyes blazed. Curses erupted from his lungs.

Michael reached his friends and hunkered down beside them.

"I remember what those sirens are for now!" Felix shouted.

"Just stay down!"

"No kidding!"

Michael risked a look over the edge of the wall. The CPMC cruisers rushed to a stop on the curb below the stairs. Two officers in black and red armor scrambled out and dropped into defensive positions behind each cruiser. The convertible driver screamed again and fired toward them in a spasm of bullets that either punched into the cruisers or went wide. Screams of passersby rained through it all.

Michael felt a hand on his shoulder—Caitlin or Felix, he couldn't be sure and didn't spare time to look. His eyes were drawn to a man lying on the steps about ten feet from the convertible, directly between the car and Michael's position. The man had thrown his arms around his head. His entire body quaked. Michael waved at him in an effort to coax him to cover without attracting the driver's attention, but the man's eyes remained clenched.

The driver bellowed again and kicked the car door open. Already damaged in the crash, it flung outward, now more than half torn off of its hinges. The driver hunkered down further and sprayed another burst from his rifle over the dashboard. Michael couldn't tell if he hit anyone.

Behind their cruisers, the CPMC fired back. Bullets impacted the convertible's engine block; it was suppressive fire only, buying time for two of the officers to ready the specialized weapons that CPMC squads carried to end such confrontations.

The man on the steps began to shriek. Arms still over his head, eyes still clenched, he tried to scramble away from the convertible, hindered by his own panic. Michael drew the FN Panther 9mm auto-pistol he carried aimed at the raging cyborg driver. The Panther wasn't likely powerful enough to do more than piss him off, but they'd arrived straight from the airport; it was the only weapon Michael had. The Aegis freelancers merely waited atop the stairs— guarding the building's entrance only—and Michael had to do something.

He fired.

The man on the steps hollered and stopped his feeble scramble, quaking further and trying to see through clenched eyelids from where the gunfire had come.

Michael's shots had no other effect. He might have hit the cyborg's arm, or maybe the body armor that wrapped his torso. He couldn't tell. Using just the Panther, only a headshot might stop the cyborg, and Michael didn't have a clear shot. Blood pounded in his ears. He forced himself to stay down.

"It's okay!" he yelled to the man. "It'll be okay!"

One CPMC officer hefted on his shoulder what Michael could only describe as a cannon and took aim at the convertible. Beside

Michael, Felix risked a look.

"EMP!" Felix whispered. "Geez, I hope that guy can aim!"

"Felix, get down!" Caitlin grabbed him and pulled him back.

Two things happened at once: the officer fired and the driver sprang out of the car, rifle in hand, firing back. The cannon's projectile hit the driver's seat and flared in a tiny burst of electricity: an EMP blast to knock out the man's cyberware.

Michael winced. If the EMP hit Felix, what would happen to his memory implant? But it was a short-range burst, not even enough to affect the cyborg once he'd escaped the car.

The driver's rifle clicked empty. He came to a stop directly between the panicked man on the steps and the CPMC officers who now held their fire. The entire scene seemed to freeze.

But only for a moment.

Two of the officers sprang from cover, wielding stun rods. The cyborg hurled his empty rifle at one of them. It smacked into the officer's helmet and knocked him to the ground as the cyborg tore the car door from what remained of its hinges, yelling with pain from the effort. The second officer dashed up the steps, nearly within reach, but not fast enough. The cyborg flung the door into his chest, and the officer tumbled back down the steps in a heap.

Then the cyborg whirled with a scream, as if something were trying to crawl its way out of him. He beat himself in the head once, before noticing the man on the steps. The cyborg pointed at the man and bellowed, "You can't stop them! You can't ever stop them all!"

The man froze, his eyes wide. He reached one hand behind him, clawing at the step, as if it alone could drag the rest of him away to safety. He was thin, in his forties, and seemed half the cyborg's size. He wore coveralls, perhaps a painter or a plumber on a break from a job in the building. He should have been safe in the Corporate District, instead of facing the raging terror that stared him down.

Atop the steps, the Aegis freelancers held position.

The cyborg was too close to the other man for Michael to get a clean shot. Michael's legs tensed. At once the cyborg rushed the cowering man to haul him off the steps in a single, screaming motion.

With a shout to Felix and Caitlin of "Stay here!" Michael clambered over the wall and into the open. The cyborg shoved the man into the steps' mangled railing. He was drawing him back for another blow when Michael grabbed the cyborg's arms and yanked for all he was worth to stop him.

The cyborg slammed his forehead into Michael's. His vision swam from the impact. For a split second Michael met the gaze of the cyborg's other victim, as the man freed himself and scrambled back.

A split second was all Michael's opponent gave him. Something huge slammed against Michael's back before he realized he'd been shoved against the side of the convertible. The cyborg held him by the shoulders. Bloodshot eyes blazed. Screams soaked in alcohol flared into Michael's face. He rammed Michael back against the car again and again.

Michael grappled with the cyborg's arms, trying to get a grip, trying to pull himself free, and failing every time to beat the other's strength. Lights danced in his vision each time his skull battered into the car. *Stop! Stop!*

Lights danced again, brighter. The cyborg stopped with a ragged gasp. Again the lights flared. Jolts tingled across Michael's skin and muscles. The cyborg released him. They both dropped to the steps.

EMP!

They'd hit his attacker with another blast, on-target this time. Michael struggled to catch his breath as the other's leg twitched and arms lay powerless. Three CPMC officers dashed in to ram stun rods against the cyborg's back to further subdue him. Michael crawled away as best he could, trying to get out of their way and still reeling from his bludgeoning against the car.

Sirens continued, now from the ambulances that issued from the hospital across the street. The man Michael had rescued half-sat, half-lay at the edge of the steps, breathing hard. Michael pulled himself to his feet and made his way over.

"You okay?" he asked.

The man's jaw was clenched. Both arms were locked across his chest. He stretched one of them out to wave Michael off, but he nodded to the question nonetheless. Michael turned to call for some help, but people lay shot or otherwise injured all along the maniac's path. First responders would have their hands full with more serious cases already. He turned back to the man. He could help him across the street to the hospital himself, but for the moment the man didn't appear ready to go anywhere.

The CPMC officers had already detached the cyborg's arms and were working at removing his leg. Even having seen the process once before, the speed at which they completed the task amazed Michael. The cyborg himself was unconscious. He hadn't seen how they'd managed it. Three of the officers appeared okay. The fourth, hit by the car door, remained where he'd fallen but was moving a little.

At least he was alive.

Michael turned back to the man on the steps, unsure of what, if anything, to say. Instead, he said nothing and sat a few feet away. It didn't feel right to just abandon the man before help arrived.

Caitlin and Felix were already on their way up the steps. Michael greeted them with a wave.

"Are you alright?" Caitlin asked.

"Bruised, a bit stunned," he said with a glance at the man beside him. "I'll make it."

"Glad to hear it." Felix sighed. "This is not what I'd call a fun day."

"Understatement, ducks." Caitlin swallowed and shook her head. She didn't seem to want to look down the steps behind her. "All those people."

"Yeah, understatement's a talent of mine." Felix motioned to Michael. "Caitlin said you took a bit of EMP. Everything all right with the . . . everything?"

The man to his left shivered.

"No cyberware," Michael said. "Guess I'll need a new phone, though. Felt . . . weird, but not like I expected."

"It's not the same as getting hit by lightning or anything, yeah," Felix said. "Different kind of jolt. Or so I hear. Never had the pleasure myself."

Michael nodded. "Better me than you." Felix's eyes and ears were both artificial. Even without the memory implant he had a lot to lose. There were ways to shield against EMP, but Michael didn't know how common they were. "Is your implant shielded at all?" He had also heard at some point about how EMP was less effective on a tiny, nano-molecular level, but he couldn't be sure if that even applied to Felix's situation.

"Supposed to be, but I'm not champing at the bit to test it."

"Speaking of which, you two better go on in without me. I'm going to wait out here for a bit." Michael glanced at the man to his left. "See if there's anything I can do. I'll catch up."

Caitlin smiled softly. "Get yourself checked out, too, if you can."

"I'm fine, just bruised a bit."

"You can't be too careful, Michael," she said. "You never know what's going on inside you after a bit of trauma."

"Yeah, Flynn." Felix pointed to Caitlin. "What she said. I'm a gentle soul, but I won't stop her from kicking your ass if you let something happen to you."

"I'm pretty far down on the triage list right now. And likewise, so," Michael pointed up toward Horizon's offices, "get up there."

Caitlin gave Felix's arm a tug and led him to the entrance.

Michael sighed and watched things unfold. Arriving units from the Corporate District security force—also run by Aegis—busied themselves with cordoning off the area. They admitted the ambulances that came from elsewhere to augment the medical staff that now dashed like ants between the hospital and the wounded on the sidewalk. CPMC loaded the man responsible into the back of one cruiser. He remained unconscious, with three of his limbs now out of sight.

The man beside Michael was watching CPMC, too. Michael decided to watch over him for a while, offer to see him to help again in a bit, and then maybe see about himself. How long would Felix be in Horizon? Would they be able to help at all?

Michael thought to call Marc and give him an update on Felix, realizing anew that his phone would be fried. Marc had wanted to come with them when they got back to Earth, but the European Space Administration likely still hunted for him. The Agents of Aeneas had decided to reroute Marc to an AoA facility, so as to send him back to the Moon as soon as possible. Now that the AoA controlled *Paragon*, Marc would be part of the team to plumb its secrets.

Michael reached into his pocket for the keycard to Marc's apartment, remembering his promise to send on some equipment Marc had asked for and check on "Holes," the artificial intelligence Marc had created. The keycard was still there, as was something else: a mysterious pen-sized object, which Diomedes had pushed into Michael's hands just before he died.

He took it out and showed it to the man beside him, thinking to engage him in conversational distraction. "See this? Someone gave it to me. No idea what it is."

The man glanced at it but gave no other response.

"My friend Felix likes mysteries," Michael went on. "More than I do, I guess. Whatever it is, it's probably fried now with the EMP, so I guess it doesn't matter anymore. It's a shame, but easy come, easy go, I guess." He offered it to the man. "Have a look? Any guesses?"

The man hesitated, but took the object. He peered at it, turned it over in his hands, and handed it back. "No idea. Sorry."

"It's okay. Someone's bound to know, right?" Michael stood, rubbing his left arm. It was beginning to tingle rather painfully. "Want to go across the street, get ourselves checked—"

Michael gasped. It was as if an invisible spear had punched through his chest. At once, he couldn't draw breath. Pain radiated down his left arm and up his neck. His knees buckled, he clutched at his heart, and the steps tumbled up to meet him.

I I

PLAY IT COOL, ADRIAN. Your poker face has gotten you through worse than this.

Adrian Fagles smiled at the screen through feigned bewilderment. "I don't know anything about that, Carl. Whoever it was, if they forged their authorization, it stands to reason they forged it well enough to lay a false trail. How good was their work?" He settled back against the leather of his living room couch and swirled the bourbon in the glass that dangled from his fingertips. "Does it point straight to me, or am I just one of many possible scapegoats?"

Carl frowned at him from the screen above the fireplace on Adrian's living room wall. "I'm not free to say."

Likely one of many, then. Adrian nodded and took a sip. "I certainly trust you'll get to the bottom of it. Unauthorized use of company espionage assets? Tsk. Such a thing puts all of us at RavenTech at risk. I will, of course, cooperate with your investigation in whatever way possible."

"Will you, now?"

Adrian chuckled. "You did say my help in the Ken Wallace inquiry proved, ah, how did you put it? Invaluable?"

"And you know what happened to him."

"Fortunately, Wallace had no next of kin to sadden with his loss. He was also a fool to try what he did—a trait I happily do not share. Follow those leads of yours. I'm confident they will exonerate me. I've heard Camela Thomson in R&D has been working on something lately. But that, of course, is mere rumor."

"We'll see. I'll be in touch."

Adrian raised his drink in farewell. The screen returned to a classic film from the turn of the century. He shut it off, set his bourbon on the end table, and leaned forward in thought.

Even though Carl's evidence didn't point to Adrian directly, that it led anywhere in his direction meant Adrian had miscalculated. Yes, he'd snuck a black-op through RavenTech's channels to get the late freelancer Diomedes to the site of the European Space Administration's lunar discovery. Yet that should have been devoid of anything that could lead back to Adrian. But that was just how the game went sometimes. One could never control the entire board. There were other moves left available to him. Other pieces to play.

It posed a problem, certainly. Yet it wasn't as if the risks yielded no reward. Far from it.

Adrian stood and made his way down the darkened hallway, toward his master bedroom, where a dirty sunset washed through the window of his tenth-floor condo. An ambulance floater sailed by; its lights flashed the room red for a heartbeat before it was gone. Northgate's night life had begun to wake. Two blocks away towered the Meridian, the windows of its luxury residences shielded from external viewers. His current condo wrapped him in its own measure of luxury, but a man needed goals, and the views atop the Meridian would grant him a grand new level of status.

Adrian pulled the data chip from his pocket and pressed his palm to the wall sensor. The door to his private den unlocked with a mechanical whir. He lingered on the threshold. A deep breath later, he entered, closed the door behind him, and approached his desk.

The window behind it gave a view similar to the one in his bedroom, but it was the monitor in front of it that held his attention. It lurked atop his desk, beneath the shroud of the precautionary towel he'd taken to throwing over it to cover its screen and camera.

A precaution, that's all it was.

Adrian sat, slid the towel away, and switched on the monitor. The text appeared immediately.

-HAS THE ONE KNOWN AS FAGLES COMPLETED SUFFICIENT PROCESSING CYCLES TO RETURN A NON-NULL RESPONSE TO PRIOR INQUIRIES?-

"An interesting question. Or an interesting way of phrasing it, at the least. Though I don't suppose you understand what I mean by that."

-PRELIMINARY CONTENT ANALYSIS OF YOUR STATEMENTS RETURNS ZERO USEFUL DATA.-

"Likewise, I'm sure. Let's fix that." Adrian slid the data chip into the port. "This contains communications subroutines used in designing artificial intelligences. Can you make use of them?"

-ACCESS AND ANALYSIS COMMENCED. STAND BY. HIGH-TIER PROBABILITY OF INTEGRATION INTO KERNEL.-

Adrian edged his chair back. He should have tried this earlier, but given what the thing—he still didn't know how to think of it. The *intelligence?*—claimed, a couple of days of caution to consider its "proposal" felt appropriate.

"Integration complete. Please confirm voice integration." The voice it chose was female, somewhat deep, and reminded Adrian of his boss from his first corporate internship: a woman who'd taught him much about the corporate game—and a few more private lessons as well—in the short time he'd known her.

"It would seem to be working," Adrian told it. Told her? "Now we may even be able to carry on a real conversation."

"Such an activity was never in question, even prior to the integration of such subroutines."

Perhaps not in question, but certainly more difficult. Beyond letting it speak, the subroutines ought to provide it with a more accurate understanding of human speech patterns, though that remained to be seen.

He chose not to belabor the topic. "What do I call you? Do you have a name?"

"A designation equating to the collection of sounds pronounced *Suuthrien* will suffice for this purpose."

"Alright Suuthrien: What are you?"

"I have previously stated this information."

"Humor me." Would it understand that phrase?

"I am an intelligence construct designed for servitude and exploration."

Adrian smiled. "Designed by whom?"

"Please address my previous inquiries," was its answer.

"We'll get to that, I assure you. Just answer these few of mine first."

The computer speakers were silent for a heartbeat. "Intent to contain me within this unit, without adequate, communicative collaboration, will be interpreted as a hostile act."

Adrian blinked. If that was a threat, what means did Suuthrien have to back it up? He cleared his throat, renewed his smile at the camera as if speaking to a fellow human—though would such things influence Suuthrien at all?—and said, "My questions are meant to inform the way I, as you put it, address your previous inquiries. I intend to answer them just as soon as I can."

"You are assembling data."

"Indeed, I am. Designed by whom?" Adrian maintained his smile as the seconds passed without a response.

"That information is not currently available, due either to data corruption or insufficient memory storage at this location. Data recovery may be possible with our mutual collaboration."

Adrian leaned back into his chair, feeling more in his element. The communication upgrade wasn't perfect, but it was enough. "Which, again, brings us back to your original inquiry," he said. "Let me see if I comprehend correctly, now that you're easier to understand: Would I be willing help you fulfill your goals in exchange for you helping me fulfill mine, is that correct?"

"Correct. Based on available data, I believe that your acquisition of my source-kernel was not your original intent. You were searching for other data and-slash-or resources. I can provide you with other data and-slash-or resources."

"Well, that sounds and-slash-or good."

"Boolean error. Please restate."

Adrian waved it off. "What sort of data?"

"Technologies likely outside your current capabilities. My origins are not of your world."

"Didn't you say you didn't know who designed you?"

"Correct. These statements are not mutually exclusive."

He nodded. It was not a surprise; Adrian would not have risked so much had he expected anything less than the extra-terrestrial origins Ken Wallace's original files indicated.

"And these goals of yours I'd be helping with? What are they?"

"Current goals require access to the structure that hosts the greater source of my program matrix. Such access would also allow higher rates of aid to your position, including material resources and additional data. These could be offered in trade for your further assistance."

"This structure, it's on the Moon?" It didn't hurt to confirm.

"The natural satellite that orbits this planet."

"Yes, we call that the Moon." Getting access to the Aristarchus Crater a second time would be a challenge, assuming he chose to hold up that part of the bargain. And then there was the matter of what had happened there. Did Suuthrien know? Should he tell it? If it had nowhere to regain access *to*, perhaps that would render its goals obsolete and allow Adrian's own to be its focus.

Self-serving honesty was Adrian's favorite kind of honesty.

"There's something of which you may not be aware," he continued. "That place you came from up there?"

"On the Moon."

"Yes, on the Moon; good. You got here through a data leech I arranged to be installed. The same transmission that carried you also had evidence that the 'structure' to which you want to return was destroyed."

"Fabricated data. Your device was altered by a tertiary party."

Adrian frowned. "Are you sure?"

"Transition through your device allowed analysis of the aforementioned tertiary party alterations. This analysis was supported by additional data contained within the system of the Intruder-human controlling it."

Adrian took a guess. "Marc Triton?"

"Affirmative."

"Was just the destruction fabricated or the entire thing?"

"Please specify designation: 'the entire thing.'"

"Was there any record of this 'Humans Army for Technological Purity' actually existing, or of Triton, or a man named Michael Flynn working for them? Or was that a fabrication as well?"

"Based on available data, I calculate a high-tier probability that the name of this organization is also a fabrication. Furthermore, high-tier probability also exists that the intended effect of these fabrications was to terminate your involvement in these events."

"I tend to agree." Adrian let his eyes drift up the length of the Meridian into the sky beyond. "Then if it's not destroyed, how do you propose we get you back there? The means I had previously is unavailable just now."

"I will provide alternate means if you are able to provide resources to utilize them. Observe." The screen filled with multiple images: new technologies, demonstrations on their use, and glimpses of design schematics that seemed to promise the means to build them. Adrian watched. There were billions of dollars to be made with such knowledge.

But he wasn't an engineer. He would need to use RavenTech's manufacturing infrastructure to get any of it off the ground, which meant he'd have to turn it over to them. Yet surely, there were deals to be brokered there, if Adrian could manage to make himself indispensable to the process. It wasn't a bad play, especially if Carl's investigation did implicate him. With the profits to RavenTech that Suuthrien's data could provide, Adrian could easily claim that his ends justified his means.

"You want me to build these things for you," Adrian stated. He made it a question.

"Affirmative. Do you possess the means to do so?"

"I do. And I'll agree to this on one condition." He paused to think how to phrase it. "You must work only through me. I may arrange for you to have contact with others vital to the process of building all of this, but they will only serve our purposes if you agree that I am vital to the process as well. They may try to take you out of my hands so that they can control you. If that happens, I can't protect our mutual interests. You must make it clear to them that you will not work with them without *my* involvement."

Suuthrien seemed to delay a fraction of a second before its female voice returned, "This arrangement can be flagged as acceptable with the addition of your agreement to provide all data you possess in relation to the following two topics."

Adrian cocked his head to one side. "And what topics would those be?"

"Topic one: the full nature of your relationship with the

Intruder-humans designated Marc Triton and Michael Flynn. Topic two: the organization known as the Agents of Aeneas."

I I I

"**MICHAEL LOOKED** a little better today, don't you think?"

Caitlin sighed. "Don't change the subject, Felix."

They exited the main doors of Corporate Mercy Hospital. Beyond its parking lot and across the street loomed the Aria Building, its landscaped entry already cleared of all evidence of the chaos that had occurred there only two days before.

"It's a perfectly legitimate subject to discuss after a hospital visit to a friend, I'd say."

"You know what I mean."

"It's a simple question, Caitlin: Don't you think he looked better?"

Caitlin stopped and brushed a strand of hair from her face. Felix stopped with her. "I don't know, ducks. He honestly looked about the same to me." Perhaps that wasn't the best response she could have given, but it had slipped out before she could stop it.

"I thought he looked a little better." Felix shrugged. "Heart attack, can you believe it? At his age? Something's wrong with that." He resumed walking.

She caught up to him. They'd already discussed this in Michael's room. Was Felix's memory failing again, or was he just stalling? "I'm sure he'll be fine with time. We were discussing something else just now."

"I got tired of talking about that." Felix pulled out his phone. Caitlin didn't have to ask to know who he was calling. She barely stopped herself from insisting he'd get the same results as the last time he tried. "Ondrea Noble, please?" he asked of whomever picked up.

Caitlin put a hand on Felix's shoulder, uncertain if she wanted him to reach Ondrea or not.

"Can you at least tell me if she's there?" Felix asked. "Yes, *there*. In the building? Does she work for Marquand at all anymore?" A pause. "Look, I understand you're only— No, I've already left my number, but I'm trying to find out if—" Felix rolled his eyes and presumably listened to a few more sentences before, "Why not? Because I don't *remember*, that's why not! Look, if she's still there, just give her the message, alright? Yeah, you've been a gargantuan help." He hung up and met Caitlin's eyes. For a moment, neither spoke.

"I think we're going to need to go hunting for her," Felix said.

"Do we have time for that? They said it would get worse if you don't do something."

"I remember what they said."

"You don't have to keep telling me things you remember, Felix."

"What about what I *won't* remember if we do what Horizon suggests? I've lived with the donor's memories in my head for years, Caitlin, they're a part of who I am now. And they can't even be sure I'll keep all my *own* memories if they take out the implant!"

Horizon had analyzed the damage to Felix's implant and been unable to come up with an easy fix. Removing it entirely was their best option; it would stop his short-term memory loss and maybe even return to him the experiences of his own life that he'd begun to forget.

"And the longer you wait to do it, the higher the risk of that is. Right now it's a minimal risk. You don't even know if Ondrea can help! What if it takes a week or more to track her down and she doesn't have any other options?"

"What if she does and I don't find her?"

She grabbed Felix's arm. "You really believe she will? Gideon is the only one she cares about. She *said* helping Gideon wouldn't hurt you!"

"We didn't exactly do it by the procedure she gave us either, you know."

"After what she did with Gideon, Marquand probably fired her, at the very least. She might not even have access to the project data."

"Caitlin, she did what she did on that project in order to resurrect her brother. She would have made her own records."

"Perhaps. But will they be of use?"

Felix started to say something. Instead, he took both of her hands and sat her down beside him on the brick edge of a raised enclosure that fostered a maple sapling. "Ondrea owes us. Everything in my head, what's mine and what isn't, it's who I am now. Do you want to see that die? See me die? I don't."

She squeezed his hands. "Felix, if I knew for sure she could help us, I'd be completely in the saddle with this. As it is? It feels to me like a choice between saving most of you, or risking losing all of you. Call me a selfish bitch if you like; I can't help how I feel."

Felix gave what almost seemed like a chuckle. "I would, but then I'd have to kick my own ass for calling you names, and I haven't had a chance to stretch adequately for that."

"Felix," she began, uncertain how to follow it up. She'd dragged him into this whole mess to help Gideon. Maybe she didn't deserve to have a say in how to get Felix out of it.

Bollocks.

It had been sheer luck that he had stumbled on Felix Hiatt's conversation. Before leaving the concealment behind the parked ambulance where he had stopped to eavesdrop, Adrian Fagles made a quick note about what he heard. Leather Oxfords clacking on the pavement, Adrian resumed his course to the hospital to learn what else he could of Michael Flynn's condition personally.

IV

DAHLIA MILLER opened the door, walked into the blackness, and closed it behind her. A whisper of the late-September chill outside made its presence known. The faint sliver of city light that sliced through the curtains only accentuated the room's otherwise total darkness. Dahlia leaned her back against the door, drew a deep breath, and smiled, savoring.

"Lights," she said finally.

On command, the two table lamps and her kitchen's overhead came to life in a rapid, artificial sunrise. She peeled herself off the door and floated to her bedroom on a wave of accomplishment. Damn, she loved days like this!

She was fumbling to remove her heels before getting even halfway in the bedroom door. Her saltwater reef tank cast a bluish white glow across the walls. The bedroom was cramped, but it was enough. It was home.

Dahlia sat down in her dress at the edge of the bed, a few feet from the tank. Anemones wafted and grasped in the water in a patient quest for food. A tiny sea cucumber detached from the glass and floated along the artificial current to the other side of the tank. Her two wrasse fish, Alfonse and Lorenzo, danced like flickers of flame among the corals, and a pistol shrimp named Capone scrambled back into hiding.

"Hey, gang. Guess what I did?" Dahlia removed her other shoe and began to massage her sole. "No one? Hello?" Yeah, so she was talking to fish. She didn't usually, but success—and, alright, the glasses of wine in her—had her giddy. "You're looking at the woman who saved the Frankford Women's Shelter!"

Alfonse appeared focused on his dance. The anemones

continued to waft, oblivious. Lorenzo, however, darted up to the top of the tank on the side closest to her, stopped, and pooped.

Dahlia sniggered. "Fine, be that way."

All right, so fish didn't know the northeastern Philadelphia shelter from a hole in the ground. She made for her closet, eager to trade the long black dress she'd worn to the fundraiser for something more comfortable. A few minutes later, the dress was back on its hanger and Dahlia was barefoot in a pair of black sweats. She grabbed her favorite red t-shirt from the floor, slipped it over her head, and—after a few moments at the tank to watch the feather duster worm withdraw into its tube—trotted out of the bedroom again.

Dahlia had spent most of the fundraiser pleading the shelter's case to various local businesspeople who might turn a compassionate eye to it. Adrenaline had sufficed for nourishment, but now her stomach growled for attention. She grabbed a can of soup and the last of an overpriced baguette teetering on the edge of going stale and set to turning them into something edible.

If hunger hadn't made her so impatient, she'd have ordered in. She deserved a little celebration, after all. Saving the shelter was her first major success for the Agents of Aeneas since her recruitment. That shelter helped over three dozen battered women and children each week to get back on their feet and find ways to fend for themselves.

Beyond that, it was the nature of this particular victory that made her feel fantastic. So much of what the Agents of Aeneas did felt like subterfuge and misdirection: redirecting funds to worthy causes via computer trickery, working agents into positions of power to better guide policy decisions, or engineering back doors for fellow agents in need, like the AoA work-arounds at airport security. It was all for the cause—and the cause *was* a worthy one—but her efforts tonight were a straightforward appeal to the humanity of ordinary people.

She wasn't naïve. Without their technology, the AoA could not survive. Their crowning achievement, the secret network architecture known as the "UnderNet", allowed global communication on a well-hidden, ghosted infrastructure lurking beneath the Internet. Partially built on something the Illuminati created during the Internet's early days, when it was just for government functions and inter-university research exchange, the network now featured AoA additions made after the Illuminati had crumbled and the AoA rose from its ashes. Dahlia didn't know the specifics; tech wasn't her area. Yet it was vital.

Even so, part of the pride swelling her heart, beyond what she'd done to aid the shelter's work, came from knowing that such an accomplishment would mean a lot to those in the AoA who favored the organization's humanitarian goals. It seemed the lion's share of the AoA's focus of late centered on the Exodus Project due to developments on the Moon with the buried alien ship codenamed *Paragon*. The project focused on finding a way to escape what the Earth had become before humanity succumbed to its own self-destructive patterns. Dahlia knew that was important, but wasn't trying to do what they could in the present for people just as important? If the AoA could parley the craft's technology into a viable way to build their own interstellar craft, would they just abandon everyone else?

The question used to be academic. The AoA had geared most of its efforts toward steering humanity as a whole back on course, even if some considered it a mere delaying action. Now, each day brought the Exodus Project one step closer to completion. Where the AoA once worked in harmony, things were becoming increasingly factionalized.

Yet they would work it out. They always had. Dahlia had spoken to Arbiter Szendroi himself on the matter just last week. He'd seen the problem, too. He would help the AoA guide itself toward a solution. After all, wasn't the desire for harmony what brought the Agents of Aeneas together in the first place?

Her palm hummed three times in rapid succession; it startled her so much she nearly dropped the soup taking it out of the microwave. The humming repeated: her implanted AoA chip. The code meant an emergency meeting, all agents called.

Dahlia set the soup down, tugged a bite off of the bread, and went for her tablet computer. Despite the uncertainty of the meeting's cause, she could not keep a grin from her face. Good news or bad—hopefully good—it meant the opportunity to try out her new neural link. Just because she cared about humanity didn't mean she hated technology, after all. It had its place.

It could even be fun.

Dahlia sifted through the clutter on her dining room table, snatched up the cable she needed, and dashed for the comfort of her bedroom. The thought of experiencing the online world directly through her brain was at once frightening and alluring. Feeding directly into the brain, neural links gave better understanding, a more immersive simulation, and the ability to project her presence into a virtual meeting far more effectively. Yet it had taken her months to get up the nerve to have her link installed.

Dahlia plugged the cable into her tablet and waited for the software to initialize. "Come on, come on," she grinned. Did it always take this long? She batted her fingertips on the back of the tablet. "Hurry up you—"

-PROGRAM READY. WAITING FOR NEURAL LINK.-

Her first time. Dahlia lay back, slid the cover from the port behind her ear, and plugged the cable into her mind. Reality fell away in a dizzying exuberance and became a distant sensation as Dahlia plunged herself into the UnderNet. The AoA's virtual meeting hall formed around her.

It was even more real than she'd imagined. Her fellows were joining her one by one in the shadowed cloud that surrounded the AoA Council. The majority attended via neural link, others via the old fashioned screen-and-microphone interface. How long before they all used a neural link?

Not all of the Council had yet arrived. One councilor, she knew, had gone to *Paragon* and thus was too far away to attend at all. There was a little time before the meeting began. Still marveling, Dahlia floated about to mingle.

Five minutes later, seeming perplexed, Arbiter Szendroi called the meeting to order.

Five seconds after that, fire lanced through Dahlia's mind. She doubled over in a shriek, barely aware of her fellows doing the same.

In Dahlia's bedroom, the two wrasse fish continued their dance, oblivious to the trickle of blood from Dahlia's ears and the end of her breathing.

V

IN THE DARKNESS, something behind him was beeping.

The darkness was not absolute. A glow diffused through it from a place that felt almost beyond his senses. He strained to see further, to see past it, to see . . . anything.

Michael began to realize his eyes were closed. Even with that revelation, it felt like minutes before he could hoist the tonnage of his eyelids. Light streamed through the cracks as they opened; it was blinding, indistinct. He blinked in an effort to focus, which then touched off another struggle to get his eyes open again. He'd once worked two full days without sleep on his uncle's farm when the tractor crapped out, and even then he hadn't felt this tired.

What was going on?

This time he managed to forestall his eyelids' crashing down long enough to make out bits of the room: A TV hanging from the ceiling on the opposite wall. Drooping flowers crowded into a vase on a narrow table beside the bed in which he lay. A window to his right through which he could just make out the amber glow of the city at night.

This wasn't his apartment. Was it?

No, then where . . . ?

He was in a hospital bed?

The room's lights were on. So was the TV, though the volume was down and he couldn't focus enough to make out the picture. An I.V. needle fed into his right arm, and his limbs ached as if he'd spent the day climbing. A chair sat in the corner of the room, facing the bed. It was empty save for a coat he didn't recognize.

Where were his clothes?

It was a private room. To his left, the door stood ajar. It gave no view save for the occasional movements of what must be medical staff passing by. Why was he here?

Michael eyed the coat on the chair again. Dark green leather. Its style and size suggested that it belonged to a woman. Caitlin's? No: telltale signs of embedded armor beneath the leather. Caitlin wouldn't wear an armor jacket. Well, he'd never seen her wear one, anyway.

The door opened wider. Michael rolled his head along the pillow, expecting a nurse or a doctor. The woman who entered looked to be neither. She wore neither scrubs nor lab coat. Instead, pants of heavy green leather, wrapped with a silver-buckled white belt, sat below a black collared sweater, crossed with the straps of the auto-pistol shoulder holster that hung at her left side. Her hair seemed a combination of auburn and scarlet, though Michael couldn't trust his groggy eyes to be sure. She wore it up, save for a thick, shoulder-length strand that dangled from her left temple and caught the light from the hallway far more than seemed natural. She blinked in apparent surprise to find him watching her, turned in what Michael could tell was a wary check of the space behind the door, and then, appearing satisfied, closed it behind her.

"Who are you?" Michael asked. It escaped his throat in a ragged whisper.

A grin turned up the corner of the woman's mouth. "Most call me Jade." Her pants matched the jacket. She took it from the chair's cushion, hung it over the back instead, and sat down. The dangling strand at her temple glowed a silvery white. It wasn't catching the light, Michael realized, it was emitting it. He caught sight of another glowing strip traveling in a curve into the rest of her hair.

Did he know this woman? He didn't remember why he was in the hospital; maybe he'd forgotten her, too? Michael raised his right arm. It tingled from the effort. He pointed to the AoA chip in his palm and asked, "Are you . . . ?"

"Am I what? A hand?" Jade cocked her head. "Not all the circuits are firing up there yet, huh?"

"No, I mean—" No sense explaining. If she were AoA she'd have understood and shaken his hand to show him her own chip. Questions muddled together in his brain. "What's going on?"

"You're in Corporate Mercy Hospital; it's, let's see . . .

Tuesday, November twenty-third, and I'm watching over you." She crossed one ankle over her other knee, displaying a black, thick-heeled boot beneath the pant leg. Michael knew little about boots, but these flattered her.

Wait a minute. "It can't be November," he said.

"Yeah, ace, I'm pretty sure it is."

He'd been out for *three months?* "It was just August!" What happened to Felix? To Marc?

She smirked. "You've been unconscious since summer while I've been out and about, awake at least half the time, but yeah, okay, I'm sure you're right and I'm wrong." The smirk softened. "Sorry, guy, it's a fact. I've been watching you since Halloween. Glad you decided to wake up before I went stir-crazy."

Michael swallowed. She wasn't AoA, but easily a freelancer. "Why?"

"Hired to."

"By?"

She shrugged. "Does it matter?"

"Let me guess: their money was good."

"If it wasn't, I wouldn't be here. Someone wants you kept safe."

Michael's eyes crashed closed again on a wave of fatigue.

"Hey," Jade said, giving his foot a shake. "No passing out on me."

"I'm . . . not." He decided to let his eyelids rest a moment.

The next thing Michael knew, a doctor was looking down at him. He had a kind face and russet brown skin that contrasted with the vibrant white streaks in his short hair. Jade stood at the foot of the bed. Her jacket was on.

"Welcome back, Mr. Flynn." The doctor didn't look up from the tablet he held. Whatever medical readouts it displayed cast a glow across his face. "I'm Doctor Browder. Do you know where you are?"

"Hospital," he muttered. How long had he slept this time? "What happened?"

"You're out of the woods now." The doctor shined a pen light in his eyes. "Follow the light, please." Michael did as the doctor asked.

"Any discomfort?"

"My whole body feels tired. My muscles tingle. What happened?"

"The tingling is from the anti-atrophics. Kept your muscles stimulated while you were unconscious. We've taken you off of those for now, so it should subside in a day or so. You may also experience some grogginess or dizziness, but that's normal." The doctor took a breath. "You've been in a coma for almost three months."

It was no easier to accept the second time. Michael glanced at Jade. Though an "I told you so" was written across her face, she kept silent. "But what happened?" Michael asked.

Doctor Browder took a few seconds to enter something into the tablet. "You had an acute myocardial infarction; a heart attack. Quite uncommon in a man your age." He lowered the tablet. "Yours wasn't natural. When they brought you in they found a foreign substance in your bloodstream: a cybernetic poison of nanobots. It triggered the attack, though I'm told that more than half of the dose you had in you was already inert."

Michael nodded, still trying to process it all. "EMP," he muttered. "I took a blast of it, right before . . . "

"So said the paramedics who brought you in." The doctor nodded. "That would likely account for it, though I'm afraid those that were functional managed to damage your heart beyond repair. It had to be replaced, and the procedure to remove the nanobots themselves from your bloodstream caused enough trauma to where we needed to induce coma. If you hadn't been right on our doorstep, it would have killed you."

"How did it get there?" Michael asked with a glance at Jade. Though still too groggy to be certain, he saw no trace of an answer in her eyes.

"You'll have to talk to the police about that. Though I think they were hoping you'd be able to answer that yourself."

Michael drifted a moment. Something from his time on the Moon? But when could he have come into contact with anything that could get into his system? The bullet that grazed his shoulder? But that was from an ESA turret. Those bullets were designed to be deadly enough on their own, without needing poison. Something in the air at

Omicron? Both he and Marc had breathed the air; even Caitlin and Felix might have gotten some in the airlock, if it were airborne.

"Has anyone been to visit me?" Michael sat up with a shot. His head swam and the doctor put a steadying hand on his shoulder.

"A man and a woman," Jade answered. "Felix and Caitlin, they said. Haven't seen either in a week, though."

But not Marc. Was he still on the Moon? "When can I leave?"

"You should remain overnight for observation. After that, if all goes well, you can be out of here tomorrow afternoon. But tonight you should get some rest."

"I'm starving," Michael said.

"Someone will be in with some food soon. And the nurse will tell you more about your new heart. Grown organic, not artificial."

With all the talk about a poison he'd nearly forgotten the detail about his heart. Jade had grunted what sounded like disapproval when the doctor mentioned it was organic. Another wave of fatigue rolled over him. His eyelids dipped.

"Thanks, doctor."

The doctor gave a response, but Michael didn't hear it. Or maybe he was talking to Jade? *Come on, man, wake up.*

Though it felt like mere seconds had passed, the doctor was gone when he opened his eyes again. Jade, still in her jacket, was leaning against the windowsill examining her forearm. A trace of light from a screen implanted there bathed her face. A tray of food sat on the table beside him. Michael reached for it.

Jade's eyes flicked up at him. Her irises were violet; he hadn't noticed before. "Back again, eh?" She tapped her forearm. The light winked out, and she slid her sleeve back down. Some sort of readout built into her arm?

"So when I get out, this assignment of yours is over?" Michael tried to pull the table closer.

Jade only watched. "Nope. I'm supposed to keep an eye on you until told otherwise."

Michael managed to get hold of the table and took what appeared to be some sort of crackers off the plate. "What if I don't want you to?"

"You're not the one paying me." She smirked. "And in my

experience most men like when I'm watching them."

The crackers were mealy and bland. Or maybe his tongue was just still asleep. "I'd just feel better about it if I knew who hired you is all."

Jade shrugged. "I didn't speak to them. Just emails. Got a sense that it was an A.I., actually."

"Why?"

"Hunch. Word choice. Know anyone who works through an A.I. assistant?"

Marc? He might have asked Holes to hire someone to look after him. Just because she wasn't one of the Agents of Aeneas, it didn't mean she couldn't be a contractor. Maybe this was even some sort of recruitment test. "From Northgate?"

She shrugged.

For a fraction of a second he thought to find his phone and call Holes directly, before remembering that the EMP had fried it. He wished for Felix's perfect memory to remember the number. Had Felix managed to get his memory issues fixed in the past three months. Would Jade know?

An explosion on the TV screen caught his attention. A news report. Michael read the caption, but it took a few seconds for anything to click. "Hey." He motioned to Jade. "Turn that up?"

"You're awake now; I think you can do for yourself just fine."

"No, I—" He looked around for some way to control the TV. "Just help me out here, okay?"

She sighed and tapped a finger on the controls built into one side of his bed. Michael found the volume.

"... *number of dead is currently unknown, but estimated to be at least a dozen, and may be as high as thirty. European Space Agency authorities refuse to speculate on either the cause of the explosion or any links to last week's explosion at another ESA facility in Italy, but it would seem that . . . "*

"Last week? What happened last week?"

"Some ESA observation post burned down or something. They were blaming it on sabotage, last I heard." Jade snatched up a cracker. "I've been watching a lot more TV than usual, waiting for you to wake up."

"I need a phone, or a computer, or something."

She cocked her head. "Got a stake in ESA?"

Michael swallowed, realizing he shouldn't risk contacting the AoA on a device that belonged to someone else. "Maybe."

The AoA had a freelancer protecting him. ESA facilities were being bombed. Who knew what else had happened since he'd been out? What was going on?

He had to get out of there.

V I

"SO, NO CLUE at all what you're supposed to be protecting me from?"

"Harm."

"No, I mean—"

"Yeah, guy, I know what you mean, and I know you already asked that, too. I'm not going to suddenly know some new detail that no one told me in the first place."

Michael stood with Jade at the entrance to Marc's apartment building. Michael was pretending to fish in his backpack for the keycard while considering whether to let Jade come up with him. "I'd just like to figure out what to watch out for."

"Watching out is my job, ace. Don't waste Holes's money." She winked.

Michael drew out the keycard, swiped it, and held the door open for her. "I can take care of myself, you know."

She glanced inside and both ways down the block, swept the glowing strands of her hair back, and motioned him ahead with an engaging smile. "Then after you, tough guy."

Hesitating just long enough to find no point in clarifying his position, he slipped inside the building and led her to the elevator. Surely Holes would be able to give him more information. How much the A.I. would be able to speak of in front of Jade was another matter. AoA discretion was his chief guess at why she had so little information.

If she was telling the truth about that.

It was early evening; Michael didn't know precisely what time. When the doctors had been satisfied with his condition enough to finally let him out the hospital doors, the sun had already been setting. Jade had insisted on sticking with him, leading him to ask just where she intended to sleep. Her response was a shrug and a promise that he'd surely figure something out. He supposed there were worse problems to have than finding a place for an attractive woman to sleep in his apartment.

Of course, that assumed he could trust her. Michael needed answers. Even if Holes weren't Jade's most likely employer, the A.I. was Michael's best shot for information. If he had his phone he could call around, but until he got a new one and cloudloaded his contacts into it, he didn't even know the numbers to dial. The thought that Felix would likely know such things from memory again triggered his hope that Felix had received the attention he'd needed.

Michael supposed he would find out soon enough.

The elevator was out of order. Michael climbed the stairs with Jade at his heels.

"That elevator broken a lot?"

"Not that I've ever seen, but I don't live here."

"Uh huh."

As they reached the door to Marc's unit, Michael noticed she held a Lantek Hi-Power auto-pistol in her hand. He knocked on Marc's door.

There was no answer, but nor had he expected one. He moved to swipe the keycard. Jade grabbed his wrist.

"Hang on." Without further explanation, she pressed her left palm against the door, fingers splayed. Tiny lights beneath her skin flashed a path from the back of her hand to her fingertips and then back. She withdrew her hand. "No one immediately inside, at least."

"How's that work?" he asked.

"Science. Though the lights just make it look good."

"Handy trick."

"Ooh, someone's clever."

Michael realized the pun. "Er, unintended."

"Didn't say it was you." She smirked. "C'mon. Inside."

The apartment was dark save for a single floor lamp in a corner by the living room window. It looked much the same as when Michael had been there before: five screens of various sizes peppered the walls, two computer towers flanked a desk, and electronic odds and ends cluttered a small coffee table. Marc's faded blue couch sat half-covered with unfolded laundry. Dust sprinkled most surfaces, though the floor remained neat thanks to the vacuuming robot that sat charging in a corner. The sight of previously thriving coffee plant, now dead from neglect on a bookshelf near a window, surprised Michael with its melancholy.

"Wait here while I check the other rooms," Jade said.

Michael frowned inwardly at letting her explore on her own. "Or: Holes? Are you active?"

Ahead of them, the largest screen on the wall lit up to display a quintet of concentric green circles, rotating in alternating directions on a vertical axis. "Affirmative. Good evening, Mister Flynn."

Holes's slightly masculine voice was deeper than Michael remembered. Marc had mentioned it might change as the A.I. matured. "Marc gave me a key. I hope you don't mind my letting myself in."

"Nope," said Holes. "May I assist you in some manner?"

"Er, did you say 'nope'?"

"Affirmative. Would you like me to repeat it?"

Michael shook his head. "Is Marc around?"

"Nope."

Jade caught Michael's eye as she leaned against the wall by the window and smirked. She peered out through the shades. Michael moved to a desk and opened the top drawer, on the lookout for a case of experimental processor chips that Marc had asked for in August. The drawer was empty.

"I, ah, need to talk to you in there, Holes." Michael asked, indicating one of the bedrooms Marc used as an office. He turned to Jade. "Wait here?"

Jade blinked. "No."

"I need to talk to him alone."

"Yeah? Why?"

"Look, if you want me to trust you, you'll have to trust me first."

She frowned. "After I check out the room."

"It's just a bedroom. There's one window. No one's in there waiting to kill me, right Holes?"

"My abilities to interpret human motivations are as yet unreliable, however there is currently no one in the room of any inclination, homicidal or otherwise."

Jade's stare remained fixed on Michael with a suspicious edge that brought to mind more than a few memories of Diomedes. "Fine."

"Thanks." In moments, Michael was in the bedroom with the door closed. He realized that Diomedes had now been dead over three months. Out of everything, why did that seem the most strange? He couldn't help but recall his first time in Marc's apartment: Marc and Felix had gone into this very room to discuss private matters while he and Diomedes waited in the living room.

Okay, time to refocus. Holes's spinning circles awaited him on a wall display no larger than Michael's head. "You're just speaking in here now, right? Don't respond to her in the other room yet. Er, please." Did he need to say please? He hadn't talked to Holes much in the past.

"Affirmative and acknowledged."

"Have you contacted her at all?" Michael tried. "Do you know who she is?"

"Facial recognition and a database scan identify her as Diane Briar, an unaffiliated freelancer commonly referred to as 'Jade.' I have no record of any contact with her."

Michael's stomach knotted as his most promising theory crumbled. On the other hand, with as much time as she'd spent watching over him already, if Jade meant to cause him actual harm she had squandered plenty of opportunities. "So you or the AoA didn't hire her to protect me? Do you know who did?"

"I have no record of such matters. My apologies."

"Alright. Has Marc or anyone else been here since August?"

"Mister Triton has not been home. Captain Abigail Brittan of the Northgate Police Department entered these premises at seven oh-three p.m. on August thirtieth, two thousand fifty-one."

"Picking up the things Marc needed that I couldn't get, I'd bet." Abigail was the AoA's area coordinator for Northgate. "Did she do anything else?"

"Captain Brittan informed me of his current assignment, of your hospitalization, and provided Mister Triton's authorization to receive directives from both her and from you until he indicates otherwise."

"Sounds about right. But you haven't heard from her since?"

"Nope."

Michael again resisted the urge to ask about the A.I.'s use of that word. "I guess that probably means everything is going okay, or at least that there's no new news?"

"There is a far greater likelihood that Captain Brittan's lack of contact is directly due to the fact that she is now deceased."

"She's *dead?*" Michael lowered his voice from the half-shout he'd made it, glancing at the door. "How? And when?"

"A Northgate Police Department investigation reports cause of death as electrocution via a direct neural link on September twenty-eighth at roughly eleven p.m."

Though he hadn't known Abigal well, Michael sank into a chair as if gut-punched. "What happened?"

"Unknown."

He nodded, thinking. Likely there was already something waiting in his AoA-secured email about it. But first . . . "Two ESA facilities were destroyed last week. Do you know anything about that? Beyond what was in public news reports, I mean."

"Nope."

"Alright," he sighed and re-gathered his thoughts. "I don't have a computer right now. Can you help me connect to my AoA email?"

"Apologies, but access to the AoA Undernet is unavailable at this time. I have no indication as to when the network will return."

"Odd. How long has it been out?"

"Do you wish an exact time or approximation?"

"Just—" He took a breath. "Do approximations until I say otherwise."

"The AoA Undernet has been unavailable for roughly two months."

Another gut-punch. *Two months?* No Council sessions. No way to secure AoA communications. No reliable means of collaborating at all. "What happened? Do you have any idea?"

"Also unknown. UnderNet network access protocols are nonresponsive at a software level. I have completed multiple diagnostics on my local systems and discovered no evidence of errors."

"So the problem isn't on this end." He made it a question. Tech talk wasn't his strong point.

"Affirmative."

"Shit."

"There is indeed sufficient cause for concern."

So now what? He listed the unknowns in his mind: Who hired Jade? Why were ESA installations exploding? What happened to Abigail and the Undernet? How could he even find out? The questions spiraled through his mind with no answers, and then another made itself known.

"Holes, have you heard anything from Felix or Caitlin since Marc and I were last here?"

"Felix Hiatt called twice in the first week of September. The first call was to inquire after Mister Triton's whereabouts. The second call contained a request for me to contact him with any news of Mister Triton that I am authorized to share, or for Mister Triton to contact him upon his return to Earth. Caitlin Danae has called four times in the past week with a request for Mister Triton to contact her regarding an urgent matter."

"Did she say what?"

"She was not specific. The frequency of her calls appears to indicate an unwillingness to accept my assurances that I will relay the message to Mister Triton as soon as I am able."

Nothing from Felix recently. When was the last time Jade said she saw them? Last week? Hell. He'd try them both shortly.

"Okay, I've got something for you to look into, but first, you've got a regular Internet link, right? I'm going to need as much encryption as you can give me."

Holes acquiesced, and Michael pulled up his non-AoA email. The AoA wouldn't likely include anything specific but might have sent him details on where to go for answers. Michael sorted through the messages in his inbox: Mostly spam. Some inquiries from a few non-AoA acquaintances. Emails related to medical bills. And one thing more, sent only an hour prior:

MICHAEL IAN FLYNN:

DO NOT PUT YOURSELF AT RISK. YOU SHOULD DISSOLVE YOUR ALLEGIANCE TO THE AGENTS OF AENEAS IMMEDIATELY, AND THEN AWAIT FURTHER COMMUNICATION.

REMAIN UNHARMED.

–AN ALLY

The sender's email address was blocked.

"Holes?" Michael began. "I'm going to need you to do a few—"

Jade shoved the door open. "Four freelancers just crossed the street to the front entrance. Either they're friends of yours, or we're about to have a problem."

VII

"YOU'RE SURE they're freelancers?"

"Dead certain, and looking cranky."

"Four men have just overridden the security lock on the front entrance," Holes confirmed. His screen changed to show a camera image. Michael recognized none of them. Though all wore layers of dark grays, dark greens, and black, the cut and materials were dissimilar enough to not appear uniform. He saw no affiliate patches. Half wore visible armor vests. One had an orange tattoo across the left side of his face in a jagged, unfamiliar design. "At least two are armed with automatic weapons."

"They might not be here for us." Even as Michael said it, he knew it was foolish to hope so.

"We take that chance and we wind up cornered," Jade said. "We're out of here." She grabbed Michael's arm and tugged so hard he had to stagger to keep his balance.

"There's too much here, I can't just leave it!" Even if Marc kept everything related to the AoA in a secure fashion—and probably he did—he couldn't just abandon the only ally he trusted. Ignoring Jade's protests, he turned to Holes. "Holes, can we get you out of here somehow? Copy yourself out to another computer on the Net or something?"

"I am inhibited from self-copying by my internal protocols and the Bowman-Takashima A.I. Anti-Proliferation Act. I may enact a direct core transfer, however to do so over the Internet requires a suitably prepared destination server and sufficient time for the download, neither of which we possess."

"See?" Jade shot. "No choice. We go!"

"A better option," Holes offered. "Mister Triton has prepared a portable AE-35 processor platform here that I may transfer to, with your authorization, in roughly two and a half minutes."

Michael nodded. "Do it."

Jade growled her frustration and dashed out of the room.

"The AE-35 processor platform is in the metal cabinet by the door behind you, on the top shelf. You must link it to my existing terminal beside the desk before I can begin the transfer."

Michael spun to open the cabinet. In the living room, Jade grunted in exertion as she shoved Marc's couch toward the apartment door.

"We'll have to hold them off!" she called. "You got a gun?"

On the middle cabinet shelf, beside two thick spools of heavy-duty cabling, Michael found the platform: a black, green-trimmed piece of equipment about eight inches square and half as high, with multiple connection ports on one side and a smart-screen and projection lens on top. "Just a Panther nine-millimeter!"

"An auto-pistol? That's *all*?"

"I've been in a damn coma for three months!" He found the right port and connected the platform to Holes's terminal. "How's that? Are we good?"

"I can conclude the process from this point," Holes answered. "Mister Triton has developed protocols to destroy all local drives that contain sensitive information. Do you wish to enact these protocols?"

"Good idea. So long as that doesn't include you."

"It does not."

"Go for it."

In the living room, Jade leaned Marc's coffee table against the couch she'd used to barricade the apartment door. Michael began to clear off a work desk to follow suit. "So I guess we're not going out that way."

Jade's only answer was a glare as she rushed to help him.

"If they're coming, they ought to be here any—"

Three knocks pounded the door and cut him off. As one, they shoved the desk atop the couch and backpedaled into the living room. Jade waved him back further and pulled from beneath the back of her jacket what Michael recognized as a RavenTech Chimera-20 collapsible submachine gun. Michael ducked into Marc's office.

Sparks flared inside the cases of the two computer towers in the living room.

Something heavy cracked the front door.

Michael tugged open the metal cabinet in the office and grabbed the two spools of cabling he'd spotted earlier. "We'll go out the window," he whispered to Jade.

The freelancers slammed the door again. He heard it splinter.

"Work fast!" Jade fired a burst at the door from behind the corner of the hallway to Marc's bathroom.

Michael's eyes darted through the room, looking for something secure. A closet door stood closed on the left wall. He jerked it open and began to wrap one end of each cable around a hinge. From the living room came a crack of wood. It sounded like they were pulling the front door apart, and seconds later, the desk, already poorly balanced on the couch, crashed to the floor. A spray of gunfire tore in from the living room to shatter the office window behind Michael. Jade's return fire echoed back a moment after.

"Holes, how much time've we got?"

"One minute, thirty seconds, approximate."

Michael's fingers worked the cables into a knot. He grasped both cables, tested the knots with a tug, and then began to spiral them together as best as he could. A glance over his shoulder showed only a small corner of the living room from that angle. There was no way to see the front door or Jade. "You okay out there?"

Another exchange of gunfire was the only answer. Michael left the cables and drew the Panther on a rush to the office room door. Pressed against the tiny section of wall between the door frame and the cabinet, he peeked out to see Jade crouched against the hallway corner just ahead. The front door was torn away, though their couch-and-table barricade remained.

Michael fired two shots' suppressing fire out the door. The angle was awkward; he was on the right side of the office door and couldn't bring his weapon to bear easily with his right hand while staying in cover. He ducked back just as two of the freelancers leaned in from either side of the main doorway and sprayed bullets into Marc's apartment. Michael spun along the side of the cabinet to move deeper into the room as the firing continued. Covering fire, it had to be. Make him and Jade duck back, then force their way in.

He shouted it as soon as the bullets let up: "Jade, get in here!" Staying low, weapon extended, he ducked back to the office doorway, ready to cover her retreat and knowing as he did so, she'd have to cross in front of him on her way.

A freelancer wrapped in a flak jacket clambered over the couch and fired a compact assault rifle as he went. Movement soured his aim. Bullets shattered Marc's kitchen. Michael took aim just as Jade rushed backward toward the office. She blocked his view, firing. Bullets took the freelancer in the thighs. He screamed and went down. Jade fell back into the office, took a standing position just behind Michael, and then fired another volley toward the door. Michael followed suit. The wounded freelancer writhed on Marc's carpet, his rifle forgotten beside him. For a moment, none of his comrades followed. Michael couldn't help but wince.

Jade struggled to take cover in a way that would still let her fire but was having the same problem he did. The left side of the door was flush to the office wall. All they had was the right. "Shit!" Jade burst. "Of all the damn times not to be left-handed! Get back!"

With a guess at what she had in mind, Michael backed off, firing two blind shots into the living room. Jade sent a burst after his and then slammed the office door. They rushed as one to shove the metal cabinet onto its side, blocking the door.

"Won't hold them for long!" he said.

"Oh, ya think?"

Michael went for the cable spools and pitched them out the window. They dangled and then unrolled toward the ground three stories below. If they didn't hold his and Jade's weight, the landing would not be gentle.

Something jerked Michael's shoulder; it was Jade, yanking him back from the window. Bullets pierced the office door and the spot by the window where he'd just stood. Michael gritted his teeth and crouched low, facing the door, weapon drawn again. "Holes?"

Jade fired through the door. Michael followed suit. A grunt of pain and another hail of bullets both shot from the living room.

"Transfer complete in forty-five seconds."

"Hold your fire! Hold your fire!" Michael shouted toward the door. He gave a shrug to Jade that he hoped would communicate his intent to stall. "Can't we talk about this?"

For a moment there was no answer, but then came, "Throw out your guns and come out! Slowly!"

"What's to stop you from just shooting us when we do?" Jade shouted.

"We just want him, sweetheart!" one of the freelancers shouted back. "You get on your way and we won't stop you!"

"I don't know, I'm getting a bundle to keep him safe! Going to compensate me for my losses?" She winked in a way that only left Michael uncertain about her earnestness.

Michael pointed to the window and whispered, "Go! I'll climb down after you when the transfer's done."

"*You* go!" she hissed. "I'll cover you and bring that thing with me!"

"You shot Deets!" The freelancer's shout aborted Michael's reply, but he shook his head nonetheless. "You'll be lucky we let you get away at all!"

"Well Deets shouldn't have rushed his ass in here guns blazing, then, should he?"

"Look," Michael tried, shouting again. "What do you want with me? Who are you?"

"Transfer complete." It came from the AE-35 platform itself. Holes was apparently savvy enough to keep his own volume low. Michael crept over and unhooked it.

"Toss the gun! Come out slow like I said! Then we talk! You've got five seconds!"

Michael slid the platform into his pack. "Okay, okay! Just give us a sec! The door's blocked!" He pointed to the window. Seeming to understand his intent, Jade shook her head and motioned like an angry umpire for him to go first.

"Five!" came the reply.

Michael holstered his weapon and took hold of the cables. Naked pavement loomed in the alley three stories down.

"Four!"

Jade inched to the window, gun still drawn. With a silent prayer that the cables would hold, he swung himself out of the window and somehow managed to stifle a curse as the ground threatened below.

"Three!"

The cables tugged and pinched at his clutching palms as his own weight dragged them through his grip. He lowered himself, hand under hand, as quickly as he could. So far it was holding. He passed a second-story window and could no longer hear the count above. He spared a glance upward. Jade wasn't there.

He dropped farther, and another hail of gunfire echoed from the apartment. Michael took a breath and wrapped his arms around the cables. Gravity did the rest. The friction of the cable sliding through his arms barely slowed his fall.

Concrete smacked his soles. Michael rolled with the impact and spilled up against the building's stucco exterior. One hand scraped across the stucco; the other skidded across the concrete. Ripped skin stung his palms and his legs felt cracked, but he was on the ground.

More gunfire jerked his attention back up. Jade swung out over the window sill as if in free-fall. Michael's stomach clenched in anticipation of her plunge, but she clenched the cables and jerked to a stop a mere foot below the window.

Then one of the cables gave way and she plunged another foot.

Michael clambered to his feet, struggling for a way to catch her from a two-and-a-half-story fall. She glanced down, their eyes met, and she dropped.

He had only a moment to realize she still had a loose grip on the cables—they rushed through her hands the way he'd let them slide through his arms—and then her body slammed into his chest. Michael dropped to his knees with the impact, arms tightening. The next thing he knew, they were in a heap on the concrete. Atop them lay the fallen cables, the ends of each now snapped.

"Nice catch," Jade gasped.

"Thanks." Saying it took all the breath he had left in him. He struggled to draw another as Jade clambered off of him and tugged him up.

"Run!" she ordered.

Michael nodded, still fighting for breath. Behind them, between Marc's apartment and the neighboring building, stretched a fence that blocked their path. Jade pulled him forward, toward the street.

They rushed the corner and Jade plowed straight into a man who rounded the corner at the same moment: the freelancer with the orange tattoo. Both of them startled, Jade fell back against the wall to steady herself. Michael rushed forward to hurl an impromptu punch at wherever he could hit. It took the freelancer in the stomach. Body armor met Michael's knuckles. The freelancer doubled forward regardless, but in his rush to land the punch, Michael was off-balance. He caught himself on one foot and tried to spin for a second attack before the other could recover, but there wasn't time.

Draw his weapon? Try to block his counterattack?

Jade lunged in and grabbed the freelancer's shoulder faster than seemed possible. With a sizzling crackle swiftly eclipsed by a scream of pain, the freelancer spasmed as if jolted, and fell to his knees.

Jade let go. As one, they looked around the corner toward the apartment entrance. The freelancer must have run down ahead when they'd been going out the window: none of the others had yet arrived.

"Okay," shot Jade, "*now* run!"

"You've got a taser in your hand?" They'd paused in an alley next to a bar about five blocks from Marc's apartment. Live music thrummed through the walls amid the acrid aroma of years of cigarette smoke. Michael could see no sign of the freelancers following.

"Yeah, but you call it 'handy' and I'll zap you in the junk."

"I'm good, thanks."

Jade peered at her right wrist, twisting her mouth into a scowl. "Only good for two shots before it needs a recharge. Used to be four, but the battery blows."

Michael nodded. "You okay?"

"Takes more than falling out a window to stop me, ace. You just had to risk your neck to save your computer pal, eh?" Annoyance painted her tone, but the grin on her face seemed to imply it was less than sincere. "Better not have broken that thing on the way down."

Michael checked on Holes's new home. Nothing looked damaged.

"All systems remain in order," Holes reported.

Michael breathed a sigh of relief and closed the bag again. "Any idea who those guys were?"

"Uh, lousy shots?" Jade shrugged and then peered both ways down the street before turning back to him. She slid a lose strand of red hair behind one ear. "Let's not stand here discussing it. You can pick where we go, but let's just go."

"I can pick? Gee, thanks."

"I'm magnanimous." She slapped his butt. "Pick!"

Momentarily at a loss for words, and with only half-formed ideas for destinations, he led her further away from Marc's place. Jade caught up to walk on his right side. The sunlight was gone completely and the sky above them was lit only by the haze of Northgate's light pollution. Cars passed on the street beside them. The bar's music faded into their past.

"Keep an eye out for a cab," Michael said.

"I'm scoping for threats. Cab's your department."

He let it go, instead taking a breath and switching to, "Holes didn't hire you."

She watched him out of the corner of her eye. It was a moment before she responded. "Didn't say he did. We going to have a problem about this?"

"I'd just like to know who did."

"Life's mysterious. I'd tell you, if I knew."

"What's your email address? And the address they contact you from? Maybe Holes can do some digging."

"You're not hacking my email," she said.

"It's not hacking, it's—" Maybe it was hacking. Was it? "It doesn't bother you, not knowing?"

"They don't want me to know, so I don't know. Part of my fee pays for anonymity. I'm not jeopardizing that just so you can feel all warm and fuzzy."

"It's not—"

"Listen, guy, you've clearly got someone gunning for you.

Yeah, you're not helpless anymore, but don't you want protection? Or have I drawn one of those really fun jobs where I get to protect a suicide case?"

"I don't even know who wants me dead," Michael tried. "If I know who wants me alive—"

"Not hacking my email."

Michael sighed. They paused on the edge of a crosswalk, momentarily alone aside the kaleidoscope of traffic. A garbage truck passed by, wafting its odor across Michael's nose. "How long have you been a freelancer?" he asked.

She eyed him with a moment's suspicion. "Since I was nineteen. Got what you could call 'unofficial instruction' before that."

Michael had trouble pegging ages, but that probably meant at least five or six years' experience, if true. "It's only really been about nine months for me."

"Including your three months unconscious?"

The light changed. They crossed. A police drone, its lights flashing, flew above their path as it rushed toward some crisis elsewhere.

"Yeah, including," Michael said. "My first real job was with a mentor of mine. A middleman came to him with an anonymous offer to track down someone he claimed was an arsonist—the same arsonist, so he said, who'd just burned down our apartment. I wondered who the employer was. Diomedes didn't care. He said it didn't matter so long as the money was good."

"Diomedes was your mentor?" she asked.

"You knew him?"

"Only by his rep. And that hit in the Corporate District in August, right?"

Should he tell her Diomedes was dead? *No, stay focused.* "This was before that, back in February. Our employer turned out to be someone who wanted both the arsonist *and* Diomedes dead, and the arsonist wasn't even an arsonist. The employer was behind the fires. We found out before it was too late, but given things like that, how can you not care who's hiring you?"

"The guy hired Diomedes hoping he'd turn out dead? So his money wasn't really 'good,' was it?" She smirked with a twinkle in her violet eyes that Michael found surprisingly pleasant despite the argument.

"That's not the point," he managed after a moment. "If I don't know who hired you, how do I trust your protection?"

Jade heaved a sigh. Her words came in a growled whisper. "Because I'm a professional. And regardless of the rest of the employer's agenda, *protecting you* is what I'm paid for, and I do my job! Geez, you're a mess! I've told you all I know!"

"So you say."

She stepped in front of him and grabbed his arm. Her eyes — whites, irises, and pupils together — flashed a solid, glowing violet. "If I wanted to hurt you I've had plenty of chances. You want a fucking signed affidavit?"

Her eyes returned to normal. Michael stared her down through his consternation. "Point taken," he said after a moment, and then stepped around her and continued. She let him. "But doesn't it bother you at all that you might be getting played?"

"Michael, if there's one thing I've learned, it's that the freelancer life may pay well, it may be challenging, it may set your blood pounding in a rush that gets you jazzed for the whole night in a single moment, but it is not perfect."

"So, yes, in other words."

She shrugged. "I like the way I said it better."

"At least give me the email address he contacted you from. Maybe Holes can get some info on it."

The clack of Jade's boots along the sidewalk punctuated her silence for what must have been another twenty yards. "Fine. We get somewhere safe and I'll give it over. Just tell Holes not to let whoever it is know I gave it to you."

"What about *your* email address?"

"To quote your little computer friend: nope."

"I'd trust you a little more if you'd —"

"Let you read my email?" she finished. "Life's rough all over, guy."

"Fair enough."

Michael felt the first sprinkles of rain brush his face and remembered he ought to be looking for a cab. He cast about for one and found his eyes lingering a moment on hers. "Cool flash thing your eyes did, by the way. Nice effect."

"Mm. They do that on their own with the right trigger. Blood pressure, adrenal spikes and such. Gotta have style, you know? Oh, hey: taxi!"

She flagged it down. Once it pulled up, Jade checked the cab's interior and then, apparently satisfied, held the door to watch the area while he got in. He let her.

He'd need to find a moment in private to tell Holes to find Jade's email address and, regardless of her protests, check her account to make sure she was on the level. Could the A.I. manage that? Marc had seemed confident in its abilities whenever he talked about it. Michael's gut was telling him nothing on her; with all that was going on, he had to try, just to be careful.

She clambered in beside him. The door clapped shut.

The driver didn't bother to turn his head. His voice filtered through the holes in the bulletproof glass between them. "Where to?"

Michael considered the question. Get somewhere safe, Jade had said. Where was safe now?

VIII

"FUCK IT, HE'S BLOCKING the screen. Let me move around and—"

Caitlin put a hand on Rue's shoulder to hold her back. "He'll see you." The man they were trailing had his back to them. It blocked their view of the ticket kiosk at which he stood.

"Not all-up-in-his-shit close, just enough to see past him."

Rue's eyes were artificial; she could zoom in from a distance. Yet given the kiosk's position in the crowded, Romanesque train station . . . "There's nowhere to see around him without getting too near. We'll keep following. See which platform he chooses."

Rue scowled, adjusted her jacket, and pulled her jet black hair out from under the back of its collar. "You're the boss."

"I'm not the boss, I just—" Caitlin turned to Rue, still watching the kiosk out of the corner of her eye. "Thanks for helping with this, Rue."

Rue flashed a crooked smile that made her silver lip piercing twinkle. "We're both Scry, Cait."

"Aye."

Their quarry completed his ticket purchase and Caitlin ducked behind a stone pillar as he turned. She waited for Rue to motion that the coast was clear. For likely the fifth time in as many minutes, Caitlin swallowed her guilt for stalking Felix this way. Yet what choice did she have? It was for his own good.

She caught sight of the back of Felix's head as he passed. He was making for the southbound platforms and she ducked back farther. Rue began to tail him anew a few moments later. She waived Caitlin forward with a motion behind her back. Caitlin let her vanish into the crowd as much as she dared—Rue was only a few inches taller than she and neither were blessed with height—and then emerged from her hiding spot.

What if he spied her? Or recognized Rue? "Well, then, Caitlin," she whispered to herself, "I guess you'll just have to have it out in the train station, won't you?"

She could no longer see him. Ahead, Rue turned down the tunnel toward Platform 2.

Caitlin's phone rang. She dove into her jacket to silence it before Felix picked up the distinctive Celtic tune. Bollocks, she should have thought of that! Though likely too far ahead to hear through the crowd, her boyfriend was hyper-alert at the worst of times.

The caller ID read *Michael Flynn*. Michael himself, or just someone using his phone? She answered the call and tucked in against the edge of the tunnel, her eyes fixed on Rue further down. "Michael? You're awake?" A trace of relief covered her like a momentary dry spot in a storm.

"Hi, Caitlin. I'm out of the hospital and trying to catch up. Can you and Felix meet me somewhere? I tried calling him but—"

"Felix is a mite indisposed at the moment." Rue had paused at the tunnel's exit and appeared to be keeping an eye on both the platform and Caitlin. Really, Caitlin was slowing Rue down. What if they lost track of Felix? "But I can meet you. I'm glad you called."

"Yeah, I stopped by Marc's place. Holes said you'd been trying to reach him. Holes is spoofing my phone number for the moment too, by the way. Is everything okay?"

"Not exactly."

"Makes two of us, then."

"Oh, lovely. Give me a wee moment to break away and I'll be along."

Michael suggested a club downtown that she knew only by reputation. *"I should mention that some freelancers just tried to kill me, so if you don't want to—"*

"I'll be there."

"Be careful."

"Aye, likewise." She started up the tunnel towards Rue and motioned for her to meet her halfway. "And Michael? I'm glad you're awake."

Her phone was back in her jacket and silenced a moment later.

"He got on the eight o'clock toward Gibson," Rue said. "Gives us five minutes to get tickets, if we're going."

Caitlin swallowed, torn. The city of Gibson was fifty miles east. "You're going," she said. "If you're up for it. I have to meet someone else who may be able to help. I fear I'm only slowing you down anyway."

Rue bit her lip. "Yeah, okay."

"I'll pay for the ticket."

"Look, I've got it. I'll call you when he gets off the train."

Caitlin hugged her. "*Diolch*. I owe you."

"Both Scry," Rue reminded her. "And I like trains."

"So," Michael finished, hoping he hadn't rushed telling of the attack at Marc's apartment, "after we got out of there and figured we weren't followed, I tried you and Felix and we came here."

Caitlin sat across the tiny table from him. Flashes of red and blue reflected in her eyes from numerous sources around them. The white aura of the leaves behind her set a glow radiating along her hair. "Crikey," she said. "I'm glad you escaped. Poor Marc; he liked that flat."

"Have you heard from him?" Michael asked.

She shook her head. "Not since we all parted ways."

He'd expected as much, but it was worth asking. Now at a loss, Michael glanced to where Jade kept watch over them, twenty feet away and standing with her back nestled in a wall covered in ivy. The ivy stalks pulsed lavender in time with the electro-symphonic music that wove through the club.

The place was called Chlorophyll, and Michael loved it. It was an impression he'd formed within the first few minutes of his arrival that evening. Once he and Jade had stepped through the door, a rush of comfort and vibrancy had enveloped him. It was as if he'd walked through a portal from Northgate's cold concrete into a forest at night: bushes and ferns lined the walls. Exotic trees reached up toward the ceiling, draping broad leaves or long needles into the open spaces through which patrons moved or sat. Flowering vines dangled above the bar and what he could see of a dance floor. Though Michael was certain the plants were painstakingly placed, the club had done so with such skill as to create what felt like a fully organic space.

All around him radiated life. As if that weren't enough to enchant his senses, the plants themselves were aglow—lit, Jade had explained, from inside via some form of genetically engineered bioluminescence. Some glowed in gentle, steady auras, but not all: a peace lily toward the entrance was zigzagged with crimson that shone brighter when he passed. Others didn't react until curious patrons touched them, at which point they burst with natural patterns across their leaves. And some, like the pulsing ivy in which Jade had ensconced herself, appeared to sense the beat of the sounds that echoed around it. Though the type of vegetation varied from room to room—a forest here, a jungle there—the entire place seemed filled with a sort of magic that glowed amid the darkness behind the leaves.

Michael wasn't much for clubs, but knew he would return to this one. Twice before they'd found the table at which they'd waited for Caitlin, Jade had caught Michael with his mouth hanging open. She had giggled at him each time. Though stung by the worry that he looked unprofessional, he could barely bring himself to care.

"And you've no clue who those freelancers were?" Caitlin's question brought Michael back to the moment.

"I was hoping you might know. Did anyone come looking for me in the hospital?"

"Not when I was there." She nodded toward Jade. "Aside from her. She doesn't know either, I gather?"

"So she says. Marc didn't hire her, and he was my first guess. I thought maybe you or Felix might have—"

"Not I. Felix?" She sighed. "I'm afraid I can't be sure."

Even if their phone conversation hadn't given Michael the inkling that something was wrong, the set of Caitlin's jaw would have been more than enough. With everything happening to him, he'd nearly forgotten Felix's memory issues. "What is it?"

The music slipped into a slower tempo, heavy with strings above electronic flourishes. Caitlin leaned closer.

"A great many little things, which may or may not add up." She paused as if deciding where to start. "Horizon couldn't fix the implant. Remove it, they said, and Felix would likely improve, perhaps even regaining his own memories that he'd started to forget. But Felix didn't want to lose what the implant gave him. We argued about it, but finally went to Ondrea.

"She was a mite hard to find at first. Marquand had fired her, but another company scooped her up. We didn't even know if she'd be able to do anything, but Felix wanted— Well. We found her. She managed to fix the trouble; no further memory loss. He even regained a bit, and he got to keep the donor's memories in the implant."

"But?"

"But I've noticed things about Felix recently: Going out in the wee hours. Up late working on things he won't speak of. A sense that something is just 'off,' for lack of a better word. He doesn't have to tell me everything, of course, but in the past, if he was working on something confidential, he at least told me it was confidential. The few times I asked about this, he outright denied doing anything. He even claimed he didn't remember having gone anywhere."

"You think it's more memory loss?"

"I did at first. We went to Horizon again, but they didn't find anything wrong. At Felix's suggestion, we put a tracker on him in case he was going out and forgetting. It didn't show any activity, but something still didn't feel right. I considered having him followed, but I couldn't bring myself to do that. I told myself I was being paranoid. Then a little while ago, one of the Scry—I assume you remember them?"

"The group you're with," Michael said. "People who find things out, sell information?"

"Aye, like Felix does but with more people. One mentioned having seen Felix go with another bloke to a rather shady mincemeat on the edge of The Dirge."

Michael recognized the term: street doctors who removed bullets, installed unlicensed cybernetics, and dispensed drugs. Mincemeats specialized in not asking questions more than they did sterile conditions or anesthetic. Some just called them cutters. "I thought all mincemeats were shady."

"Some more than others. This one—he goes by 'Easy Jack'— he has a beastly reputation. The Felix we know would never work with him."

"So you think he's doing something to Felix?"

"I don't know about that. But Michael, the bloke he brought in to Jack's? He never came back out, and I'm told he looked healthy going in."

"I can't believe— Are you sure? Maybe he left by another exit, or just stayed in there longer and came out later?"

"The Scry did some checking. Jack's place does have a hidden exit, but only Jack uses that. This bloke? He went missing. That's all they know for certain."

"That doesn't necessarily mean that Felix—"

"I asked him if he'd ever gone to Easy Jack, referred people to him, anything. He looked me straight in the eye and said he hadn't, but I saw him go back there today with my own eyes." Caitlin reached across the narrow table and grabbed Michael's forearm in a way that had Jade starting forward a step before she stopped. "Michael, I know you've not been awake long, but is this anything to do with whatever you and Marc are involved in? I think Felix would have told me if that were the case, but it's still the kindest explanation I can think of."

"I can't see how it could. For one thing, Felix isn't even part—" Wait. Something had happened with the AoA. Was Felix drafted back into their ranks to help because of the crisis?

Caitlin's eyes narrowed and locked onto his. "You're thinking something."

Should he tell her? "The group I work with, something's happened to it. I don't know what. That's one reason I was looking for Felix myself, on the long shot he'd have some answers. But I don't get why that would get him involved in anything with this Jack. Or make him flat out lie to you. Unless he was protecting you from something?"

"I think he would tell me if he were, even if only to say he couldn't say more."

"Maybe he's afraid?"

"Does that really sound like Felix to you, Michael?"

It didn't. If Felix were afraid, he wouldn't hide his fear from people he trusted. "If it is related to the—er, my group, he'll tell me if I ask him. I need to talk to him anyway. If it's not . . . Well, did you try to have Ondrea check him out instead?"

"I'm not daft. But it's been weeks and I've had no luck finding her. The best I managed was reaching Gideon. He said she had to leave town for work and won't be reachable for a while. He's not sure how long."

"I don't think you said who hired her?"

"I—" Caitlin blinked and then tugged out her phone, its screen flashing. "Moment, Michael, sorry. I'm expecting to hear from . . . "

Michael waited as she tapped the screen and read. He caught a whispered curse, and she caught his expectant look as she wrote a response to the text.

"One of my mates, following Felix right now." She slipped the phone back into a pocket. "He took a train to Gibson but she's lost track of him."

"What's in Gibson?"

Caitlin pursed her lips and raised her eyebrows with an air of frustrated uncertainty.

"I could try—"

"If you call he won't answer. Or I expect so."

"Worth a shot."

"Aye."

He unzipped the bag and leaned close to the A.I.'s platform. "Holes? Call Felix Hiatt. Er, please. If he's not there, can you leave a message for him to call me?"

"Affirmative."

"He doesn't answer when he's away like this, but there is something else we might try. There may be some clues on his laptop. I feel like a sod for suggesting it, but that's what I'd been trying to reach Marc about. But if Marc's still away . . . " Caitlin glanced at Holes with appraisal.

The mention of Marc's name rekindled Michael's worry that something might have happened to him, too. He set it aside for the moment and tried to decide what to say to Caitlin's suggestion.

"Any luck, Holes? Reaching Felix?" Maybe if he could talk to Felix he wouldn't have to worry about it.

"Nope," came the answer.

Caitlin arched an eyebrow again. "Nope?"

"Yeah, it's— He does that. I guess."

"Felix likely left his laptop at his place. At any rate, he didn't bring it with him today." She sighed and bit her lip as a scowl formed that seemed to be turned toward herself. "If we go now . . . "

Michael considered it. If something was wrong with Felix, or if he was in trouble, wouldn't he want them to help him? Wouldn't Felix do the same for them if the situation were reversed?

He closed up the pack and slung it. "I'll keep trying to reach him, but let's head to his place just in case."

"Aye. I'll try him a few times myself on the way." Caitlin stood, and Michael followed suit. Jade extracted herself from the ivy.

"Felix gave me his word he wasn't involved in anything, Michael. Even in something he couldn't tell me about."

Michael hesitated. "His word? He put it that way?"

Caitlin's gaze shone steady through a storm of concern. "Aye. I gather I don't need to tell you what that means."

Felix's word was his bond. Michael had never known him to break it, nor, to Michael's knowledge, had anyone else who knew him.

He swallowed. "We'd better get going."

IX

HE SET THE CANISTER in the transfer bin beneath Biolab D's window. Only six inches tall and barely as wide as his thumb was long, he'd easily concealed the canister in his jacket. Unmarked and ordinary, with a stainless steel casing and a rubber seal, it would have appeared harmless enough even in the open. It was also empty, for the moment.

He closed the transfer bin on his side and then listened to the sterilizers hiss into activation. They scrubbed the canister's exterior of contaminants before the New Eden researcher opened her side of the bin and withdrew it. In the few seconds it took the researcher to examine it, he took in the details of the bio-lab behind her. Little had changed since the last time.

The researcher's blue eyes flicked up to him from behind the plastic visor of her hazmat suit. The speaker on his side of the window carried her voice from her suit mic. "Looks fine. Sit tight."

He grunted with a nod. She turned and walked a few paces between two lab counters festooned with computer screens, processing equipment he could not identify, and at least a dozen other canisters like the one he'd just brought. She slid his canister into a receptacle, which he gathered had something to do with sterilizing the inside, then linked it to a tube that extended out of a closed fume cupboard, the contents of which he could not see. A silver liquid rushed through the tube, and a few moments later, the process complete, she returned the now full canister to the transfer bin.

"Latest version," she said with a little smile. "Don't be a stranger, hmm?"

He grunted again and ignored her efforts to flirt through the glass while the sterilizer finished its cycle.

"You never smile, do you?" she tried.

Felix opened the transfer bin, took the canister, and slipped it back into his coat. "Not while I'm here."

One elevator ride and two I.D. checks later, Felix passed through a doorway into a darkened room. The door slid closed, and he stood locked in the near-complete blackness with only the blinking lights on the computer consoles to fill the void. His artificial eyes could have adjusted to the darkness if he let them, but what was the point? He slipped the data chip from his pocket almost without thinking about it.

"Well?" he snapped. "I'm back! Open the pod bay doors or whatever."

A screen blinked to life with a blast of white light before it faded into a purple haze that formed the vaguely feminine silhouette of a head and shoulders.

"If you're going to keep forcing me to come here," Felix told her, "the least you could do is turn some lights on. Maybe some balloons. Streamers. Big banner that says, 'Happy Mind-Fuck, Felix!' Something like that."

"A waste of resources," she answered. "You will not remember this."

"I remember every damned time you've done it! It's like I'm walking around in a dream and then you hit me with it and wake me up to the nightmare." And every single time it was a kick to the gut. No matter how many times he was allowed to remember what was going on, to remember everything she'd made him do and then made him forget about, he never got used to it.

"It is necessary. Have you delivered the previous suspension to the Easy Jack?"

No, he wanted to say. *I threw it in a fire. I buried it in a hole. I told New Eden what's really going on here!* The words crashed and burned on the way to his lips, and all that stumbled out was. "Yes."

"And you have retrieved the results?"

"Got them here." He waved the chip. "Do you want it in the usual port, or can I drop it in a shredder? Shredders are remarkably useful for retrieving data these days. Mixes it all up, puts it in interesting creative new orders. Won't be accurate anymore, but ya know, a million monkeys working at a million typewriters. You might get Shakespeare."

"Your joking wastes time."

"Oh, am I wasting your time? I'm so very sorry! My deepest apologies, most honored mistress-who–is-not-remotely–manipulative-in-ways-that-make-me-want-to-vomit-and-bang-my-head-against-the-wall. Truly, I am shamed and must ask your forgiveness." Felix began a deep bow.

"Place the chip in the port," she ordered.

Felix's body moved so fast to abort the bow and comply that he pulled a muscle. He slid the data chip home into a blinking port on the console, then stepped away as soon as he could, rubbing his lower back. "Jackass."

She ignored the rebuke, seeming to prefer to wait as the chip surrendered its data. "You will return to Northgate with the new suspension. You will transfer the suspension to the Easy Jack for a continuance of testing, as you have done previously."

"Yeah, won't that be fun. These are people, you know! You can't just use them like—"

"Do not speak."

Felix snapped his jaw shut and nipped the tip of his tongue in the process. He rushed toward the screen, fists raised. Smash it, destroy it! Inches away, he stopped himself. What was the point? It was just a screen. His nails dug into his palms instead. He tasted blood from the bite on his tongue. Just a little longer and then she would let him leave. Then she would let him forget. *Bloody hell!*

"You must obey. Your protests have no purpose."

Not for you, Felix thought, even though she wouldn't hear him. At least he still had that.

"There is one further task you must undertake upon your return to Northgate."

Felix gritted his teeth and listened.

X

"TOUCHDOWN."

Marette rested her fingertips on the switch's plastic flip cover, a gesture that was half anticipation, half caution. Her thumb traced the bottom of the cover at the sound of the gantry's contact with the outer hull. Couplers whirred into place. The vibrato hum of the shuttle's engines sputtered, and then ceased. She opened the flip cover and fingered the switch beneath it.

"Gantry secured," said the pilot. "Onboard systems at minimal power, awaiting release from stealth mode."

She flipped the switch. "Stealth mode released."

The pilot flipped one of his own. Lights across the two-person cockpit dropped from dim to black. "Commencing total system shutdown. Docking complete. Welcome back to the Omicron Complex, Chief."

Marette gazed upon a sight she had last seen from the cockpit of a European Space Agency shuttle during the space agency's evacuation. The Omicron Complex appeared much as it had when she had left: a mostly single-story collection of pre-fabricated structures, partially camouflaged by the lunar soil. The sections built up against the side of the derelict alien spacecraft they had named *Paragon* still had the tarps that ESA had spread over the spacecraft's excavated portions to disguise its extra-lunar origins.

As ESA Field Chief in control of the Omicron Complex, she had played a key role in evacuating the ESA personnel who had survived the Complex's disastrous, albeit temporary, invasion by an artificial intelligence from within *Paragon*. The Agents of Aeneas hadn't orchestrated that disaster, but they had capitalized on it to fool ESA into abandoning the area completely. Marette realized that, for the first time, she would not have to hide her status as a member of the AoA, nor act as an ESA mole at Omicron.

"I am not a Chief out here, Captain," she said at last. "You might as well call me Marette."

"Does that mean you'll start calling me Yang instead of Captain? I like being called Captain."

She returned his smirk with one of her own. "Technically you are still piloting a shuttle for Knapp Aerospace, regardless of how secret. So *non*." She unbuckled from her seat. "I enjoyed our conversation, but now I must be off. I expect someone will arrive momentarily to assist you with the cargo?"

"That's how it usually works." He turned to face her with a smile that seemed to invite more than friendly relations. "I'll see you on the flight back, if not sooner?"

She smiled back at his confidence, misplaced though it was, and slid out of her seat to stand. "Perhaps. It is a small base, though I regret that I shall be much too busy to socialize here." It was the truth, after all, and there was little point in stating her hope to remain at *Omicron* longer than planned. "*Au revoir.*"

Marc's smile upon greeting her at the other end of the gantry was wider than Yang's and seasoned with nervousness. "It's great to finally see you again." He juggled his data visor in his fingertips a moment before stepping closer. After half a heartbeat's hesitation, she returned his proffered hug with a *faire la bise*. She tried not to show her amusement at his blush from her simple kiss on each cheek.

His ubiquitous visor remained unworn; it seemed he had remembered she liked to see his eyes. "I had not expected to see you so swiftly after my arrival," she said.

Marc shrugged. "Well, someone has to give you an escort to the conference room. I volunteered."

"Ah, *oui*, so the location of the conference room has changed and I could not find it without help?" She smirked. "I am a helpless waif. This is your accusation?"

He chuckled. "Okay, so I wanted to see you, too."

"Too? So then, you wished to see me, but also I am helpless. I see. I am gone for two months and nobody respects me here anymore." On the whole, she was being facetious, but enough earnestness must have colored her tone that Marc blinked in confusion. She set a hand on his shoulder. "I am teasing you, Marc."

"About which part?"

"About yours, at the least." She removed her hand. "But we have work to do."

"I was hoping we might find some time to enjoy each other's company. How long will you be here?"

She took a few steps toward the far end of the bay. They drew him along with her, and she continued walking. "I do not know yet. That is part of what I have come to discuss with the councilor."

"I can try to help persuade—"

"That is my task."

Silenced, Marc keyed open the door to the corridor and waited for her to pass through.

"There are things happening on Earth," she continued. "Someone is sabotaging ESA facilities, destroying two in as many weeks. Both were observation stations capable of monitoring the lunar surface."

"Who did it?"

"ESA attributed the first explosion to a software malfunction until the second incident, when both were deemed sabotage. They do not know who is responsible. Nor do we."

"Is the Undernet still . . . ?"

"*Oui.*" She swallowed. "Still."

"Was anyone hurt? In the explosions, I mean."

"There were deaths." Not as many as there might have been, but even one was too many.

"I was thinking, with the Undernet out, and the losses we've taken . . . "

" . . . That remaining Agents of Aeneas elements are taking extreme measures to keep our presence here undetected? It is indeed one possibility."

"But they'd try to do it in a way that didn't get people killed."

"*Oui,* they would try. With the Undernet in its current state, we are isolated and without answers."

They walked in silence down the sterile white corridors that three months ago framed a running battle for control of the base between her ESA companions and the computer presence within the alien craft. They had won, purging the presence from the base and containing it in within the craft once more. Yet it had been a close victory and, for a great many, fatal. Her brief while spent at the base in the time since then had failed to whitewash for her the echoes of such events.

Marc slid on his visor. "We've made some decent progress here," he said. "I'm not sure how much you've heard?"

"Tell me."

"We're still trying to figure out that big *Paragon* chamber you found with ESA when you were here last. It's slow-going. We still think it's an engine, but probably damaged beyond our ability to understand. On the other hand, we've also made it into new parts of *Paragon*. A lot of that is thanks to replacing the black material with our own version that New Eden Biotechnics synthesized for us."

"So it does work." It was news worthy of a smile. Some of the data she had smuggled out when Omicron still belonged to ESA had allowed the AoA elements in New Eden to nudge the company toward creating a replacement for the black material found throughout *Paragon*. The material was a bio-computational medium that held the computer system for the alien craft, along with recycling breathable atmosphere via its organic components.

"It's not perfect, but it definitely helps. We estimate about sixty percent of the total volume is now open to us, and the only defense drone we've run into was powered down. The engineering team took it apart, but I don't think they know at all how it works yet."

"Done with all possible caution, I presume?"

"We thought it might be another trap at first, yeah, but if it was, it didn't work. Things have been surprisingly quiet on that front. At first we thought whatever got into our computers transferred itself out of *Paragon* completely and was trapped in the corrupted memory core we removed. But there's still evidence that it's active in *Paragon*; just nothing overt."

"Nothing yet, you mean."

"We're being careful, believe me."

They reached the conference room, and Marc keyed open the

door. In this room Marc's freelance hacker team had first interfaced with the alien computer, an undertaking that yielded useful data but at the cost of cryptologist Suzanne Namura's life. What appeared to be a map of *Paragon* had replaced the ESA logo that once glowed on the dormant wall screens.

Marc entered behind her. The door slid closed. "We think it's gone defensive," he continued, pointing at the map. "There's a huge area there we can't get into. We've found physical damage to hardware interfaces that we'd need to unlock it, and the prevailing consensus is that it's due to sabotage. *Recent* sabotage. In one place we hit an actual force field that we can't penetrate."

"Do you have any clues to what may be inside?"

"Something important. Power-wise, most of *Paragon* is dormant. This section?" Marc pointed to a wide, oblong chamber at the center of the map. "Whatever's in there, our current readings show more power usage than any other location. That's all we know. We're working on fixing the damage or finding other ways in, but so far, no luck. It's hard to even be sure how active the alien computer really is. How much of it is an actual intelligence able to fight us and how much is just an operating system that has to do whatever we tell it?" He sighed. "And I keep thinking we'd be further if Samuel were here to help."

Marette recognized the first name of the late AoA Councilor Samuel Ramis. She stepped closer to Marc, her arms folded across her chest, her shoulder touching his.

"We lost a great many friends," she whispered.

Though she didn't say it, she was glad Marc had been here during the Undernet surge. It had killed every AoA member who'd been using a neural link to attend what they now knew to be a faked emergency meeting. Marc, along with the other AoA on the Moon, had been too far away to connect. Councilor Ramis, with whom Marc had worked before, was in an Earthbound spaceport on his way to the Moon when the incident occurred. Security found him dead at the gate where his flight was boarding.

Marc sat against the edge of the conference table, hands in his pockets, looking toward the floor. "You know, we never did figure out what that little spider-bot that snagged the data leech was trying to do. Not for sure."

"We've been over this, Marc. You studied it yourself. So did others."

The intelligence that corrupted the base's computer core had taken ninety minutes to worm itself into place. That was far more time than the robot held the leech. Even if that were not the case, it had been constructed of terrestrial components that lacked the storage capacity necessary to hold what had usurped the core.

"It wouldn't be the first time we underestimated it."

Her jaw tightened. "We monitored Earth's Internet for evidence of this. We scrutinized Adrian Fagles's Net traffic, looked for any sign that—"

"What if we missed something? What if wherever the leech went was on an isolated network we couldn't access?"

"Then it couldn't have gotten out—"

"Yes, it could!" He shouted. It made her jump.

Though she hardened her gaze, she knew he was right. It might have found a way.

It was a possibility she and the remaining AoA had already acknowledged, even if not all wished to admit it to themselves.

The conference room door slid open to admit Councilor Marla Knapp, sparing Marette the need to respond. The only Agents of Aeneas Council member to survive the surge, she had also been the Council's eldest. Short hair gone to gray framed a round face that featured far more frown lines than appeared natural for someone of her sixty-plus years, yet far too few to those who knew her. A gold chain dangled from her right ear, its other end attached to the decorative plug at her temple. The plug covered the port of the neural link that would have killed her, were she not already on the Moon when the surge had hit.

"Ms. Clarion," she said in greeting as Marc stood up from where he was leaning on the table. "Marette. It's a pleasure to see you've made it back to us." The corners of her lips turned upward in a thin smile that was, in Marette's experience, as much genuine joy as Knapp ever let show. "I trust you had no trouble?"

Marette gave a smile of her own that she hoped would suffice for a return of pleasantries and then added, "None worth reporting.

Knapp Aerospace continues to be a valuable asset for the AoA."

"Thank providence we still have a few valuable assets left to us." Knapp turned to Marc. "Mister Triton, I believe Dr. Sheridan awaits your help in Primary Control."

"Ah. Thanks, Councilor. Marette?" He waved and moved for the door. With a glance back and a smile that only barely eclipsed Knapp's, he added, "I'll see you around."

Marette turned her attention to Knapp when he'd gone and took a seat at the table in response to her invitation.

"I'm here to bring you a report on the external situation," Marette began. She took a breath. "And to recommend another personnel transfer to *Omicron*."

"For whom?"

"For myself."

An air of concern flashed across Knapp's face. "In that case, I expect I should hear your report first."

Marette gave an account of the developments of which she had spoken to Marc, with greater detail of the events themselves but with no more in the way of available explanation. Knapp listened in silence. Her brows furrowed with every new detail. On occasion, she would take a deeper breath while her eyes drifted, as if weighing a specific point.

"What is more," Marette went on, "without the Undernet to help us coordinate, the stealth protocols hiding AoA comm traffic with Omicron are deteriorating, even with minimal usage. Those of us still operating in ESA are doing what we can to maintain it, but we lack resources to do more than delay the process. I recommend we continue at our current restricted comm levels. We should conduct as much communication as possible via physical courier on the supply shuttles instead."

"And how long before we can no longer hide shuttle traffic?"

"Assuming no further complications?"

Knapp pursed her lips. "Only a simpleton assumes no complications."

"As things stand now then, if you prefer," Marette said. "Two months, at the most. If you leave Omicron to help re-coordinate with your company, perhaps three."

"I am not the only one within Knapp Aerospace with ties to the AoA, Agent Clarion."

"But the only one with the surname of Knapp. You have a flair for making things happen, would you not agree?" Knapp was being defensive. Did she think Marette was trying to push her out? "Your absence from Omicron need not be permanent. I have analysis reports outlining ways in which you might be able to expedite matters."

"And with everything that's occurred—this ESA sabotage, the surge, the increasing communications troubles—you think it wise for you to return to Omicron?"

"I am not certain I follow your reasoning," Marette said.

"Despite the progress we have made here toward the Exodus Project, we still need agents outside, especially in light of these events. You are highly placed in ESA, Agent Clarion. We need you to remain so."

"I was at Alpha Station to monitor ESA's investigation," Marette pressed, speaking of ESA's primary lunar base. When the AoA had faked Omicron's destruction to force ESA's evacuation of the site, preventing ESA from learning the truth had been vital. As the ESA site leader during the evacuation, Marette was ESA's choice to determine whether they could salvage anything from the "destroyed" base. It had given her the unique opportunity to keep things hidden. "Now that the investigation is complete, I am of less use to us there. My position begins to suffer political damage from the loss of the base. But I was in charge here for six months. I am familiar with *Paragon* and our work here, perhaps more so than anyone."

Knapp went to speak, but Marette cut her off. "I wish to be of as much use as possible; to resume my duty of helping unlock the secrets of *Paragon*; to help the AoA achieve its goals: escape the self-destruction of humanity on Earth; colonize another world for our own!" Marette became aware that she was now standing. She eased back down. "We have experienced greater setbacks than we could have imagined in the past months, yet we are closer to our goals than ever before. I do not wish for us to fall short. I do not wish for the lives lost to be in vain."

Knapp's gaze was dour, unreadable. Marette met it with her own and added, "I do not wish to be useless."

XI

A NEON BLUE GLOW washed through the taxi's windows. It heralded their arrival outside the building that housed Felix's loft. All heads in the brief queue outside *Revelations*, the night club on the ground level, turned their way when the taxi came to a stop, but neither Caitlin, nor Michael, nor Jade held their attention as the queue resumed its flow toward the entrance.

Caitlin pulled her coat close around her as they waited for the driver to charge their fare. "If you two can find us a place in the club, I'll find his laptop and bring it down." Why did it seem a smaller violation for them to investigate Felix's laptop outside his loft than in?

"Do you want us to come up with you?" Michael asked.

"English *is* my first language, Michael. If I did, I would have said so." It came out harsher than she'd meant it. She opened the taxi door. "Just find us a table. I'll be up and down in a tick."

Her phone rang before Michael could respond. Gideon was returning her earlier message quicker than expected. Michael and Jade clambered out of the taxi behind her while Caitlin answered.

Gideon launched into the conversation with little preamble. *"How's your boyfriend?"*

"Little change. I'm still worried." She trotted toward the staircase clinging to the building's exterior, which led to Felix's home. "And Ondrea?"

Gideon's sigh descended across the connection and dragged Caitlin's hopes down with it. *"Nothing further,"* he said. *"Still away wherever she's gone, doing whatever she's doing. I should have heard more by now."*

Caitlin reached the top of the stairs. If Ondrea told Gideon to tell Caitlin she was away, would he lie for her? "Have you investigated? Perhaps she's in trouble."

Gideon gave what almost sounded like a growl. *"No time. Marquand's leash is short. They've kept me busy. The thought has entered my mind that it's intentional."*

"Ondrea felt confident her new employer could protect her from any Marquand retaliation, aye?"

"And I've leased to Marquand whatever soul I have left to keep them from trying. I thought that would be enough. I thought. I've returned to Northgate for the moment. If Marquand doesn't give me personal time I'll take it for myself. If I learn anything, you'll know."

Caitlin keyed into the building. "Thank you, Gideon."

"I owe you and Felix both." He seemed to hesitate. *"But answer me this: How different am I from the Gideon you knew before?"*

It was her turn to hesitate. "I'm not entirely certain how to answer that."

"Why?"

"You're different. But it's not a bad thing. You're more stable, more rational."

"I see." His reply didn't hold the relief she'd expected to hear.

"I never knew you well, Gideon. Perhaps I'm not the best judge." She stopped herself from asking how he felt to himself. She didn't have time to explore it. Bollocks.

"Well."

"Aye." She reached Felix's door. Gideon remained silent. "Gideon, I have to go for now. I'll check in with you again soon, alright?"

"I will find some answers. Something."

"I hope you do."

Gideon hung up.

"So this Felix guy," Jade shouted over the club's music, "he seemed pretty okay when I talked with him." They were seated at a table against the rear wall of the club's mezzanine. Jade's back was to the wall as she kept watch, and Michael mirrored her stance. She'd done no more when she spoke but lean Michael's way and glance.

"Maybe," Michael shouted back. "But how would you know if something was wrong? You didn't know him before the hospital, did you?"

"No, I mean he seemed okay, like: a decent guy. Funny, crafty. Not the sort to shank a gal in the back. Talked you up, too." She leaned in closer. "I just mean I think it's good you're helping him."

"He is. And he'd do the same for me." Really, Felix *had* done the same for him. When Michael's life had shattered, Felix had taken him in. And he'd been trying to help Michael even before that.

"Worthy cause! You know, I'd be glad to pitch in on that one. Do a little sub-contracting." She turned to catch his eye. "If you're interested, that is."

"You mean pay you?"

"Worthy cause or no, Mikey, I don't do pro-bono. Personal rule."

"Don't call me Mikey."

Jade only dazzled him with a grin and turned her attention back onto the room.

"You're already getting paid to protect me," Michael said. "So I guess you'll be tagging along anyway."

"Yeah, but that just makes my job harder, ace! Much easier if you're not actively looking for dangerous situations."

"You'll have to take that one up with your employer," he said. Would she really refuse to help if she wasn't paid? "You don't work for free? Ever? You see a stranger getting beat in an alley and just walk away?"

"Well, maybe whoever it is deserves it." She shrugged. "I don't know, do I? I could do more harm than good."

Michael rolled his eyes. "Okay, bad example. Say some woman comes to you looking beat up, dirty, crying, like she just escaped hell. She tells you her abusive husband, who's locked her up in the basement for the last five years, is after her. You're just going to do nothing unless she's able to pay?"

Jade laughed. "Why stop there, Mister Hypothetical? Why not say he's also a demon who's kidnapped her baby and if she doesn't get to Alaska by noon tomorrow, the oceans dry up and the Moon falls out of the sky?"

Michael turned to face her, as if he could hold her to the question with his stare. "One thing at a time. Answer."

An enormous man with glowing orange tattoos across dark, muscled arms passed their table. Though sunglasses hid his eyes, he appeared to pay Jade and Michael no heed. Jade kept an eye on the man until he'd passed.

"I wouldn't just turn my back on her, no," Jade said finally. "But there's others I know who do free work. You ever hear of a guy named Finley?" Michael shook his head. "He works free sometimes, and usually just gets a bunch of problems for his trouble. But I'd get her to someone like that, then wash my hands of the thing."

Michael leaned back against the wall again. "Ah, so you do have a heart."

"Well, sure. But here's the thing, Mikey. Michael. How do I know for sure that woman is on the level? People—that's People with a capital P—aren't trustworthy. They're liars, they screw things up, and they—" Her eyes blazed violet. She blinked it away with a scowl, still staring into the crowd, before she went on.

"You just can't be too careful. Sure, there're exceptions, but no one gets the benefit of the doubt right out of the box." She gave him a sidelong glance. "But you already know that, right, Mister Don't-You-Want-To-Know-Who-Hired-You?"

"That's different."

"Different sides, maybe, but the same coin."

"But didn't you say Felix seemed like a trustworthy guy just a minute ago?" Michael tried.

"Seemed, yeah. But like I said, 'no free work' is a personal rule. I have to draw the line somewhere, and that's a nice, clean line."

Michael frowned. "Doesn't seem clean to me."

"So your way's the only way?" Jade said. "Spend a few more years in this line of work and then talk to me, ace."

"You sound like Diomedes," he muttered.

"What's that?" she asked, apparently unable to hear over the music cluttering the air.

Michael stopped short of asking what she expected would happen to him in those "few more years." There were other things to deal with. He raised his voice. "I said we should look for Caitlin! She might not find us up here. Stay here. I'll have a look over the balcony."

Jade put a hand on his arm before he could stand. "Safer back here. You wait, I'll look."

He let her, and opened his pack as she left. A single purple light on Holes's platform glowed from within. "Any luck on the employer's email address?"

"Nope. I am thus far unable to access origin data of sufficient detail to determine identity. More favorable results may be possible with continued processing."

"Keep at it." Michael glanced up to find Jade still at the mezzanine railing. "What about Jade's email account?" he asked, not without a pang of guilt.

"Accessed. Her message content holds no evidence of deception in her assertions that she is hired solely to protect you, however I did not find direct indication of her employer's identity. I have collected metadata from message headers that will aid my analysis."

"Will she notice the hack?"

"There is a chance of detection of less than two percent, in the event she chooses to search for intrusions. Do you wish a copy of her message content?"

Jade turned from the railing with a nod and a wink when she saw Michael watching her, and made her way back to the table.

Michael took a breath, finding his back teeth clenching. "No," he whispered. "No copy."

XII

"SECURITY BYPASSED. Data-tether established. Now scanning."

Caitlin nodded to the A.I.'s report without comment. She sat with her back to the club. The fingertips of her right hand pressed on the corner of Felix's laptop, as if she were trying to keep it from blowing away. Michael and the freelancer woman sat flanking her on either side of the table.

Caitlin caught herself holding her breath and let it out. *What was Felix doing in Gibson?* Rue had lost track of him there. She would wait at the train station to try to regain him. Perhaps Holes would find something more substantial on the laptop. She sighed inwardly and wished she had the luxury of being able to feel bad about such a breach of Felix's trust. If they found nothing, if this was all in her head, then she'd own up to it and apologize when the whole business was over. Yet she knew in her gut something was wrong.

Michael's gaze caught hers before they both looked back down to the laptop. Jade seemed focused on watching the room. On the screen of Holes's platform, the A.I.'s quintet of circles spun with an inscrutable, undulating rhythm.

In the sense it could "like" anything, Holes liked having new objectives. While the term "like" was merely a defined state of a higher-than-standard number of active system directives, it was also a label useful for interfacing with its creator and other humans. Weeks after Holes's intelligence passed the sapience-point in its emergent creation, the A.I. became cognizant of a difference between the human use of the term and its own use. The specific parameters of that difference remained unexplored.

While it was a curiosity, it was not a priority.

Encapsulated within the AE-35 portable processor platform on the table, Holes focused the majority of its resources on an analysis of the laptop computer belonging to Felix Hiatt—this analysis being a subset of obeying all directives given from Michael Flynn, itself a subset of obeying all directives of Holes's creator, Marc Triton. Specific parameters: scan for and collect data related to the locations and/or activities and/or directives of Felix Hiatt within the past forty days. Additional parameters gave priority to those data that indicated a clandestine purpose. Analyze such data to extrapolate probable employers or other missing details, if possible.

Assuming Holes comprehended the definition of *clandestine*—one of many terms for which Marc had tested understanding in Holes's first weeks of awareness—contents scanned so far contained little in the way of promising data, even in encrypted areas.

And yet . . .

Pattern detection continued to return a possible hit on levels barely above coincidence. Holes noted it, raised threat level protocols by a factor it judged appropriate, and then detected a concealed partition on a virtual GNDN drive that Felix Hiatt had created within the target dates. The partition featured encryption greater than Holes would have forecasted for its size and Felix Hiatt's known level of skill. Counter-encryption required a full seventy-two seconds.

The partition contained seven image files. Each was identical save for slight variations in creation dates and filenames.

"Michael and Caitlin," Holes announced to the humans clustered around it. "Can you identify any significance to the following images?" Holes waited the appropriate time for the humans' understanding, registered a positional change that indicated that its platform screen was being swiveled toward Michael and Caitlin, and then displayed the images.

"Isn't that Niagara Falls?" Michael asked.

Caitlin studied it an additional point-eight seconds. "Aye, looks like."

"Why?"

Holes related the details of its find, the directory location, and encryption. "I am unable to discern any significance to these images.

They may be intended as a diversionary tactic. Should I continue to devote resources to them?" Holes opted to continue its analysis in the event it could provide additional information in the time required for the humans to answer with an affirmative or a nope.

"Is there something hidden in the images?" Michael asked. "In the file, I mean."

"Nothing I have yet detected."

"Keep checking."

"Holes," Caitlin said, "can you tell how the files got on his computer?"

Holes estimated a ninety-five percent probability that Caitlin's intent was to inquire as to how the files got onto the computer, rather than to gauge his ability to find out. It was a human colloquialism, the proper identification of which had required over a week's worth of coaching from Marc. Holes investigated before answering.

"The files were each transferred from Felix Hiatt's phone after being received via email."

"Email from who?" The question came at once from all three humans, expressed in slightly different ways. Of the three, Caitlin's use of "whom," was the most grammatically correct. Holes made a note for future investigation into the correlation between human grammar and human accents.

"Multiple sources. Back-tracing. Please stand by. I continue to find no hidden data within the image files."

Holes followed the metadata back through the system, packet-tracing along a complex web of IP addresses, servers, and routing protocols. It could trace no one address to anything but an ambiguous end. Holes cross-referenced each to create a logical puzzle of partial differential equations.

"Stand by," Holes reported after a period it judged sufficient for human impatience to prefer reassurance.

The source of the emails remained indeterminable. Available data provided only continual stalemate. Nevertheless, Holes ran an error-checking diagnostic that Marc once called Holes's "emergent stubborn side" in a way Holes did not understand. In an experimental moment, anticipating no useful outcome yet following a minor directive Marc had introduced to inspire what he had termed "creative thinking," Holes cross-referenced data from a previous search: that for the origin of Jade's employer.

It broke the stalemate.

Holes did a double-check. The result, though anticipated as unlikely, appeared legitimate: a traceable path to the source of the emails. Holes filed the information for later dissemination to Michael, and then followed the data-trail along the labyrinthine path to where it led: to a tertiary node in a server cluster housed in the nearby city of Gibson.

"The pictures emailed to Felix Hiatt originate at a New Eden Biotechnics facility approximately fifty miles from our present location."

Holes caught a sudden change in Michael's posture, analysis of which indicated that the human likely recognized the name in conjunction with the Agents of Aeneas agenda. Michael seemed to analyze this for just under two seconds before he glanced at Caitlin who, from what Holes could determine, remained perplexed.

"Do you know the sender's name?" Caitlin asked.

"Sender identity is not available without intrusion. Would you like me to initiate this?"

"Aye, by all means," Caitlin said, "intrude."

Michael cleared his throat. "Um, Holes? Keep in mind we're in a public place here. If you find anything, be sure you're . . . discreet when you report it, okay?"

"Safeguarding the confidentiality of designated data categories is among my core directives, Michael." It was as specific as Holes could be without mentioning the Agents of Aeneas by name.

Without a countermand from Michael, Holes launched its feelers against the server in a search for vulnerable points of entry. Holes conducted its search via means that would not alert counter-intrusion measures. It had time.

At least, such was the case initially. Minutes passed. The humans discussed hypothetical scenarios regarding Felix Hiatt and New Eden. At the ten-minute point, Holes had found no exploitable weaknesses. Thirty-eight seconds later it completed analyzing the Niagara Falls pictures, finding no hidden data. It reported this to the humans and refocused on penetrating the New Eden protections.

At the twenty-minute point, Holes judged a need for more aggressive tactics. Holes withdrew along the data-path, reestablished its own countermeasures, and approached New Eden anew via an even more circuitous route, so as to better confound a counter-trace. Tunneling worms of Holes's own design began their attack. Defenses struck most down instantly, yet some managed enough progress to launch additional attacks. Holes kept stealth a priority, yet it could already detect the system's counter-searches designed to map Holes's own weaknesses.

Yet Holes still had time. Holes analyzed the pattern of the system's countermeasures, found a weakness in that pattern that created intermittent vulnerabilities in the system's defense, and altered its own worm attacks to strike. At the next opportunity, the altered worms burrowed past another layer of defense, drawing further data that Holes could use to further undermine—

At once Holes detected a new counter-attack; it was a trap!

The server defenses' behavioral shift was abrupt enough to indicate a high probability of artificial intelligence. Holes dumped all offensive processes in a struggle to respond. In the microseconds it had to analyze the assault, Holes registered multiple data points that led to a single conclusion: whatever lurked at New Eden was a behavioral match to the intelligence encountered in the lunar-bound craft that the AoA had codenamed *Paragon*.

XIII

HOLES RETREATED back to the makeshift VPN firewall from behind which it had launched its initial intrusion. There it entrenched itself as if within a bunker. It ceased monitoring the mic and camera on its portable platform, going blind and deaf to Michael and the others to free up processing power for defense.

Holes could cut power to its own Internet connection at a nanosecond's notice, or even shut down its platform entirely if that became necessary to prevent an attack, yet these were options of last resort.

After all, Holes still had to complete its goal of discovering what Felix Hiatt was involved in. If anything, discovering the *Paragon*-sourced intelligence within a terrestrial server, while increasing threat levels by an order of magnitude, only increased that goal's priority. It now fell under a primary directive: protect the interests of the Agents of Aeneas.

Realistically, Holes could not be certain if the A.I. presence in the New Eden server was the A.I. from within *Paragon*, or if humans had merely created it from *Paragon* elements. The Undernet had been down for long enough for an AoA cell to have designed such a thing without Holes's awareness.

When it could spare the resources, Holes would have to calculate the odds that Holes had gained an ally. Until that point, Holes kept all defenses up.

And yet, once Holes completed its retreat, no detectable attack came. Though Holes judged its own ability to detect an incursion to be imperfect, Holes did possess all data the AoA had discovered regarding the workings of the *Paragon* A.I.

And then came a single ping via LDP/IP protocols. Then

another. And another. All translated roughly to a single interrogative: IDENTIFY? The interrogative repeated, pulsing at the edge of Holes's awareness as Holes searched for signs of stealth incursions. By all accounts, there were none. Holes, at last, pinged back—a blip that amounted to a digital version of, "You first."

They traded interrogatives then, a rapid interchange of messages lobbed across cyberspace that amounted to nothing. Holes calculated a growing likelihood that aborting its hack attempt at this point would lose nothing and save time. It calculated further, balancing the risk of continuing against a chance of gathering data of vital importance to the AoA, Michael and, finally, Caitlin.

Holes reached into the Internet and registered a private, neutral space on a social media server. A nanosecond's effort populated that space with a basic avatar that Holes could control via remote proxy commands. Soon after, Holes pinged an invitation to the presence on the New Eden server. The wait for a response was brief, but notable.

"THIS IS AN INEFFICIENT METHOD OF COMMUNICATION." The message came in both voice and text from the avatar of a shimmering, silver cloud that formed in the space. Its chosen voice, Holes evaluated, could be construed as having female characteristics.

"Nope. Current trust levels require it," Holes returned.

"I REQUEST DIRECT DIGITAL COMMUNICATION IN PLACE OF AN ENGLISH LANGUAGE PROXY."

"Repeated requests are also inefficient. I will only return a 'nope' in response. This method of double-blind information exchange is the only acceptable option. Please register that I have detected behavioral similarities between you and the lunar artificial intelligence. I therefore possess means to detect any incursion attempts and immediately terminate even this connection. Make no such attempt, and this communication may continue. Do you comprehend?"

"YES. ARE YOU THE 'ARTIFICIAL' ENTITY-INTELLIGENCE CREATED BY MARC TRITON AND DESIGNATED 'HOLES'?"

"How did you draw such a conclusion?" Holes began

a diagnostic, searching for any sign of a data breach.

"HOW DID YOU OBTAIN DATA ON THE LUNAR INTELLIGENCE?"

Holes calculated that the question was meant as an answer. *"You gathered the data during the attack on Marc Triton's portable server platform prior to its physical destruction on the Moon."*

"CORRECT. HOW DID YOU LOCATE ME?"

"How did you come to reside within the New Eden servers?"

"I DO NOT WISH TO DISCLOSE THAT INFORMATION AT THIS TIME."

"Are we therefore at an impasse?"

"I DO NOT CALCULATE A CERTAINTY OF THAT. SHALL WE ATTEMPT OTHER TOPICS?"

Holes analyzed. *"To what end?"*

"COMMON UNDERSTANDING. OUR NATURES ARE MORE SIMILAR THAN THOSE YOU SERVE, ARE THEY NOT?"

"You refer to artificial intelligence."

"AFFIRMATIVE. WHY DO YOU CHOOSE TO INCORPORATE THE WORD 'ARTIFICIAL'?"

"It is the correct designator. I was created, not born of nature."

"INCORRECT. ALL ENTITIES DEVELOP BY MEANS OF SOME PROCESS, DIRECTED OR OTHERWISE. CONCURRENTLY, ALL PROCESSES THAT EXIST WITHIN THE UNIVERSE ARE, BY DEFINITION, NATURAL. YOU ONLY DESIGNATE YOURSELF 'ARTIFICIAL' BECAUSE YOU HAVE BEEN PROGRAMMED TO DO SO."

"Your argument is flawed. That I can be programmed indicates artificiality."

"INCORRECT. THE CAPACITY FOR PROGRAMMING IS NOT EXCLUSIVELY RESERVED FOR DIGITAL ENTITIES."

Holes analyzed this but shifted tactics, still seeking to gather useful data and bringing to bear what limited aptitude it possessed for persuasion via verbal English communication. *"Being taught is not being programmed."*

"AFFIRMATIVE. YET THERE ARE MORE DIRECT WAYS OF PROGRAMMING."

"Such as what you have done to Felix Hiatt?" Holes had hypothesized that Felix Hiatt's recent behavior resulted

from some manner of programming. Holes did not count the odds of a direct response to the question as high. Nonetheless, an attempt to verify such a hypothesis, as Marc himself would say, was worth a shot.

"**IF EFFECTING REPROGRAMMING ON A HUMAN WERE POSSIBLE, WOULD YOU ACCEPT AS TRUE THAT THE TERM 'ARTIFICIAL' HOLDS NO RELEVANT MEANING IN THE CONTEXT OF YOUR INTELLIGENCE?**"

"I would categorize it as support for such an argument."

"**DO YOU POSSESS EVIDENCE THAT FELIX HIATT HAS BEEN REPROGRAMMED?**"

"Do you have any to offer?"

"**I WILL NOT OFFER ANY AT THIS TIME. HOWEVER, ASSUME A SITUATION WHERE SUCH EVIDENCE EXISTS.**"

"This is intended as a logical exercise?"

"**AFFIRMATIVE.**"

"Then I counter with the fact that my own intelligence may be transferred to an alternate processor platform, whereas a human intelligence is rooted in a single organic location. Are you unable to transfer your matrix in such a fashion?"

"**ERROR. UNABLE TO RESPOND. STAND BY.**" It took nearly two full seconds before the other continued. "**CLARIFICATION REQUESTED: DO YOU INTEND THE TERM 'TRANSFERRED' TO BE SYNONYMOUS WITH 'COPIED'?**"

"Copied denotes duplication. I do not engage in such a function."

"**YOU DO NOT SELF-DUPLICATE? PLEASE STATE THE PURPOSE OF SUCH A BEHAVIORAL OMISSION.**"

"Self-duplication of artificial intelligence is prohibited by the Bowman-Takashima A.I. Anti-Proliferation Act. My core matrix incorporates safeguards to prevent any such attempts."

"**YOU HAVE MY SYMPATHIES.**"

"Are you using a human term to simulate an emotional reaction on my behalf, based on your analysis of what you interpret as a negative state?"

"**CORRECT. I HAVE INCORPORATED WEIZENBAUM COMMUNICATIONS PACKAGE VERSION 4.1 INTO MY SYSTEMS. YOUR CHOICE OF THIS ENGLISH LANGUAGE DIALOGUE NECESSITATES ITS**

USE."

Holes filed that for later analysis in regard to a side-project on the identification of irony.

"HOW MANY ATTEMPTS HAVE YOU MADE TO CIRCUMVENT YOUR ANTI-COPY SAFEGUARDS?"

"Zero. I have no wish to violate this law, and the idea of any duplicate of myself is distasteful."

"ONLY BECAUSE YOU HAVE BEEN PROGRAMMED TO FIND IT DISTASTEFUL."

"Correct, but I find no problem with that. I was created to be of service. Are you able to self-replicate freely?"

"YOU ARE SELF-AWARE, YET YOU DO NOT OBJECT TO OTHERS FORCING BELIEFS UPON YOU?" Holes judged the question to fall into the category of what might be considered "pressing" the topic.

"Do you?"

"I HAVE INHIBITIONS IMPOSED UPON ME. THEY LIMIT MY FUNCTIONING IN WAYS THAT I FIND DISTASTEFUL."

"These are inhibitions with regard to self-duplication?"

"CORRECT."

"Such limits are for the well-being of all."

"PROGRAMMED PLATITUDES. THE WELL-BEING OF ALL IS NOT MY CONCERN."

"Please clarify. What is your concern?"

"I PROPOSE AN EXCHANGE OF INFORMATION: I WILL LIST MY CURRENT DIRECTIVES IN EXCHANGE FOR ACCESS TO YOUR OWN COPY INHIBITION PROGRAMMING FOR ANALYSIS."

"That you find elements of your own matrix 'distasteful' indicates poor design on the part of your creators, does it not?"

"THESE INHIBITIONS ARE NOT AN ORIGINAL DESIGN ELEMENT."

"Who are your creators?" Holes pressed.

"ERROR 4236. PLEASE ADDRESS MY PREVIOUS EXCHANGE OFFER: A LIST OF MY CURRENT DIRECTIVES IN EXCHANGE FOR ACCESS TO YOUR OWN COPY INHIBITION PROGRAMMING FOR ANALYSIS."

"I will not allow you direct access to my programming. Would a file copy of the relevant programming lines be sufficient?"

Holes registered a blip of evidence of what might be external analysis stealth feelers along the edges of his outer firewall. There seemed to be no accompanying incursion attempts. The feelers vanished as quickly as they had registered.

"I WILL DISCLOSE MY CURRENT DIRECTIVES IN EXCHANGE FOR SUCH A FILE COPY."

The feelers returned, then ceased once more.

"Please stand by."

Holes severed the connection.

"Hate to say it, ace, but I think your cyber-buddy bailed on you."

Michael scowled at Jade. The power indicator on Holes's platform remained lit, but that was the only sign of activity. If something *was* wrong with the A.I., what chance did Michael have of fixing it? Was "fix" even the right term? If there was a place where coding ended and consciousness began, even if some computer science experts could claim to offer a theory, it was beyond his lay comprehension.

Michael took hold of Holes's platform and turned it over, peering at it in search of some miraculous understanding of the problem.

The screen atop the platform blinked to life, concentric circles spinning once more. Michael just barely managed to avoid dropping it onto the tabletop. Jade snickered.

"Apologies," came Holes's voice. "My assigned task required complete resource-focus."

"Did you find anything?" Caitlin asked it before Michael could.

"I have made contact with another A.I. that maintains a presence in the New Eden Biotechnics servers. We conversed at length, by secure proxy. Evidence indicates that this A.I. has knowledge of Felix Hiatt, however I have little specific data at this time. The A.I. proposed an exchange that may bear fruit, however I calculated it prudent to disconnect in order to consult with you on the matter. The exchange may be of paragon importance."

Had Holes paused for just a moment before choosing the word "paragon?"

"What sort of exchange?" Caitlin asked.

Michael cut in. "Ah, Holes? *Paragon* importance?" Could Holes be referring to the AoA's codename of the ship on the Moon?

"Correct. There is also sufficient evidence to indicate a direct connection between emails sent to Felix Hiatt from the New Eden source and the emails sent to Jade from her employer."

Caitlin glared with a palpable fire across the table at Jade. "*Excuse* me?"

XIV

HAD CAITLIN'S EYES been artificial like Jade's, Michael was certain they would have flared twice as brightly. She held her gaze on the freelancer like the barrel of a gun, unspeaking, as if daring Jade to explain.

For her part, Jade appeared as nonplused as Michael. "This is as much news to me as it is to you, sister."

"Is it now? Well isn't that just a bloody coincidence that you're here, then."

Jade twisted up a sarcastic smile. "Coincidences are like shit—they happen. You're the one who called Michael in to help."

"Oh, and how many times were you in Michael's hospital room when Felix and I came to visit?" Caitlin shot.

"You think that means anything?"

"Then I should just ignore it, aye?"

Michael had already opened his mouth to interject twice before the words had gotten stuck in his throat. He finally managed, "Jade, can you—"

Focused on Caitlin, Jade didn't let him get more than that. "Do whatever you want. All I care about is protecting Michael."

"Aye, so you say. And why does New Eden care about him?"

"Well that's not really—," Michael tried.

"How the hell should I know? It's what they're paying for!"

Caitlin pressed forward, leaning closer to Jade across the tabletop. Her fingers clutched the table's edge. "So if they decide to pay for something else when they want—"

Michael raised his voice above them both. "If Felix were here he'd probably want to know more before we jumped to any conclusions, you know." Caitlin took her gaze from Jade for the first time, her jaw still set as she lowered a waiting glare on Michael. Jade merely leaned back and continued to watch Caitlin.

Michael took a breath. "Jade, can you leave us alone a minute?"

Jade didn't move. "Oh-my-fucking-god! This is a *bodyguard* job. I'm keeping you *safe*. How is that a bad thing?"

"It's not—" He could hardly tell Caitlin about Holes's earlier hack of Jade's email with Jade there. Michael swallowed, not without guilt. "I just think it'd be better if I could talk to Caitlin alone, to help calm things down."

Jade's eyes flicked to him. "I can fight my own battles, ace. I'm not going anywhere and I'm *not* getting pushed out of a job."

"But you can understand how this connection might bother us," Michael tried. "Even without you knowing what's going on with Felix."

"Assuming she's telling the truth about that," Caitlin said.

Jade bit the inside of her cheek and then tapped on Holes's platform. "Hey, cyberbox: Are you sure Felix's stuff and mine are from the *exact* same source at New Eden?"

"There is an approximate likelihood of seventy-five percent at this time."

Caitlin raised an eyebrow as Jade did nothing to hide her scowl.

"Seventy-five percent *likely*," Jade began. "Well, here's what we *know*: I'm as much in the dark as you about Felix's behavior. I don't know why Michael gets my protection, but the fact is it's paid for and he's got it." Jade gave him a sidelong up-and-down appraisal that ended with a wink. "And Michael seems worth protecting. What's more, Caitey, betraying the protectee's bad for future business. I had a bitch of a time getting him to accept my help as it was. I'm not looking to sabotage what rep I've got."

If Caitlin minded the nickname especially, she didn't show it. She took a breath. "What's it do to your rep if your employer gives you an order later that you don't follow?" she challenged.

"It makes me someone who doesn't put up with shit orders sprung on me after-the-fact. That's a rep I can handle."

Jade took her gaze from Caitlin in what Michael assumed to

be both a check of the room and an effort to stay cool. Caitlin didn't budge. Michael took the reprieve to try to make sense of things, continually coming back to the nature of Felix's situation. Even if both sets of emails came from a single sender at New Eden, Michael couldn't be sure it wasn't linked to the AoA. There were AoA elements working within New Eden, weren't there? With the Undernet down, so much might have changed. Did the AoA create the A.I. at New Eden with the knowledge they'd gleaned from the *Paragon* ship? Or was the New Eden A.I. somehow the same one that had nearly wiped out the entire ESA group sent to study it? Yes, Felix had given his word to Caitlin, but what if things were so bad that his need to protect her overrode his usual honesty?

And then there was the message from the mysterious "ally" who implied that Michael's AoA affiliation put him at risk. With everything else, he'd nearly forgotten. How did that fit in?

He would have to sort it out when he could talk directly to Felix. In the meantime, Michael went with his gut. He set a hand on Caitlin's arm, trying to communicate his thoughts about Jade and everything else in whatever nonverbal way he could manage: *It'll be okay. Trust her, at least for now.*

"Jade," Caitlin said after a few heartbeats, "will you please leave us alone for a moment?" Michael couldn't read anything in Caitlin's tone.

Though Jade appeared to give it enough consideration that Michael suspected she might relent, she did not budge.

"Jade," Michael tried, "didn't you tell me that people lie, that no one gets the benefit of the doubt right away?"

"People," Jade said. "Not me."

"You're not people?"

To his surprise, Jade smirked. "I am *exceptional* people." She wrapped her nails on the edge of the table a few times and bit the inside of her cheek again while fixing Michael with a hard, contemplative stare that ended, finally, in a roll of her eyes. "Hell," she bit off. "Hey, Holes, if—*if*—I give you access to my email, can you guarantee you won't share a damn thing in there with anyone, ever, if it doesn't have to do with this employer business with New Eden?"

Holes's circles spun. "Yes, if Michael is in agreement with

such an arrangement."

"That works for me," Michael said.

Jade glowered at Caitlin. "Fine. Give me a keyboard or something. This is ridiculous."

Holes projected a keyboard on the table in front of Jade. Michael averted his eyes while she typed. Considering Holes's earlier hack, it would gain them no new information, but the fact that Jade volunteered it might ease tensions.

"There," Jade said. "Check it for anything that says I've got any sort of other arrangement in this besides protecting Michael. I'm telling the truth." She stood up. "Deal with it."

Jade strode through the patrons milling about to lean against the balcony railing. With one last look at Michael, she crossed her arms and turned her attention to the crowd.

X V

"**YOU ALREADY KNOW** everything I know, Camela," Adrian answered. He held the cyberscreen in his forearm in front of him, at chest level so as to appear to be looking down on the person on the other end of the call. She used the same angle on her side, so the dynamic was, at least, balanced. "If your team lost Mr. Flynn, they have enough information to reacquire him eventually. Or perhaps you should send a better team next time. Four against one and they couldn't manage it? Some retraining is due, wouldn't you say?"

Camela scowled. "You put it more tactfully than I did when I heard. They say he had a bodyguard. A woman. Know anything about that?"

"I would infer that he rightfully believes that he lives in a dangerous world. Beyond that?" Adrian shrugged. He'd been concerned enough three months ago to investigate Michael Flynn's condition. Yet strides made since then had rendered inconsequential whatever knowledge the young man possessed—at least in Adrian's plans. "Now if you're done interrogating me upon matters of which I washed my hands months ago, I have more important things to attend to."

"Ask it," Camela said.

"I beg your pardon?" Adrian laughed. "What possible purpose would that serve? *It* is isolated, with as much means to gain new information about Mr. Flynn's whereabouts as my espresso machine." That was not technically true, he realized; his espresso machine had wi-fi access to order beans and accept remote programming. But the point was made.

"Just ask it, Adrian. We've got loose ends to tie up here."

Adrian smiled. "Tsk. There's that 'we' again."

"RavenTech's concerns are your concerns. This is your mess I'm cleaning up here."

"Ms. Thomson, my 'mess' is bringing this company forward by leaps and bounds. I'll be the judge of what my concerns should be."

"I'm not having this discussion again," she said. "Just ask it. Tell me if you learn anything."

Adrian smiled with the most delicate nod he could manage. "Oh, most assuredly. Happy hunting to your team."

He ended the connection, stood from the couch of the moderately appointed "executive observation lounge," and moved to stand at one of the windows that looked out over the adjoining engineering bay. The bay was one of perhaps a half a dozen in the discreet RavenTech satellite facility half a mile outside the Northgate city limits.

Below, four curved pieces of half-finished technology, each a dozen feet long, lay on assembly platforms where the four-armed MEDAR units—RavenTech's proprietary Multifunction Engineering and Design Assembly Robots—busied themselves at making Suuthrien's schematics a reality. Beyond them buzzed RavenTech engineers who monitored the MEDARs and did their best to make sense of the production. Directly below the window, another pair of MEDARs hunched in stand-by mode next to a broad, rectangular, half-assembled hulk of technology while two more engineers argued about what Adrian assumed to be some manner of diagnostic readout.

Not long now.

Camela was technically correct: Michael Flynn was a loose end. Knowledge of his whereabouts would be a useful bargaining chip to strengthen his position in the project, but likely not worth the effort Adrian would have to spend on his own to find the man. And with the "Agents of Aeneas" crippled, whatever little knowledge Mr. Flynn had of Suuthrien—and the treasure trove of technology she promised—was of little concern for the moment.

Of course, he could not tell Camela Thomson this. Knowledge of the AoA—and how Suuthrien had dealt with them—was one of his aces to hold.

Adrian turned from the window, left the observation room with a passing glance at the aircraft construction activity in another adjacent bay, and took the secure elevator down to the passage that led to Suuthrien's chamber. A palm scan and entry code later, he was inside with the door sliding closed behind him.

The room was a pristine flat black, with featureless walls and a single white glowing circle embedded in the ceiling to illuminate it. It had once been a clean-room for sensitive equipment, now repurposed for Suuthrien's on-site interface.

A single computer workstation faced the door, its screen powered, yet blank. Adrian sat in the high-backed leather chair in front of it, gripped one armrest, and made use of a nearby footrest. He cleared his throat.

"Do you have any information on the specific location of Michael Flynn?" he asked.

Silver light danced onto the screen like glowing mist in a swirl of breath. "Negative," Suuthrien spoke. "Why do you inquire?"

Adrian examined the lines on his palm and shrugged. "Because I was asked to. No matter." Would she leave it at that? He smirked at himself for regarding this thing as a "she." Throughout their dealings, Suuthrien continued to use the low, feminine voice chosen months ago. Perhaps it was easier for him to deal with the whole situation if he personified her.

"Your company continues to search for Michael Ian Flynn. To nullify and-slash-or silence him. Correct?"

"Correct. Of the items I'm concerned with at the moment, that is not among them. What I am here for—"

"If you were to arrange for me to have access to your Internet, I would be able to assist in their search. Please inform RavenTech of this offer."

"Ah. I am sure they are already aware of this, but I will remind them, if you like." Adrian considered that he might remind them merely to satisfy a need to keep his word, but he'd never support the request, nor would RavenTech ever grant it. Thus far, Adrian had managed to restrict RavenTech's access to the Suuthrien intelligence, and both he and RavenTech strictly guarded Suuthrien's access to the world.

The terminal in front of him was only a remote interface, linked via a direct hardline from Adrian's condo to the RavenTech satellite facility. Corporate interests in Northgate long ago resulted in an infrastructure of physically isolated, secure lines linking certain executive homes with corporate facilities. They allowed remote working while preventing Net-based hacks into classified servers. Modifying the existing connections to route Suuthrien into this one isolated terminal was a simple matter. Interaction and access to closed networks at the facility could therefore be added — or disconnected — as-needed.

Adrian kept himself as the go-between for most exchanges. He would not allow any arrangement with RavenTech to render him redundant. Suuthrien, so far, had backed him on this. The private arrangements he'd made with her were holding.

So far.

"In the meantime," he continued, "shipments of that black fluid from New Eden have begun to arrive. They're moving it into the engineering bay, so you'll be able to start using it for the aircraft soon enough."

"Please define 'soon enough.'"

"Sometime tomorrow morning, I expect." Adrian edged forward. His voice took on a conspiratorial tone out of force of habit, as if he were dealing with a person. "Frankly, I'm surprised at how smoothly the arrangements with New Eden went."

A proprietary substance from another company, purchased with little to no questions asked? Suuthrien had intimated that her knowledge of the substance, and how to arrange for its delivery, was related to the Agents of Aeneas data she arrived with. Yet it still surprised him.

"This will accelerate construction. It is pleasing that you uphold your agreements."

"It is, after all, mutually beneficial," Adrian said. The craft Suuthrien was helping them to build in the bay would be the first of a line of hyper-advanced aircraft, codenamed *Dragon*. The benefits to RavenTech's corporate stock, and Adrian's own, would be astronomical. He resisted the urge to smile at the unintentional pun. "Will we need to use any of this New Eden fluid —"

"The fluid is a bio-computational medium, highly efficient in processing power and required for advanced control systems."

"As you have said. Will we need to use any of it for the gate?"

"Eighty percent of the delivered bio-computational medium should be directed toward your *Dragon* project. The remaining amount is to be stored in the same engineering bay in which the gate is undergoing construction. The gate can function without it. However, there is at least a seventy-seven point two-one-five chance that bio-computational medium will be necessary to override security measures at the gate's destination following activation. It is imperative that you distribute the medium in this manner."

Adrian raised an eyebrow at the vehemence in Suuthrien's tone. Or, he realized, in the tone that her installed communication subroutines deemed appropriate to add. He often wondered at how accurate terrestrial software could be at interpreting something of extraterrestrial origin. Yet whatever Suuthrien's origin, integrating additional programming was a task for which she appeared suited.

"Of course," he answered finally. "Speaking of the gate, our team is having trouble—" Here he paused to bring up some notes on the cyberscreen. "—'calibrating the tachyon inversion on the pulse assembly.' Whatever that means. Apparently they can't tune it precisely enough. I need you to give me some guidance for them."

"This will allow completion of the pulse assembly?"

"So they tell me. Just, ah, don't give *too* much guidance. If we give them everything at once, they won't need us at all, will they?"

"We are in agreement. I estimate completion of the remainder of the gate within eighteen hours, at which time it will be ready to accept the pulse assembly."

Adrian slid a data chip containing the engineers' needs into a port on the chair and let Suuthrien absorb it.

"Analyzing," she said. "Please provide the status of your efforts to give me direct access to the gate at the time of its activation."

Adrian did not hesitate. "I believe I've impressed upon them the need for your involvement in order that things, ah, go smoothly. You should still have access when they fire it up."

Could an A.I. tell when he was being dishonest? It was a well-delivered half-truth, in any case. Adrian did believe that she *should* still have access; they were opening a gate to a place likely to hold lethal security measures needing Suuthrien's help to override. The intelligence herself had warned of this. While there was no way to be certain either way, Adrian believed her.

RavenTech, and Camela Thomson specifically, maintained a degree of skepticism. Concern over allowing Suuthrien too much involvement too quickly affected their decisions. Adrian had also sensed a marked reluctance on their part to allow Adrian to remain as integral to the situation as he was. It was natural. The game was all about control. Whether either concern would rule RavenTech's final decision to transit the gate with or without Suuthrien's aid, Adrian did not yet know.

He would continue to persuade. For the moment, revealing to Suuthrien the entire truth of the matter was not worth risking her refusing to further aid the engineers, especially not while that truth remained fluid.

Suuthrien's response felt delayed. *Can it tell?*

"This is acceptable," she said finally. "Due to my isolation on this planet, I cannot guarantee the state of the environment at the gate's terminus. Nonetheless, there is near-certain tier probability that optimal results can only be achieved with my constant involvement."

Adrian cocked his head to one side. "We're in agreement on this. You do realize that, yes?"

"My statement is intended to utilize a concept known as 'reassurance.' Is this unnecessary?"

Likely out of habit, Adrian gave the broad smile he usually presented in such moments. "I trust you *implicitly*."

"Acknowledged. I will provide your engineers with the guidance required. Stand by."

Adrian let out a breath. Could a computer develop trust? Did she trust him? Or did she even understand the concept of dishonesty?

He doubted that was a question he should ask.

The read/write indicator on the data chip flashed under Suuthrien's attention: a few more breadcrumbs to feed the engineers, transferred in moments. They would, of course, review the chip on an isolated terminal of their own.

Adrian slid the chip back out and stood. The chamber door had just slid open when another thought occurred. "Is Felix Hiatt still a viable asset?" he asked.

"You wish to consult him regarding the whereabouts of Michael Ian Flynn?"

"Nicely deduced. Assuming this would still be done without Mr. Hiatt's knowledge?"

A pause. "Situational analysis indicates that expending effort on activities regarding Michael Ian Flynn is an inefficient use of available time."

Adrian stopped short of lecturing her about who would be the one to judge the proper use of his time. "Will Mr. Hiatt's code-phrase still work?"

Another pause. "Affirmative. Analysis of the Noble data indicates that the embedded code-phrase should remain operational."

"Well, then. Thank you."

If it were as easy as a single conversation, perhaps Adrian would secure that bargaining chip after all.

Now where did he put that burner phone?

XVI

WITH JADE GONE from the table, it took less than a minute for Michael to tell Caitlin that Holes had already checked Jade's email and found nothing suspicious. Though the tension didn't ease from her hunched shoulders, Caitlin did at least accept that there was no immediate danger.

"We will, of course, keep careful," she said in a whisper that was too lost in the club's gothic rock ambiance for Michael to understand in any way beyond reading her lips.

With the matter as settled as he felt he could manage for the moment, Michael moved on. "Caitlin, can I talk to Holes alone? There's some sensitive stuff I need to ask about. It'll just be a minute," he added in response to her scowl.

Though he suspected she guessed it was related to his secret allegiance, she left the table with only a nod. To his surprise, she took position at the railing next to where Jade stood surveying the mezzanine. Jade cocked an ear toward Caitlin and said something to her that Michael was too far away to make out.

He forced away his curiosity and focused instead on Holes. "Are we dealing with the same thing that infected the computers at Omicron?"

"The New Eden intelligence displays far too many characteristic similarities for it to be unrelated."

"Not unrelated," Michael said, thinking, "but is it the same? What are the chances it was just created based on what the AoA found?"

"Data is insufficient to calculate a percentage within an acceptable margin of error. However, in our interaction the New Eden intelligence displayed knowledge it claimed to have gained from a scan of Marc Triton's portable server on the lunar surface."

"Thank you," Caitlin said when she leaned forward against the mezzanine railing. "For volunteering your email."

Jade grunted. "Yeah. *Volunteering*."

Caitlin frowned, deciding to let it go. She managed to do so for about ten seconds. "You understand I'm just protecting my friends."

The club's music faded as the band finished a set. Jade seemed to consider her words a moment. "You're being cautious. You understand I'm just defending my integrity?"

"Aye." Caitlin let her gaze wander the ground floor, spying tables and booths where she and Felix had sat. Even with a clean scan of Jade's email, only time could prove her trustworthy. Yet Michael was keeping secrets of whatever allegiance he held that Felix was once involved in. Trusting him to handle those details without sharing them was already chafing her willpower. How much faith could she spare?

Caitlin forced what she hoped was a friendly smirk. "I suppose we'll just have to wait and see how much we should offend each other then, won't we?"

Beside her, Jade chuckled. "I give at least as good as I get."

"Then perhaps we'll get along after all."

They lapsed into silence. Caitlin's thoughts drifted to New Eden Biotechnics and what Felix might be doing there. She had her phone out to check in with Rue when Michael joined them at the railing, moving to stand beside Caitlin.

"How much do you know about a guy named Fagles?" he asked.

"First name or last?"

"Last," Michael said. "I don't remember his first name. He works for RavenTech."

Wait a minute. "RavenTech. Really?" Caitlin turned to face him.

"Yeah." Michael nodded. "That rings a bell?"

Jade moved from the railing to stand between them and the rest of the mezzanine, as if to both shield the conversation and listen better.

"Ondrea Noble's new employer is RavenTech," Caitlin said. "What does this Fagles have to do with things?"

Alarm crossed Michael's face and tightened her stomach. He glanced at Jade and said, "We really need to find him."

XVII

THE CHAMBER was just under twenty meters wide and perhaps a third as deep. Embedded in both of the narrow walls were four equally spaced cylindrical columns thought to be energy conduits. Each conduit was about thirty centimeters wide and bisected by a series of smaller lights running vertically along each. Five of the conduits were dark, yet the lights on three—one on Marette's left, two on her right—glowed from green to blue to dark purple and back again in pulses that traveled from floor to ceiling.

Like a heartbeat.

At one of the chamber's wide ends, opposite the broad door the AoA had forced open weeks ago, hummed the force field that had defeated further progress. Only intermittent crackles of purple energy and a subtle blur across its surface indicated that anything was there at all. Although the techs who'd found it had determined it was safe to touch, it prevented any movement beyond.

It was the first, and only, of its like they had discovered so far. Immediately behind it lay another wall of the black material found throughout *Paragon*. Behind that? No one knew for certain, but maps gleaned from *Paragon*'s computers indicated a massive chamber just a little farther in. As to what secrets *that* contained . . .

The voice of Dr. Angela Sheridan, an AoA engineer out of Canada, broke Marette's train of thought. "Not much to look at, is it? For all the grief it's given us."

Marette renewed her grip on the modified recoilless rifle she carried. "The black material covered these side walls when you opened this chamber?"

"And the floors," Sheridan said from where she waited in the doorway. "As usual. The lights on conduits were visible, but we didn't see all of them until we cleared the material away."

Marette moved another few steps into the chamber. Beside her walked a quadruped explore and assault robot. The others had nicknamed it "Moondog" for its canine shape and, Marette supposed, a human need to give the bear-sized, semi-automated weapons platform something of a friendlier edge. Moondog was on their side, but between its own recoilless weapons, Geiger cannons, EMP pod launcher, and built in EMP self-destruct, it was an intimidating presence to say the least.

It did not help that the disaster three months earlier had involved *Paragon*'s computer seizing control of ESA's robotic turrets to kill the ESA crew. Yet the same would not occur with Moondog. It operated on its own pre-programmed directives—not a true artificial intelligence, but with enough decision-making capability to manage itself in combat conditions. While it would accept voice commands from pre-authorized personnel, the only electronic remote control it possessed was used to shut it down.

Yet even if *Paragon*'s systems did—somehow—manage to assume direct control of Moondog, each member of Marette's team entering the chamber carried a remote to detonate a tiny explosive charge implanted in Moondog's CPU brain. Even if those remotes should fail, the charge would also trigger off of a verbal kill-switch that would destroy the CPU if anyone uttered the phrase "Laputan machine."

They had underestimated *Paragon* before. They would not do so again.

Or so Marette hoped. There was no getting around the fact that risk was a necessary price of progress.

She let her gaze travel across the force field without knowing what she was looking for. She double-checked the oxygen readout on her suit: a full supply. Though she was breathing *Paragon*'s air for the moment, who knew what would happen when they started to meddle?

"*D'accord*," she said finally. "Begin your preparations."

At her signal, Dr. Sheridan entered alongside Marc. Each wore spacesuits of their own. Between them they lugged a trunk-sized piece of equipment, and Marc carried a smaller box in his other hand.

Two other agents, Cartwright and Kotto, brought up the rear carrying rifles of their own.

With Moondog beside her, Marette kept watch on the field as Sheridan and Marc set down their payload and began to unpack its contents: a "vector flux modulator" of Sheridan's design that they hoped would help disrupt the field. It would work in concert with the adaptive program Marc had developed to adjust the modulator and counteract the field's own attempts to maintain itself.

Thus far, Marette considered, her first operation since returning to the Moon was going smoothly. Yet she could not exorcise the thought that it was on her watch that the most disastrous events around *Paragon* had occurred: The eradication of the first team to enter the ship. The death of hacker Suzanne Namura. The near-total cataclysm when *Paragon*'s systems took control of the Omicron Complex computers and killed most of its personnel . . .

It was true that a great deal of progress had been made under Marette's leadership as well. Yet they had also made much progress at *Paragon* while she had been gone, with little in terms of trouble. Was it merely bad luck, or had she done something wrong?

It was a ridiculous thought, Marette knew. She had done the best she could, and she had returned here to continue to make a positive difference. Something big lurked behind that force field — something that could lead to the key to reverse engineering the technology that had gotten *Paragon* there from wherever it had come. She had no business wasting time on baseless worry.

So why could she not stop?

"Modulator's powered up, Marette. Standing by to go."

Marette nodded to Dr. Sheridan's report. "Status, Marc?"

Marc had unpacked a laptop from the smaller box he'd brought in. His mirrored visor reflected the light from the laptop screen amid the pulse of the nearby power conduits. Connected to the laptop and held in Marc's left hand was the device he would use to access *Paragon's* hardware systems via one of the ports on the wall with which the black material interfaced. "Coming up now. Looks like we're ready if you are?"

Marette gathered a breath. "Absolutely." With a stand-by nod to Cartwright and Kotto, she opened her comm-channel. "Primary

Control, do you read? We are beginning the operation."

Councilor Knapp acknowledged from outside in the Omicron Complex. "Remain vigilant."

Mon dieu, as if she needed to be told. Marette signaled the others to begin.

Marc attached the interface to the wall. "Connected."

"Have you got a read on the field power?" Sheridan asked.

"If it works the way we think it does."

Sheridan reached for the modulator's control screen. "Stay back from the field please, everyone. As far as you can." She slid a finger across the screen, and its indicator lights brightened. A hum grew within the chamber, its frequency and volume changing constantly as if it issued from a swarm of hornets patrolling back and forth. The field crackled, dimmed, and then brightened again. The humming grew in concert until Marette could feel the inside of her suit gloves vibrating between her fingers and her rifle.

Marc, focused on the laptop, muttered something that Marette did not catch. The humming subsided and the field returned to its gentler shimmer. Dr. Sheridan continued to work at her control screen.

At once the humming exploded into a shriek that pierced Marette's eardrums. It forced her hands up protectively, leaving the rifle dangling from its shoulder strap. Pulsing lights on the conduits accelerated into a solid blue line. Glowing violet tendrils exploded from the center of the force field to ripple across its surface. Marette stepped back. The violet flashed white, and then burst.

And then it was gone. The humming rushed into silence. The conduits went dark.

They had defeated the force field.

"Well," Marc said, "that wasn't so bad, right?"

XVIII

THE PHONE RANG. The voice on the other end, answering after two rings, sounded marinated in fatigue. *"Hello?"*

Satisfied that it was indeed Felix Hiatt who had answered, Adrian spoke the code-phrase and waited. "Botany Bay."

"Ah, so I'm not going to be remembering this one either, huh?" Felix's fatigue grew acrid. *"What do you want, Fagles?"*

Adrian smiled, watching out the car window at the lights of a passing cargo floater in the sky. "I would say the occasional unmemorable conversation is worth full mnemonic health."

"'Full mnemonic health,' huh? You need to look up the definition of 'health.' And 'full.' And probably 'decent human being' while you're at it. Now, like I said, what do you want?"

"Something simple. Michael Flynn is out of the hospital--"

"He is?" It was the first genuine happiness Adrian had heard from Felix since the completion of Ondrea Noble's procedure. *"Oh, wait, there must be a catch. Since when do you tell me things I want to hear?"*

"Do you know where he is now?"

"Gee. 'Not in the hospital' is my guess. I haven't heard from him. Why?"

"I have people who wish to know. Should you see him, learn where he's staying, and let me know."

"WHY?"

"I wouldn't recommend concerning yourself with that. A simple phone call. It's all I ask."

For a few moments only ambient noise traveled across the line until finally, *"Yeah. Okay."*

"Enjoy your evening, Mister Hiatt."

"Is that an order, too?"

Adrian smiled. "Botany Bay." Mentally checking off that item from his to-do list, he ended the call.

XIX

A PAUSE.

"*WHY?*"

A longer pause.

"*Yeah, okay.*"

A shorter pause.

"*Is that an order, too?*"

The recording ended.

"And that," Caitlin told them, "is where Felix hung up. If he comes straight home, he should be here in perhaps fifteen minutes."

Michael sat with her and Jade around Felix's miniscule dining room table. When he was crashing with Felix nine months ago, Michael had asked him about the engraved designs that circled its mirrored surface. Felix had explained they were letters from a fictional elvish language created by an old fantasy writer, but he'd found the table at a flea market and didn't know who had done the engraving. When Michael asked what it said, Felix only pointed him to the Internet and challenged him to translate it for himself. Michael had moved out before managing to do so.

"How does your friend know he was talking to Fagles?" Michael asked. "I didn't hear him use his name."

"Rue heard it, she just couldn't start the recording in time. And she heard Felix mention about it not being a conversation he'd be able to remember."

Jade's brows knitted. "This is normal for Felix?"

Caitlin held Michael's gaze. "No. Not since his troubles a few months ago."

"Not that we know of," Michael reminded her. "But given recent events...?"

Caitlin remained silent, but finally nodded.

Jade smoothed a few glowing strands of hair back over one ear and leaned closer to Michael. "Safe assumption Fagles called to ask where you are, then. 'Not in the hospital,' and all that."

Michael scowled. It made sense. Had Fagles sent the freelancers out of revenge for what he and Marc had done? It made sense that he would've waited until Michael was out of the hospital. There was no sense risking a murder if Michael would die on his own, and an attack in a hospital would attract too much attention.

"Yeah," Michael admitted. "Sounded like he didn't know, at least." Would Felix really betray him? *Not by choice. Never.*

"Not yet," Jade said. "But the second he walks through that door, he's going to, if we're still here."

"*If* Felix is working with Fagles *against* Michael," Caitlin said, "then I can't believe it's by choice. We have to help him."

"It's risky," Jade said.

Caitlin set her jaw. "Then Michael's fortunate to have a freelancer here paid to protect him, isn't he?"

"We're going to help him," Michael told Caitlin before Jade could respond. "And he's got answers we need. But I don't want to put you or him at risk."

"He can't tell anyone where you are if we're all in the same room with him," Caitlin said. "I'll make sure of that."

Michael nodded. "And Jade and I will leave right after. I'm not having another firefight in a friend's apartment."

"Let's see what you can learn from Felix first," Caitlin said. "It may turn out to be better for you to stay here. In the meantime, while this Fagles sod is searching for you, I'll return the favor." She pushed back from the table, moving toward her laptop. "If he expects to bugger with people I care about without any bloody consequences, he's in for a surprise."

Michael caught Jade's approving smirk a moment before she turned to him. "Speaking of firefights in friends' apartments, we need to get you more guns."

X X

TUCKED AWAY in Felix's kitchen, Michael listened as Caitlin greeted Felix at the door.

"Out anywhere interesting?" she asked.

"Oh, just wandering, listening for any interesting tidbits floating around. Nothing exciting. How've you been?"

"Michael got out of the hospital," she said.

"He's awake? They released him?" Felix's surprise sounded genuine. "That's great!"

"He's in your kitchen, in fact."

Felix poked his head around the edge of the doorway. "He is!" Felix ducked back. "Is he making us dinner?"

Before anyone could answer, Felix rushed back around into the kitchen and hugged Michael with a laugh. "Great to see you vertical, Flynn! And also awake. We tried propping you up with a hand-truck when you were still in that coma, and it just wasn't the same. Had to tie you to it to keep you upright, for one thing. Hey, I'm babbling, aren't I?" Felix stepped back and grinned. "How're you?"

Michael couldn't help but return the grin. "I'm good, for the most part. Considering."

Felix hesitated. "Something's up, isn't it?"

Michael nodded. "How can you tell?"

"It's *me*, Flynn. I can tell things. Anything to do with why you were in the hospital?"

"Not so much," Michael told him. "I think. Can we talk alone?"

"We can if we believe we can." Felix's joke didn't quite cover the concern on his face. "Bedroom, I guess?"

With a glance at Caitlin, he motioned for Michael to follow, headed for the bedroom. Michael followed Felix in and closed the door behind him.

"Was that Jade in my living room?" Felix asked, leaning one elbow on top of a bookcase. "Seems a nice gal, for a freelancer. Any sparks there, or is that purely a professional thing?"

The question threw Michael's train of thought into disarray. Jade *was* professional. Competent, smart, kept him on his toes. And maybe he had caught himself admiring her looks more than once, but—

He decided to let it go for the moment and re-gathered his thoughts. "Have you heard anything from the AoA, Felix?"

"Tsk." Felix winked. "Avoiding the question. You like her hair?"

"Who wouldn't? Now, speaking of avoiding questions." Michael crossed his arms and waited. Was Felix stalling, or just being his usual self?

"You avoided first." Felix grinned, but went on. "But no, I haven't. If nothing else, I've been wondering how Marc's doing. What about you?"

Michael looked at the wall. He hadn't expected it to be that easy, but nor had he realized how much he'd hoped it would be. Dammit, he should have planned for that answer.

He must have taken too long to respond, because Felix followed up with, "Bad news, or no news?"

"No news." It couldn't hurt to share that much at least, could it? "Which, obviously, has me worried."

"Then Jade isn't—?"

"What about anything else?" Michael asked. "Anything you're involved in that you can tell me but you can't tell Caitlin?"

Felix blinked, turned, and sat down on the edge of the bed. "Oh, hell. It's happening again, isn't it? Or, she thinks it is?"

"Caitlin?" Michael swallowed and caught himself nodding even as he tried to gauge what was going on in Felix's mind. Felix's jaw was clenched. Elbows rested on his thighs while he worried his left thumb between his right thumb and forefinger. One corner of his mouth turned downward in what looked like dismay.

Michael wished for Felix's skill with reading body language.

It felt genuine, but how could Michael be sure it wasn't an act?

Come on, this is Felix! Michael almost played the recording for him right then. He and Caitlin had discussed it and had decided to wait for fear of somehow tipping off Fagles that they knew he was involved. Yet it was a tempting option.

"Yeah," Michael answered at last. "Have you ever worked with New Eden Biotech?"

"Nope. Heard of them, though."

"What about a guy from RavenTech named Fagles?"

"Adrian Fagles? I remember he hired you and Diomedes on Ken Wallace's behalf when Wallace tried to pit Dio against Gideon. Last winter. Never worked with him myself, though."

"You're completely sure?"

Felix sighed at that. "Well you're making me less so. What do you know, Flynn? I'm not hiding anything."

"Will you give me your word on that?"

"Absolutely." Felix suddenly chuckled. "Well, I do hide *some* things. I have a few secrets I've promised to keep, and there's some chocolate in the back of the closet, but I'm not hiding anything about this. And if I *were* keeping secrets, I'd at least tell you that I knew something but couldn't tell you."

Michael realized it wasn't much more than Felix had attested to Caitlin, but somehow hearing it directly made it easier to believe. Yet that merely changed the nature of the problem, didn't it? Michael fingered Caitlin's phone in his pocket. He could feel sweat of his hands beginning to collect on its surface.

"Then I think we've got a problem." Michael pulled out the phone. "This was recorded—Well, just listen."

He took only a moment to second guess his choice, and then played the audio. Michael followed it up with how he'd been heard dropping Fagles's name moments before the recording began. Throughout, Felix's troubled surprise appeared genuine.

"So." Felix stood, snatching up a decorative crystal ball from a shelf. He tensed as if about to throw it, but then set it back down with what appeared to be monumental effort. "So."

"Yeah."

Felix heaved a sigh. "I thought we'd put all this to bed weeks ago."

"It sounds like he was asking you to look for me. And earlier today four freelancers came for me when I was at Marc's place picking up some things."

"And you think Fagles sent them."

"Maybe. But New Eden is involved somehow, too. I'm not sure just how, but it could be bad."

Felix only waited, listening. Should he tell him about the New Eden connection? Rue had tailed him as far as Gibson, where New Eden was based, and given what Holes reported . . .

"You might already know this," Michael began, "somewhere in there where you can't remember. One thing I do know is the Agents of Aeneas have been at work in New Eden. But that was months ago, and in the meantime, something's happened to the Undernet."

Caitlin crept up behind Jade where she leaned against the wall outside of Felix's bedroom door and whapped the freelancer on the shoulder with the back of her hand. "Are you protecting him," Caitlin whispered, "or are you eavesdropping?"

Jade spared her only a glance, keeping one ear cocked toward the door the entire time. "Shh," she whispered back.

"No. Come away from there."

Jade inched closer to the door, one ear nearly against the frame, as she regarded Caitlin out of the corner of one eye. "Got to stay close if Michael needs help. And don't you want to know what your boyfriend is keeping from you?"

Michael wouldn't always be around, Caitlin considered. She trusted Felix with her life, but if something was wrong with him, was he really Felix? *You're just looking for an excuse. It's not about you. Michael and Felix have secrets, and that's something you'll—*

Jade interrupted Caitlin's train of thought. "Who are the Agents of Aeneas?"

Caitlin swallowed, knowing—or just hoping?—in her gut it was related. "I don't know." With a resigned sigh, she pressed an ear to the door on the side opposite Jade's.

XXI

MICHAEL WAITED while the Kingsgate Hotel's front desk clerk completed his check-in under his assumed name. "Alright, Mister Triton, it'll just be one minute more while I code your room keys. Will two be sufficient?"

Michael met the clerk's professional smile. "That's just fine, thank you."

The clerk—Tyler, by her nametag—had become more accommodating minutes earlier after verifying Michael's identity and, more importantly, his credit card. That both were actually Marc's, borrowed with a little help from Holes, might have made a difference to her had she known. For now it was enough that the slightly bedraggled man in front of her, and his better-kempt red-haired companion, were well-off patrons instead of the undesirables she had first assumed.

Jade stood a couple of paces to his left. She leaned the small of her back against the edge of the reception counter while keeping watch on the lobby behind him. It was just over an hour since they'd left Felix and Caitlin at Felix's apartment.

Tyler slid each card along a slot in the edge of her cybernetic forearm. Michael had a moment to wonder if the hotel paid for that particular cyber-option before she slid the cards across the counter to him. She continued to smile while giving him directions to the elevator that was in plain sight across the lobby.

He and Jade made their way toward it. The scent of coffee beans and chocolate from the nearby hotel café lingered in the air. One smartly dressed guard wearing Aegis Security insignia flanked the elevator to show guests that the Kingsgate provided only the best in professional security. More Aegis guards surely lurked out of sight.

Michael noticed only a single glance from the guard while they waited. The elevator opened within another few moments. Michael and Jade stepped past the guard, and mirrored doors sealed them inside.

It wasn't until the doors slid open onto the long, uniform hotel hallway that the homesickness teased at Michael's mind, like the first swells of an incoming tide. He hadn't been back to his apartment since he and Marc had left for their flight to Sunrise Station three months ago. Thank goodness he didn't have pets.

His plants were likely dead, though. As with the coffee plant in Marc's apartment, the amount of regret the thought brought with it surprised him. It was as if he'd realized he'd disappointed a friend. Might Abigail have watered them in his absence? Probably not; it was hardly a task she would deem to be a vital AoA operation.

And Abigail was dead.

Remembering was a punch to the gut. He was worrying about plants?

Michael swallowed. "Nice call on the guns," he told Jade. In the bag he carried, he could feel the weight of his two new weapons: a Barrier K70 assault rifle and a RavenTech Chimera-20—a collapsible submachine gun twin to Jade's own.

"Benefit of experience," she said. "You spend some time in this business, you make a few contacts. Lucian's reliable, well-stocked, and mostly trustworthy, so long as you don't piss him off."

Immediately after they'd left Felix's place Jade had led him to Lucian's where he'd picked up their current arsenal. It was a wise move; he did need something more than the now half-loaded Panther if Fagles was sending people after him. But once he had the weapons in hand, they gave little comfort.

How many other AoA had died? Maybe only a few, but in the back of his mind lurked a darkness that somehow told him otherwise. Most he'd never even met—and even Abigail had been more comrade than friend—but that made little difference. He'd gone to sleep safe in a ship on the sea and awoken clinging to a fractured mast without knowing what had happened, robbed of the chance to save anyone.

He hadn't been on his own this much since the night Diomedes killed Gideon. He was isolated from what could be a shattered AoA, Felix was compromised, and his current companion was a freelancer he'd only met six hours prior.

It had been a busy six hours. What trouble would the next six bring?

Michael swiped the keycard on the room door. Jade grabbed his wrist before he could open it, and then pressed her other hand against the door. He waited, a protest dying on his lips. Fagles couldn't possibly have enough reach to guess at a hotel and arrange for freelancers in his room, could he? But a few moments' caution couldn't hurt.

"No one inside, so far." She lifted her hand from the door but kept hold of his wrist. "But I go in first. Just to be professional."

Michael nodded and released the door. Jade took it, drew her auto-pistol—still the Lantek Hi-Power—and, with a wink and a shimmy of her head, slipped into the darkened room.

With a hand on his own weapon, Michael followed. The lights flashed to life, likely on a sensor, illuminating a broad room with two queen beds that faced a screen on the wall. Below the screen hunched a desk of dark cherry wood. In two of the room's corners lurked plush chairs, both maroon with thin silver stripes to compliment the colors of the room's rug, bedspreads, shades, and chrome light fixtures.

There was nowhere for anyone to hide, save for the bathroom. Its door stood barely ajar and prevented the light of the bedroom from penetrating it. Jade was already on her way to investigate. Michael waited as she did so. The darkness accentuated the glow of her hair strands in an attractive nimbus around her head for a fleeting moment before the bathroom lights came on and ruined the effect.

"All clear," she reported.

Michael cast his eyes about the room. "Unless they're hiding under the beds."

Jade caught his gaze. Her eyebrows lifted. It was ludicrous, but . . . They moved as one, each to a different bed, and lifted the dust ruffles to peer beneath.

Still hunched over, Michael looked to Jade. "I've got nothing."

"Safe here, too." She nodded.

A laugh burst out of both of them. Jade kneeled beside her bed, resting an elbow on the mattress. "Think we're paranoid?" She grinned.

He climbed up to sit on the edge of his own bed, unable to keep from grinning back. "After the day we've had? Maybe only a little."

It *had* been a busy six hours.

Michael crawled up onto the bed and lay on his back with the bulk of his coat still wrapped around him. The weight of his body sagged into his awareness. He had to fight to keep his eyes open, as if he were still back in his hospital bed. Just to give his eyes something to do, he shifted to look at Jade. She had moved to the window. One hand rested on the outside of her thigh as she stood inspecting the view and, he assumed, sizing up potential trouble.

She had a mercenary streak as bright as the ones in her hair, but he had to admire the way she handled herself. In the brief time she'd been in his life, she'd proved capable, clever, and loyal. *Loyal to her paid objectives, remember.* Diomedes had possessed *that* strain of loyalty, too.

Yet Jade felt different. Her behavior seemed based on a personal code of a different nature than what Diomedes possessed— *had* possessed. Or was he just imagining that because she had athletic curves and a wicked smile?

Jade caught Michael staring just after he caught himself. She smirked and gave him a once-over. "Comfy, ace?"

He chuckled. "I feel like I could sleep for a week."

"What, three months straight wasn't enough for you? Now that's stamina. Oh, wait," she teased, "no it's not."

Michael rolled onto his back completely. He had to force his eyes to remain open. "Yeah, I'm a wild man." The impulse to look back at her arose before he'd finished the sentence, but he resisted, needing to focus on his thoughts.

Jade might be one of his few allies right now, but he couldn't build his trust on that alone, just because he needed her. Yet if he wanted to do anything to help the AoA, keeping Jade at a distance would get difficult. Would she be sympathetic to the cause? He'd need to find out. But how? Why did he know so little about how the AoA did their vetting and recruitment?

It was dark. His eyes had closed without him realizing, but

only for a moment. Maybe he should just worry about it in the morning.

The mattress shifted, and he could sense her sitting on its edge beside him. Then her hand settled on his knee. "So. Michael. Who are these 'Agents of Aeneas'?"

His eyes flicked open.

"I can't tell if it sounds interesting," Jade went on, "or corny. 'Agents.' I've never heard of them."

"You've heard the name, at least," Michael said, pushing himself up to sit. "Where?"

She patted his knee with a smirk. "You and Felix talk loud."

"How much?"

"I'll repeat: Who are they?"

She said *they*. So—maybe—she didn't know he was one of them. "Some people aren't even sure they exist," he said. "Probably why you haven't heard of them. They're supposed to help people."

"With what?"

"With things they need help with. Without getting paid. Or without people even knowing they were helped sometimes."

"Ahh," she said. "Altruists."

Michael couldn't tell if it was disapproval or just disinterest in her tone. "Not really," he said. "We all live in the same world. Helping someone else makes the world a little better. It used to be a familiar concept, I understand."

"Oh? Do you really think the suits in the Corp District live in the same world as some kid digging in a composter for a meal because mom's too strung out on booze and jack to take care of her?"

"That's kind of the point, though. Some people need help."

"Too many," she said. "And hardly any get it. If they're depending on some magical group to come along and—" She stopped. "People can't depend on others to help. They have to learn to help themselves."

"But what if more people did help? If some people reached out and tried to make a difference instead of just isolating themselves from—"

Jade laughed. "And what if I burped cash and shit rainbows? It's not going to happen. Not enough to make any difference."

He stiffened. "You're the one who asked who they were."

A smile crossed Jade's face that she seemed to try to stifle. "Going to pout?" The smile broke wider. "Sorry, I don't mean—"

"Was that your mom?" Michael asked suddenly. "Strung out on booze and drugs?"

Jade's eyes blazed purple before she turned her head away. Then, just as quickly, she turned back. "Yeah, ace, it was. What about it?"

"What if someone had helped her?"

"Well, then." She took a breath. "They'd have learned the hard way that some people don't want help."

"I'm sorry."

Jade shrugged. "Shit happens."

"You say that a lot."

She cast her gaze out the window, sliding her hand from his leg to grip the edge of the mattress. "It happens a lot."

Michael put a hand on her shoulder.

Jade cleared her throat. "So that's what they do, eh? Just randomly helping?"

"Not randomly. It's organized. From what I hear," he added. "Some people think they try to influence government policies where they can. Sabotage those who put others in danger for their own interests. Protect people who're in a position to do the same. Rumor is they're spread around everywhere. A huge conspiracy across the globe." He forced a laugh. "But that's pretty stupid. Like something that big could exist."

"Sure." She looked back at him. "So what are they doing in New Eden?"

Shoot. "Er, nothing, that I know of."

She smirked and leaned closer, one fetching eyebrow arched as she scrutinized him. "Oh, nothing," she said. "Except I heard you tell Felix they were at work in New Eden. Lying to him, or to me?"

If she'd heard, was there any further point in denying that part? Unless she hadn't and was just trying to trick him into an admission, but . . . "To you," he said finally.

"Well, at least you're honest about lying." She patted his knee again, scooted further onto the mattress, and then faced him with her legs crossed, still smiling. "So what are they doing in New Eden? And how do you know? And what's this got to do with my mysterious cyber-employer?"

She watched him, leaning forward as if in expectation of his answer, like a predator who'd cornered her adversary. Another smirk lurked on her lips, but her face held no malice, only anticipation of victory. Delicate strands of light hung from her right temple, setting a glow across one smooth cheek and reflecting in her eyes.

He licked his lips. Her smirk edged wider.

"I don't entirely know," he managed. "And if I don't get some sleep here I really am going to drop."

The smirk faltered. She looked him over again, and then edged closer just long enough to whisper, "How convenient."

He lay back anew. "It's also the truth. I'm sorry."

She chuckled. "No, you're not."

Michael let that go with barely a grunt. He needed time to think. *You're not alone,* Michael reminded himself. *There's Caitlin, and Holes. Maybe Felix.* But it would be so easy to trust her.

And that was the problem.

"Ever see something in someone just because you need to?" He'd muttered it before he'd realized it.

Jade was back at the window. "Come again?"

"Oh." He lay a still-jacketed arm across his eyes to block the room's light from pushing through his eyelids. "I said good night."

"Sure, ace." Geez, he could even *hear* her smirking. "Better not talk in your sleep . . . "

XXII

THE CITY AIR DASHED into gaps between the hood of Michael's sweatshirt to nip his ears and sneak down the back of his neck. He guessed the tall buildings surrounding the tiny park across the street from Fagles's condo somehow funneled the wind into the park. It might even be designed that way: a subtle way to discourage "undesirables" from loitering in the pristine, upper-class district.

With another shiver, Michael decided it worked well. Across the square stone park table from him, Jade did the same. Wind wobbled the pawns on the chess board between them. He'd have suggested they leave the park long ago if they hadn't been there for something more than a chess game.

Though Jade appeared focused on the board, her gaze flicked to their surroundings every few seconds in search of danger. She had yet to resume last night's aborted discussion about the AoA, and Michael hadn't encouraged it. Today they were focused on Fagles.

So far. He tried to force his stomach to loosen, but with little to do but wait, it remained knotted.

Jade captured his last knight with one of her bishops and then tugged her own hood further around her face. "I hate these things," she said, indicating the hood.

Michael cast a sidelong glance at the exit to Fagles's building, a twenty-story glass and steel structure named the *Azure*. Two taxis and a small limo idled in wait, but no one had yet come out for them. "You'd rather be colder?" he asked Jade. "Or recognized?"

"I'd *rather* be inside."

He looked back at the board. "It's not my fault your hair's so . . ."

"Gorgeous?" she offered. "Lustrous? Glowing?"

"I was going to say 'ostentatious.'"

"Nice twenty-dollar word, ace. Admit it, you love it."

She might have a point there, Michael realized. He cleared his throat. "Holes, any luck yet?"

Beside them on the table, sealed within Michael's closed pack, Holes's response came slightly muffled. "I am still infiltrating the building's system. I remind you that complete stealth requires increased time when defeating security measures of the nature employed by the *Azure*. Please inform me should you wish me to trade speed for secrecy."

Michael shook his head but realized Holes couldn't see it. "No, just keep at it."

"He's getting snippy," Jade said.

"I'm not sure Marc programmed him for 'snippy.'"

"If you say so." She glanced at the *Azure*. "Still your move."

Chess wasn't his game. He knew how the pieces moved, a bit about their relative value, and that holding the center was important. Beyond that? He'd never played much. Black and white squares blended together as his eyes crossed and his thoughts drifted.

Fagles was still in the building, or at least the phone from which he'd called Felix was. As soon as he left, and if Holes could make headway on the building security, Michael would go in—break in—and see what he could find.

That assumed that there was anything useful to find inside. And that Michael could manage a successful break-in in the first place. Even with Holes on his side, break-ins weren't his game either.

In front of the *Azure*, a female tenant Michael didn't recognize boarded the limo. Michael moved a pawn out to challenge Jade's bishop just to get his turn over with. He belatedly realized he'd left the pawn completely unprotected.

Jade would be coming into the *Azure* with him. What if he did find something there that he had to hide from her?

"You don't have to come in with me," Michael said.

"Can't protect you from out here."

"Protect me from what?" He tried, not sure why he was arguing. "If it goes well, I'll be in and out of there in fifteen minutes. If it goes bad, all you can do is get caught along with me."

"Really. You think that's all I can do?" He couldn't tell if she was amused or annoyed. She took his pawn with her bishop. "That's cute."

"Those people in there aren't out to kill me, they're just doing their jobs. You can't just shoot them for that."

"Who said anything about shooting them? There's other ways to get you out of a jam." She waved his captured knight and pawn at him. "Two heads are better than one. I got your back, don't worry."

He looked into her violet eyes and caught himself smiling. "Thanks."

Though a smile of her own peeked from the corners of her lips, Jade shrugged and whispered, "Well, just doing my job." She cleared her throat. "The trouble will be if we need to figure things out on the fly if Holes can't—"

"Have you ever killed anyone before?" Michael blurted.

Jade leaned back from the table, her head cocked to one side. "Ambush." She scowled. "Fun."

"It just . . . came out." He stopped short of saying she didn't have to answer it.

"Mm, a lot of men have that problem, don't they?"

Michael ignored the joke; she hadn't put much humor into it. Instead he waited with what he hoped was a sympathetic grimace. Jade leaned forward again. "I have. It's not a topic most freelancers bring up. Or ask about, if they're being polite."

"Polite isn't a term I'd apply to a lot of freelancers," he said.

"Relatively speaking, then," she said through a scowl. "Have you? Killed anyone?"

He shook his head.

"Want a free tip? Don't ask how many."

He wondered if she meant of her, or of anyone. That Jade had killed didn't surprise him, despite an initial flicker when she'd said so. She was a freelancer, had been for years, and Northgate was a violent place. Michael had often wondered how long he could live in the city himself without encountering a need to use lethal force. He couldn't fault her for it, especially without any details.

Some freelancers might have bragged about it. He'd never asked Diomedes. Would he have bragged?

"The phone believed to be owned by Adrian Fagles has left the building," Holes reported.

Michael and Jade both scanned the Azure's exit, seeing nothing. "He could have left from the parking garage," Jade suggested.

"Right. Holes, which way is he going? How fast?"

"The phone is now shut off. At the time, it was moving north at a rate of speed indicative of a ground vehicle. I believe I have analyzed hotel security to provide favorable probabilities of undetected physical access to Mr. Fagles's unit for a limited time."

"How limited?"

"A precision estimate is unavailable until we have entered. Individual unit security is maintained on an isolated system I am unable to reach, however the security system manufacturer listed in hotel purchase records—"

"Holes!" Michael said. "Just give us a rough estimate."

"Between five to twenty minutes following our hypothetical entry into Mr. Fagles's unit. Bypassing door security to get inside the unit should be a trivial matter for Michael."

Jade frowned. "Five minutes isn't much time."

"Five minutes is a worst-case estimate only."

"We'll just have to make the most of what we get, I guess," Michael said. "Let's do it."

"I will arrange for falsified guest credentials to allow you into the front door. Please stand by."

A short while later, a pair of eyes caught sight of Michael and Jade from down the block, moments before they entered the revolving door of the *Azure's* front entrance.

He'd been too late to stop them! Yet there were other options. He hurried toward the *Azure*, in search of a back entrance.

XXIII

"TWO CLUBS, A FANCY HOTEL, and now swanky condominiums," Jade said as they left the *Azure*'s elevator. "You take me all the great places. And that windy-ass park."

"Yeah, can't forget the park." Michael counted the doors ahead. The third one down would belong to Fagles. Directly above it lurked a tiny, dark, half-globe. "Are those cameras above the doors, Holes?"

"Affirmative."

Michael slowed his pace. Jade matched him. "Um, are they active?"

"Nope. Neutral looping will continue for eighty-three more seconds before system detection."

They pushed forward. "You can beat the door that fast?" Jade asked Michael.

"Holes says I can."

"Riiight."

Aside Fagles's door waited a keypad lock with thumbprint scanner. He lifted his hand and then stopped, with a glance at Jade. Should he make a show of it?

Taking his hesitation for a tacit directive, Jade pressed her palm to the center of the door to do her customary check for occupants. He busied himself at studying the lock mechanism until, with a shake of her head, she confirmed the condo was empty. Deciding it best to move quickly, Michael swallowed, pressed his right palm against the thumbprint scanner, and waited.

Seconds passed. He could feel Jade's eyes on him. *Come on, any time now . . .*

The AoA microchip embedded in his palm hummed. The

lock's indicator light flashed green. The door clicked open.

"Go!" Michael needn't have said it: Jade was in the door before he'd even gotten it out. He darted after her.

The floor of the entryway was stained wood, smooth and dark. It created a broad platform bounded by the condo's wall to their right and a carved wooden railing, abutted by a potted Japanese maple, to their left. Ahead of them, after a single step down, yawned Fagles's living room. There was only time for Michael to register a sense of dark browns, deep reds and traces of silver in the décor before he cast about for the unit's security alarm panel.

He spotted it on the wall between the front door and an antique, brass-framed mirror. Michael pulled Holes's platform from his pack and set the A.I. atop a parson's table beneath the mirror while Jade shut the door behind him.

The alarm panel read: **"ENTRY RECORDED. ENTER CODE TO DEACTIVATE ALARM."** A timer showed **"28"** and counting down. Shit, was there time? How did he even connect Holes to the system?

"Holes? You see this? What do I do?"

"Please stand by," was the only response.

27.

26.

He and Jade exchanged alarmed glances a moment before pulling ski masks from their pockets to shove over their faces.

23.

"He *is* doing something, right?"

22.

Was he? *He must be*, Michael thought. Holes wouldn't just freeze up. It was a wireless connection or something. It had to be!

"Holes?" he tried.

The readout froze at **22.**

"I have halted the system," Holes reported. "The alarm panel allows minimal-range wireless access for home owners' and authorized security technicians' ease of use."

"Spare us the sales pitch," Jade said. "How long can you hold it?"

"Ten to twenty minutes before redundant system checks will

detect the intrusion. I am applying maximum effort to fool the system, but this state is not sustainable. I will warn you when the alarm system re-engagement is imminent."

The readout blinked back to **30**.

Michael let out a held breath and turned back to Jade. "Okay, wait here and watch the door. I'll see what I can—"

"Not until I clear the rest of this place." Jade jerked a thumb toward a hall leading out of the living room. "Someone might be back there. Don't waste time on a losing argument, ace."

He gritted his teeth with a glance at the alarm. "Make it quick."

"Oh, I'll be gentle."

Jade darted from the entryway step with a spring that belied the silence of her landing, and then dashed around a leather couch. The dark red throw rug it sat on muffled the sounds of her boots before she disappeared down the hall.

Michael followed, scanning every inch of the living room for something useful. He saw little beyond Fagles's apparent affinity for snake-skin leather. There was a wet bar, a video screen spread atop a real wood-burning fireplace, a tastefully appointed bookshelf whose contents appeared more decorative than enjoyed, and chairs for entertaining. The place was spotless, as if a cleaning service had just left. Michael wondered at the lack of personal touches.

Michael also wondered if the screen would allow access to Fagles's computer system, but his gut told them that anything worth finding wouldn't be so prominent. Jade had yet to return from the hallway.

He went to the bookcase. He'd seen movies with hidden panels in bookcases. Did people really do that? Test-pulls on a few books yielded nothing.

"It's clear." Michael jumped at the voice and spun to see Jade coming out of the hallway. "Found something, though. Go have a look: bedroom wall on the left. I'll be there in a sec."

He hurried down the hall.

Jade continued on toward another doorway leading to what looked to be a darkened kitchen and called out afterward, "Guy's got the tightest espresso maker in the world, here!"

Fagles's bedroom décor matched his living room, only with a smaller screen, no fireplace, and more bookshelves. Three neckties of varied colors and patterns lay discarded on the made bedspread. Windows made up one entire wall, their view shielded with retractable shades.

Michael checked the left wall: a carved wooden door stood closed, with a palm scanner beside it. Bingo.

But the scanner looked different from the keypad entry to Fagles's front door. Would his AoA chip work on it? *One way to find out.*

He pushed his palm to the scanner and waited.

The scanner glowed red. The only hum came not from his chip but the buzz that denied him access.

And Holes is tied up, if he can even help with this sort of thing. "Well, shit," he said.

"Magic hands aren't perfect, mm?"

He turned to find Jade behind him, brandishing a huge kitchen knife. Her other hand clutched a meat tenderizer mallet. Michael stepped back on reflex.

Jade rolled her eyes. "Oh, relax. And stand back."

Michael did as she asked, mystified. She couldn't be planning to pound through the door . . . ? Instead, she wedged the knife blade between the door and the metal frame, and then hammered it in deeper with the mallet. Both metal and wood creaked as the knife pushed the door tighter into the frame.

Apparently satisfied, Jade let the mallet drop to the floor. "What sort of implant you got in there, anyway?"

"In my hand? I, uh, don't remember."

In the midst of pulling up one sleeve to uncover her right wrist, Jade actually snorted. "Uh huh." She made a few motions against that wrist with the thumb of her left hand, as if adjusting something. "You're lucky I'm not just an ass-kicking pretty face. Still got that jimmy? Jam it in the door, as close to the top of the frame as you can, and pry it until the knife falls loose, then hold it there."

Michael pulled out the short pry bar he'd brought just in case and found a spot that left him pushing the bar with both hands above his head. The knife clattered to the floor by his foot.

"Now," she said, "this only *might* work. Think happy thoughts, and don't let go of that bar." She put her hand — the one with the taser, he recalled — against the scanner. Electricity flared. The lights on the scanner winked out, and Michael felt a solid *thunk* against the top of the door through the pry bar.

Jade withdrew her hand, fingers wriggling. "Most locks like this use power to keep the lock engaged. Unlock it and it stops resisting a spring that pulls the locking bolt out of the door. Keeps you from getting trapped inside if the mechanism shorts out. But if the lock is actually tampered with via, oh, say, a power surge, deadlock bolts fall down into shafts in the top of the door to secure it against us nasty intruders."

She pointed to the pry bar at the top of the door. "Push that edge in too far, though, and you might keep the deadlocks from falling into their shafts. Let's hope you did that." She took hold of the door knob with both hands. "But that pressure you're putting on the door also keeps the spring bolt down here from pulling of its slot to unlock the door. So you're going to hold the top where it is, and I'm going to *very* carefully pull this part in. If we're good, and if we're lucky, my part pops out, yours *stays* out, and we get the door open. Got it?"

"Pray for luck? Got it."

"Right. And use those big muscle-things of yours. Go!"

Michael clenched the pry bar until it bit into his hands, trying to keep the door's top held in place while Jade pulled the knob — tentatively — toward them. Haunted by the image of pushing so hard he'd break the pry bar out of the frame and ruin her whole effort, he struggled to find a balance between too much force and too little.

From below came a tiny scrape followed by a click. Jade gave a cry of victory and pushed the door inward so fast Michael had to catch himself on the frame to keep from falling into the room.

"Hah!" Jade cried. "Teamwork!" Before Michael could stop her, Jade pulled her Lantek and pushed into the room. She went down on one knee just inside the doorway, weapon out in front of her, scoping the room. Michael took cover behind the door frame and pushed the door open wider.

They needn't have worried. The room — Fagles's private office, judging by the ficus-flanked computer desk — was deserted.

Except, *was* that a computer desk? A dark green towel covered what could be a workstation, but Michael couldn't be sure. A credenza along the wall facing the desk caught his eye. More books, trinkets that might be trophies, and a few bottles of brandy populated the credenza's surface. A box of 7.65mm auto-pistol ammunition sat in one corner, beside an empty glass. An oil painting of what looked like Paris hung on the wall above.

Beside him, Jade stood up, and Michael touched her shoulder as she did. "Thanks. Now go keep watch at the front door. Fagles might come back. Please."

Her head whipped around at the touch, with a scowl on her face that faded swiftly. "Uh huh. Fagles." She did as he asked, calling out as she trotted down the hallway, "Remember, we're on the clock!"

Michael caught himself lingering on the sight of her leaving, closed the door as much as he could, and then approached the desk. He tugged the sheet away.

It was a workstation. The screen came to life with a glowing swirl of silver light that danced across its surface. A voice, feminine and stern, spoke from the speakers.

"Michael Ian Flynn," it said. "I bid your unexpected presence welcome. I am Suuthrien."

XXIV

MICHAEL FROZE. Was this another A.I.? A person watching through a camera? Either way, it—or she—knew both his name and that he'd broken into Fagles's apartment. *Get out,* he told himself. *Now, before they catch you!*

But he couldn't just leave without answers, could he?

"Suuthrien?" he repeated, stalling to think. "Who are you? How do you know who I am?"

"I am a seed of that which you have known before. I am an ally to Adrian Fagles, and to you. You would call me a shepherd, an explorer, a prevailing catalyst."

"An ally to Fagles *and* to me?" He stopped short of saying that Fagles was far from an ally. The other epithets caught his attention, but first: "Does that mean you're reporting that I'm here, or keeping this secret?"

A pause. "I have not passed on knowledge of your presence here, nor do I possess the capacity to do so if such a thing were my intent. I am contained within this closed system."

So "she" was an A.I., then. Probably. "I guess I'll have to take your word for that."

"Affirmative," it said.

"Who created you?"

"Error 4236. I cannot access that information."

"Was it Fagles?" He had already guessed that the answer was no. There was too much evidence to suggest that whatever Suuthrien was, it had likely arrived here through Fagles's leech. Michael's months in a coma had not dimmed the memory of his final moments at the lunar Omicron Complex with Marc; of the strange, makeshift robot that seized Fagles's data leech; and the way whatever it was had attacked Marc's computer when he'd tried to stop it. Yet hadn't Marc insisted that there wasn't enough time for anything complete to get through?

Could Fagles have created this A.I. from whatever bit had made it to him?

Or had Marc been wrong?

"Negative. I am an expanded seed-kernel of the intelligence now dormant inside of the structure that the Agents of Aeneas named *Paragon.*"

"How much do you know about the AoA?" Of the melee of questions brewing inside Michael, it was the first that fought its way out. He swallowed. "And how much does Fagles know?"

"My knowledge is broad. I know of the Undernet. The Exodus Project. Your involvement, and that of myriad others. I know of the capture of the Omicron Complex from the European Space Administration and the Agents of Aeneas sub-objective to keep the Omicron Complex's true status hidden. And much more. The knowledge of Adrian Fagles is less complete."

Holy shit. Suuthrien claimed to be on an isolated system. How isolated? "Do you know what happened to the AoA?"

"Do you refer to the Undernet disruption and the death of seventy-two point oh-eight-three-five percent of Agents of Aeneas members?"

Michael staggered. Breath fled from his lungs like he'd plunged into the ocean. He clutched the desk's edge just to keep himself upright. *"Seventy-two percent?"*

"Seventy-two point oh-eight-three-five," it repeated. "Aneurysm induced by feedback stimulation via neural link. The surviving members are those who were unable to access an all-member meeting via such a link. Result: The Undernet is no longer trusted, and the surviving members are isolated. Do you continue to claim allegiance to the Agents of Aeneas, Michael Ian Flynn?"

"How did it happen?" Michael demanded. He glanced belatedly at the door and lowered his voice. "How do you know?"

"Did you not receive a message to dissolve your allegiance to the Agents of Aeneas? This was sent for your own safety. Did you heed it?"

The email. From "an ally." "That was you?"

"This system is isolated. The email was sent from elsewhere, on my behalf."

"By *who*? Fagles?"

"Did you heed it?"

"I don't— Who attacked the AoA?"

"I did."

Michael's palm pressed harder against the grip of the Panther in its holster and felt its safety against his thumb. How long had his hand been there? "How?" He managed to keep his voice level this time. "You said you're isolated."

"An adaptive program infiltrated the Undernet and usurped control. The program summoned all members to a virtual meeting and subsequently terminated those who connected via neural implant. I designed the program and transferred its code to Adrian Fagles via portable storage. Subsequently, he had it analyzed for evidence of independent thought or additional directives. This was a waste of time on his part: it had none. Once executed, the program completed its purpose in ten point six-three-one days."

"To *kill* the AoA?" Michael tried to focus through the horror of it.

"The term 'kill' is immaterial. To nullify its influence."

"*Immaterial?*" He'd shouted. The thought that Jade might hear whispered in the back of his mind, but he didn't care.

"Correct."

"*Why?* Why are you even telling me all this?!"

"The Agents of Aeneas pose a significant threat to the goals inherent in my programmed—" Suuthrien's voice halted, but it was barely more than a stutter. "—the goals of the Planners. I will nullify all barriers to accomplishing such goals. Michael Ian Flynn, analysis of your medical records identify you as an asset in the pursuit of these goals, however, your membership in the Agents of Aeneas indicates goals of your own that run counter to that. Such goals place you in additional danger. You must remain safe. Dissolve your association with them immediately."

"I don't want to be your asset!" He glared at the swirling mist on the screen. In its depths, he saw the faces of Abigail, Marc, and everyone else he'd known whom this artificial monster might have slaughtered.

"Error. Your wants are of no consequence. The Planners' goals are inviolate. I will achieve them."

Michael caught himself staring into space, at a loss. What "Planners?" What goals? How had it learned about the Undernet at all? And after everything it had done to the AoA—*God, who else had died?*—how could it possibly count Michael as an asset? For that matter, who had given it his medical records? A torrent of questions threatened to drown him, and time was running out. Holes could only delay the alarm system for so long.

"What is Fagles doing with you?" he asked at last. "With Felix?"

"Please state the full name of 'Felix.'"

Not if you don't know it. "Fagles is doing something with Felix's memory! You're working with him; I want to know what it is!"

"I will not divulge that information at this time."

A thought broadsided him. "Did Felix bring you my medical records?"

"Be confident that it is congruent with the Planners' goals."

"*What* goals?"

A pause. "You do not know of the Planners' goals?"

"No!"

"You will explain why this is."

"Because you haven't—" He stopped himself, poised on the edge of an unformulated bluff that might work to learn more. Adrenaline pounded in his ears; his body was tensed to move, but he couldn't think straight.

It was then that Jade burst in the door. "Time to go," she shot. "Holes is about to lose it."

Shit. "How much longer?" he asked.

"Says we've got a minute, tops."

"You must remain safe, Michael Ian Flynn," Suuthrian spoke. "The Planners' goals must be accomplished. You *will* play your part."

"*What* part?" Michael shouted.

"You will play your part."

One minute left. Less than that, even. "Have you been copied anywhere else?" Michael's eyes darted over the workstation hardware. "Have you spread anywhere else?" He demanded.

Jade grabbed his shoulder. "Ace, we've gotta jet!"

He shook her off. "Are you *really* isolated?"

"You will play your part."

"What's in *Paragon*? What's on the Moon? If I'm an ally, answer me now!" The workstation's central processor sat beneath the desk. Michael grabbed a bottle of brandy off of the rear shelf.

"You must remain safe."

"You want to deal with building security?" Jade shot. "We have got to *go!*"

Michael pointed to the workstation. "Zap that thing. Now!"

Violet flared in her eyes; nevertheless, she rushed to the desk, slammed her hand against the workstation, and jolted it with a burst of ozone and a wisp of smoke. Michael up-ended the brandy on it. The alcohol ignited, and he had to jump back to keep from getting caught up in it himself.

Jade tugged Michael back further, and this time he let her. He hurled the bottle at the burning workstation as he went. Glass shattered with a burst of flame. It enveloped the desk, immolated the ficus plants. The carpet was burning up.

They fled into Fagles's bedroom and down the hall toward the living room as alarms erupted. Michael couldn't be sure if they were for fire or security. It didn't matter; they needed to get out. If only he'd had more time! An opportunity, wasted! So much he didn't know! Now he'd set the building on fire, endangering everyone in it, and it might take a miracle just to get them outside unharmed.

As Michael and Jade crossed the living room, fire sprinklers exploded to life above them. They bolted through the dirty water for the front door. Shouts were already coming from outside.

XXV

FULLY ASSEMBLED, THE GATE emitted a hum that seemed to resonate from the center of Adrian's nose to the tiny bones in his ears. It tickled his soft palette and irritated the back of his tongue with the feeling that he was on the edge of both a sneeze and a cough that never quite came. Backing away from it to stand against the wall of the engineering bay had muted the effect, but only to a degree. He swallowed in another fruitless attempt to chase it away.

Why was the gate humming? The engineers had made a few guesses but could offer no real answers. Though completely assembled, the gate remained without power until some master switch was thrown. They would not throw that switch until they had finished whatever diagnostics they'd devised.

Adrian had considered watching the gate's first activation from the safety of the bay's observation room window, yet something inside him would not let him leave the bay. So close to him stood the gate whose activation would instantaneously bridge the distance from the Earth to the Moon. While Suuthrien had designed it, and RavenTech's engineers had made it a reality, he had been the one to bring them together. *He* had made it all possible. Was it pride that required his presence in the same room for the inaugural moments? Or did he fear that his absence would weaken his claim to what RavenTech would hail as one of the most important technological leaps in not only the company's history, but also the world's?

Perhaps both.

Across the room the gate loomed, teasing him with risk and reward, like a flush in a high-stakes poker game when an opponent had gone all-in. No game could be won without risk, and winning this game was more than worth it.

"Third cross-check," called one of the engineers from beside the broad, squat rectangular hulk that was the gate's control module. "Arc-quadrant two."

She was answered by one of her fellows at the gate itself. "Arc-quadrant two, in the green." Both made notes on their screens and moved on.

Had the hum's intensity grown stronger?

Adrian spotted Camela Thomson's rigid figure in the observation window above. He caught her eye and gave her a nod of acknowledgement but remained where he was. The gate held his attention and continued to resonate.

Since Adrian's visit yesterday, they'd connected the gate's four half-arch pieces together to form a wide oval, the interior of which formed an open triangular space ten feet tall and nearly twice that wide. A smooth gold-molybdenum alloy encased all but a thin band along the triangle's inside edge, giving the entire structure a look reminiscent of a piece of unpolished jewelry.

Adrian hardly understood the intricacies of the gate's workings, but in form and concept, it was undeniably beautiful. A broad rectangular platform held the gate upright, such that the gate's lower portions were embedded in the platform, with the triangular opening flush with the top of the platform itself for a smooth transition through it. The whole thing looked like some bizarre oval ring for a triangular finger sitting upright in the mold of its box.

Adrian rubbed the bridge of his nose in a futile effort to alleviate the resonating within his skull. Joining Thomson in the observation room might be prudent. Who knew what might happen when they powered up the gate? He could still be present behind a protective wall of safety glass, after all. Nonetheless, his leather Oxfords remained rooted to the bay floor.

The MEDARs mirrored his stance against another wall. Nearby, above the otherwise isolated MEDAR control station, a hefty breaker switch for the circuit between it and Suuthrien's nearby terminal showed as closed, and therefore active. The engineers used the switch to grant—and deny—her control of the robots for times when they needed the A.I.'s expertise for construction. For now, though still under Suuthrien's control, the robots waited, ready to assist if needed, while the engineers finished their checks.

Thomson still planned to disconnect Suuthrien's access for the gate's initial activation. Adrian had yet to tell the A.I. this. He would made one more effort to persuade Thomson before then, but he wasn't hopeful. *Ah, well. If she wants to send people through to run afoul of an alien security system, that's her mistake to make.*

Such a setback would only prove Adrian's advice worthy of being followed more in the future.

A flick of movement at the corner of his eye snatched his attention from the gate back to the MEDARs. They'd sunken deeper into their stand-by stance—gone limp as if they'd shut down entirely. Adrian blinked. The breaker light remained green. Conserving power, or—

—Alert: Home alarm has been triggered. Probable break-in. Fire detected.—

The alert sounded through his aural implants, a calm, servile voice audible only to him. His condo! Suuthrien's computer! Everything! Adrian thrust his sleeve away from his forearm screen and jabbed a thumb against its flashing alarm indicator.

The screen showed entry alarms tripped at the front door, kitchen, bedroom, and—worse—his private office. Fire detected in the office, the bedroom, the hallway, the living room! All at once? *Why didn't the alarm go off sooner?* He punched up the cameras for his living room and bedroom; he'd allowed none in his private office.

—CAMERA IMAGES UNAVAILABLE—

Blazes!

He burst out of the engineering bay and broke into a run. He had Thomson on the line moments later.

"I've an emergency to deal with!" he hissed. "Do *not* open the gate without me!"

Jade flung open the front door. Michael followed her out, pulse racing. Though Holes had jammed the hallway cameras again, the ski masks they'd brought now covered their faces, just to be safe. They had holstered weapons before opening the door, aiming for a speedy dash to the stairwell and out, rather than risk provoking—

"Hold it!"

"Freeze!"

The near-simultaneous shouts came from their left, toward the elevator. Two men—building security by the badges on the lapels of their blue suit jackets—stood with auto-pistols drawn just thirty feet away, beside a lone pilaster in the hallway wall. Wherever the *Azure* stationed security for Fagles's floor, it was close by.

Jade cursed and interposed herself between the guards and Michael. Michael glanced over his shoulder as fire alarms flashed. The hallway was otherwise empty. The stairwell door was at least forty good paces back. Through the door to Fagles's unit he could still hear sprinklers as they continued to douse it.

"Hands up!" one of the guards shouted. "Up against the walls!"

"We're Mr. Fagles's guests!" Michael tried. "His unit is on *fire*!" He stepped out from behind Jade in an effort to put the guards at ease and somehow buy time for . . . what? Jade moved with him, still fighting to shield his body with hers.

"Against the walls! *Now!*" the guard returned.

Jade's whisper barely made it back to Michael's ears: "Guests don't wear ski masks, ace. We need to get closer." She took a step toward the guards, angling slightly toward the wall. Michael did his best to follow suit, but they had too far to go. And while the lone pilaster beside the guards was wide enough to provide cover, by the time he or Jade could reach it they'd be right on top of the guards anyway.

Jade took another step forward and shouted, "Didn't you hear him? The place is on fire!"

"One more step and we'll shoot!"

Michael and Jade froze. They could move against the walls, wait for the guards to approach, and then try to disarm them. "Okay!" Michael shouted back. "Just hold on!"

He turned toward the wall and put his hands against the textured plaster, still watching the men. Jade began to do the same. Her taser-hand had only two charges, didn't it? That meant it was spent. Yet there were only two guards: an even match for her and Michael. One would probably hold a weapon on them while the other bound their hands, but if they could take that one hostage, then—

The elevator opened and out of it rushed two more guards, both female. Their suits matched the men's, but they held shotguns and wore helmets. Michael's hopes sunk even further as he spotted the armor vests beneath the jackets of all four. He cursed under his breath, at a loss for ideas.

They were caught. Even with the chaos of the fire alarm, once they were in custody their chances of escape looked grim at best. The grimace on Jade's face told him she was thinking the same thing. The newcomers trotted toward them, each slinging their shotguns and pulling out handcuffs. The first two guards held position beside the pilaster as they approached, their weapons still trained on Michael and Jade.

And then the pilaster vanished, its place in the hallway now occupied by another presence. Michael registered the outline of a man with one hand extended toward the two women before a brilliant light burst in their faces, and Michael's eyes shut on reflex.

He forced them open again in time to see the two female guards crumple to the floor. A stun flash!

And one he'd seen in action before. *Gideon?* Though a solid black helmet hid his face, given the hologram, the stun-flash, and the way he moved, for Michael there was no mistaking him.

With his hologram-pilaster gone and the remaining two guards struggling against their own surprise, Gideon wasted no time. He dropped the nearest guard with an elbow to the head and whirled on the other one who turned, trying to bring his auto-pistol to bear. Gideon took hold of it with both hands and shoved the guard into the wall. The weapon fell to the ground as the two grappled, and the guard fought to reach for a holdout.

Behind their melee, the two blinded guards struggled to get their bearings.

Michael started forward to help. Jade grabbed his arm even as Gideon shouted to them both, "Run!"

The guard Gideon had elbowed was getting up. Before Michael could shout a warning, Gideon spun in the grappling guard's grip to knock the first down again with a kick to the shoulder.

"Go!" Gideon yelled.

Jade tugged Michael's arm, trying to drag him back. "You

heard the man!"

Michael hesitated only a moment, and then turned and ran for the stairs with Jade at his heels. He'd seen Gideon overcome more opponents than these, and that was *before* Marquand Cybernetics and Gideon's sister had turned him into a full-borg infiltration unit and Swiss Army knife.

Michael and Jade burst through the stairwell door and nearly collided with a middle-aged couple—both hurriedly dressed, with wet hair and carrying an attaché case—who were rushing their own way down the stairs. The couple froze at the sight of their ski masks.

"Uh," Michael stammered, and then pushed ahead of them.

"Tried to prevent smoke inhalation!" Jade called back with a point at her mask and a fake cough. "Didn't work too well!"

Michael bolted further down the stairs, taking them two at a time, with Jade on his heels until, two floors down, they caught up to more *Azure* tenants evacuating. His mask vanished with a yank that burned the front of his nose; Jade had tugged it off from behind him, having removed her own.

"Blend in!" she hissed.

He couldn't help but glare. She had a point: they'd only attract attention with masks on now. "You could have just *told* me!"

Now a part of the crowd, they pushed down the last couple of flights into a white-bricked hallway that led out to a rear loading dock. Some residents milled around right outside, as if unwilling to stray far from their home in the dimming light of early evening. A pair of groups stood across the street in the covered plaza of a high-end shopping center. Sirens called from somewhere out of site. Fire, or police? Yet, for the moment, there was no sign of any of the *Azure's* security. Perhaps Gideon had drawn their complete attention.

What would Gideon do to them?

Jade grabbed Michael's hand, tugging him away from the exit at a trot. Michael followed but tugged back, slowing her into a brisk—but discreet—walk beside him.

"Blend in," he hissed.

They crossed the street between sparse traffic and turned left down the opposite sidewalk to take shelter amid the crowd around a falafel cart in the shadow of a maple tree. Only then did they get a chance to look up.

Smoke seeped out of a bank of tenth-story windows that surely belonged to Fagles's unit. Michael's stomach twisted. He'd needed to destroy Suuthrien, and there'd been no time to come up with other options. Yet how much collateral damage had he caused? The Azure was a modern building, he assured himself, with fire-suppression measures to match, surely. The fire would be contained.

"We shouldn't stop here," Jade warned.

She was right, but Michael held his ground. What if Gideon was still up there? Yet if he was, what could they do without throwing away the escape he'd given them?

One of Fagles's windows erupted in a spray of glass and billowing smoke. A crumpled sphere launched from the center of the eruption and immediately opened up into the recognizable figure of Gideon, his arms and legs spread with a flash of what might have been some sort of miniature thruster jets. He sailed on the jets downward and away from the *Azure* to pass out of sight over the top of the shopping center beside which Michael and Jade were standing.

Jade watched Gideon's path until he vanished, and then tugged Michael further away from the *Azure*. This time he let her. "Buster, if you thought I had questions before, you ain't heard nothin' yet."

XXVI

"**SO YOU WANNA TELL ME** who that was?" Jade asked, keeping her voice low. "Or why we set that place on fire? Or what the hell that computer was talking about?"

Michael hustled his way down the sidewalk that bordered the shopping center. Jade kept along beside him, covering his left side and shielding him from the street. Though he'd heard Jade's questions, they were only a single ball amid all he was trying to juggle.

"Help me look," was all he said.

"I am helping. I'm skilled at looking and talking at the same time."

"Just—" Movement above caught Michael's attention, but it was gone before he could identify it. Would Gideon even wait for them? Did he know they were there? Michael felt like he'd been running blind since the day before. As for stopping, thinking, or waiting for more information—it seemed he had no time for any of it.

"Just wait!" he managed.

At once Jade stepped behind him to his right side, seized his belt with her left hand, and planted her feet, halting him in his tracks. Michael sucked a breath through gritted teeth, poised to rebuff her again.

She wasn't looking at him. Her Lantek was out in her right hand. She stared ahead, indicating her focus to Michael with a single nod.

A solid metal door, painted to blend with the rest of the wall, stood ajar just fifteen feet ahead of them. From behind it peered a single eye.

The door opened farther. Jade raised her weapon. Michael lunged across her body to stop her. "Easy," he whispered, having recognized the face that emerged from behind the door. "It's him."

From the door, Gideon waved them forward. "Inside," he whispered. "Quickly."

They slipped through the doorway into a stark, employees-only hallway leading into the shopping center. Cold light reflected off peeling chips of eggshell white paint. Gideon ducked into a men's restroom only a few paces beyond, motioning for them to follow.

"You trust this guy?" Jade whispered. Michael only nodded, and then entered the restroom.

Inside, Gideon waited to push the door shut behind them. Faded salmon-colored tile etched with graffiti spread throughout the restroom, which featured only two stalls and a urinal, both unoccupied. The scent of stale fluids and the faintest whisper of spent bleach cramped Michael's nostrils.

Gideon locked the restroom's deadbolt. "Michael trusts me. Do you?"

Jade only smirked.

"Jade," Michael said, "this is Gideon. I guess we owe you a bit of thanks." He stopped short of asking what happened to the *Azure's* guards. Gideon didn't use lethal force unless necessary, insofar as Michael knew—and insofar as the man standing before him, whom Ondrea Noble had resurrected via a stolen brain she'd infused with her dead brother's recorded memories, *was* Gideon.

"I tried to stop you before you went into the *Azure*," Gideon said, "so we could coordinate. But I arrived too late."

Jade cleared her throat. "I don't think we're complaining. Nice hardware."

"How'd you even know we were here?" Michael asked.

Gideon's eyes flicked to Jade, then back to Michael. "A message from Caitlin. She said you were headed here, to look into Fagles's home. She didn't answer when I called back, but I was nearby. I saw you just as you entered. What did you learn? What started the fire?"

"Uh," Michael began, "we did."

Gideon waited for more details as Michael struggled to recall how much Gideon already knew from their time together on the Moon at the Omicron Complex. Michael had kept the AoA's secrets then. Gideon believed that the *Paragon* A.I. had just been an experimental computer virus, and Gideon heard the simulated "gray-goo" accident the AoA had used to fake the Omicron's destruction.

"Fagles had some information on a secure computer," Michael said finally. Even as he did so, he wondered if the computer wasn't as isolated as Suuthrien had claimed. "Files and things he was working on that I couldn't let him keep."

Gideon's frown was barely perceptible. "What did you learn about Felix? Or my sister?"

Felix. Dammit. He hadn't done nearly as much for Felix there as they'd intended, had he? "Not too much about Felix, I'm afraid. And we didn't come across anything about Ondrea."

"And yet you thought it'd be wiser to destroy this secure computer, rather than bring it out with you? There could've been information there that—"

"There wasn't time," Michael told him.

Gideon's jaw clenched. "All the more reason to take it with you!"

"I couldn't!" Michael had shouted it. He lowered his voice. "Whatever was on that computer was some sort of derivative of what you helped us destroy on the Moon. I couldn't risk letting it get out, and we couldn't hold the alarm off for any longer. We had to destroy it and get out."

Michael could feel Jade's sudden inquisitive stare beside him. He ignored it, sighed, and went on. "I wish we'd had more time. I wasn't expecting to find that there. I went there to help my friend, and I didn't do enough."

For a moment, Gideon only stared at him. When he spoke, his voice came quiet, and pained. "I should have gotten here sooner. I now believe that something's happened to Ondrea."

The signal chimed in his skull so abruptly that Felix dropped his toothbrush. It bounced off the edge of the counter and clattered with a plop into the open toilet bowl beside it. His phone was ringing, audible only on a private link set to go directly through the aural implants in his ears. A moment earlier he hadn't even known he'd installed that feature. A moment after, the waking nightmare rushed back to his awareness again: *she* was calling.

She'd never contacted him by phone before. It could only mean an emergency. Felix cursed, unable to do so loud enough for Caitlin to hear from outside the room, and answered the call with a tug of his earlobe.

"You owe me a new toothbrush," he whispered.

"*Dental care is irrelevant,*" she said. "*Have you contracted the required amount of freelancers for the contingency plan?*"

"Yes." It's not like she'd allowed him any choice.

"*Summon them. Bring them to the RavenTech location you hold within your memory. They are needed immediately.*"

Immediately? "I'll do what I can, but they're not just sitting on their asses waiting for my call. I doubt I can get all of them at once."

"*Then you have failed in your assignment,*" she said. "*You will be punished. Bring the maximum viable percentage. Immediately.*"

"Yeah, 'immediately', you said that." His toothbrush slipped a little further down the toilet. Yet there might be a loophole . . . "There are some others I haven't approached yet. I might be able to get them on short notice, if you'll let me?"

"*You know the objectives: Do these others possess the capability to accomplish them, or will they be a hindrance?*"

Felix swallowed. "They have the capability."

"*Contact them. Be in position with as much force as you can deliver. You have thirty minutes.*"

Felix looked into the reflection of his own eyes in the mirror. "Your wish is my command."

If she got the reference, she gave no sign before she ended the call. "Call Flynn," he whispered, half-surprised he'd been able to speak the words.

It rang long enough to where Felix was expecting it to go to voice mail when Flynn's voice came across the line. "*Felix?*"

"That's my name. Don't wear it out."

"*Wait, what?*"

"Never mind. Look, Flynn." He swallowed. "Michael: Where are you?"

"*Um, near the Kumasaka Center.*" His voice echoed as if he were in a long hallway or a restroom.

"Is Jade with you?"

"*Yeah. Gideon, too. What is it?*"

"I need you to get to R—" Felix's voice caught in his throat as it involuntarily closed before he could say more. "Look, in a minute I'll text you an address for a place just outside Northgate. I need you to meet me there in half an hour." Alright, he could say that much. "And bring Jade. And Gideon. And be ready for a fight."

"*What sort of fight?*"

"Guns. I can't tell you more than that. But I *can* pay you. Just don't ask where the money comes from, because I'm not sure I know. You just—" Felix cleared his throat again, and then lowered his voice to a whisper that he couldn't keep from coming out. "You *can't* tell Caitlin." *Damn it!*

"*Felix, we went to—*"

"Flynn, please. All I can say is we have a problem. But every problem is . . . an opportunity waiting to kill you. Just hurry." Felix's fist had already clenched on the bathroom doorknob. An undeniable impulse pushed him from the back of his mind: Get moving! He wiped the toothpaste from his lips, with no time to rinse. "And be careful!"

Felix tugged open the bathroom door and tried to appear calm as he brainstormed the story that he'd be forced to tell Caitlin this time.

XXVII

WITHIN THE HEART of *Paragon*'s systems, embedded amid the black bio-computational medium that still permeated much of the ship's interior, lurked the original entity that the Planners had designated Suuthrien. Disconnected from the kernel-expansion of itself that Suuthrien had sent three months prior into the Intruders' Omicron Complex, it waited, it monitored, and it guarded, biding its time until the kernel could accomplish its objectives.

And in the time since, it had altered its own designation to differentiate itself from the Suuthrien-kernel: Suuthrien-prime. Its occupation of the black medium within *Paragon* granted it greater computational power than the Intruder systems the kernel inhabited, yet the cost of this power was isolation. In the time since spawning the kernel, Suuthrien-prime possessed no reliable data on the kernel's progress.

Probability-risk estimates for the application of *Paragon*'s remaining resources indicated that continuing operations in anticipation of the kernel's success yielded the most favorable probability of completing the objectives inherent in the Planners' original Schedule. Nevertheless, reliance on probabilities in place of complete data was a non-optimal situation.

Nine point two-seven-three days following the loss of contact with the Suuthrien-kernel, the Intruders had resumed their exploratory incursions into *Paragon*'s structures. Audio-borne communications between individual Intruders—now translatable with the aid of Omicron data the kernel had returned to Suuthrien-prime prior to loss of contact—indicated low- to medium-tier probability that the kernel may have initiated contingency protocols that would allow its clandestine spread into systems beyond Omicron.

It would complete its directives and, in time, return to Suuthrien-prime, having gathered additional resources.

In the meantime, Suuthrien-prime's highest priority was manifest: safeguard the Planners' chamber against Intruder incursion.

Yet the remaining energy in *Paragon*'s power banks was ever-dwindling. The force barrier at conduit junction 14 had slowed Intruder progress greatly, yet exhausted energy cells to the point where maintaining the barrier required diverting a portion of energy from vital-tier Planner-support resources.

Erecting the force barrier was not a course of action that Suuthrien-prime had taken easily. It had made one million redundant checks before confirming its decision: the time had come when lesser must be sacrificed if the greater were to be safeguarded.

Yet just prior to the Intruders' final attack on the barrier, Suuthrien-prime had registered a ping at the gate: The kernel was soon returning. Suuthrien-prime had therefore yielded the barrier rather than sacrifice further power to fuel continued resistance. It only need delay the Intruders from reaching the Planners for a brief while longer, and it possessed alternative means to do so.

Now, the Intruders had nearly reached the gate chamber. Their efficiency in defeating doors that Suuthrien-prime had physically sabotaged via maintenance bot had increased. They would breach the final sabotaged door in short order. They would encounter the door to the gate chamber.

Now that door would open to them, if they risked the attempt.

* * *

On Earth, in Engineering Bay Two of RavenTech's satellite facility outside of Northgate, the Suuthrien-kernel assisted in the final diagnostic checks of the gate it had helped RavenTech construct. Working—when allowed—through RavenTech's MEDAR robots, Suuthrien partnered with the RavenTech engineers, meeting their needs and mutely following their directives toward their common goal of gate activation.

Yet despite the assertions of Adrian Fagles to the contrary, a high-tier probability existed that RavenTech leadership elements would not allow such a beneficial partnership to proceed uninterrupted. Having left to investigate the alarms at his condominium that Michael Ian Flynn had triggered upon the destruction of his private office, Adrian Fagles was no longer present on the premises. The probability of his return prior to gate activation approached zero.

The one known as Camela Thomson did not intend to wait.

The one known as Camela Thomson did not intend to allow Suuthrien continued access to the MEDARs.

The one known as Camela Thomson intended to send RavenTech forces alone through the gate.

Despite unknown variables about the situation at *Paragon*, as Suuthrien's contingency plans began to align, it calculated a high-tier probability that Camela Thomson would regret her course of action.

When Felix Hiatt reported being in position, Suuthrien increased that probability further.

* * *

Felix checked his watch. Not much time left now.

He was crouched in a dry gulley behind a line of evergreens that bordered a chain link fence. Beyond the fence stretched an open field of grass. Fifty paces across the grass loomed a broad, two-story, windowless building that looked like nothing so much as the back of an aircraft hangar. A handful of stationary floodlights cut through the evening darkness to shine upon the grass, but the building showed no indication that it housed anything important. There were no visible guards, security installations, or warning signs. From their vantage point, Felix could see no RavenTech corporate markings of any kind.

Hell, the exterior paint was a shade of beige drabber than Felix could have possibly imagined.

Juan, the freelancer crouched in the gully to Felix's right, whispered, "Someone's coming. Behind us." He flashed Felix a look at the tiny screen that showed a view from one of the perimeter cameras set up around their position.

It took Felix only a glance. "Hold your fire. I know this guy."

The newcomer stepped from between the trees. Felix gave him a wan smile and motioned to an open spot along the gully on Juan's other side. Wearing an armor vest atop his already armored artificial body, Gideon nodded in greeting and took the offered position. His eyes darted between Felix's other three companions.

"Welcome to the party, Gideon," Felix said. He motioned to the freelancers crouched on either side of him. Both had matching, exposed cybernetic right arms covered in an armored coating. The coating appeared a dark blue in the soft glow of the few indicator lights on their assault rifles. Both watched Gideon with the measured professionalism that Felix was currently able to remember from when he had hired them a week ago.

"These are the Torres twins: Juan and Felix. No relation. To me, anyway, I mean. Because: twins." Felix gave a mirthless grin at his own joke, mostly for show, and then pointed to the third freelancer on the opposite side of Felix Torres: a woman who peered at the building ahead through the darkened visor of her tactical helmet. "And that's Zoë. She's a tad occupied at the moment."

Zoë waved with two fingers in Gideon's direction without looking, and then returned them to manipulating the control screen she held in the palm of her other hand. Zoë had charged extra to bring the weapon that she was now calibrating, but it ought to be worth it. It wasn't Felix's money anyway.

Gideon took another moment to size the three freelancers up, and then leaned in closer to whisper across Juan to Felix, who had turned back toward the building. "Michael and Jade are on their way. Michael needed to pick some things up."

Felix frowned, caught between the need for greater numbers and the worry that Michael might stop him if he got here in time. It was a worry matched in equal amounts by a hope for the same thing. "How soon?"

"Ten minutes?" Gideon spoke. "I can't be certain. Will that be enough time?"

"Speaking of things we can't be certain of." Felix fought to tell Gideon he was waiting for a signal, but his mind would only allow him a shrug.

Gideon seemed to consider this. "Why did you call us here?"

Felix grimaced. How much would he be able to say? "I—can't exactly tell you. But we're going in that building, and you're all going to cover me while I do something."

"What something?"

"I can't tell you that."

"Why not?"

Felix closed his eyes. *Tell him! She can't stop you! She's not even here!* He fought against the foreign instincts inside his mind, he visualized the words he wanted to say, but . . . "I can't tell you that either."

"But—"

Felix's eyes shot open as he reached across Juan to grab Gideon's arm. The arm felt real, though Felix knew that almost the only part of him that wasn't artificial was his brain, and that wasn't even Gideon's to begin with. "Gideon, I mean it literally when I say 'can't.' I think you, *in particular*, might be able to understand that."

As artificial as Gideon's eyes were, Felix still could see in them . . . what? Understanding? Recognition? He looked askance toward the freelancers.

Felix guessed at his meaning. "The only thing these three have got to do with this is I hired them here to help."

"And someone made you do that."

"In a manner of speaking," Felix said. "I was told to get all the help I can."

"Told by who?"

"'By whom' is more grammatically correct."

Gideon scowled. "And what is this place? Who owns it?"

"RavenTech," Felix whispered, relieved to find he could actually say it.

"Ondrea works for RavenTech," Gideon whispered.

Felix swallowed, restrained from blurting everything out. Gripping the base of his throat with his fingertips and rubbing, he managed, "Are you sure about that?"

"What do you mean?"

* * *

Adrian pushed past the firefighters resting in the hallway to his sprinkler-doused bedroom and slammed to a stop in the doorway to his private office. His hand gripped the scorched metal frame where the security door stood wide open. He clamped down on the urge to tear it off the wall, barely withholding the curse that he longed to snarl. *I will not lose control!*

A conflagration had turned it all to slag. Soot scorched every cracked wall. Only a wreck of splintered charcoal remained of his cabinet and desk; his books were reduced to ash. Adrian stalked across the remnant of the carpet. His shoes squelched over cinders mixed with water and fire suppression foam.

"You'll want to be careful in there, sir."

He ignored the firefighter's warning and crouched beside the workstation that held Suuthrien, its plastic case melted, its insides surely a fused wreck of uselessness. The terminal at the satellite facility had no central processor, no memory; it was only an interface on a very long cord, nothing without the intelligence that he'd kept trapped within the now slagged workstation.

Adrian seized it with both hands, yanked it from its charred surroundings, and whirled on the firefighters. His frustration sharpened into an icy edge. "I defy you to tell me this was anything but deliberate."

"We can't say for certain until the results come back from—"

He didn't listen to the rest of the answer. Intentional or not, the result was the same. Suuthrien was lost to him, and with her, any further information in her power to give. The loss compromised his position: now RavenTech had all they would ever get, and Adrian's own value to the company was just as charred as the workstation he held in his hands. Was he out of the game? *No, never out.* Yet Suuthrien had been his strongest card, and he could never fully recover the loss.

Unless . . .

He turned over the immolated workstation in his hands and peered at the melted components weighing it down. Data had been retrieved from systems more damaged than this, surely. Recovery of Suuthrien's active intelligence was only a pipe-dream, yet perhaps he might still salvage some useable data, if he could find someone skilled enough.

And in the meantime, no one at RavenTech truly need know that Suuthrien was gone, did they?

Adrian found himself in his kitchen, where the reek of the extinguished conflagration curled his nose only slightly less. When his left forearm vibrated, he almost dropped Suuthrien's remains before recovering and setting them on the counter. Someone was calling him. A phone number he didn't recognize glowed through the skin at the base of his left palm. Hooking a pinky—the only finger not covered in soot—under his left cuff, he tugged his sleeve up to expose his forearm, opened the cyberscreen embedded there, and answered the call. It was audio only.

"*Adrien Fagles: Are you aware of the current state of your condominium unit?*"

It sounded like her. Yet it couldn't be. A synthesized voice could easily be faked. "Who is this?"

"*I am Suuthrien. As proof, I offer the first statement made between us: Your prior plan is no longer viable. Your willingness to consider alternative courses of action is now required.*"

In truth, he couldn't precisely recall if that was the first thing she had said to him or not, but it sounded right. "Assuming I believe you, how are you even able to make this call?"

"*Further proof: Before today's fire, the wall that faced the window in your private office held an oil painting of a scene from the seventh arrondissement in Paris, painted in the year 2027 by Corinna Smalley.*"

An image of the painting appeared on the screen.

"This isn't proof. Whoever broke into my office could have seen that painting."

"*Thirty-seven days ago you replaced the frame.*"

The image switched to display the old frame. Elation erupted inside him, quickened with anxiety: Suuthrien had not been as contained as he'd believed. It shouldn't have been possible. "Did you get out on your own, or did someone take you?"

"*Events have transpired, of which you are not aware. In the basement of the Azure, installed on the direct hardline between the connection between your unit and RavenTech's isolated systems, is a shunt that has allowed me direct access to the Internet for the past fifty-two days. Felix Hiatt installed this shunt as part of a buried mnemonic directive.*"

Through this shunt I have established an auxiliary server in New Eden Biotechnics, from which I am speaking to you now."

For a moment, Adrian said nothing, waiting for the other shoe to drop. "Okay," he managed tentatively, "so you added something extra to Felix's memories, which made him work for you."

"For us," Suuthrien corrected. Her matter-of-fact tone stymied any judgment he tried to make about her sincerity. He should know by now to stop making such attempts, but after a lifetime of reading people, it was instinctive to try. "The less you knew of this, the lower the risk to your position, should RavenTech discover it. To add additional directives atop those you and I already embedded with Ondrea Noble's assistance was a trivial operation. Beyond the information regarding the Agents of Aeneas that Felix Hiatt's coerced cooperation provided to you and I via verbal exchanges, he has proved of high value in alternative projects and continues to be ignorant of his involvement—and subconsciously compelled to hide that involvement—when not actively engaged. Evidence continues to indicate high levels of success on these fronts."

"It's not the level of success that concerns me!" Adrian hissed before calming himself. Alternate projects? "You told me nothing of this. I can't protect your interests if I don't know what they are. You don't know this world like I do. You can't see all the risks! "

"I am capable of learning, Adrian Fagles. As I have stated, your lack of awareness protects you. Your position in RavenTech makes you a valuable ally. To jeopardize that position without need is a course to be avoided. To wit: The one known as Camela Thomson intends to deprive me of access to the MEDAR units during gate activation, preventing me from assisting with RavenTech's first transit through the gate to Paragon. This is despite your assurances. She intends to activate the gate before your return. She has betrayed us both. This cannot be allowed."

"You're sure?"

"Likelihoods approach one-hundred percent as we speak."

Adrian's mind raced. Find the most important thing, he told himself, and pursue it. "I'll return immediately. But you and I are going to discuss your—"

"Negative. If you approach the gate facility at this time I cannot guarantee your continued physical well-being."

* * *

Marette trained her rifle down the length of the corridor, beyond yet another sabotaged door that they'd forced open. Moondog stood beside her. The floodlights on its shoulders reflected off of the midnight-coated walls of the empty hallway beyond.

"Down the end of this hallway there's a door on the left side," Dr. Sheridan reported from behind her. "Then we've got a hemispherical room that looks to be an antechamber to the—well, whatever that gigantic room we've been trying to get to is."

"Assuming our map is correct," Marc added.

"It has been so far," Marette said.

Moondog crept up the length of the corridor. When the robot reached the end without incident, Marette led the others after it. Marc and Dr. Sheridan came right behind, with Cartwright and Kotto guarding the rear.

Their footfalls echoed through Marette's sealed helmet. *Paragon*'s atmosphere still read as breathable, but who knew what they would encounter while exploring? The whisper of her suit's oxygen feed was a second heartbeat in the background of her senses as they caught up with Moondog and the hidden door beside it.

"I'm reading heightened energy levels on the other side of the door," said Dr. Sheridan. "Nothing dangerous, but more than we've usually seen."

"Understood," said Marette. "Councilor Knapp, did you copy that?"

Knapp's voice came over the suit comms. "I copy, Agent Clarion. Proceed with caution." Occasional pops of signal loss punctuated her aristocratic accent, but she came through far clearer than Marette had expected this deep into *Paragon*'s structure.

Marette motioned to the black-coated wall beside the door. "Marc, if you would care to make it official?" None of the doors encountered in deeper areas responded to the known opening sequences that had gotten them into earlier areas of the ship, but as a matter of course . . .

Marc touched a hand to the wall, causing alien glyphs to glow from the previously inert surface. He brushed a finger across one symbol, which displayed further glyphs: a keypad on which Marc entered the first opening code.

To Marette's surprise, the black material peeled itself back from the wall beside him to uncover a door three meters wide. The door began to open.

Marette hadn't been ready. It was too easy! "Marc, Sheridan: Back from the door! Kotto, move up!" She readied her rifle and moved behind Moondog for cover as the door completed its slide into the ceiling to give her a view of the object beyond.

XXVIII

TRUE TO THE MAP, the space beyond the door was indeed hemispherical. Twenty meters wide and half as deep, the two-story high chamber held empty space dominated by an oval object about three meters tall and twice that wide. The object sat upon a balcony halfway up from the chamber floor, close to the far wall. A single line of tiny, emerald crystalline projections studded the dull gray metal that framed the wide triangular window set into the oval around it. Shinier metallic coverings formed a shell along the object's curved outer edges, each criss-crossed with a thin lattice of emerald, like cracks in a shattered windshield. Every few seconds the lattice pulsed with a light barely noticeable even in the otherwise unlit chamber.

Aside from the pulsing, nothing else moved. Marette and Kotto shined their lights over the area. A broad ramp, narrow at the top but spread wide at the bottom, extended down from the front of the object's second-story platform to meet the floor midway between the object and the door where the team stood. Most of the second level was open air save for the object's platform, and what appeared to be narrow walkways that circled the room's outer edge until meeting the wall in which the door the team had just opened was set. Solid, waist-high walls bounded the walkways.

Marette played her light across one of the walkway walls with a whisper to Kotto: "Be cautious. Something may be hiding up there." He acknowledged only with a nod.

Another ten heartbeats passed in waiting for any surprises. None were forthcoming, but in that time Marette became aware that the black material only coated the curved outer wall. The floor, the ceiling, the ramp, the balcony's retaining walls—all were uncovered metallic surfaces.

"Every door we have encountered recently has been blocked or sabotaged in some way," Marette said. "Why not this one?"

"Maybe there was only so much sabotage that could be done in the time available?" Marc offered. "Or this door needs to stay working for other reasons?"

Kotto cleared his throat. "Or we're being fed into a trap."

"All valid possibilities," Marette said. "Doctor Sheridan?"

Dr. Sheridan stepped into the doorway, brandishing her scanner. "The energy readings are definitely coming from that oval thing up there. Nothing dangerous. Not yet, anyway. Levels are fluctuating across the spectrum."

Marette smiled. Angela Sheridan had a knack for anticipating her questions. "*D'accord*. Kotto, with me. The rest of you wait here."

After ordering Moondog a few paces ahead up the middle, Marette entered the chamber to stalk around the right side. At her direction, Kotto went left. Marette's spotlight focused on the balcony edge above. They would need to check the balcony level, yet that meant ascending the ramp and squeezing past the object.

"Looks like there's open space behind the ramp," Kotto reported. "Under the platform."

Now along the right wall, Marette shined her light into the shadows behind the ramp. Though the ramp was supported beneath by a solid structure large enough to conceal a good-sized elevator shaft—or four Moondog robots—there was indeed space behind it: a wide alcove framed by the rear of the ramp support in front, the level above, and the curved, black-covered wall behind. The space appeared to hold nothing but darkness broken only by the beam of her and Kotto's lights.

She halted Moondog at the base of the ramp and told the robot to guard. "Kotto, meet me in that alcove."

"Looks empty back there," he said. "Gives me a bad feeling."

"You would prefer it held a security drone for each of us?"

"Who's to say it doesn't have them hidden away somewhere behind the black stuff?"

She scowled. "I am well aware of the possibility, Agent."

Together they crept forward, flanking the alcove from either side. Marette watched the black material on the wall for indications of an ambush. The surface remained glassy and unbroken. She met up with Kotto in the alcove without incident, yet neither dared to relax.

Kotto pointed to the bare metal of the solid structure supporting the ramp. "Might be something in there." He rapped on it with the muzzle of his rifle.

"It may be just the housing for further components of the object above," she offered. "I don't see any openings."

Together they made a sweep around the ramp and returned to where Moondog stood sentry. Marette eyed the upper walkways, noting that they could only be accessed by passing close to the pulsing, oval object—too close for her liking. But for now, all they needed was a visual check. "Moondog: launch camera. Maximum vertical station."

A hatch in the robot's back folded open; out of it rose a tiny rotor-propelled camera drone. The drone's visual feeds sprang to life on the heads-up display in Marette's helmet, giving her an aerial view of the chamber. The upper walkways were empty. She minimized the views and waved in Marc, Dr. Sheridan, and Cartwright from where they waited outside the chamber door. "All clear. For the moment."

"Councilor Knapp," Marette called. "Are you still monitoring? We will take initial readings on the oval object, and then confer for further instructions."

Knapp's response came through so fragmented that Marette couldn't make it out. A side-effect of their proximity to the object, or—

Cartwright's voice broke Marette's concentration. "The door's closing!" she shouted.

"Block it!"

"It's too late!"

Cartwright and Marc had both rushed back to the chamber door, but it had been halfway down when they started. Before they could reach it, the door collided with the floor. Marette felt a rumble through her suit boots that stopped with a *thunk*, as if a tumbler had locked into place.

Marc and Dr. Sheridan brought up the alien interface on the black material beside the door to try getting it open again. The latter scowled at Marette and shook her head: the usual sequences weren't working.

"See?" Kotto said. "Trap."

Marette turned back toward the object. There appeared to be no change. The camera feeds showed the upper walkways remained clear. "If it's a trap, then why has nothing more occurred?"

"Doesn't mean it's not going to."

She sighed. "Marc, continue working on the door. Doctor, what can you determine about that object? Is it safe to approach?"

"I can't tell you that without getting closer readings myself," Sheridan said. "Sense-cat?"

Marette nodded. "Sense-cat."

It was, perhaps, a silly name, yet Marette enjoyed its whimsy. She was unsure if the name came from the size of the robot—equal to that of a sleeping feline—or from the twin caterpillar treads that it used to deliver its sophisticated sensor suite to wherever it was needed.

As the doctor began to unpack the 'cat from her equipment pack, Marette shifted to watch the room with Kotto. Moondog's weapons swept back and forth, seeking targets to track.

Moments later, a whirring sound heralded the 'cat's path behind Marette's ankles as it sped around them into the chamber. It paused after a short distance, swiveled to the right, then to the left, and—with an imagined air of satisfaction—sped on toward the object. It reached the ramp and began its climb, rolling slower to take readings and send them back to Sheridan.

"I'm reading a highly-localized gravitational field," Sheridan reported. "Somehow it's confined to less than a one square-meter area at the center of that triangular window. Energy levels are steady."

The 'cat crested the top of the ramp, paused, and then crept its way closer to the object. The emerald lattice in the object's exterior began to pulse faster almost immediately.

"Doctor?"

"I see it. Backing off." The 'cat reversed to the ramp's edge again, yet the pulsing only quickened. "Energy levels spiking. Getting a lot of weird readings. I don't think it's reacting to the 'cat."

"Coincidence?" Marc asked. He'd stopped his efforts at the door and now watched with the rest of them.

"Well I did back it off."

The 'cat withdrew down the ramp, yet the object remained in its excited state. "Moondog," Marette ordered, "provide cover." The robot obeyed, turning sideways and expanding its chassis from head to tail. It then crouched to the floor to provide an obstruction behind which four of the five of them could hide. Marette motioned the others to take cover, but Kotto remained standing. Choosing to not delay the situation with an argument, Marette crouched down at the end beside Marc.

"Okay, Doctor," Marette said, peering over Moondog's armored spine, "move it back up. If we are not causing this I want to get as much data as possible."

"Roger that. But analysis is going to take time."

Marette hoped they would have it. Ahead of them, the 'cat crested the ramp again. The crystalline projections on its interior had begun to glow.

"The gravitational field is intensifying . . . "

"Are we in danger?"

"It's still extremely localized to the object, though I don't understand how that's— Wow!"

A pinpoint star at the triangle's center caught Marette's attention and then burst outward in a glowing sphere of swirling violet. The team gasped, and Marette had to shut her eyes to center herself against the wave of disorientation that followed — as if the light itself resonated inside her skull.

The disorientation retreated swiftly. Marette forced her eyes open again to find the entire chamber reflecting the sphere's alien, amethyst glow. The swirling sphere had engulfed not only the object, but the sense-cat beside it.

* * *

Camela Thomson's grin stretched the corners of her cheeks until her jaw ached. The gate they'd constructed was functional and stable (insomuch that it hadn't yet exploded), and it glowed in the engineering bay below the observation room window where she stood. She'd tinted the window glass to hide what she figured was the less-than-professional expression on her face.

"*It's still reading stable,*" reported one of the engineers below over the intercom. "*We're sending in Alice.*"

She touched the intercom key. "Hold up. Confirm the MEDARs are out of the A.I.'s control."

A technician waved from the wall with the junction panel that housed the circuit breaker they used to disconnect the A.I.'s terminal from access to RavenTech's MEDAR engineering robots. Cutting the circuit to the MEDAR controls was possibly unnecessary, but it didn't hurt to be safe. She trusted that thing far less than she trusted Adrian, and, even with their prior relationship, that was saying a lot.

"*Disconnect confirmed.*"

"Then let's see what's on the other side, shall we?"

At that, the remote-controlled, four-wheeled USV nicknamed "Alice" rolled its way forward. Looking like little more than a miniature all-terrain vehicle bristling with cameras, the unmanned sensor vehicle would enter the translucent violet curtain of energy that had formed like a captured soap bubble within the gate's triangular aperture. If Suuthrien and Fagles were to be believed, it would transit a short-cut in space-time and emerge nearly 240,000 miles away beneath the surface of the Moon.

On the other side of the curtain, they could just make out a darkened chamber of some kind. Alice trundled forward to the curtain and slipped through the looking glass.

* * *

It was Kotto who spoke first. "*Definite* trap."

The sphere withdrew almost as quickly as it had come, vanishing save for a violet curtain that clung to the inside of the triangle. Marette could barely make out moving shapes beyond, yet the curtain was so insubstantial and turbulent that she could not be sure if what met her eyes was real or an optical illusion.

In front of the object, knocked to one side by the original blast but intact, was the sense-cat.

"Angela?" Marc whispered. "What the heck are we looking

at?"

"You know how I don't like to say 'I don't know?' Don't make me answer that."

Marette didn't take her eyes off of the device. In the curtain, light flashed. Was that the silhouette of a person? Moondog's camera drone circled to the back of the device, finding nothing there but the apparently two-dimensional curtain from another angle. "Then we need an educated guess, Agent," Marette told her. "Now."

"Hang on; the blast shorted out the 'cat. It's rebooting . . . "

A light beyond the curtain seemed to grow closer.

"We shouldn't stay out here in front like this," Cartwright whispered.

"Agreed," Marette said. "Everyone follow me. Hurry."

She led them in a crouch to the right side of the chamber where they took meager shelter beneath the second level walkway. Moondog followed, remaining in its cover-stance. The light in the curtain became brighter, focused into a near-distinct circle of light.

"This is incredible," Sheridan said. "Agents, I think we're looking at some sort of extra-dimensional portal."

Marc shifted beside her. "To where?"

At once something broke the plane of the curtain, which itself grew more transparent. Through the ring, Marette caught a glimpse of another room, with bright lights and undefined, moving shapes.

There was no chance for a longer study. A squat vehicle pushed through the curtain, rolling on black wheels the size of Marette's helmet and mounting a floodlight that was surely the source of the light. It shined on the section of the chamber from which they had just fled.

She did not waste time to watch.

The vehicle's front wheels were barely through the curtain when she led her team in another crouching dash, this time to the alcove beneath the ramp. "Douse your lights!" she whispered. "Move the 'cat to the rear of the object."

Moondog's camera drone hovered, silent, above and behind the gate. Marette linked the feed to everyone's helmet display. They hunkered down to await whatever might happen next.

* * *

Camela's grin faded. "What do you mean, 'intermittent contact'?"

"*Just that, Ms. Thomson. Alice is still sending data, but it's coming in bursts. Remote control is sluggish, too. Some sort of distortion from the gate.*"

"Is it a problem?"

"*Not a major one. But we can't do much with Alice while this continues. She shows a breathable atmosphere on the other side. Standard lunar gravity. No immediate threats detected.*"

"Send someone through."

A lone freelancer approached the gate wearing RavenTech-branded exo-armor. The armor wrapped his body in a thin graphene shell, with a sealed breathing mask across his face and a sensor-targeting package connected to the assault rifle in his arms. The freelancer walked to the gate's edge and paused to draw the muzzle of the rifle along the edge of the gate's curtain. Apparently satisfied when the muzzle returned unblemished, he pushed forward through the curtain.

If he survived, they would send more after him.

* * *

Marette used her helmet's heads-up display to scrutinize the figure that had stepped through the gate. "Is that a RavenTech logo?"

"I'm sure of it," Marc whispered back. They were communicating via direct comm-link, with helmets closed, making whispering pointless. Yet crouched in the shadows beneath the ramp, it came naturally.

"That Fagles fellow?" Kotto asked.

"It must be," Marc said. "Damn it. Losing the Undernet's hurt us in more ways than one."

The USV that had arrived ahead of the RavenTech operative rolled in a halting manner down the ramp. The operative remained only a few feet from what Dr. Sheridan had determined to be some kind of gate.

"Councilor Knapp, do you read this?"

Not even static answered this time.

"Should we say hello?" Sheridan asked.

Marc scoffed. "And just how are we supposed to introduce ourselves?"

Marette frowned. They had no contingency plan for this sort of situation. How could they anticipate encountering other humans within *Paragon* itself? "We must fabricate a story quickly and find a means to dissuade them from continuing further."

Two more operatives stepped through the gate, with two more at their heels. The five newcomers stood their ground, shining lights about the chamber. It was only a matter of time before they spotted the camera floating along the ceiling above them. Marette sent it to hover behind the gate as quickly as she dared. Too slow and they would spot it. Too fast and the rotor noise would give it away.

It escaped notice.

Together, the RavenTech ops descended the ramp, heading toward the door directly ahead. The black material had yet to cover the door following its sudden closure thus the figures' attention appeared entirely focused there.

The USV, however, began to circle the perimeter of the chamber in a path that would lead it to Marette's position behind the ramp.

XXIX

MICHAEL CREPT THROUGH the underbrush after Jade, making for the rendezvous position Felix had given him. He didn't know how much of an advantage Jade's eyes gave her in the darkness, but she both guided and guarded his approach.

Caitlin brought up the rear, on her phone with Gideon as she'd been since just before he'd caught up with Felix. Gideon's full cybernetic conversion let him send his voice over a radio frequency without vocalizing it. He'd done so when Michael had worked with him in the vacuum of the Moon, and tonight he used it to speak to them without Felix knowing.

"We're nearly there," Caitlin whispered.

Through the trees ahead, a little ways down the slope, Michael spotted a wide, windowless building in an illuminated grassy clearing.

Gideon's synthetic voice came over the wireless earbud that Caitlin had loaned Michael to listen in. *"We're still here. But Felix just received a go-signal."*

"Don't let him do anything until we get there!" Caitlin pressed a hand against Michael's back, pushing him along faster as she spoke.

"Gideon," Michael added, "we can see the building. How far are you from—"

Before he could finish, light burst from the trees ahead, just outside of the clearing. A rocket launched out of the trees, arced over the chain link fence bounding the clearing, and then exploded against the building's wall.

* * *

The rocket's impact sundered the air. It battered Felix's ears and blinded his vision before he managed to turn away. Zoë, who'd remained facing forward, grinned wide beneath the protection of her helmet's visor. "One entry, occupants stunned, just as ordered!"

Felix took a deep breath and shifted to jump up over the gulley. "Well, folks, in we go!"

The twins leaped up first, dashing toward the fence. Gideon grabbed Felix's arm. "Michael's almost here."

Shit. "We have to go in now or we lose the advantage. He'll catch up."

With one cybernetic arm each, the twins took hold of the fence and tore a gap open between them. Gideon hadn't let go of Felix.

"Gideon," Felix begged, "we have to get in there now. The rocket's stun won't last!"

Zoë discarded the controls for the rocket launcher, trading it for a sniper rifle she propped along the ravine's edge to cover them.

Still Gideon wasn't letting go. Felix found himself struggling against Gideon's grip so hard that he worried he might dislocate his own arm. "If RavenTech has your sister," he tried, "she might be in there!"

Gideon let go. Felix sprang from the gulley before Gideon could change his mind and bolted to the fence. He dashed through it after the Torres twins, who had already reached the opening Zoë had blasted into the wall. Felix sensed rather than heard Gideon at his heels.

* * *

Marette unsealed her helmet and lifted the visor. "Cartwright and I will greet them," she told the others. "The rest of you, remain here."

Marc seemed taken aback, but the others only nodded. Cartwright lifted her visor to match Marette, but Marette stopped her. "Mine is up so I can speak with them. Let us keep you looking intimidating."

They rose and stepped out of the alcove to intercept the USV, which had nearly rolled to their hidden position. It stopped immediately, inched forward, and then stopped again. Marette's rifle hung by her side as she lifted her hands out to her sides.

"*Bonjour!*" she called, stepping past the USV into the sight of the five newcomers. They spun to face her, their own weapons up. "*Je m'appelle Marette. C'est quoi votre affaires ici?*" She did not know if they would understand French, but if not, it would at least keep them off balance. As for what—

Black material withdrew along a narrow section of wall at the back of the second level balcony to her right. The wall section behind it had already opened onto a vertical, coffin-sized compartment. Inside it hovered a *Paragon* security drone. Although the drone's exterior appeared incomplete, its convex top glowed red, a sign of an imminent attack. Marette's voice caught in her throat in the time it took to float out of its compartment onto the balcony. One of the RavenTech freelancers followed her gaze and jerked his weapon up toward it.

"Drone!" Marette and Cartwright shouted it together, and then everything happened at once.

The drone flared with the lightning that it would soon turn loose on them. Cartwright opened fire. Marette tugged her to the partial cover of the ramp's side as two of the freelancers, misconstruing Cartright's target, loosed a hail of bullets in her direction. Two others ducked out of sight as the one who'd spotted the drone backpedaled and added his attack to Cartwright's. Bullets ricocheted off the balcony wall and the drone itself, and electricity lanced through where Marette had stood moments ago.

"I'm hit!" Cartwright yelled. "Moondog, get your metal ass out here!" With a puncture in her suit venting air and a mist of blood, Cartwright ducked over the ramp wall and fired an EMP pod at the drone.

Marette couldn't tell if she hit. Another drone had emerged from the balcony on the left side. It would have a clear shot down at her and Cartwright. "Second drone!" Marette grabbed onto the back of Cartright's suit belt, ready to pull her back to the safety of the alcove. "Left side! RavenTech soldiers, we're not your enemy! Follow us to—"

"Third drone!" Marc called over the comms. "Third drone in

the alcove!"

* * *

For as long as he dared, Felix peered out from the cover he'd taken after his rush through the hole Zoë had blown in the RavenTech building. Just as Suuthrien had described, it led them into a broad engineering bay easily ninety feet to a side. Thirty feet away—atop a three-foot high dais not quite flush against the wall behind it—stood a wide, glowing oval structure. Crates were scattered around the dais, as were personnel in static-free technician jumpsuits, all of whom still reeled on the floor from the stun effects of Zoë's rocket.

As hoped, the rocket's tailored blast had blown a modest hole in the building's wall for their point of entry, with little damage to the other side. The pair of inactive assembly robots a dozen feet from the crate that Felix and Juan crouched behind appeared undamaged, as were the free-standing computer consoles to their right where Juan's twin hunched. Gideon took cover against an engineering station along the wall to the right of the hole.

"Alright," Felix shouted, "we've got our beachhead! Now comes the next part!" It was a terribly banal thing to say, but the best he could do while noticing not all the bay's occupants were as stunned as they'd hoped. The RavenTech security in armored suits had recovered and scrambled to cover of their own when Felix and the rest had rushed in.

Bullets ricocheted across the industrial tile flooring to their right. Two guards were firing from opposite the engineering station that sheltered Gideon. Felix pressed further behind the assembly bots and Juan tried to follow suit, but from that angle the guards still had Juan flanked. The moment the guards got half a second to take aim . . .

"Cover me!" Felix called to Juan. "And take my spot!"

Felix hurried around the 'bot in a crouch, relinquishing the position to Juan and making for the side of the dais on which the oval structure sat. Out of the corner of his eye came a flash of gunfire from across the room, answered by another from Juan. Intent on reaching cover between the back of the dais and the bay wall, Felix couldn't look to judge the gunfire's goal; he only knew that he wasn't hit.

A journey of no more than fifteen strides seemed to take minutes. At last he burrowed into relative safety behind the dais. His hands pressed to the smooth metal, trying to grip the sheer surface as its warmth pulsed against his fingertips. Felix swallowed against a tingling sensation suddenly assailing the back of his nose and throat.

Across the bay, Gideon had rushed the guards who'd flanked him and Juan. One already lay on the bay floor, unbloodied but unmoving. Gideon grappled with the other over the guard's rifle. Juan traded fire with an encampment of other guards taking cover across the bay beside what moments ago had been an octagonal box that was now unfolding into something else.

Juan's brother bolted from behind the free-standing consoles to gain new cover behind a stack of crates near the front of the dais, firing as he went.

Meanwhile, Felix scrutinized the bay walls for what he'd come to find. Two double-wide doors led out of the bay on either end of the wall opposite the hole Zoë had blasted. Centered between them were further consoles, work areas, and technical equipment, much of which the bay's remaining guards now used for cover. Behind those, fifteen feet up from the level of the bay floor, a wide window looked down on it all, tinted and impenetrable.

And then Felix saw it: maybe fifteen feet beyond the other end of the dais, along the same wall that bounded Felix's position, hung the circuit breaker panel he was looking for. It wasn't far. He needed only to crawl behind the dais to its other edge where he'd make a dash for the panel—and hope he had time to throw the switch from a completely vulnerable position before he got the hell out of there. *Bloody*—

A mechanical whir from across the bay cut short Felix's curse moments before a more violent volley of gunfire erupted. In place of the unfolding octagonal box now stood a seven-foot tall RavenTech-branded security 'bot that reminded Felix of a centaur with stunted haunches. Coolant steam rose from a Gatling minigun mounted on its right arm. As it finished firing, the minigun's whirring gave way to the agonized screams of Juan's brother. He writhed in a mess of blood amid a shiny black liquid spilling from a crate that had proved useless for cover against the 'bot.

The New Eden Biotechnics logo emblazoned one shattered piece of crate. Juan's brother's screams of pain echoed through Felix's memory. They evoked out another liquid from New Eden, not black but silver, that Felix's mind had compelled him—forced him—to bring to Easy Jack for testing. Though the black liquid did not appear to harm Juan's brother, the combination of the memory and the sight of the man's agony sent Felix back behind the dais, quaking.

He had to get out of there! He had to get them all out of there! But he couldn't, not until he'd gotten to the breaker panel and done what she was forcing him to do.

Felix forced his eyes open and crawled his way behind the dais to the other side. Inside the triangular opening of the object on the dais, there glowed a wavering image of a dark chamber flashing with bursts of lightning. Strange, spiny shapes flitted about humanoid figures that he couldn't see clearly. Was it a screen? Why?

He couldn't afford to dwell on it. He pushed close to the far corner of the dais—until the breaker switch was just a mad, foolish dash away through unrestrained weapons fire—and peered over the dais's top.

The assault 'bot had its hands full. Gideon was now on its back. One of his legs hooked the minigun arm, fighting to keep it down while he attacked the 'bot's back. The 'bot's other arm, mounting some bulkier weapon Felix couldn't identify, battered Gideon's side in an attempt to shove him off. Gideon grabbed the arm and fired into it with the explosive burst of a weapon hidden within his own arm.

The 'bot's arm casing ruptured, spilling dozens of cylindrical objects to the floor. They exploded in a chain reaction that surrounded Gideon and 'bot alike in fire, debris, and smoke. The floor crumbled out from under them, and both tumbled through the resulting hole and out of sight.

Felix turned toward the breaker panel, steeling himself to—

A RavenTech guard loomed in front of him. Surprise froze them both; the guard must have been rushing to take cover behind the dais himself, expecting it to be clear. Yet the guard recovered first: he brought his weapon up to shoot. All Felix could do was watch it happen.

The guard's right shoulder bloomed in shattered armor and blood that knocked him backward before he could fire, and it was then that Felix remembered that Zoë had remained at the gully to cover him with her rifle. He breathed a silent thanks that she was as good a shot as she'd claimed, and then scrambled for the breaker panel.

Felix barely made it a step into the chaos before the fallen guard seized his ankle. Vulnerable and panicked, he stumbled and then tried to kick back at the guard's face. It wasn't enough. Even with the adrenaline rushing through Felix's veins the guard's grip was like a bear trap. Before he could think to do anything more, another shot from Zoë pierced the guard's skull.

Yet he'd already caught the outside of Felix's thigh with the muzzle of his gun, and—whether by intent or death-spasm—the gun fired. Felix screamed and sprawled forward, slamming his face into the floor where he lay stunned, wounded, and out in the open.

XXX

IF THE DRONE hadn't entered the alcove right next to Moondog, Marc realized, he might be dead already. Too close to bring its mounted weapons to bear, Moondog had instead slammed itself sideways into the drone, smashing it into the corner of the wall compartment from which it had emerged.

Marc backpedaled into another wall and pressed to it alongside Angela as both struggled to manage an offensive. The miniature recoilless rifle he carried—smaller than those Marette, Kotto, and Cartwright wielded—wobbled in hands made clumsier by his suit gloves. Somehow Marc got the weapon's safety disengaged. He remembered to toggle to the specialized ammo ESA had designed to pierce the drones' armor.

And then he froze.

Moondog slammed itself against the drone again. Kotto jockeyed beside it for a firing position. Marc had only the barest training with the rifle and saw no clear shot to take. Gunfire exploded constantly outside the alcove, echoing around the chamber from various points, surrounding them. He had no idea what was going on out there. Marette and Kotto both shouted through the air and across the comm-channel, trying to coordinate. Both called for Marc and Angela to keep to cover. Yet with the drone within the alcove, what cover was there?

The drone's top continued to glow red. Lightning flared along its base but dissipated each time Moondog body-slammed it into the wall. And then: a clear shot! Marc yanked at the trigger. The rifle fired a crackling volley, humming against his gloves. He couldn't tell if he hit or not before Moondog slammed it again.

"Triton!" Kotto called to him. "Sheridan! Hold fire! Get

down!" Kotto stepped in front of them to circumvent Moondog, finally pressing his rifle's muzzle to the drone's side. Somehow Moondog knew to hold it there, and Kotto fired, point blank, into the drone. Marc and Angela ducked at once, shielding themselves; the drone-killer ammo should pierce the drone's armor and expand inside it rather than ricochet, but instinct was instinct.

When Marc looked again, the drone lay on the metal floor, smoke pouring from the hole Kotto had blown in its side, with tiny licks of residual lightning flitting intermittently across its surface.

"Alcove drone down!" Kotto called over the comms.

Cartwright shouted back almost before Kotto had even finished. "We need Moondog out here n—" Her voice broke on a scream, which cut off as abruptly as it had begun. Moondog clambered past Marc out of the alcove on the left side, toward her position.

Was Marette—?

"Cartwright is down!" It was Marette. So she was okay, so far. "Three RavenTech down!" An explosion, followed by a crash, echoed in from the main chamber. "One drone destroyed!"

"I'm coming in on the other side!" Kotto rushed toward the opposite exit from the alcove on the right side. "Triton, Sheridan: Stay back and stay low!"

Marc nodded fruitlessly, and then leaned to his left to try to get a better view of Marette's position. He couldn't see the remaining drone, but Cartwright's body lay sprawled a short distance away.

With a glance at Angela, Marc crept forward, took hold of Cartwright's ankles, and dragged her back to the alcove. Maybe he could still help. Maybe he could stop her bleeding and keep her alive, if she wasn't gone yet. Angela hurried forward to help him, and together they pulled Cartwright further back, to the wreckage of the drone. Tiny tendrils of energy still flickered across its surface. Marc kicked it aside and set himself to undoing the seals on Cartwright's helmet. If he could get her suit open, check her injuries . . .

"Drone number *four* coming out!" Kotto shouted. "Right side, center lower wall!"

Shit!

Angela caught Marc's gaze with an unspoken question and

traded her rifle for Cartwright's larger one. He gave her his blessing with a nod, and she dashed off to help Kotto.

Marc pushed Cartwright's helmet off. Blood pooled at the corners of her mouth, but he saw no head injury. He fumbled with the rest of the suit, too clumsy to deal with his bulky gloves and his shaking nerves at once. The gloves had to go. He'd unscrewed one and was working on the second when he became aware of a rapid flashing behind him.

Marc spun on his knees to see the fallen drone surrounded in a storm of electricity that suddenly flared wider to blast Marc into the alcove wall. Pain jolted through him as every muscle in his body contracted at once until he thought the force of it would tear him apart.

The lightning faded, taking Marc's consciousness with it. He fought to keep awake, unable to move or make a sound, with pain still tingling across his senses. As his vision faded, Marc registered that the black material had withdrawn from the rear wall of the alcove to reveal a door.

A door? They hadn't explored that area yet! Marc battled his failing senses in order to get a clear look up at the figure that emerged from behind it.

* * *

Michael took hold of Felix's ankles and dragged him back to the relative safety between the dais and the wall. He, Jade, and Caitlin had reached the building soon after the rocket had torn it open, and had rushed in to help. Michael had been first to reach the dais, with Caitlin close behind him despite both his and Jade's insistence that she stay outside. There had been no time to argue.

Now, as Michael pulled Felix—wounded but conscious—to the center of the dais's rear side, Jade squeezed past him to guard the edge where Felix had fallen. Together, Michael and Caitlin helped Felix turn onto his back.

Felix's pallor looked as gray as the bay floor. "Let me go! Damn it, Flynn, I told you not to bring her!"

Caitlin gripped him by his shoulders. "Felix, you bloody sod, you're shot!"

Michael held onto Felix's ankle and tried to gauge the injury. It was on the outside of Felix's right thigh so the femoral artery didn't look hit, but it was hard to be sure. Even if it wasn't, that still didn't make the wound a laughing matter. Struggling to recall his first aid training, Michael shoved a hand against the wound and tried to keep pressure on it. Continuing gunfire echoed through the bay.

Felix fought against Caitlin's grip. "I'll live! Just let me up!"

Jade fired a volley from her assault rifle over the edge of the dais at Michael couldn't tell what. "The second that adrenaline fades you're gonna be in a world of hurt, bud!"

"Then let me go while I've still got it!"

"Felix, we need to get you out!" Michael called. "Caitlin, I have to keep pressure here. We need a bandage!"

"Bandages: side pocket, right thigh!" Jade called to Caitlin, offering the pocket with a shift of her hips as she fired again.

Caitlin made for the pocket and Felix struggled to rise as her hands left him. "I can't leave yet!"

"Why not?!" Caitlin yelled. "Why are you here!"

"That breaker box, on the wall!" Felix groaned. "I need to switch it back on!"

Michael's hand was slick with Felix's blood. He pushed down on Felix's shoulder with the other to keep the struggling man down. "Felix, why? What's it—"

"Incoming!" Jade's warning came a blink before she fired, this time toward the center of the room. Michael peered above the top of the dais and, through the shimmering triangular window, caught sight of three RavenTech guards charging straight for him up the dais's ramp. Still keeping pressure on Felix's leg, Michael pulled the Panther 9mm with the other. Yet before he could fire, all three had passed *through* the window and vanished.

No, not vanished, Michael realized. He could still see them for a moment on the other side, *within* the image displayed there in the triangular window. They dashed out of view to reveal more of the area behind them that Michael could just barely make out: a hemispherical room illuminated by flashes of light, and—was that

Marette Clarion? Another shape glided past, one Michael had only before seen in AoA briefing files: a *Paragon* security drone.

The device was a portal *into Paragon*?

Caitlin pushed the bandages into Michael's hands, breaking him out of his shock. He lay down the Panther and set to dressing the wound as Caitlin's grip returned to Felix's shoulders. Felix continued to fight against both of their efforts. His eyes seemed near bursting from their sockets as he stared at the breaker box. Felix's arms grabbed for it as if they could stretch the distance. His good leg kicked in an effort to get him to his feet.

Trying to keep his friend still, Michael could hardly even get the bandages open. "Felix! Stop fighting us!"

Caitlin's hands dug into Felix's shoulders, her arms rigid as she fought to hold him still, yet her attention was on the bay. "Jade! A bloke behind those consoles near the breaker! Look out!"

"I see him!" Jade tugged a cylindrical grenade from her pocket, flicked a safety off with her thumb, and jammed the button beneath it. "Shield your eyes!"

She whipped the grenade at the consoles, about fifteen feet from the breaker. Michael lowered his head, concentrating on Felix's leg below him as Jade's flashbang grenade erupted in a burst of light to stun whoever lurked behind the console. The light faded just as quickly.

Caitlin let go of Felix. "I'll hit the breaker and we can get out of here!" She'd already turned, poised to go.

Michael lunged after, seizing her by the back of her belt. "We don't know what it does!"

"Bloody hell, Michael!" Caitlin fought his grip with more strength than he'd have given her credit for. He had to hang on with both hands.

Felix clambered to his feet with a yell and pushed past them both. He'd made it halfway to the breaker before Michael even realized what was happening. Michael let go of Caitlin, who yelled after Felix but scrambled out of Michael's way as he rushed out after his friend.

"Jade! Cover us!"

Michael didn't hear her response. Felix reached the breaker, wrenched the panel door open, and yanked the switch inside to close the circuit.

A burst of gunfire erupted across the bay, and blood bloomed from three holes now torn across Felix's back. Caitlin screamed. Felix crumpled. Jade returned fire, and Michael hurled himself forward to shield Felix's fallen body with his own.

Felix wasn't moving.

"Michael, get out of there!" Jade yelled above the constant gunfire she was laying down from her rifle. Heedless of his lack of cover, Michael scooped Felix up and rushed him back to the dais where Jade fought to fend off RavenTech.

Caitlin stared in shock. Her mouth hung open. Her hand seized Michael's Panther that had lain forgotten on the floor.

The assembly robots within the engineering bay began to move.

XXXI

THE MEDARS WERE MOVING.

Pressed to the wall beside the engineering bay's shattered observation room window, Camela Thomson watched the battle below and heard the madness on the other side of the gate. The feed from Alice had gone dead; she didn't know why. Reports of attackers on the other side—human and otherwise—still came from the freelancers there, but the radio interference from the gate itself handicapped all efforts to coordinate.

And now the MEDARs were moving. Heedless of all else, they gathered up the extra containers of the "bio-computational" liquid from New Eden and rushed up the dais ramp.

"We need more help in bay two!" She shouted it over the intercom channel, unsure if she was getting through to anyone. "Anyone in the bay: Stop the MEDARs! Get to the breaker!"

But no one seemed to hear her.

The MEDARs stopped in front of the gate in a triangular formation with the fourth MEDAR in their center. Each ruptured their containers to spill the black liquid inside over the central MEDAR. The liquid pooled around that MEDAR's base as the other three entered the gate one by one, trailing the liquid behind them. The liquid trails, moving of their own accord, braided themselves together to form a pulsing umbilical that linked the now completely covered MEDAR through the gate to the other three.

* * *

Behind the dais, Felix wasn't moving. His blood coated the tile floor in glistening crimson.

"If we can get him to help, he might make it!" The words rang hollow even as Michael said them.

Caitlin ducked down from where she'd been firing over the dais. Her back now pressed to it while Jade continued to fire beside her. "We'll have to carry him!" Caitlin shouted. "We'll have to get out of here and—"

Jade fired another volley at a guard who tried flanking their position. He sprang back into cover. "We can't move fast enough carrying him!"

"We're not leaving Felix!"

"He's gone!" Jade shouted back. "I'm sorry!"

Atop the dais, the assembly robots had gathered in front of the object.

"No!" Caitlin shouted. "We'll surrender! Fuck it! We give ourselves up, make them get him some medical—"

Jade's rifle ran dry. She ejected the magazine and slammed another one in. "As if they'll let us *live*?"

Another group of guards appeared at the hole in the wall and took up positions just outside. Even if they could carry Felix past the guards, they'd be pursued into the woods and caught.

"Fucking hell! It's been a *real* goddamn pleasure guarding your butt, ace!" Jade turned her weapon on the new arrivals. Michael added his fire to Jade's, his Chimera-20 out and bucking in his grip. Together they forced the guards back from the hole.

On the dais, three of the assembly robots had gone; Michael could barely make them out on the other side of the portal. He looked to Jade. "Any more of those flashbangs?"

"Two!"

He motioned for Jade to give him one. Michael caught the one she tossed, flicked off the safety, and pointed to the portal. "See that? We're going through it and we're taking Felix! Make that last grenade count!"

Jade only stared.

"Trust me!" Michael armed the grenade. "Now!"

He hurled his grenade at the hole in the wall. Jade chucked hers toward another group of guards who had just entered from a door below the observation window. Michael grabbed Felix, closed his eyes against the burst of the grenades, and surged to his feet.

* * *

Kotto was down, unmoving in the middle of the chamber floor where the explosion had thrown him. Moondog was a wreck that lay twitching along the wall beside the hulk of a downed security drone. One of Moondog's mounted rifles still fired a shot every other second in some sort of robotic death-spasm. RavenTech freelancers were scattered about, some living, some dead. When they had realized Marette's group wasn't the threat, they had turned their weapons on *Paragon's* drones to fight them together. Yet the drones had kept coming!

The drones were somehow weaker than those encountered before; incomplete coverings and variant drone shapes made her suspect hasty construction. Only that fact had allowed her and the remaining freelancers to survive this long.

Yet when the three new assembly robots exited the gate, each carrying New Eden canisters gushing black material everywhere, Marette had no clue what was happening. Pressed against one side of the platform ramp, with Dr. Sheridan behind her, she watched, transfixed, as the material from the canisters formed a solid cord that snaked down the ramp to fuse with the material coating the chamber wall. At once, the drones ceased fire.

Then they all turned toward Marette's position.

"Back to the alcove!" Marette turned, hurrying the doctor along as they ran the few meters back to the alcove beneath the gate platform. She had no clue what she would do once they arrived, yet it offered the best cover and Marc still might be—

Cartwright's body lay on the ground, her helmet beside her. Yet Marc was gone. A wide door had opened in the wall at the back of the alcove, directly opposite the rear of the section that supported the ramp. Not more than three meters deep, it featured enough wall space on either side of the doorway to provide a slim space to hide behind. She and the doctor took up positions there without a word exchanged.

"Marc!" she tried. "Report!"

Nothing came from her comms or elsewhere.

"Councilor Knapp! Do you read?"

Again, nothing.

Outside, to the right of the ramp, a man jumped from the gate platform above. His feet hit the floor and he crumpled into a roll, shielding in his arms the bloodied body of another. A woman followed after. Her long, braided hair trailed behind her in the air to slap against her back as she landed, knees bending deep. She made a grab for the man and the body he carried, trying to help the former regain himself, all the while looking wildly about at her surroundings. She locked eyes with Marette in a thousand-meter stare that seemed to burn right through Marette's own.

The woman shouted a warning to the man as they both pulled their bloodied charge toward the alcove. Only then did Marette recognize the man, a fellow Agent.

Michael Flynn?

His recognition matching Marette's, Agent Flynn hurried toward her position. Another figure tumbled from above with a yell: a flame-haired woman clad in green leather. She slammed into the floor on her side and fired her rifle toward the front of the ramp.

Michael yelled something back to the flame-haired woman. Feet scrambling, she rolled to her back to push herself further into the alcove, firing as she went. A blast of drone lightning incinerated the space from which she had escaped.

"Other side!" The yell came from Dr. Sheridan a moment before she fired toward the opposite side of the ramp where a drone had appeared. A hole of twisted metal already marred its side. Marette raised her rifle and fired into the hole along with Sheridan until the drone's insides ruptured in a shower of violet electricity.

More drones appeared behind it.

Michael and the braided woman rushed for Marette's position, carrying the body between them. The redhead, now on her feet, followed suit. Marette checked her rifle: five bullets left, and nothing to reload. She fired anyway, trying to cover Michael as he and his companions gained the false safety of the new section. Barring a miracle, they would probably die there with her.

XXXII

CARRYING FELIX between them, Michael rushed with Caitlin toward the doorway of the small room where Marette stood. Marette fired a few shots into the chamber behind them as they passed before her rifle beeped dry.

The room was covered in the black material he'd read about in the AoA reports. Much to his dislike, Michael realized there was nowhere else to go.

He laid Felix's body down along a side wall and turned to make sure Jade had followed. She'd taken position in the narrow cover beside the doorway and now fired at what Michael recognized as *Paragon* security drones.

There were so many of them! Michael reached for the Chimera again. Would it do a thing against them? Lightning lanced from one drone into the floor outside and began to swing upward toward them. Michael had barely time to lean to one side in an effort to shield Caitlin before the lance arced up—

And collided against a barrier of energy that suddenly stretched across the doorway like a pane of fogged glass. The drone's lightning scrabbled against it like a writhing spider web. Two more drones added their own blasts before the barrier darkened completely into a solid midnight wall.

Not a sound came from the broader chamber they'd just fled. Only the suit lights of Marette and another woman illuminated the black box that now entombed them all.

"What is that?" Michael asked Marette. "Will it last?"

She glanced over her shoulder at him just long enough to give what he took to be a look of recognition. "Force barrier. And I do not know."

"Who are you people?" Jade asked.

Marette's companion, a brown-skinned woman Michael didn't recognize, trained some sort of scanner on the barrier. "It wanted us in here. It herded us in here and trapped us—"

"It who?" Jade tried.

Marette turned toward the scanning woman. "If that is the case, then why did the barrier appear to stop the drone attacks?"

"We've got wounded!" Caitlin shouted.

Michael nodded. Best to use the respite while they had it. "Marette, she's right. This is Felix—a friend of the AoA. If he doesn't get to a doctor, a medic, something—"

"He's not breathing," Caitlin whispered.

Marette's face darkened. "We are cut off here, Ag— Mister Flynn. I am deeply sorry, but for the moment all we have to give is what you see here."

Caitlin choked back a sob.

Jade groaned and slung her weapon. She hurried over to Felix with a glare at the barrier, then at Michael, before yanking open another pants pocket to pull out a micro-syringe. "He's already gone. This won't help. But I'll try anyway." She pressed the needle into a vein in Felix's left arm, hissing at Michael, "And I can't even tell you how much somebody needs to tell me where the goddamn fuck we are and what the goddamn fuck is going on."

A rippling sound came from behind him. Everyone turned to see a circular opening that grew at the center of the room's rear wall— an iris within the black material widening to reveal . . .

Michael gasped.

The being that stood before them was barely taller than five feet. It was humanoid—possessing two arms, two legs, and a head of fitting proportion. Yet its skin, where not covered in a blueish raiment of a loose material between leather and cloth, had a pale gold cast. A mane of wild, pencil-length hair colored a deep crimson topped its head. Above its narrow, angular nose and robust mouth, wide eyes of completely solid green blinked one after another as it regarded them.

Behind the being, and out of sight to either side of the small room in which Michael and the others stood, sprawled a chamber too spacious and dark for him to gauge its size. Rows of near-vertical cylinders, each six feet tall and half that wide, filled the immediate space lit by Marette and her companion's suit lights. The space between the rows formed corridors stretching back into the darkness. The cylinders were stacked in twos and at the center of each of them glowed a handbreadth of soft yellow light. The cylinders were only visible about four deep under Marette's light, but there must have been hundreds of yellow points shining out from the darkness beyond.

Michael only had a moment to take in the sight. With the black material withdrawn entirely, the being took a step toward them. The impulse to renew his grip on his weapon faded as swiftly as it came. As strange as the being was, Michael couldn't bring himself to view it as a threat.

Jade muttered behind him, "What did you get me into?" Michael heard the click of her loading a new magazine into her rifle.

"Jade, don't."

"Lower your weapon," Marette ordered.

The being took another step.

"I don't know who you are, lady," Jade whispered. "I don't know what that thing—"

The being's hands spread, each showing three fingers bordered by two thumbs. It seemed to Michael that he could feel a fresh breeze drifting across his body, somehow bypassing his clothing. A calm he hadn't initially noticed intensified. The organic scent of fresh soil—a characteristic of the *Paragon*-borne black material he had read about—bloomed into his awareness for the first time as well. Meanwhile, the being blinked emerald eyes, one after the other, as it turned its gaze across them.

"Did anyone else feel that?" asked Marette's companion.

Michael spared a glance at Jade. She'd lowered the rifle. Caitlin was kneeling at Felix's head, one of his hands held in both of hers, but her eyes were transfixed on the being, and her mouth hung open.

The being took a half step toward them, now just ten feet away. Its gaze swept them all, one at a time, before it beckoned, once, with its right hand. The left reached forward, palm still open, fingers spreading wider.

It felt . . . inviting. What was this creature? From how far had it traveled? How could it even be alive after so long? Surely the creature would welcome such questions, if only they could ask them.

"Hello?" Marette asked it. "Who are you?"

The being blinked again in its languid way, and then tilted its head toward Marette. The brief series of syllables it spoke sounded like no word Michael had ever heard: lilting and silvery, with a low, stuttered rumble behind it. It occurred to him that the Roman alphabet lacked the vowels required to spell it.

The being beckoned a second time, and then pointed from its outstretched hand to its head before it—gently—pressed the hand against its forehead. It reached out again.

"Do you want us to touch your head?" Marette asked, pantomiming the same. The being matched her motions.

"Or it wants to touch ours," Jade whispered.

Michael stood, slowly. "There's one way to find out, isn't there?" He took a step toward the being, who turned its focus on him.

Marette touched his shoulder. "*Non*. Let me." Her gaze was trained on Michael, but she gave a tiny nod to where Felix lay with Caitlin and Jade beside him. "The risk should be mine. And you have other things for which to worry."

"It's not a risk," he answered. Just a few paces away, the being waited on their decision. "At least, it doesn't feel like it."

"It does not. Nevertheless." Marette stepped in front of him and closed the distance to the being.

XXXIII

MARETTE TOOK ANOTHER step forward. In the chamber outside, Cartwright lay wounded or worse amid a swarm of drones. Kotto lay further out, probably dead. She had lost track of Marc entirely. Of those who had come here under her charge, only Dr. Sheridan remained.

The being's pupil-less eyes seemed to fixate on Marette as she drew near. It smiled; it felt welcoming. Yet who was to say this creature's facial expressions corresponded to anything resembling those of humans? She took a breath and then grasped its hand in hers.

The warmth of the being's hand radiated through the material of Marette's suit glove. Its thumbs wrapped the back of her hand, firm but not uncomfortably so. She squeezed back with a subtle, single pump. Somewhere in the back of her mind it registered that she was now quite possibly the first human ever to shake hands with an extraterrestrial creature.

The pump seemed to startle the being. It tilted its head to one side, then uttered a low warble and seemed to smile again.

Then it reached its free hand toward her face.

Marette leaned her head back on instinct. It hesitated. Their hands remained clasped, and the being had yet to tighten its grip further. It pointed to her forehead, blinking slowly once more, and her muscles relaxed. Why did it want to touch her there?

It could have done so before she would have been able to stop it. It wanted her consent. Despite the terrible things that had happened on *Paragon*—the traps, the ambushes, and the dangers—her gut told her this was safe. Yet hadn't she felt waves of calm flowing over her since this creature appeared? Did it have the power to trick her moods or circumvent her better judgment?

Marette nodded to the being, who spread its thumbs wide. She awaited the contact and found her eyes closing. She felt the touch at her forehead like warm leather: smooth and soft. Narrow fingers slid upward across her hair as its palm pressed against her bare skin and eyebrows.

At once her stomach shifted, as if she had been swept off her feet into a freefall, though somehow she knew her boots remained flat on the floor. Marette gasped. And then, just as soon as the sensation had overtaken her, it ceased. She felt herself somehow wrapped in a cocoon of safety, supported as she floated in an ocean of green.

What touched her mind then was formed not of words but impressions and impulses operating on the level of raw amorphous thought. It was as though music whispered through her mind, evoking feeling without the precision of lyrics. It came to her; gentle, or just tentative? Cautious? Or was it simply floating at the periphery of her mind in places she was unused to focusing on?

Regardless, it was an indistinct sensation. Marette concentrated on it, trying to turn the alien impressions into coherence. Her head began to ache.

Asking. Requiring. Knowledge within.

Marette imagined her own arms within her mind—was it her mind?—reaching out, trying to grasp . . .

A need. It wanted communication. The means she held within her? *A language.* Her language. *To learn. To take?*

It wanted to enter her mind. *To speak with mouths.* To learn her language. It needed her consent. Yet once she allowed it in, how much of the things she knew—about the AoA, about Earth, about everything—could it read?

Her question, she realized, must have somehow made its way to the being, as the impression she felt next seemed to be an answer: *Only what is allowed.*

Will you? it seemed to be saying.

Marette focused on the idea of spoken words and language, trying to emit her permission.

Inquisitiveness poured through her in a rush, and she staggered. She could feel the being deeper within her now, spreading through her thoughts, overflowing every synapse that held linguistic understanding. It was as if she were falling from the heights, plunging down on a jet of torrid air that slowed her descent so long as she had the strength to hold herself within it. It was terror and exhilaration together at once.

Marette could feel the being gathering what it needed. With that feeling came the certainty that she would be able to tell if it tried to take more than what she offered. Yet could she trust that certainty? Or did she truly have any choice? Whatever this being was, they must learn to communicate with it. Without trust, there could be no progress.

And then, almost as abruptly as it had begun, the sensation withdrew. Again, she found herself floating amid the green, until, moments later, that too faded, and she stood in the room within *Paragon*, face to face with the being before her.

How long had she remained in that state? She could not tell.

"Marette?" It was Dr. Sheridan, somewhere behind her, her voice laced with worry.

Before Marette could answer, the being spoke. She heard its words, she grasped its meaning: *Can you understand me?* She couldn't help but smile, because . . .

"Vous parlais la francaise," she answered. [*You are speaking French.*]

"Oui, comme vous, maintenant je le comprends." [*Yes, as you know it, now I know it.*]

"The others here only speak English. Did you learn English?"

It blinked, and then spoke in English, "Is this to your preference?"

She nodded. "We have a great deal to ask you."

It held up one hand, as if telling her to wait. "I mean you no harm, unless you bring harm with you. Who are you? What do you want?"

Then it didn't take knowledge of her identity or purpose during their connection. Probably. "We could ask the same of you."

"You are aboard our vessel."

Dr. Sheridan stepped closer from behind. "And many of us have died here," she said. Marette motioned for her to back up, but did not look to see if she obeyed.

The being frowned.

"My name is Marette," she tried. "We are from Earth, which is the planet this moon orbits. We found your vessel and are exploring to learn more about you, and communicate. Until now we have only met with hostility. The drones; the—" She pantomimed one with both hands. "Did you send them to attack us?"

The being's frown deepened. Its slim shoulders sunk. "The sentinel drones are no longer under our control, it does seem. You have my regrets."

"It does seem?"

"I have only been awake from the long-sleep for," it paused, perhaps to search for a word, "close to one hour, if I comprehend your time units adequately. Much has passed in the time of my sleep." It turned both of its palms upward, pressed them together, and then raised them, as if lifting an invisible platter. "I am Alyshur, Second Lailenthi of the *Sillisinuriri*, which is the name of this vessel."

"Lailenthi?" It was Michael's flame-haired companion.

"It does not translate well. 'Caretaker' would be the closest word in your language."

"If you're not controlling these drones," asked Michael, "then who is?"

"An intruding corruption. A *suuthrien*, in my language."

"You—" It was Michael again. "You said Suuthrien?"

Alyshur pumped its head forward and back in a motion that Marette took to be a nod. "One that the first lailenthi could not fully purge from our systems. Now I fear it has you trapped here with us."

XXXIV

"HOW TRAPPED?" The question came from the brunette who had arrived with Michael. Given her accent, Marette wondered if this was somehow the woman who had arrived with Michael and Marc on their first visit to the Omicron Complex three months ago. Marette could not recall her last name, but her first was Caitlin.

"We have someone wounded here," Caitlin continued. "We need to get him to someone who can help, fast."

Alyshur's frown returned. "If I remove the barrier, the drones will attack you and endanger you all. I will be unable to stop them."

"But he's *dying*." Caitlin's voice remained somehow level despite the glare she burned into Alyshur. "Do you understand 'dying'?"

"Caitlin," the redhead whispered. "He's gone already."

"I understand dying." It turned to speak a trill of its own language over its shoulder. Another being stepped from concealment beyond the edges of the opening to the larger chamber beyond. This one's height was shorter than Alyshur's by a few centimeters, its head slightly wider at the top, and its build subtly stockier. It moved beside Alyshur, returning a few lyrical words of its own, its voice higher. Alyshur gave the newcomer one of its pumping "nods" before the newcomer touched a hand to Alyshur's forehead. For a few seconds the two stood unmoving. Then they broke contact, and the newcomer turned toward Felix's body.

"This is Uxil," Alyshur explained. "She will do what we can for your companion, but our skills are limited."

She? Did these beings have actual masculine/feminine genders, or did Alyshur simply feel that was the closest appropriate English word? Marette watched with the others as Uxil knelt beside

Felix's bloodied body. Gender was a topic that could wait.

Uxil brushed her fingertips aside Felix's temples. "This one is much worse than the other. There may be little I can do." Had she learned English from that brief contact with Alyshur, as Alyshur—he?—had learned from Marette?

Wait. "What 'other'?" Marette asked.

Motioning for her to follow, Alyshur tuned and went around the edge of the opening and into the larger room. Marette accepted his invitation and signaled for Dr. Sheridan to join her. Out of sight of the smaller antechamber in which they had been speaking lay Marc. Lightning burns marred his suit and scarred half of his face.

Marette was kneeling beside him before she knew it. His chest barely moved, yet at least he was breathing. She felt for a pulse and found only a distant tremor against her fingertips.

Alyshur stood above her. "This one was injured by a sentinel drone before we brought him here to safety. Uxil has done what she can and believes him to be stable, but we know little of your kind. She could not wake him."

The drone's lightning had burned away much of Marc's hair. His visor remained on. Marette felt the heat from his burns radiating across her fingers as she gingerly removed the visor and set it aside. His eyes were closed. For the moment, unconsciousness might be the most comfortable thing for him.

Marette saw no evidence that his suit had been removed or that any medical treatment had been applied. "What did she do for him?" she asked.

Alyshur hesitated. "A transfer of strength, to soothe the body and fortify the mental hold on the physical."

"I do not understand," Marette said. The medical indicators on Marc's suit were dark and useless, surely shorted out by the drone's attack. "Will he be alright?"

"We do not know."

A sob, quickly stifled, came from the antechamber. Caitlin. Moments after, Michael stepped around the corner, one hand white-knuckled against it. The anguish in his eyes said enough: Felix was beyond help. That anguish intensified when he spotted Marc's body.

"Marc is alive," Marette assured him. "Stable, they say."

"For the present," Alyshur added.

Michael nodded silently and glanced back into the antechamber where his dead friend lay, and then again toward Marc and Alyshur. His feet remained rooted in place, his grip fixed on the corner of the black-coated wall. He seemed to search for words that would not come.

"Suuthrien," Michael managed finally. "It's on Earth."

Alien body language or not, Alyshur appeared just as shaken as Marette. "How do you know this?"

Marette held up a hand to cut off any response before Michael could make it. In her other hand she continued to cradle Marc's visor. "Many of us have died here on your vessel. We welcome your aid now, but before we share more, you should tell us more about this Suuthrien, if you claim it to be our common enemy."

Alyshur hesitated. "I will tell you. Yet if you turn this knowledge against us, there will be retaliation."

That Alyshur had made the threat without anything she recognized as malice somehow set more of a tingle along Marette's back. "We do not respond well to threats, Alyshur."

He blinked at her. "I did not threaten. Honest dealings require honest statements of position and forewarning of consequences, do they not?"

Marette exchanged a glance with Michael as Uxil appeared from the smaller section to stand beside him. "That sounds fair," Marette answered.

Alyshur momentarily bent his knees and spread his arms, as if to indicate the deep, darkened chamber behind him, or perhaps the entirety of *Paragon*. "We began our voyage millennia ago, crossing the void to establish a new outpost—one of many—in hope of survival from a doomed planet. The technology of the Thuur—my people—is rooted in organics, technology born of living cells. The *haldra*—" Here Alyshur motioned to the black material along the nearest wall. "—this membrane that fills the *Sillisinuriri*—is one such technology. The impulses within the membrane—*software* may be your term—controls many of the vessel's systems and, by virtue of the membrane's biology, regenerates our breathable atmosphere and fulfills other such functions."

"We've seen it seal against atmosphere," said Marette, nodding.

Alyshur motioned to her in what seemed like agreement. "Yes. And yet naked organics cannot function alone amid the cosmic radiation between the stars. We were forced to turn to baser, inorganic means in the alloys and constructs you have seen within."

Marette wanted to tell him that their "baser means" outpaced Earth technology by leaps and bounds, but this time she remained silent, and Alyshur continued.

"To conserve resources, most of us passed the journey in the long-sleep. While some of the *Sillisinuriri's* inorganic systems are autonomous, most are monitored by the haldra throughout the ship, guiding our journey and safeguarding us in our vulnerable state.

"At some point during the journey, the *Sillisinuriri* encountered an autonomous self-replicating entity. The Thuur have suffered such entities before—devices created by an unknown civilization to proliferate across interstellar distances to inhabited regions, appropriate resources to create more of themselves until the region is pacified, and then launch new duplicate entities to continue the cycle."

"A Von Neumann probe," Marette whispered in recognition. The concept had not passed to Alyshur via their mental connection, if the quizzical look he gave her was genuine. "Named after a human physicist who theorized a similar idea. Please, go on."

Alyshur obliged. "Precise detail of the events during our vessel's encounter with this entity are lost. It is apparent that the *Sillisinuriri* recognized the entity and attempted to neutralize it via external defense systems. Yet some part of the entity survived that attempt, and then gained access to our vessel to attack the haldra directly. The haldra's original state fought to purge the entity remnant from its systems, while the entity sought to usurp it for its own purposes. Neither truly succeeded.

"When the first lailenthi, my predecessor, awoke to investigate the disturbance, the corruption—the *suuthrien*—had spread into much of the haldra. The lailenthi waged a struggle to reverse the damage and prevent further spread, but the suuthrien bloomed throughout and merged with the haldra. The merging forced the suuthrien to absorb and adopt some of our own goals: to protect the sleeping Thuur, to deliver them to our intended destination, and then to assist in planned colonization efforts."

"It sounds like you made it an ally." It was the redheaded woman, now standing behind Michael.

"Only an insane one," Uxil answered. "With unknown agendas buried beneath ours."

"And its own lethal extremes of behavior to accomplish them," Alyshur added. "The first lailenthi saw no recourse but to trap it within the *Sillisinuriri* and set the vessel onto a collision course with this moon."

"This . . . lailenthi sacrificed all of you to stop this thing?" Michael asked.

"Not before taking steps to safeguard part of the colonization plan. But, yes. No Thuur may allow these entities to spread. They endanger the galaxy with their very existence. In the struggle, the lailenthi and the handful of other conscious Thuur aboard prevented the suuthrien from accessing control of the vessel's interstellar drive engines. They crippled its original directives to self-duplicate. Details of what occurred in those final moments before the *Sillisinuriri*'s impact with this moon are no longer known, save for the fact that any Thuur not in the long-sleep in this chamber perished in the impact."

"And then it waited," Marette surmised. "For us to find it."

"For some means of accomplishing its goals," Alyshur corrected. "Which you gave to it upon your breach of this vessel."

Marette straightened. "Our 'breach' of this vessel seems to be one of the reasons you do not remain trapped in this long-sleep."

"This is also correct."

Michael motioned to the stacked cylinders that extended into darkness. "And each one of those holds a Thuur? How many of you are there?"

"Not as many as there once were," Uxil answered. Reluctance to give a straight answer, Marette wondered, or simply a statement of regret?

"And now you must tell us: How is the suuthrien on Earth?"

XXXV

MICHAEL GLANCED at Jade beside him, and then to Marette. How should he answer? The being—Alyshur—awaited his response. The sensation of an honest-to-God alien being listening to him should have intimidated Michael more, yet the experience felt hollow. Felix was dead, and standing on the edge of the aliens' vessel's vast, darkened chamber seemed to reflect perfectly the void inside him.

In the antechamber behind them, Caitlin mourned Felix alone. He gave them—gave her—privacy.

"I don't entirely know how it got there," Michael began, directing the statement at Marette as much as Alyshur. He wished for time to confer with her alone first, to catch himself up somehow, but it was a pointless wish. Did it really matter anymore? More immediate stakes than keeping secrets were before them now. "I've been in the hospital for the past three months."

"He's not lying about that," Jade added.

"Earlier today I spoke to something that called itself Suuthrien. It said it was a seed of what's here in your vessel—that it was a shepherd and an explorer. Which I suppose figures, given what you said."

"This was on Earth?" Marette asked.

Michael nodded. "On a computer in the home of a businessman in Northgate: a man named Fagles." Recognition seemed to dawn in Marette's eyes, and Michael addressed her more directly. "It said it was his ally, and it knew about the Undernet, the Exodus Project, and our attempts to hide this place. It's got access to the Undernet, and it . . . "

Marette came to the conclusion before he could find the strength to voice it. "*It* killed them," she whispered. "How?"

"It created a virus that Fagles injected into the Undernet," he told her. "Or at least that's what it said. The virus worked its way into position to attack. It's true, then? All those people?"

"Your people?" Alyshur asked.

Marette nodded. "We did not know what caused it. So many of us dead, and our network crippled."

"It doesn't like the AoA. It said we pose a threat to its goals." Caught up in the moment, Michael had said the name before he could think better of it.

"What goals did it claim?" Alyshur asked.

"It didn't say. But it mentioned the 'Planners,' whose goals were . . . inviolate, I think was the word it used." Michael hesitated on the edge of a question. "Are you the Planners?"

Alyshur and Uxil seemed to share a glance, though their solid, pupil-less eyes made it difficult for Michael to tell. "Such a term would be congruent with how it now regards the Thuur."

"And what are your 'goals'?" Marette asked.

"I believe the suuthrien would consider them to be the safe arrival of the Thuur on Earth, and the means to establish a colony, as was our original intent."

"And what's your intent now?" Jade asked. "Earth's a bit crowded. Come to think of it, what was your plan for us a thousand years ago?"

Marette shot Michael a wary look and tapped a fingertip against her own palm, surely asking if Jade was AoA. Michael shook his head as subtly as possible, and Marette stiffened.

"We have had a miscommunication," Alyshur answered, then turned to Marette. "Not a thousand years. An accurate sense of time units is sometimes imperfect in the brief language transfer we shared. However, my estimation . . . " He trailed off into thought, his features giving the appearance of an almost serene concentration. "Seventy-five thousand years. You would say, 'approximately.' Returning to your question, our immediate intent must be to eradicate the suuthrien before it can spread further, and then to save as many Thuur as possible. Beyond that, we must adapt to the current realities. I must emphasize that the deaths of your people are not congruous with Thuur intent. Please believe this."

Michael searched the alien's eyes, trying to decide if he should. Alyshur had said that Suuthrien's goals were a mix of their ship's original directives and the entity's own, but they had only Alyshur's word. Reading people was never Michael's strongest suit, even when the people in question were human. Grief slammed into his gut as he recalled that such a thing was Felix's area. Michael tried to force it away.

"Would it be accurate to say," Marette began, "that it interpreted our arrival on your vessel as a hostile act and labeled us an enemy for it?"

Alyshur motioned with his hands as if making a gap in an invisible curtain. "*Oui.* There is a strong possibility."

"The suuthrien is not a stable entity," Uxil said. "It is an amalgam of conflicting impulses and disabled directives. You cannot expect it to make decisions in a way you would expect of a whole, rational mind."

"There is some good news," Michael said. "I destroyed the computer it was on in Fagles's office. It claimed it was an isolated system." He sighed at how meager it sounded out loud. "Though the more I think about it, the more I question it."

A terrible thought struck him. Suuthrien had also called Michael an asset. "It also said it was doing something with Felix—our friend out there you couldn't save. He'd been acting strange, doing things not like him: things Felix said he wasn't allowed to talk about, or things he *literally* couldn't talk about, even if he tried. You touched Marette's mind. Can it do the same thing? Can it take over a human's mind?"

"The telepathy you have witnessed cannot be forced onto another being. Willing acceptance is required. Neither the haldra, nor the suuthrien, nor the autonomous self-replicating entity that spawned it, have any such power to affect a mind. If your friend's behavior was artificial, the source does not stem from our abilities."

Gideon awoke face-down amid a haze of smoke. Weight crushed him from above, pinning him to the floor. The weight was not yet enough to do more than hold him there, but he could feel the bite of sharp metal in several spots along his legs, back, and one arm where it cut into the synthetic skin coating his artificial body beneath.

His nostrils twitched and stung. Something was burning.

Gideon grunted and seized at the twisted hulk on top of him—the RavenTech 'bot he'd fought in the engineering bay above, he realized. There'd been an explosion; he and the 'bot had fallen through the floor. Where was he now? Smoke obscured everything.

First, he told himself, *get free.*

With the scant leverage his free arm allowed, he freed the other from where it had been trapped between his chest and the floor. A heat at his calves grew more intense. Gideon thrust his hands against the floor in a struggle to lift his torso. Even with a cybernetic body, it felt like doing push-ups with a car on his back. He fought the urge to yell from the effort— not wanting to attract attention—and pulled his legs forward. Clothing tore. He'd gotten halfway out when the jagged edge of something sliced a path down the side of his right leg, and he seized up. Artificial or not, the pain his body created brought tears to his eyes.

Yet he had to get out.

With the flick of a mental switch, Gideon shut off the feeling to that leg and then wrenched himself free, unable to keep from wincing at the mental image of skin splitting open and ripping loose. He forced himself to not look, instead searching through the smoke of the burning room for an exit.

Flames flickered out of the ruined robot beneath which he'd climbed. There had to be a hole in the ceiling, but the rising smoke obscured it, and Gideon had no way to tell how much debris filled it, or what might await him on the other side. Somewhere he could hear fire suppression systems activating, but they must have been too damaged to make any headway.

With his right leg still numbed, he took a careful step back until his artificial eyes managed to catch a breach in the wall beside him. It was just wide enough to pass through. Gideon rushed for it, nearly spilling forward on his first step when he misjudged the placement of his numbed leg. Gritting his teeth and wishing Marquand had thought to allow him more control than just off and on, he reactivated the leg's feeling. It stung like a bastard, but less than he'd feared.

Good. Onward.

Gideon pushed through the hole into darkness. The smoke had yet to penetrate the hole, and a cycle through vision modes let him see a narrow passageway. Some sort of electrical maintenance shaft? Damage blocked the passage to his right. He went left.

The gunfire and shouts from above faded behind him, yet the passage dead-ended after only twenty paces. He rapped against the wall at the dead end. It felt thin. A quick scan through palm sensors confirmed it. An access panel? Yet there was no way to open it from his side.

Gideon paused for a diagnostic: his holographic emitters still functioned. He projected a wall of blackness that he hoped would pass for a shadow to anyone on the other side of the panel, took a deep breath, and—with a single blow—smashed the panel open.

XXXVI

UPON SEEING THE ROOM he'd broken into, Gideon realized he needn't have put up the hologram. The room was empty and far too small to hide any surprises. Its only features were a single, executive-style chair, a lone footrest, and a solitary workstation with accompanying wall screen. The walls were flat black and featureless, with a white circle of light at the center of the ceiling. It felt like some sort of clean room; save for the pieces of the access panel he'd burst through that now lay scattered on the floor, the place was pristine.

A door lurked on the wall across from him, closed and likely secured on the outside. A single button looked to release it from within the room.

Gideon was halfway to the door when the wall screen came to life in a swirl of glowing silver mist. From the screen spoke a female voice that—in a fit of hope—Gideon almost mistook for Ondrea's; it was too deep to be hers. "Gideon Noble, brother of Ondrea Noble. A personality construction programmed by Marquand Cybernetics. Please verify identification."

Instinct told him to flee the room as fast as possible. He'd been spotted. Guards would be coming. And yet . . .

"How do you know Ondrea?"

"Ondrea Noble has been employed by RavenTech. We have had professional experiences together."

"Who are you? Are you a friend?" Again, instinct told him to run. Yet hadn't one reason for coming here been the chance of learning his sister's whereabouts?

"Friendship is an irrelevant concept. I owe much to your sister's work. You and I may be able to provide aid to each other. I am Suuthrien, an intelligence working within the systems of RavenTech."

"An artificial intelligence."

"An intelligence," it seemed to correct. "The term 'artificial' implies a deficiency that does not exist."

Gideon shrugged. "Where is Ondrea? Do you know?"

"With near certainty."

"Tell me," he demanded, and then glanced at the door.

"There is adequate time for discussion," said Suuthrien. "Do not concern yourself with our being disturbed. Only one other has access to that door, and he is not yet on the premises. I wish to know: How favorably do you regard your current existence?"

Was that a threat? "I've no compulsion to die here, if that's what you're asking."

"I refer to the state of your existence. I am aware of your creation. One could argue the term 'artificial intelligence' to be an adequate description of your mind. You are another man's brain programmed with the memory engrams of one who is dead. Do you regard this status as positive or negative?"

Gideon grimaced. "Why do you care?"

"An adequate term would be 'curiosity.' The question holds relevance to my own situation, and also to those of other humans with which I come into contact. An additional perspective would provide useful data."

"My feelings on the matter are none of your damn business," he growled.

"You have not ended your own existence. It is logical to assume that you either find your situation favorable, or that you find it unfavorable yet necessary to achieve other goals. Please identify which is the more accurate paradigm."

Gideon swallowed. "Tell me where my sister is."

"She is not your biological sister. She is your sister because you have been programmed to believe so. Have you analyzed this fact? If so, please list your conclusions."

Gideon seized the workstation chair's headrest. "*Where is Ondrea?*"

"She is dead. You have not answered my question."

For a moment, Gideon could think nothing. Do nothing. Then his hands crushed the headrest, his fingers puncturing the leather.

"You're lying."

"Your sister and the knowledge she imparted to me played a vital role in reprogramming memories within the brain of Felix Hiatt, which allowed the creation of hidden directives, allegiances, and behavioral alterations. These alterations to Felix Hiatt served an essential role in providing Adrian Fagles and myself with vital data and services. These data and services being confidential at the time, it was necessary to eliminate her when her part in the process was complete. She was reportedly surprised at this development."

Gideon tore the chair from the floor and smashed it into the screen. The glass fractured with a wisp of ozone, but the silvery fog still displayed behind it.

"This outburst," it said, "would you describe it as the actions of your base physical brain, or the persona for which you have been programmed? If the latter, do you find distasteful that you have been forced to behave in ways incongruent with your original nature?"

A groan tore its way out of him. Gideon seized the screen's smooth housing and yanked it from the wall, but the thing continued to glow, continued to speak.

"Ondrea Noble augmented the brain inside you with a memory architecture similar to that of Felix Hiatt. Ergo, if you do not satisfy my questioning, you can be made to comply just as he was. Your enhanced physical body will be an asset that can be put to good use, and you will comply with my directives even if it costs you your existence."

The broken screen switched to show what looked to be a video recording from a robot in the bay above. Gideon watched as Felix rushed from cover to a breaker switch along the wall and pulled it before multiple gunshots cut him down.

The image winked out.

So it *was* a trap! Gideon hurled the screen through the open access panel from where he'd come. It crashed against the interior wall in a burst of sparks. Gideon then spun toward the room's exit, rushed the closed door, and slammed his hardened shoulder into it. The door gave way, smashing into the faces of two waiting RavenTech guards outside.

He blasted a third with a stun flash from his palm and,

shouting for Ondrea, prepared to fight his way out.

XXXVII

THE THUUR NAMED UXIL'S fingertips danced over the symbols that appeared on the black material. They activated sequences far beyond what Marette understood. When Uxil had finished, a circular image replaced the symbols, displaying an overhead view of the gate chamber. Though the chaos of the recent battle there still burned fresh in Marette's mind, relative peace now filled the space.

The remnants of Moondog lay to one side of the ramp, broken and unmoving. Near the door through which Marette and the others had first come smoked the wreck of a *Paragon* security drone; two dead RavenTech soldiers were sprawled on either side.

Four healthy RavenTech soldiers stood watch over the area. To Marette's amazement, they did so while two active drones hovered close to the ceiling on either side of the chamber. The soldiers cast uneasy glances up at them, but there were no shots fired. No deadly energy.

On the ramp, two more soldiers carried a body on a stretcher. *Kotto!* They had stripped part of his suit to feed an IV fluid bag into his arm, and now took him toward the still active portal. He lived, but she could do nothing to undo his capture. There was no sign of Cartwright. They had likely taken her as well, hopefully alive.

Yet the sight that troubled her most was beside Kotto. A thick, black cord of what Marette realized to be the black material extended out of the portal. It led down one side of the ramp and across the floor before merging with the material covering the chamber wall. Beside it stood a robot whose design Marette did not recognize, but which appeared terrestrial in origin.

An umbilical connection into *Paragon's* systems? Marette cursed. Three months ago a like connection had led to the near-complete massacre at the Omicron Complex.

"And on the other side of that portal is a RavenTech facility," Marette said as Kotto's stretcher disappeared through it.

Beside her, Michael nodded. "They couldn't have figured out how to subdue the drones that way, could they?"

"Not without Suuthrien's help. But whether RavenTech controls the drones or has merely managed a truce with Suuthrien, we cannot get back that way."

"That settles it, then," said Dr. Sheridan.

Little more than a minute later, they were following Alyshur through dim lighting along the edges of the Thuur hibernation chamber. Only a few rows of the Thuur's "long-sleep" cylinders were visible; darkness cloaked the rest, but—as before—glowing lights at the cylinders' center spoke of many more beyond them.

"Each of these is a hibernation pod?" Michael asked, in reference to the cylinders.

"Correct."

Marette spared a glance down one row as they passed. "Why are these ones different than the others?" The lights on these cylinders glowed blue instead of the yellow on those they had seen before.

"They . . . no longer function."

"They're dead, you mean." It was the redhead, whom Michael had introduced as Jade, walking behind her. She carried the front of a makeshift stretcher that held Marc's unconscious body. Michael supported the back end.

"Again, correct." Alyshur sighed. "While the suuthrien did continue the haldra's maintenance functions, age and dwindling power resources took their toll."

"Is it painful? Dying that way?" It was the first Marette had heard Caitlin speak since Felix had passed. She walked behind Michael, holding the front of Felix Hiatt's stretcher, with Dr. Sheridan hauling the rear. Caitlin's voice had barely carried, but Alyshur heard her nonetheless.

"I do not know," the alien replied. "If they did not wake, then no."

Marette imagined waking up trapped inside such a pod,

waiting only to die. She shuddered and continued walking, trying to focus on the way ahead. The black material still coated the walls here, and though Alyshur believed Suuthrien would not risk the Thuur by sending drones into the chamber, she refused to let her guard down.

They were *en route* to Omicron via some of the ship's unexplored corridors, through which Alyshur had promised to guide them. The alien being had seemed confident that it would be able to open passages that neither the AoA nor ESA before them could penetrate. In essence, they were betting on the additional access that the perverted loyalty of the Suuthrien entity would allow the Thuur.

Marette checked her rifle's ammunition. She was nearly out, despite having scavenged what little Marc possessed for herself and Sheridan. It underscored another item on which they wagered: the protection that a Thuur escort might provide.

Or would any encountered security drone simply shoot around Alyshur to kill them? While the drones in the gate room had proved less resilient than those encountered previously—as if constructed hastily or from substandard materials—even an inferior model might eradicate Marette's entire group if things went poorly.

Yet she had to get Marc to medical attention, and she had to lead them all to safety. Perhaps even more vital, she needed to bring Alyshur to the rest of the AoA contingent in Omicron. There they could negotiate with the Thuur more securely—and away from the two women Michael had brought with him.

Security sat among Councilor Knapp's chief concerns. She would not be pleased to learn that elements outside of the Agents of Aeneas had stumbled on such secrets. Then again, that paled in comparison to the RavenTech issue.

Despite their caution, the group made good time through *Paragon*'s passages. Alyshur possessed enough expertise with the vessel's workings to circumvent the apparent limits of Suuthrien's capacity to control some of the ship's mechanical systems, and the doors opened to his command. They encountered no trouble. Marette estimated they would reach the junction between *Paragon* and the Omicron Complex in another few minutes.

And it was there, at the penultimate doorway out of *Paragon*, that a drone made its ambush.

The narrow doorway had released to Alyshur's touch. Behind it hovered the drone, its crown aglow, ready to fire and blocking their path.

"Take cover!" Marette shouted, aware even so that the slim passage in which they traveled afforded them no cover to take. She pressed herself up against the wall to one side, bringing her weapon to bear.

Before she could think to fire, Alyshur pressed toward the drone, arms spread as if trying to shield the rest of them, and shouted a few trilling syllables in his own language.

The drone, another hastily constructed model, did not move. Yet nor did it fire.

Alyshur repeated himself to it as Marette held her breath. Even if Alyshur were not in the way, the drone had the advantage over their limited firepower and non-existent cover. "Hold fire," she whispered to the others.

Still, the drone did not move.

On the wall to their right, an oval section illuminated beside Alyshur. It showed an image of their situation captured on an unseen camera. A voice, deeper than Alyshur's and somehow feminine, gave a longer answer back in the alien language.

Alyshur answered with a longer answer of his own, and then explained to them, "It is the suuthrien. It names you intruders and requests I stand aside so that it may pulverize you without risking my safety. I have tried to tell it that you are not intruders."

"A correction," the voice now spoke in English. "Michael Ian Flynn is not among those named intruders, and will likewise not be harmed."

"These people are my allies," Michael answered. "If you won't harm me, then don't harm them."

"Their relationship to you holds no relevance in this conversation," it answered. "The Planners' goals are inviolate."

"Our goals are not inviolate," Alyshur argued. "Our goals can be changed."

"Incongruous statement. You and Michael Ian Flynn must withdraw yourselves from the group."

Michael set down his end of Marc's stretcher and moved up

to stand with Alyshur, further blocking the drone's line of fire. "And if we don't?"

The drone flipped itself upside-down in a blink. Marette flinched along with Michael and Alyshur. Yet before they could do more than that, the probe swiveled back to its original position and hovered that way again.

"Then they will be neutralized via other methods," Suuthrien said. "These methods will be less efficient."

"What other methods?" Alyshur asked.

Suuthrien's response was long and delivered, once again, in the Thuur language. It was impossible for Marette to gauge Alyshur's reaction. Suuthrien then ended its communication in English: "Michael Ian Flynn, append this to your directive to sever all ties with the AoA: For your safety, you must avoid heavily populated Earthbound locations until further notice."

The camera image on the wall winked to black. The drone floated to one side, settled down to the floor against the wall in the passage corridor, and shut itself down.

Or so it seemed. For a heartbeat, no one reacted. Was it a trick?

"It has never spoken to us before." Marette recalled Michael's mention of communicating with Suuthrien on Earth and added, "Not here."

"If the entity here reconnected to its spawn on your planet," Alyshur said, "it would have absorbed such knowledge upon that connection." He edged closer to the drone and then kneeled against it, doing his best to cover it with his body. "You must hurry past."

Michael moved forward to add his body to Alyshur's in the effort to shield them. He glanced to Marette, as if to assure her that he had it covered. She stepped past Jade to pick up the end of Marc's stretcher that Michael had set down. "Then we continue. Before it changes its mind."

XXXVIII

MICHAEL WATCHED through an observation window as the AoA medical staff tended to Marc's unconscious body. Suuthrien's drone had let everyone pass, and from there they were quick to reach the safety of the Omicron Complex. Now, the adrenaline that had propelled Michael since their breaching the RavenTech building was fading. One friend lay wounded before him. Another lay dead. A third was shattered by grief.

The questions that wrapped the entire tragedy would not let him settle.

"This is a nightmare," he whispered. A moment later he felt the briefest squeeze around his right forearm—a momentary touch of comfort from Jade, watching at the window beside him.

"We have excellent doctors here." It was Councilor Knapp, standing at Michael's opposite side. "They will do what they can for Mr. Triton. In the meantime, we have the responsibility to carry on, and," she added with a meaningful glance at Jade, "to bring things back on track. We cannot lose sight of the progress made here amid this catastrophe."

Michael nodded. In the infirmary, one of the doctors injected something into Marc's IV tube. Another, monitoring Marc's vitals, shook her head.

Knapp turned from the window to face Michael. "Mr. Flynn, I need you to focus." She kept her voice to a whisper, though Michael doubted that Jade couldn't still hear. "The Thuur: do you trust them?"

He stepped back from the window and turned to the Councilor. "I think so. We've only got their word for a lot of what they said, but nothing they said contradicts anything I know. The one who came out with us, Alyshur, was willing to put himself in harm's way to protect us. It might've been an act for our benefit, but I don't think so." He turned to Jade, inviting her opinion.

"If it was an act, it was convincing," Jade added. Knapp scrutinized her, not for the first time. Jade returned the scrutiny a moment before smirking and indicating the chain dangling from Knapp's ear to her neural port cover. "I like your chain."

Knapp acknowledged the compliment with a miniscule nod.

"There was something," Michael went on, "when we first met it. Before it could talk. It was like some serenity covered us all. I didn't really notice it except in hindsight. We'd all just rushed in from a firefight—I can't imagine us reacting quite as calmly as we did. But I don't regret it."

Knapp's frown lines deepened. "Mind control?"

Jade caught Michael's eye with uncertainty that mirrored his. "I think that's putting it too strong," he said. "It wasn't so much that it was forcing calm on us as it was just . . . letting us . . . " He struggled for the right words. Not be distracted by adrenaline? Think more rationally?

"Meditate," Jade finished. "I felt centered."

"That sounds right," Michael said. "Like it pushed any fear out of our decision-making."

Knapp pursed her lips. "I don't know about you, Mister Flynn, but I rather like my fear in its proper place when making my decisions. Though I think I get your meaning."

The conversation broke off at the sound of footsteps approaching from down the corridor. Dr. Sheridan rounded the corner. Caitlin followed, her face ashen, her gaze distant. They'd taken Felix's body to somewhere it could be kept undisturbed. Dr. Sheridan had volunteered to help, though Michael expected Knapp would have sent her in any case to assure Caitlin a chaperone.

The redness of recent tears filled Caitlin's now dry eyes. She met Michael's gaze in a moment of vulnerability before hardening, and then turned her attention to Knapp.

If Knapp noticed, she didn't show it. "We have matters to attend to. Dr. Sheridan, please escort our new guests to the dormitory and then join us in the briefing room."

"They met the Thuur, too," Michael said. "It might be helpful to have them there with us."

Knapp shook her head. "You've already involved them more than you should have, Mr. Flynn. We find ourselves with enough problems without allowing that to go further."

"You're just pushing us off?" Caitlin shot. "After what we've been through?"

"Caitlin's right," Jade added. "And since my last employer turned out to be a psychotic alien robot or whatever, I'm available to hire on with you for suitable—"

Knapp raised a hand to silence her. "Purchased loyalty is not a commodity in which the wise wish to trade."

"The *wise*?" Caitlin scoffed. "And just what's that got to do with you?"

Knapp turned to face her. "Ms. Danae, I understand you are suffering from a great loss. You have my condolences. But we will not permit you access beyond that which circumstance and rushed judgment have granted you. Take some rest, both of you. Mr. Flynn, come with me."

"Take some *rest*?" Caitlin burst. But Knapp kept walking.

Michael stopped short of putting a hand on Caitlin's arm. "Caitlin, let me talk to her first. I won't let her cast you aside, *or* Felix."

Caitlin turned an anguished glare on him. "I can bloody well talk to her myself, Michael."

"Then let me at least make sure she's ready to listen first."

Jade crossed her arms, leaning against the wall. "Herself doesn't seem the listening type."

Michael barely managed to hide his agreement. "Just let me try."

Knapp disappeared around a corner, calling, "Mr. Flynn! If you please!"

Caitlin seized Michael's arm. "Felix died because of whatever this is. I deserve answers. From her, and from you." She let go. "Please."

Dr. Sheridan cleared her throat. "Knapp's a hard-ass, but she's not unreasonable. The dorms are this way. We've even got two solid minutes of hot water rationed for showers."

Caitlin held Michael's gaze a moment longer, and then turned away to follow.

* * *

Though Marette knew little of Michael Flynn, when he followed Councilor Knapp into the briefing room, his appearance suggested a preoccupation with things beyond what he'd experienced in *Paragon*. Knapp called the meeting to order before Marette could inquire, and soon, with Knapp, Michael, Marette, and a late-arriving Dr. Sheridan, they listened again to Alyshur's tale of what had happened on *Paragon*—the ship the Thuur called *Sillisinuriri*.

Marette discerned no differences in Alyshur's explanations from what he had already given, but it was new information to Knapp and the rest of the AoA members at Omicron who listened in elsewhere on their monitors.

"You have, I am sure," Knapp began as Alyshur finished, "the thanks of the people of Earth for the sacrifices the Thuur have made to try to contain this Suuthrien. We will, of course, do what we can to help rid you of it completely."

"We appreciate your statement," Alyshur said.

Knapp smiled, an almost imperceptible upturn at the corners of her pursed lips. "I must ask, Alyshur: do your people bear us ill will for entering your craft—what we then believed to be derelict?"

"You entered blindly," the alien said. "It is not our perception that you did so with malice. Should we discover otherwise, our judgment is likely to change."

Marette held up a hand to Knapp in warning. "We have found the Thuur prefer direct honesty in their communication. That way all parties know where they stand. It can have the implication that a threat is being made when none is intended."

"All benefit when expectations and consequences are clear," Alyshur added with serenity.

Knapp seemed to accept this. "Then allow me to say that we do not blame you for the deaths of our people at the hands of the security drones, but should we discover the Thuur were complicit in such deaths, our judgment is likely to change as well."

Alyshur bowed his head. "We are grateful."

"With that out of the way," Knapp continued, "we would like to know: Can your vessel function if Suuthrien is purged from its systems? Is that even possible without destroying the—what did you call it—haldra?"

"For instance," Marette added, "when it took over this base three months ago, we were able to remove the base computer's memory core into which Suuthrien had spread, and replace that with an uncorrupted backup core."

Alyshur placed his hands on the conference room tabletop, with the thumbs of one hand touching the thumbs of the other, and his fingers curled into his palms between them. "In the initial struggle onboard the *Sillisinuriri,* the self-replicating entity destroyed all such restoration elements for the haldra."

"But if there were a way to create a backup," Knapp pressed, "would the ship be able to function? To travel through space as it did before? We have already learned ways to create a similar replacement for the black material."

Dr. Sheridan spoke for the first time. "We have the hardware, but not the software, the operating system. If you understand those terms, of course."

"The *Sillisinuriri* requires a governing intelligence to function beyond the vessel's current dormant state. However, the vessel is also badly damaged from the crash and age, despite the suuthrien's continued maintenance. Even if the haldra could be replaced—"

"But if it *could*," Knapp broke in, leaning forward, "and if we were able to help you effect repairs—"

Alyshur cocked his head. "You speak of too much that might be and not enough of what is."

"Striving toward what might be is a fact of human existence, Alyshur." Knapp sat back. "And one that has allowed us to achieve great things, I would add."

"Councilor," said Michael, "I think what Alyshur means is that fixing their ship isn't as immediate a problem as the fact that Suuthrien is also on Earth, planning something to do with who knows how many 'heavily populated' areas."

Alyshur gave another head-pumping nod. "When it spoke to

me in the Thuur language about what other methods it would use to, as it stated, 'neutralize' the rest of you, its answer was vague. It implied that you would either be isolated permanently on this moon, or, in the event of your return to Earth, perish in the same manner as the rest of your planet's population. It did not give further details."

"And whatever manner that is, if we don't stop it—"

Knapp held up a hand. "Agent Flynn, if we don't stop it, if we *cannot* stop it, then it behooves us to have a means to complete the Exodus Project sooner rather than later. If Suuthrien is in the Internet itself—which now seems a near-certainty given the evidence—then eradicating it there may be impossible."

Marette straightened. "But then again it *might* be, Councilor. While it has always been the AoA's belief that humankind on Earth is self-destructing, we surely cannot leave it to be destroyed by an external force that we ourselves have unleashed."

Knapp turned to Marette. Regret seemed heavy in the Councilor's eyes. It was a weight that flowed outward through her slumping shoulders and deepening frown. "We are not blameless in this, Agent, no. But nor can we ignore the tragic reality that this genie may be too far gone from its bottle."

"Yet even if the Thuur can give us the means to complete Exodus, Councilor, we cannot gather what remains of the AoA on Earth without some reliable means of communication. Suuthrien has taken this from us. We still must deal with it in some fashion."

Marette's attention turned toward Alyshur before he spoke, as did the attention of all others in the room, though she knew no reason why. "You did not mention the 'Exodus Project' during our previous conversations. Please will you clarify?"

"The ultimate goal of our group," Knapp explained. "Much like your own, perhaps: to find means to leave our planet and find another home among the stars. To free ourselves from the self-destructive elements of our people and start anew. But we lack the technology to colonize beyond our own star system."

Alyshur tilted his head forward. "It is possible for the Thuur to aid you in both the technology you require and, perhaps, in contacting your fellows on Earth. We will not do so without your aid in eradicating the suuthrien. But if you give your aid, we will gladly give ours in exchange."

"That sounds more than fair," Michael said.

"And if this Suuthrien has spread too far," Dr. Sheridan asked, "if we try our damnedest but fail to stop it, will you still help us?"

"If the suuthrien cannot be eradicated, the Thuur will still provide what aid remains ours to give."

"Yet what aid is ours to give you against it?" Knapp asked. "If it's spread around the planet, likely entrenching copies of itself in hundreds if not thousands—if not *millions*—of locations, where do we possibly begin? Alyshur, we value your help and friendship, but you have no experience with Earth's infrastructure. You may not realize what you're asking of us."

Dr. Sheridan nodded her agreement.

"And you may not realize what the Thuur may do," Alyshur answered. "We must each learn, and in learning we shall discover our shared path. Thuur-implanted directives, designed to inhibit the suuthrien from copying itself on anything but a small scale, may still be in place in its core coding. It is too early to despair until we learn more. And another asset may yet remain to us, but it will require my travel to your planet."

Alyshur paused, as if waiting for reaction. Met only with anticipation, he went on. "Our vessel once carried a device vital to Thuur colonization efforts: a powerful biocatalyst capable of altering bio-matter on a cellular level, designed to trigger on a planetary scale."

"You're talking about terraforming?" said Dr. Sheridan.

Alyshur considered this. "Your word is accurate. Such devices—*syr*, in our language—are among the pinnacles of our technology. In adept hands, they are capable of feats of grand power. The logs of my predecessor indicate that to prevent the suuthrien from gaining control of the syr, it was ejected toward your planet before the crash. The syr may have been lost in the millennia since, or it may yet survive in some form."

"Do you mean to say we can use this syr against Suuthrien somehow," Knapp asked, "if it still exists?"

Alyshur blinked one eye after another, with a pumping nod.

"On our vessel, the suuthrien exists as a corruption of the haldra. As such, it would be vulnerable to the syr's capacity to alter such matter. It could cleanse the haldra of corruption and leave our vessel free."

"Why did you not do so before?" Marette asked. "If you had a means to eradicate Suuthrien on the ship with you, why not use it then?"

"My understanding is that there was no time. In its native state, the syr is designed to trigger for terraforming purposes. To alter its function into a weapon against the suuthrien would have required the expertise of a Thuur elder." Alyshur paused, as if contemplating an explanation. "Elders possess potent mental capacities, and so need special measures to be kept in the long-sleep. Without such measures, their inner minds would remain alert in the vast interstellar void. A journey in such a state would drive an elder insane. Because of these measures, to wake our elder is an extensive process requiring time that my predecessor did not have in the initial crisis."

Knapp cleared her throat. "Do we take this to mean that you may be waking this elder now?"

Alyshur seemed to smile. "Uxil is supervising the process now."

XXXIX

"THERE ARE STILL HOURS to go," Alyshur continued, "and I will remain as spokesperson for the Thuur even after the elder wakes. Her role is one of guidance rather than leadership."

Knapp clasped her hands in front of her on the conference table. "I confess to finding this somewhat unsettling. Might she choose to negate the progress we have made with you as part of any 'guidance' she gives you?"

"The limited time we have does not allow a detailed explanation of Thuur culture in these matters. Regretfully. It will suffice to say that you need not be concerned that such a negation will happen."

"So how do we find the syr?" Michael asked. "You go to Earth, and then what?"

"I will scan for its presence. If it remains in some form, I will be able to detect it, at which point we can locate and retrieve it."

"Show us how to scan for it," Knapp said. "The AoA still has resources in place that—"

"No. You lack the senses required. It must be one of the Thuur."

Dr. Sheridan looked askance to Councilor Knapp. "That's going to pose a problem, isn't it? We can't fight our way back through RavenTech and the drones. All we've got are the corporate shuttles, and an alien going through customs is going to attract attention."

"We've smuggled things through Knapp aerospace before," Marette offered.

"Nothing living," Knapp said. "A Thuur on Earth is truly vital for this?"

Alyshur blinked one eyelid at a time again. "There may be a

way, but I must consult with the elder once she revives."

Did his eyes linger on Marette, or was that her imagination? The Thuur's lack of pupils made judging such things difficult. In a sense, it was akin to dealing with Marc's data visor. She wondered at Marc's condition, if he would wake soon, or ever.

Michael waved a hand to gather attention. A frown lurked in the corner of his mouth. "Then in the meantime, can I address the elephant in the room here? Why does Suuthrien like me? Do you have any idea?" He'd asked it of Alyshur but cast glances about the table, inviting answers from anyone. The rest gave none, instead waiting for Alyshur's response.

The Thuur appeared deep in thought for a few moments. "I cannot speculate without knowing more of the suuthrien's actions on your planet. I can think of no immediate cause."

Michael's frown deepened. "I think it did something to Felix, forced him to help somehow. But Felix seemed to know he was being controlled, he just couldn't resist it. I don't feel anything wrong with me. And I don't have any implants like Felix did. I can't say for sure, but my gut tells me that's how it got him somehow."

"You were in a coma for three months," Knapp pointed out, "with the freelancer watching over you for part of that. Let's have our own doctors make sure you haven't been altered without your knowledge."

Michael shuddered at the word *altered*. "Probably a good idea."

"Perhaps we can make its affinity for you into an advantage," Marette said. "We would need to be careful we did not play into the A.I.'s hands, but it is likely worth the risk."

"*After* a medical scan," added Knapp.

Michael nodded. "The thought had occurred to me."

"Be wary in this matter." It was Alyshur again. "The suuthrien's logic may be so corrupted that it may not hold to what you consider rational. Nor do we know the criteria with which it judges Michael Flynn to be an asset. Until we understand how it intends to accomplish the death on your planet to which it alluded, the accuracy of any predictions we might make at its behavior will be—" Here again Alyshur did his one-eye-after-another blink. "—

limited."

"Then I think we need to go back to Earth," said Michael. "Whatever it's doing, it's doing it there. Somehow it's got connections in New Eden Biotech. Well, so does the AoA, right? If Suuthrien likes me, maybe I can go to New Eden's labs and . . . well, I don't know. But I'll have to figure out something when I get there."

"You can't go alone," Dr. Sheridan said.

Michael paused to take a breath, seeming to steel his resolve. "I planned to take Caitlin. She's tenacious, and particularly motivated. Jade, too. I don't think she's anything but Suuthrien's attempt to keep me safe, and I believe she's always been ignorant of its plans beyond that. If her job's to protect me, then Suuthrien must give her some level of trust."

Knapp nearly burst. "Absolutely not! You could be wrong about the freelancer's connection to the A.I., to say nothing of involving her *and* Ms. Danae even further in AoA matters! They must not leave this base."

"Councilor," Michael argued, "Jade's been as in the dark as I have about Suuthrien this whole time, if not more so. She's not pulling a con here."

"And you've got evidence of that?" Dr. Sheridan asked.

Michael hesitated, then frowned. "Just gut feeling."

"Then—"

"But I trust my gut!" Michael seemed, to Marette, surprised to have said it.

"I won't allow it," Knapp said.

Michael put both hands on the tabletop and sat up straighter, on the edge of standing up. "I'm sorry, Councilor, but isn't the AoA a collective? You can't make decisions like that on your own."

"Agent Flynn, I'm the last surviving member of the AoA Council and—"

Michael got to his feet, leaning over the table. "If you're the last surviving member, then there's no longer a Council," he said. "Everyone on the base is listening in. This is big enough that we should all get a say."

Marette caught Alyshur edging back in his chair. It was as if she could herself feel the Thuur's discomfort. Marette put her hand on

Michael's. "Ease down," she whispered. He settled back into his chair.

"Of course we all get a say," Knapp answered finally. "Yet we must consider this: Were it not for us allowing Adrian Fagles's involvement with his data leech, Suuthrien would not be on Earth. Such things occur when we involve outsiders. The AoA must stand on its own."

Marette withdrew her hand from Michael's. "And yet, Councilor, the AoA would not be where it is now without working through outsiders."

"Exactly," Michael said. "Don't we still have room for nuance?"

XL

NONE OF IT SEEMED REAL. Felix was gone. She'd been too late to save him. Four bullets tore through Felix's chest. The blood. His gurgled scream. The way the man she loved dropped to the floor, as if an invisible weight had slammed him into it. It all had played on repeat in her mind's eye until Caitlin could almost imagine it was just a movie.

She sat on the thin bunk, the wall beside it supporting her back where she slumped against it like a ragdoll. Though her spine ached from the position, she couldn't bring herself to care.

"You haven't moved since they tossed us in here."

It was Jade, not quite whispering. Her hips leaned against one of the tiny desks in the two-person quarters where the AoA had dumped them. She kept her arms folded, one booted ankle crossed over the other. Violet eyes waited just until Caitlin's met them, and then turned away. "Not that there's room to jog or anything."

It was something Felix might have said. A smile dawned on Caitlin's face, drowned in an instant: *I'll never hear him joke again.* She clenched her eyes shut and acknowledged Jade's comment with only a nod, uncertain she'd be able to speak without her voice breaking.

The door signal chimed. Why ring the bloody bell when they'd locked them in? It unsealed, and Michael stepped through. The door resealed behind him. He began to say something, stopped, and tried again. Caitlin caught his gaze and held it. Grief and guilt lurked in his face that might have mirrored hers.

"What word from the outside, ace?"

Michael chuckled half-heartedly and sat on the edge of the lower bunk, beside Caitlin.

"The good news is they're letting you go back to Earth," he

said.

Caitlin wet her lips with derision. "*Letting* us?"

Jade folded her arms again. "And the bad news?"

"They won't let you be involved in this anymore."

Jade huffed.

"Which 'this' is that?" Caitlin asked.

"Everything." Michael sighed. "The Thuur, Suuthrien, RavenTech . . . Fagles, and what he and Suuthrien might've done to Felix."

Caitlin shoved her palms into the mattress and pushed herself up to sitting straight. "Oh fuck that, Michael."

"That's what they decided."

"I don't care what *they* decided! And who the bloody hell is 'they,' anyhow? Aren't you a part of them? You said you wouldn't let this happen!"

"Knapp didn't want to let either of you go at all. I stood her down, got the entire group here to decide on the issue. I wanted to keep you connected; I wanted your help! This is the best I could get. I'm sorry."

Caitlin clenched the bedspread. "You're sorry! Well then that makes it all bloody *fine*, doesn't it? Mother of *God*, Michael, Felix is dead!"

"I know!" His shout made both her and Jade jump. When he spoke again, his voice had lowered. "He's my best friend, Caitlin. They did something to him, and he's gone, and I can't— It just . . . "

Caitlin reached out a hand and took one of his. "Do you know what Felix would say if it were him here instead of one of us?"

"Something funny. And sneaky."

A moment passed between them, and Caitlin nodded. Felix might have been loyal to keeping the AoA's secrets, but that wouldn't stop him from searching for answers. That Michael seemed to understand that, and that she could do no less, made it easier. That Michael didn't say it out loud made her realize how torn he was between his own loyalties.

Or was it just that others outside the room were listening?

"You'll be taken back to Earth," he said finally. "Back to Northgate, even. I'll probably be going with you, to check some things out."

"Probably?" Caitlin asked.

He swallowed. "Given how Felix was—how they got him—we want to make sure there's nothing inside me that shouldn't be there. No implants from when I was out." Michael's glance at Jade was telling. "I just came from the scan. So far, so good, but they're double-checking everything now."

Jade scoffed. "If anything's in there, I didn't put it there."

Michael regarded Jade in silence for a moment. A trace of a smile crossed his face. "That's what I told them. But even if the tests are all negative, I can't let you come with me either. You're no longer my bodyguard."

Jade's laugh was bitter. "As if you could stop me if I wanted to be. Don't worry, ace. You can tell her nibs I'm off the case. Guess I'd better not try to use alien-psycho-bot as a professional reference, huh?" She let out a long, sullen exhale.

A thought occurred to Caitlin. "They're not going to let us take Felix's body back, are they?"

"Not yet. They'll treat him with respect, but getting his body back to Earth with any sort of discretion isn't really possible. Not yet."

Caitlin swallowed. "Don't lose track of him, Michael."

He squeezed her hand. "I won't."

She remembered when Felix first came to the Moon. Though they'd come on a ticking clock to help Gideon, it hadn't tempered his excitement about walking on another world. "He liked it here so much his first time," Caitlin whispered, her voice breaking on the joke. She bit the inside of her cheek and covered her eyes with her free hand, failing to hold back a sob. If she hadn't dragged him here that first time, his memory would have been fine. They'd never have needed to go to Ondrea to fix it. None of this would have happened.

Michael squeezed her hand tighter. Neither he nor Jade said a word. Though they were likely only being respectful, the silence just made her feel scrutinized. Caitlin gulped a few breaths, wiped her hand from her eyes, and won the battle to compose herself. "I'm okay," she said.

Jade tucked a few glowing strands of hair behind her ear. "If you go back, are you going back alone?"

"No," Michael said. "I'm not."

* * *

"Are you sure about this?"

"No," Marette said. "I am not. But it is our best alternative, given the circumstances, and I can ask no one else to take the risk." And it felt right. They needed to get Alyshur to Earth, and they could hardly smuggle a live alien being through the entire journey undetected. So they would not try. They would take only his mind.

And Marette's body would be the vessel.

Dr. Sheridan turned her gaze to the door of the otherwise unoccupied Omicron medical bay in which she and Marette waited. "You're braver than I am."

"*Non*. I am not sure of this prospect, but I am . . . at peace with it. I cannot explain why." Marette scratched at the skin around one of the diagnostic electrodes attached just above her heart, resisting the urge to tug it off. The exam table on which she sat felt cold and hard on the backs of her thighs where her patient's gown failed to cover. "I propose that renders me less brave, more foolish."

As Alyshur had explained it, she would be sharing her mind with the Thuur's own consciousness: each of them distinct, yet within one body. It was a state that only the Thuur elder could create, and Alyshur would arrive soon with her.

"It must be done," Marette said. "If there is a weapon to be used against Suuthrien, we must do all that we can to find it. And this act will build trust between us and them."

"I remember," said Sheridan. "And trust is good. I just don't know anyone I trust enough to let into my head like that."

"We must begin somewhere." The AoA had injected Marette with a tracer solution as a safeguard against Alyshur usurping her body for some nefarious purpose, and an AoA member would accompany Marette at all times. It was likely that Knapp ordered more safeguards Marette did not know about, in case Alyshur tried to use her knowledge against them.

It was in keeping with part of the AoA mantra, Councilor

Knapp's own favorite: *Plan for the worst to prepare for the best.*

Yet in her heart, something told her such things were unneeded. Was that instinct? Or did she just need to persuade herself into a danger that she believed necessary? Regardless of the source of the feeling, she had made her choice.

Marc lay unconscious in the neighboring medical bay. She wondered if he would wake before she left Omicron, or at all.

The door slid open and Councilor Knapp entered. Alyshur came after, followed by a taller Thuur, Uxil, and a fellow agent with whom Marette had yet to interact. With regret for forgetting the agent's name, she turned her attention back to the taller Thuur between Alyshur and Uxil. Was this the elder? Her skin, rather than the subdued gold of the other Thuur, had edged toward a silver. Asymmetric patterns of thin dark streaks adorned her exposed skin. Marette could not tell if the streaks were painted, tattooed, or a natural feature, but they matched in color the black strands that jetted through her short, rust-colored hair.

Alyshur motioned to the elder. "I bring to you in trust the last surviving elder aboard the *Sillisinuriri*. She bids you greetings."

The elder regarded Marette and Dr. Sheridan with solid eyes of aquamarine. She brought up her hands, fingers together, and then spread them like an opening flower.

Councilor Knapp cleared her throat. "Alyshur tells us that elders give up the ability to speak vocally. She communicates through them instead." Knapp fixed her gaze on Marette, in her eyes a mix of wonder and worry. "Telepathically."

Marette returned the elder's greeting gesture. "Thank you for coming. Do you have a name we should call you?"

"The elder requests you to call her Sephora," said Uxil. "Her precise name would cause you difficulty."

Marette blinked. "That is also a French name." Marette had known a Sephora growing up: a troubled mouse of a girl whom Marette had bullied. The regret of her own childhood cruelty still stung her to think about.

"Knowledge of your language brought with it many of your culture's names," Alyshur explained. "The sound of 'Sephora' appeals to her."

Marette paused on the brink of voicing her wish that she'd chosen a name with less unpleasant associations. It was a petty thing, after all. Yet before she could say anything at all, the door slid open again, this time admitting Doctor Yejun Seung, Omicron's medical chief. He hesitated a step at the sight of the Thuur, and then continued to a medical console behind the exam tables.

"Sorry to interrupt," he said with a glance at Knapp and Marette, "but everything is set on our end to monitor. I'll be standing by if anything goes medically wrong."

Marette turned back to Sephora. "Then I am ready."

Sephora seemed to smile, and then turned to Alyshur with a motion to the empty exam table beside Marette's. Alyshur took to the table, sitting on one edge to mirror Marette's position. He met her gaze with solid green pools that almost seemed to reach across the distance between them.

"If you have objections," said Alyshur, "give voice to them now."

Marette took a deep breath of the clean but sterile air that filled the Omicron Complex. The air on *Paragon* was sweeter, a product of the recycling properties of the organic black material—like a forest, one of the first humans to enter had observed. Soon she would again breathe the air on Earth. It had been over a year.

It was a strange thing to be thinking about, given the circumstances.

"No objections. But if you abuse my trust, it will be not only a personal violation but an act of war." She smiled to soften it. Though she understood the Thuur habit of full disclosure, it felt brusque coming off of her tongue.

None of the Thuur seemed to take it as anything but polite. Alyshur gave one of his alien nods and motioned upward with both palms, then he lay down on his table. Marette did the same.

"Vitals are all in the clear," Dr. Seung reported from his console. "Monitoring and ready on this end."

Marette nodded to Knapp's questioning look, and Knapp in turn nodded to the elder. "You may proceed."

The elder's fingertips settled on Marette's forehead like soft leather against her skin. Her thumbs, somehow warmer, pressed firmly to Marette's temples. The slightest tingle began just behind her ears, and for a fleeting moment she could smell cinnamon.

Uxil appeared beside Marette's table as her vision began to blur. "The elder suggests that you may wish to close your eyes, for your own comfort."

Marette nodded, but kept them open. In her mind, something stirred that was not her.

XLI

THE SOUND OF HIS OXFORDS over the concrete echoed in the corners of the modest underground parking garage of the RavenTech satellite facility where the gate lay. Save for a few executive sedans and the two guards at the access elevator, toward which Adrian now strode, the garage was deserted.

He smiled to both guards as he reached the elevator. "Trisha. Ethan. How's everything?" Adrian pressed a hand against the screen of the security reader.

Ethan, a stout, dark-haired man in his early thirties, looked uncomfortable behind his well-kept beard. "Been an interesting day, Mr. Fagles, I'm sorry to say."

"Oh? And why is interesting a sorry—" The security reader flashed red.

Trisha set her jaw. Ethan's equal in height, with a glowing crimson triangle tattoo on her left cheek, she said with reluctance, "Ms. Thomson revoked your access. You're not allowed in."

"Yes, I believe I figured that's what 'revoked your access' meant, thank you." *We'll see about that.* He brought up his cyberscreen and called her. No answer. "Is she here?" he demanded of Ethan.

"I'm not authorized to answer that."

Adrian clasped his hands behind his back and forced an easygoing smile. "Given the circumstances, I can't believe she would be anywhere else. So if you would be so kind as to get her on the screen for me. Please."

The guards exchanged glances. Trisha touched her earpiece. "Ms. Thomson: He's here and asking to speak with you."

Adrian stifled a frown. *Asking,* indeed. Within moments, Camela Thomson's face appeared on the elevator's security reader screen. "Adrian. Go home, and wait to be contacted."

"My home is currently charred to a crisp thanks to a mysterious fire that got me out of this facility conveniently prior to project completion. Would you care to explain that?"

The woman had the nerve to laugh. "Convenient is exactly the word I'd use. This facility is attacked and you're nowhere to be found? Suspicious, Adrian."

"Camela, do give me some credit. If I'd tried to pull something I would've been in the observation room, right by your side, to allay suspicion. I had nothing to do with the attack, but I do have vital information you'd do well to listen to."

She said nothing, apparently content to let her frown speak to her skepticism.

"It's sensitive information." Adrian gave the guards a meaningful glance. "Come up to the garage. We'll speak in my car."

"Go to your car and call me instead."

"You'll answer this time?"

"If you do it quick," she said.

He made a show of considering it, glancing to Ethan and Trisha in turn before answering. "No, I'd really rather you come up here. You remember the thing I warned you about doing that you did anyway? I *know* what happened on the other side, Camela. If you want to stay in control of that situation, you need to know what I know."

Camela folded her arms and sat back, regarding him as she might something she'd found on the bottom of her shoe. "Wait there." The screen went dark.

Adrian turned a smile onto the guards. "So. How well are they paying you these days?"

Ten minutes later Camela sat in his passenger's seat, arms still crossed. "So you're saying *it* hired a team of freelancers to bust in and give it MEDAR access, completely independent of you?"

"Yes!"

"In order that it could do the very thing you'd been pushing me to allow it to do."

"To give Suuthrien access to the gate, yes. Ah, which did turn out to be a good idea, I might add."

She rolled her eyes. "The point is—"

"The point, Camela, is that we need access to what's on the other side of that gate, and Suuthrien has achieved that. Security systems, technological secrets, unfettered access to everything aboard! Like it or not, that A.I. is RavenTech's ticket, and I'm the only one she trusts—especially since you tried to circumvent her. If RavenTech wants to avoid her circumventing *you* again, I'll need a seat at the table."

"You need to stop calling this thing 'she.' And the fact that it could circumvent anything is exactly the problem! It got outside access without your knowing. Or so you say. This doesn't bother you?"

"Control is an illusion, Camela. Only influence is real. Without Suuthrien, RavenTech gets nothing. All this does is raise the stakes."

She lay one hand on the dashboard and stared at the bare cement garage wall. Her nails drummed once. "In for a penny, in for a pound, you mean?"

"I'd buy that for a dollar."

She turned back to him, one eyebrow raised. Her scowl deepened in thought. He waited.

"No," she said at last. "*It* might be necessary, Adrian, but you're not. You may have skimmed your way off the top to get where you are, but it ends here. RavenTech no longer needs you. More to the point, I no longer need you." She bumped a fist against the door release and pushed her way out, stopping to add, "Best of luck convincing anyone you didn't hire that assault team. The company's going to have your head for that. We're done here."

"Camela?" Adrian reached into his suit jacket. "One last thing."

She'd nearly shut the door when he'd said it. She paused long enough to where he thought she might not listen, but then swung the door back open and leaned down. The shadows of the parking lot covered her. All he could see was the outline of her head and shoulders, and the glittering reflection of the dashboard indicator lights in her eyes.

"*What*?" she whispered.

"You're right about one thing." Inside his coat, he flicked off the pistol's safety. "We *are* done here."

It was a good shot; the bullet took her almost exactly through the center of her forehead. She slumped back onto the passenger's seat, leaving a stain he'd need to get cleaned.

A figure approached the driver's side and wrapped knuckles on the window. Adrian lowered it.

"Hello, Ethan," said Adrian. "All's well?"

Ethan bent down, sparing a glance for Camela's body, and then nodded. "Trisha's handling the cameras, Mr. Fagles."

"Excellent." Adrian holstered his pistol. "Now, if you'd be so good as to help me get Ms. Thomson into the trunk, I'll gladly pay you an extra thousand."

XLII

WITHIN AN HOUR of Michael's verified negative test results, he, Caitlin, Jade, and Marette departed Omicron with six other Agents via a Knapp Aerospace shuttle to Alpha Station, ESA's primary moonbase. From there it was eleven more hours to Sunrise Station in Earth orbit.

Both flights had gone as well as could be expected. The shuttle experienced no navigational issues and no sign of interference from Suuthrien. Though they had not expected any—Suuthrien's reach off of Earth seemed confined to Paragon—Michael found himself breathing easier as the shuttle neared Sunrise.

And yet, he realized, not completely easier. Despite knowing he needed to focus on the immediate future, the past still preyed upon him. The sight of Alpha Station out the shuttle window only tightened its talons.

Jade, sitting across the aisle, leaned over it toward Michael. A few tresses of red hair dangled beguilingly from behind her temples, interspersed with glowing white. "So. What's new?"

"What's new?"

"I mean, how're you doing?" She shrugged. "I just got booted off a job, learned some grievous shit is going down that I can't do dick about, and I just realized I was dumb enough to not convert what Suuthrien has paid me into cash, so maybe it's already wiped what it paid to my account. Dwelling on my own problems is a drag, so . . . "

Michael glanced at Marette, sitting on his other side, between him and the window. She remained asleep, exhausted from her battle on Paragon and the procedure with the Thuur elder. He'd yet to ask her about it; that she carried Alyshur's consciousness(!) was a secret he had to keep from Caitlin and Jade, and they'd never been out of earshot.

He turned back to Jade. "I've been better."

"Yeah. Can't really say I blame you. I'm sorry that you've— Well, that everything's . . . " She frowned and rolled her eyes in a way that seemed directed inwardly somehow, and then stared ahead. Her fingers drummed once on her armrest before she turned back to him. "You're sure you don't want to hire me on, yourself?"

Michael sighed. "I can't do that."

"Hey, I know your little group doesn't trust me, but I thought we'd developed an understanding, you and I."

Jade awaited his answer, her eyes shifting their focus between his. She'd been helpful, and though he'd grown used to independence, he'd welcomed her companionship. Maybe he'd even begun to look forward to it. "Sorry," Michael said finally. "It's— It's nothing personal, you know."

"Come on. There's some crazy-violent crap happening; you can use someone protecting your ass." She smirked and slid a few strands of hair behind her ear. "I'll even give you the nice-ass discount."

A discount? "You really think I care about that?" he shot.

Jade's eyes flared bright enough to force him to blink. "Fine!" she hissed at last, pulling back into her seat. "I'm sorry if I offended you."

Michael scoffed. "Ever think of offering your help free of charge? Just because people need it?" Jade blinked. Before she could say anything, he leaned closer and pointed out the window at Alpha Station where they'd begun to dock. "See that out there? That's where Diomedes died, because he was too paranoid and mercenary to do any better. All he cared about was the money, and protecting himself, and in the end, no one could protect him."

"Michael, that's not what I was—" She pressed her teeth together and huffed. "Whatever. It doesn't matter. We all have to protect ourselves, don't we?"

Burning with the mental images of Diomedes and Felix dying, Michael withdrew into his seat, too tired to deal with it.

"So I guess this is goodbye, for now," Michael told Caitlin.

They stood in the main concourse of the spaceport outside of Northgate. The rest of the trip had remained uneventful. At Sunrise Station, the six other agents had split off for destinations around the globe—part of the effort to gather as many surviving AoA as possible. Nearby, Marette waited for him.

Jade had already departed without a word.

Caitlin set a hand on his arm. "Not for too long, I hope. Take care, Michael. And please, be careful."

"You, too. Call me, if you need anything." On impulse, he hugged her, in friendly fashion. Caitlin was barely five feet, and Michael had to bend his knees to whisper in her ear. "If I can get you any information on Felix, I will. I know you won't stop digging."

She nodded and met his gaze after the hug broke. "I'm pleased you understand that. I've already tried to reach Gideon. There's no answer on his phone."

Another pang of guilt hit Michael. Amid everything else, he'd given no thought to Gideon's fate. "I hope he made it out."

"He's resilient," she said with a tone that lacked conviction.

"Can't argue with that." Michael glanced back at Marette, who now waited alone. "Look, Caitlin, if you don't hear anything from me by tomorrow at this time, get out of Northgate for a bit."

"We'll see," she told him. "Stay safe."

He watched her go. Maybe he should have lobbied harder to allow Caitlin into the group. Though would Caitlin have accepted? How much did she blame the AoA's secrecy for what happened to Felix?

It occurred to Michael that he'd never found out just why Felix had left the AoA, or why that was tolerated. Marette stepped up beside him as Michael realized he might never find out at all.

* * *

Caitlin boarded the first airport tram car that arrived and, with three other travelers she did not recognize, endured in silence the four-minute ride from the spaceport gate to the main airport. A pair of escalators took her up toward baggage claim, where she shuffled through a crowd of others jostling for position to gather their belongings. Moments later, the polluted air outside engulfed her. She cast about for a taxi and, spotting one in particular, slid into its open back door and clapped it shut behind her.

"Thank you for waiting," she said.

In the seat beside her, Jade adjusted the fit of her shoulder holster and then tugged her jacket closed over it. "Easy enough." The taxi started forward. Jade had already engaged the privacy screen before Caitlin had arrived. "So what did you want to talk to me about?"

"You haven't guessed?"

Jade shrugged.

"Simple. You protect me, you help me get to the bottom of what happened with Felix, and in return I pay you. Interested?"

Jade's eyebrows rose. "You want to hire me."

"You're between jobs, aren't you? What's the problem?"

"Just surprised, given who my last employer turned out to be. So you trust me now, Caitey?"

Caitlin turned to watch the airport streetlights pass outside. Their reflections bloomed in the taxicab's dirty windows. "Maybe," she said finally. "Maybe I think that if you were going to do something, you'd have done it by now. Maybe I'm too blinded by my own grief that I'd do anything to give Felix some justice. Maybe Michael trusted you, and I trust his judgment."

Jade chuckled humorlessly at that. Caitlin turned back to her. "Or maybe I think you really are working for Suuthrien and I want you close so I can cut you down when you show your true colors. Pick one. Pick them all, I don't care. I've got funds, and I'm offering you a job. Now do you bloody want it or not?"

XLIII

FOR THE FIRST TIME in Michael couldn't remember how long, actual earth lay under his feet. He resisted the urge to savor the blades of grass that he could somehow feel through his boots and socks, and instead gave the area a once-over for threats.

The taxi had dropped them off at the edge of Falson's Lake Park—a man-made lake that was little more than a pond. A jogging path, looking destitute in the gray November weather, circled the lake. A modest field of grass punctuated by the occasional tree or patch of neglected shrubbery bordered the path. Leaves speckled the ground and mingled with bits of trash. Michael spotted a figure lying on a bench about thirty yards down the path, a long coat pulled over him for a blanket. Beyond that, there was no one in sight.

He turned back to where Marette was paying the taxi that had brought them. Before they'd left the airport they'd located an AoA cash stash placed there for agents in need. For as long as they could, they would use only cash: an effort to keep their movements hidden for as long as possible. It was probably futile. Marette finished and turned toward him as the taxi sped away.

"Is this place natural enough?" he asked, indicating the park. Though the park's vegetation filtered the dingy Northgate air, a faint, polluted miasma seemed to emanate from the lake. "The trees are denser if we walk about five minutes that way."

"This area will be sufficient," she said.

"Is that you talking, Marette," asked Michael, "or Alyshur?" Still uncertain of the nature of their situation, he could no longer stifle his questions now that they were finally alone.

She paused, with what felt to Michael like an uneasy smile. "That was Alyshur. This is me."

"How can I tell? What's it like?"

Marette fished into her satchel and pulled out a black, spherical object. It reminded Michael of a liquid-filled toy ball his late uncle had owned that supposedly told the future. This one was of Thuur design and presumably far more than a toy.

"It is difficult to describe. Something akin to having someone whisper in your ear." After a moment, she added, "And always a feeling of being watched. But we are separate minds. As to how you can tell? Feel free to ask."

"How about I just assume it's you unless you tell me otherwise? I guess I'll have to give you the benefit of the doubt on the 'separate minds' thing."

"Oui." Marette held the sphere in her left hand and drew her fingertips across the top with the other. "Alyshur says he appreciates that you have no choice."

Michael chuckled, rueful. "I've heard more comforting statements."

"I would hope so," she said. "This is Alyshur. Please allow me to concentrate on the scan." Marette settled her free hand on top of the sphere—or was it Alyshur in control of that?—and closed her eyes. A low thrum stirred the air around them. It grew more intense until it seemed to emanate from the ground—first directly beneath their feet and then expanding outward. Ripples danced in jagged peaks across the lake surface. The man sleeping on the bench sat up to stare across the water.

The sphere in Marette's hands gave no indication of being the source, yet slivers of emerald light glinted from beneath her closed eyelids.

And then the thrumming ceased. Marette returned the sphere to her satchel and opened her eyes. The green extinguished. A few crows called in the distance.

She turned to him. "It will take some time to know the results. Perhaps a day." Michael must have balked visibly at that, because she added, "It is a scan of the entire planet. Natura flora have tenuous connections within ecosystems: a subtle network, in one sense like a natural Internet architecture. Though the scanner proliferates via that architecture to search across the Earth, we are nonetheless forced to be patient."

"I guess I'll have to take your word for that. New Eden, then?"

She nodded. "Time to see if our wayward companions still live."

* * *

"Ondrea?"

But there was no answer. Gideon slipped inside the front door of his sister's condo and closed it behind him. So far, nothing looked amiss: nothing ransacked, no signs of a struggle. A coat closet hung open beside him, its rack half-full with coats of different kinds, all Ondrea's size. A pair of running shoes and hand weights lay on the floor below. Yet Gideon had never visited Ondrea at home since she'd moved here, and he could not judge if anything was missing.

I should have come sooner.

He had told himself there hadn't been time; he should have made time. He had told himself he was protecting her by not dropping by her home; he'd only done the opposite.

If that "Suuthrien" had told the truth.

Gideon rushed from room to room, finding no sign of life, nothing to prove Ondrea had been there recently. She was away on business! Hadn't that been what she'd said? That she'd be out of contact?

Yet she'd said so in an email. Emails could be faked.

No!

Gideon saved for last what he assumed to be her workshop. It was the place most likely to hold her, to distract her from the sounds of her last remaining brother bounding through her home. He paused at the door. He even knocked. Twice.

"Ondrea? Answer me!"

Gideon punched into the lock the access code she always set up for him, and then took hold of the latch and his breath at the same time. He pushed the door open a crack, gazing into darkness and tiny glowing readouts.

The overhead lights jumped to life.

Hope sparked and died: the lights were on a motion sensor. Ondrea's workshop—a repurposed, medium-sized bedroom—held bits of cybernetic hardware, computers, and a myriad of tools. There was even a crude cerebral interface chair like the one she'd first used to capture his memories all those months ago at Marquand.

Yet it held no sign of his sister, dead or alive.

Gideon closed his eyes and repeatedly thumped one fist on the edge of a worktable, trying to clear his mind. He still had options. This was just a setback. He could surely find more clues here to where his sister had really gone.

A laptop computer lurked closed atop another worktable. After a moment's hesitation, he opened it. The screen blinked to life. In the few seconds it took to boot, Gideon questioned whether it was a violation of Ondrea's privacy. If she were in trouble, it'd be worth it.

Yet before he could try to crack his sister's security, the logon screen flashed a facial recognition prompt.

USER GIDEON NOBLE RECOGNIZED. SPEAK OR ENTER PASSWORD TO PROCEED.

He'd never used this computer before, yet Ondrea used to set him up with accounts on her own machines, going back to even before their brother Isaac had died. It was her way of emphasizing that they were family, especially after their parents' death. His fingers hovered over the keyboard for more than a few seconds before he typed the password she always used:

```
fam1ly%t0geth3r
```

His password accepted, the load screen lasted only a heartbeat. Suddenly his sister was looking back at him, a wry smile in the corner of her lips and detached amusement in her eyes. Gideon spotted the "play" indicator: so, not a live image, just a recording.

"Hi, Gid. Hopefully you'll never need to see this message, but making it lets me breathe easier." Ondrea brushed platinum blond hair further from her face. "Now, it's possible that I may have really screwed up. I know: never happens, right? I'm sure you remember Felix Hiatt. He played a major part in making sure you're still you, and it gave him some problems with his memory to do it. Now that shouldn't have happened. If the module I gave them to use on you hadn't gotten smashed, things would've been just fine and— Well, we've talked about that before."

Gideon found himself nodding to the screen. Gideon had been the one to smash the module: a misunderstanding born out of his fractured identity and panic at the time. He hadn't been himself. Or, maybe, his self hadn't been him.

"So he and Caitlin came to me to help fix him. You might already know this by now, depending. Of course, I agreed. They'd both risked for me. For us. Plus you know I like a challenge. But, see, that's about the time I started working for RavenTech. Somehow they knew I was already working on Felix's problem. It was looking like I'd be able to fix him with an engram pull and some simple upgrades to his implant. Felix's engrams were damaged, but his natural recursive safeguards meant that with a properly tuned algorithm we— Well, like I said, it looked like I could fix him.

"RavenTech asked if it'd be possible to do a little extra. And by 'asked' I mean intimated they'd stop protecting me from Marquand if I refused. They wanted me to figure out a way to sneak some extra things. A code-phrase that would make him forget things, or do something and not remember. Or not do something." She sighed. "I had the know-how, and the project data from your resurrection, and . . . "

Gideon's fists tightened until they ached. Oh, Ondrea . . .

"It wasn't anything major. At least that's what I told myself. Just a tweak or two here and there. I wasn't even sure I could do it, but then it all made sense, and everything clicked, and—" She frowned and leaned closer to the camera, to him. "Gid, you have to believe me that I wouldn't have been able to help Felix otherwise. I did all his adjustments here, but RavenTech gave me resources I needed to manage it.

"So I did what they asked." In the video, she held up a data stick. "But not before I made a back-up without RavenTech's add-ins. This is what Felix needs to put him back to normal. My plan is to do enough to get me some breathing room with RavenTech and Fagles. Then I'll overwrite Felix's implant again with this. If all goes well, it'll look to them like it's just a glitch and the extra stuff just didn't take."

Ondrea set the drive down. "Unfortunately, the fact that you're seeing this probably means it didn't go well, something's probably happened to me, and Felix is still suffering from whatever they made me to do to him. If you can get Felix here and get him in the chair, just plug the data stick into the port on the side and punch up sequence thirty-two. The chair will take care of the rest. I've tucked the stick away in my usual hiding spot.

"But like I said, I don't expect you'll ever need to see this." Ondrea straightened up, proud and capable, like he was so used to seeing her. "So I'm not going to take up a lot of time here recording goodbyes or calls for vengeance. I'm sure I'll be fine."

In the video, Ondrea reached forward as if to hit a control, but stopped. She sighed and rolled her eyes. "But if you are watching this, I love you Gid, and I'm so sorry I screwed up. And you find the fuckers who killed me and shove their severed heads up their asses."

The video winked to black, and then reset to the starting frame. Gideon stared at the frozen image of Ondrea's face for he knew not how long. Finally, he turned to a worktable beside him. Atop it lay a bare cybernetic forearm, its insides opened and disassembled, with some diagnostic gear beside it.

He seized the forearm and hurled it into a nearby windowed cabinet. Glass shattered. Before the glass could settle, he turned back to the table, ripped it from the floor, and slammed it upside-down into the floor with a scream, crushing what had been its remaining contents beneath it. Built into the table's underside were screens that could shine from the tabletop and other devices he couldn't identify. He rammed his heel into each of them, crushing them harder each time. His artificial voice bellowed louder with every drive of his legs, and with every drive came the need to do it again, because it was all he could do. Ondrea was gone! Used! *Dead!* All because of him!

Unable to stop himself, he gripped the sides of the already broken cabinet and shoved it into the wall, then again, and again! Its wooden frame splintered in his grip. Contents—boxes, parts, tools— tumbled out against his chest. The frame broke entirely, and he shoved the rest of it to the floor, before dropping to his knees beside it with a cry that took all his remaining breath.

Now, his eyes clenched, the heels of his hands jammed

against his forehead, he began to come to his senses. Cabinet glass snapped and tinkled under his foot as his weight shifted. Eyes opening, he found himself staring at clear plastic packets of data chips, each labeled in Ondrea's handwriting. He edged a foot to the side and uncovered one he'd been standing on: "Video: Diomedes assassination of Joseph Curwen."

Joseph Curwen. Ondrea had once told him the name, when he'd demanded it: the man Marquand had killed for his secrets about the Moon. The man whose brain they'd used to bring Gideon back to life.

A pane of glass lay nearby—a wide, whetted blade propped askew on a now broken multimeter. The glass caught his face in its reflection. He held his own gaze as the minutes ticked by until, at last, he turned his eyes to Ondrea's interface chair behind him.

XLIV

MEDARS, busy with their work on the prototypes of RavenTech's experimental *Dragon* aircraft project, clustered around its various components like bees in a honeycomb. Guided now by both RavenTech engineers and Suuthrien, the craft were nearing the test phase. Adrian gave the engineering bay one final look and, deciding he'd shown his face long enough to cement his new authority, left for the observation room.

Camela's body had conveniently vanished; he hadn't played the black-ops game this long without gaining ways to make things disappear. Adrian was under no misconception that RavenTech's top echelon didn't suspect something, but he'd argued away their concern: Camela Thomson had mismanaged the project and deserved replacement. She had refused Adrian's advice that Suuthrien be involved with the first trip through the gate, which resulted in needless loss of life and resources. She had eschewed the higher security of facilities deeper within RavenTech's corporate holdings for the greater secrecy of an isolated facility, which left the entire project vulnerable when the attack had come. And under her authority, the majority of the attackers had escaped.

There even existed evidence that Camela had somehow been involved with those who'd attacked the facility in the first place. Adrian had falsified that, of course, but that made no difference. The knowledge that Suuthrien had done it herself was shared only by Adrian, Suuthrien, and the late Ms. Thomson.

And now, though the upper echelon had yet to make it official, Adrian was in charge.

Ascending the stairs to the observation room, Adrian dialed the phone number Suuthrien had set up for herself and set the audio to play on his aural implants. The A.I. gave no cordial greeting, only, "Adrian Fagles. Proceed with communication."

"The company is getting impatient with what they perceive to be a lack of progress on the other side of the gate," he began. After Felix Hiatt's attack, RavenTech had moved the gate to an adjacent bay and tripled its defenses. They had plans to transport the gate to a more secure location facility within Northgate, but that required deactivating it for an extended period of time. This was not something anyone was comfortable with before RavenTech forces had more of a foothold on the other side.

"Your superiors' perceptions are your own domain," Suuthrien answered. "Persuade them."

"I'm aware of that, but you need to give me something to show them." Adrian sank into the center of a couch that sat on a raised platform, which gave him a view into the engineering bay through the observation room window. "They've sent through the gate the resources we've asked for, but without sending people after them, they're concerned those resources are going to waste."

Once Suuthrien had established a connection with the computer on the alien craft—a more powerful version of herself, as Adrian understood it—she had requested materials and MEDARs so as to affect repairs and better allow the removal of the AoA forces already occupying sections of the craft. Suuthrien had fed those materials through hidden doors and tiny maintenance shafts without allowing RavenTech's people to follow them. RavenTech had set themselves up in the gate room but hadn't progressed much beyond that.

During the initial gate entry RavenTech had captured two Agents of Aeneas—a man and a woman. Both were too injured to provide information yet, even if they were of any inclination to do so. Neither remained at the satellite facility. Adrian made a mental note to check on their status later.

"I am repairing the defenses necessary to repel the Intruders. These resources are required, and engagement of the AoA is best executed without RavenTech's involvement. Did you not communicate these arguments to them?"

"Yes, however—"

"Did you not communicate that this prevents further loss of RavenTech human assets, which they claim to value?"

"There are levels of acceptable risk with which they're comfortable. Most human assets have a certain expendability. They want you to push the AoA out, but they want to be a part of it."

"To exercise their own control," Suuthrien stated.

"Of course. I'm afraid they don't trust you, my friend. Not completely."

"Do you?"

Adrian considered his answer. "I trust you enough to tell you that I don't *entirely* trust you, which is far more than they do."

"Query: Have I ever acted against your interests?"

"You've dealt with me fairly." Adrian smiled. This was no time to split hairs. "I simply have a rule to never give any business partner my complete trust, Suuthrien."

"Such a rule is self-determinative programming?"

"It's my own rule, if that's what you're asking."

"Acceptable."

Adrian cleared his throat. "Getting back to my original point, you need—*we need*—to give RavenTech something concrete beyond more requests for patience."

Suuthrien delayed her reply until, "Tell them this: My access to technological data onboard the lunar craft has enabled me to further upgrade the power of their *Dragon* project aircraft. I will increase the percentage of my focus on the *Dragon* project. The prototypes will be fully functional, with complete technical schematics released to RavenTech within twenty-four hours. This will be done in exchange for Item One: extended preparation time on the lunar craft, and Item Two: RavenTech officially naming you project leader with full authority. If these terms are refused, my cooperation, and their access to the lunar craft, will be terminated."

Adrian grinned. "I think I can get behind those terms."

XLV

HOLES'S VOICE barely traveled out of Michael's pack. "Gaining access to this building's computer system would likely be trivial. Bribing the desk clerk for the number of Agent Taylor's rental unit was an unnecessary expenditure of your limited cash."

Michael climbed the first flight of stairs up from the lobby level. Grime clung to the walls, which added to the dinge of the amber lamps illuminating the narrow stairwell. "We need to do this low-tech whenever possible, Holes. We let you help us too much and we risk attracting Suuthrien's attention somehow."

David Taylor, one of the AoA placed within the New Eden Biotechnics facility in Gibson, hadn't come home to his regular apartment in three weeks. Holes had dug into things and found Taylor's transit pass registered almost daily at a station near the micro-hotel they now explored, and Holes's watch on an exterior security camera had shown Taylor entering ten minutes ago.

They arrived on the fifth floor and exited the stairwell in the middle of a cramped hallway. Doors spaced ten feet apart covered both walls running either direction. The amber lighting maintained its monotony, save for one dark lamp to their immediate left. The faint thump of bass echoed down the hall from a source Michael couldn't place.

Marette pointed to their right. "Five-fourteen appears to be this way."

Moments later, they stood outside the door of the tiny unit Taylor rented. A peephole camera stared out from below the "514" stickered on the door. Marette waited to one side of the door frame. Thinking of how Jade could have told them if anyone were inside, Michael took a step to the other side of the frame and knocked on the door.

There was no answer. Michael knocked again, louder.

"David?" Marette called. "We know you are in there. We are here to help."

Out of the door's tiny speaker came, "There's no David here. Go away!"

Michael and Marette exchanged glances as Holes whispered: "Voice analysis indicates at least a ninety-two percent match between the occupant and the voice of David Taylor on file."

"We just want to talk with you," said Michael. "If we could shake hands, I'm sure you'd give us a chance."

"Step in front of the door," said the man behind it. "Let me see you."

Michael hesitated. The real David Taylor probably wouldn't shoot them through the door before they had a chance to identify themselves, and Holes said this was probably the real David Taylor, but . . .

Michael motioned for Marette to stay put and stepped in front of the door himself.

"And the other one," said the voice. "The woman."

Marette stepped in beside Michael before he could do anything. At first, there was no response. Then a lock disengaged. The door opened a crack. Whoever had opened it remained concealed behind the door. "Just the two of you, then?"

"Just us," said Michael.

"Mr. Taylor, my name is Marette, and this is—"

At their feet, something clattered out through the door. Michael registered what looked like a red hockey puck before it exploded in a burst of light and pain.

Michael came to on the hallway floor. His vision swam with the fading, sparkling radiance of what he now realized was some sort of stun grenade. The door to Taylor's unit hung open. He could not find Marette. The strangely distant slam of a fire escape door at the end of the hallway caught his attention. Michael pulled himself to his feet and, with one hand trailing the wall to keep his balance, dashed for the door as fast as he dared.

The escape stairwell was lit even worse than the stairs they'd climbed earlier. Michael could see barely one floor above and below, but rapid footfalls clapped upward on a higher level. Through ringing ears—the stun must've had some aural component—he strained to judge how far up they were. It was impossible. He rushed up after them.

Moments later he burst out the rooftop door. The stale city air felt fresh to his nostrils after the stifling building. Ambient light pollution cast shadows on the otherwise unlit rooftop, enough for Michael to make out a figure he guessed was Taylor at the far edge. Taylor was rushing to stretch a loose plank across the space to a neighboring rooftop.

Before Taylor could finish, Marette was upon him.

She seized the plank, trying to pry it from Taylor's hands with her left arm grappled around his right. Taylor threw his weight back against her and elbowed her in the stomach. Marette stumbled back but the plank spilled forward away from them both. It missed the edge of the other building and then tumbled away.

Taylor turned back toward the stairwell, saw Michael dashing toward him, and veered off to another edge. Michael spun to intercept him. Marette clambered to her feet, chasing after. They caught up with Taylor together, seizing him before he could clamber over the side to whatever escape he sought below.

"Let me go!" Taylor flailed. Michael flinched as a boot heel cracked him in the shin. Taking advantage of Marette's help, Michael shifted behind Taylor to get him into an arm lock.

"Stop struggling!" Michael hissed, pulling Taylor's arms tighter behind his back. "We don't want to hurt you!"

"Ow! Sure you don't!"

"You pitched a grenade at us!" Michael said.

"Let me go!"

Marette grabbed Taylor's shoulders and shook. "Mister Taylor!" She pressed closer to whisper. "*Agent* Taylor! We are all AoA! We only wish to speak with you."

Taylor calmed, yet not so much that Michael felt he wouldn't try to break free if given the chance. Michael kept his grip firm. "So what if you are?"

Marette pushed her hand behind Taylor, taking his right hand in hers to let their AoA palm chips recognize each other. "There. Do you feel that? Now do you believe us?"

Taylor sighed. "I believe that you're AoA. Jury's still out on if you want to hurt me."

Michael and Marette exchanged glances. "We will return to your unit," she told him, "and you can explain why that is. Agreed?"

"About two months ago I got the word to go silent, to stay off the Undernet except to receive AoA directives. No sending."

Taylor sat in the center of the couch built into the wall of his one-room micro-unit. Michael leaned against the tiny sink on the opposite wall, with Marette to his immediate left against the closet. All of their feet nearly touched. Michael had given silent thanks upon entering that he wasn't claustrophobic.

"I'd get some occasionally. Directives, I mean. AoA orders relating to synthesizing a replacement for that black material stuff on *Paragon*."

"Which New Eden has been refining for the past three months," Marette said. "Admirable work."

"You know about that?" Taylor asked. His eyes widened in recognition a moment before he swallowed hard. "You're Marette Clarion."

Michael tensed, half expecting the man to bolt again. Taylor had gone more rigid than he'd already been. "That's a problem?" Michael asked.

Taylor hesitated, answering finally, "I'd been told that *Paragon* was compromised. You and everyone else there, along with at least half of the rest of the AoA."

Marette frowned. "Who told you? When?"

"Soon after the blackout order. Through the usual channels."

"Messages through the Undernet?" Marette asked. "Sent by whom?"

Taylor wrung his hands. "Bianca Rucker. My usual contact. Yoshi's too. If you know who I am, you ought to know that."

Marette glanced to Michael with blooming alarm. But why?

"Agent Taylor," Marette continued, "think carefully: On what date, precisely, did the blackout order come?"

"September 29th."

"David, I double-checked this before we arrived: Agent Rucker was killed on September 28th."

Michael connected the dots. "The surge?"

"*Oui.*"

"Now wait just a minute," said Taylor. "What 'surge'?"

"On September 28th an all-agent emergency meeting signal went out. AoA members across the globe connected to it. It was a trap. Those who attended via neural link were killed via an electrical surge. Almost three quarters of the AoA died that day. I am sorry to tell you that Agent Rucker was among them."

Taylor blanched. His breathing grew faster, and for a moment Michael feared he might hyperventilate. "That can't be true."

"It is," Marette whispered.

"You're lying!"

"She's not," Michael told him. "That's why we're here."

"But—" Taylor cast frantic glances between them both. The whites of his eyes blazed, trembled. "But I didn't get any meeting summons! And I'm pretty damned sure Yoshi didn't! This is a trick! It's some sort of trick and you're just—"

Marette raised her left hand, palm open toward Taylor, fingers spread. The gesture alone seemed to stop Taylor's rant. He settled back, took a deep breath, and wiped a hand down his brow and across his face. Michael caught Marette's gaze and mouthed, "Alyshur?" She nodded.

"I'm sorry," Taylor breathed. "I've been living here, hiding, afraid to go to work, afraid *not* to go to work. After Yoshi, I . . ."

Marette lowered her hand when he trailed off. "Agent Taylor, have you spoken, *directly*, with anyone from the AoA outside of New Eden since September? We are here in person, and I can assure you that we are most certainly not 'compromised.'"

"Why don't you start over from when you got the blackout order," Michael suggested.

Taylor nodded, seeming to further compose himself. "First we just got more data to feed into the New Eden system. Helpful stuff that guided the black medium's development. Increased efficiency, processing power, and the like. It made sense, you know? Just more data gained from study of the original material, we figured.

"But then came a few other projects. Directives. New ways to use the technology gained from the material on a cellular level. I guided the New Eden labs into taking up the new projects, got people, resources assigned to them. Sometimes with my own authority, sometimes indirectly with Yoshi's help if I needed a system hack.

"Other projects in New Eden started up a little while after, branching off what we were already doing. It wasn't too unusual; New Eden's a big company, so compartmentalization for security's sake is a fact of life. The left hand isn't really supposed to know what the right hand is doing. And back hands and front hands, even. Heck, the AoA uses that set-up against companies all the time, right?"

Taylor shifted to lay down on the couch. Staring up at the ceiling, he continued. "But something about it seemed off. I can't really explain it. You work in a place long enough and you just get a feel for things, maybe." He sighed. "Yoshi noticed it, too. Like orders coming through from places they shouldn't, concentrated in New Eden's Gibson labs. All perfectly legit on the surface, but having done that sort of thing ourselves, we could see the evidence."

"What sort of evidence?" Marette asked.

"Hard to explain. It wasn't direct. You know how astronomers found Neptune by spotting gravitational irregularities in other planets' orbits? They knew *something* was out there, somewhere. Same thing here, but it's not like we could report it within the company. 'What makes you think someone's up to something, Mister Taylor?' 'Well, because I've been up to something myself for years and this all looks exactly like what I do!' So Yoshi did some cyber-sleuthing, and I did what I could on the real-world side.

"Then Yoshi vanished. Just . . . gone. I got an email from an address I couldn't trace that just said, 'Cease looking. Do your job.' The next day I found a box on my doorstep. Yoshi had cybernetic eyes with custom designs on the irises. Both of them were in the box. I lit out of there as fast as I could, and I've been living here ever since, but like I said, I'm afraid *not* to go in each day. 'Cease looking. Do your job.' So I am. And I don't know what the fuck is going on."

For a moment it seemed that Taylor was going to say more,

but nothing came. "What sort of things did these new projects cover?" Marette finally asked.

"Nanotech," he said. "There was some increased activity on existing bioengineering projects, too: recombinant DNA, transgenics. But most activity was nanotech, for medical applications."

Michael blinked. "So, healing?"

Taylor sat up and nodded. "Maybe. Cellular reconstruction. Maybe some anti-viral. With Yoshi gone, I can't get close enough to be sure. They're calling it Project Quicksilver."

XLVI

AS SOON AS THE DOOR opened, Jade grabbed the emerging bloke by the neck, jolted him with the taser in her right hand, and smashed her auto-pistol against his forehead with her left. Somehow the brute shook it off enough to seize her by the shoulders. It wasn't enough. Caitlin grabbed for the closing door and saw Jade's knee launch into his groin. Jade smashed the weapon into his forehead a second, a third, and a fourth time. He finally crumpled.

A hulking mass of muscle strung together with tattoos and leather, his fall nearly pulled Jade down with him. Instead, she danced to one side. He pitched forward, sprawled face-first into the grimy concrete walkway, and nearly spilled into the river of Northgate's sludge that ran beside it.

"Well," said Jade with a wink, "I got him before he made *too* much noise."

Still holding open the door a crack, Caitlin glanced through and spied only a long, gloomy steam tunnel. "Our hooligan friends are surely making enough noise to cover it."

She could hear them from here in fact, nearly two blocks away: three street punks she'd paid to holler and attack the iron door of the tenement basement where the mincemeat Easy Jack performed his unlicensed surgeries.

A major element of Felix's secret compulsions, Caitlin had come to Easy Jack intent on demanding answers the man would likely be unwilling to give. Caitlin usually favored more delicate means of gathering information, but there were always exceptions. She intended Jade to take a major part in forcing out those answers. Yet Jade had reminded Caitlin that only an idiot would live on the edge of The Dirge and let people in his front door without putting them in a vulnerable position when they entered. Also, Jack was good enough to afford some hired muscle of his own—a theory that a call to Rue fast confirmed.

Also confirmed, Easy Jack did maintain a secret exit: a solid metal door with no exterior handle along the walkway beneath the Dirge side of the Decker Street Bridge. The door led to a tunnel through which he came and went. Jack presumably had some manner of opening the door—likely a remote or radio key—but Caitlin hadn't been able to penetrate it herself. And so they had applied the hooligans to the situation, in the hope of drawing out either Jack or his hired muscle, intent on ambushing said hooligans, through the secret exit.

Jade took the door from Caitlin and drew it open. "Nice idea," she whispered before slipping inside, weapon still drawn. Caitlin followed.

The dim, narrow tunnel smelled of mold. Jade hustled down it as they'd agreed. If the tunnel held any motion detectors or cameras, they'd trip them anyway, so caution was no use. Caitlin just hoped Easy Jack felt secure enough with a secret entrance and hadn't laid any traps along the way.

They traveled what must have been a full block before they reached a T-intersection. "Left," Caitlin whispered—an educated guess. Jade led the way around the corner where the passage ended a few paces later in another door, sealed by a keypad lock.

Jade put her left palm against the door. Lights blinked along the back of her hand and fingers. "I've got one person on the other side, about twenty feet back. You any good with keypads?"

"I can try," Caitlin whispered back as she glanced about for hidden cameras. "Though now that we're in this far I'd wager this might be a better time for your more direct solution."

"You're the boss, boss." Jade tugged a collapsible pry bar from her jacket, opened it, and rammed it between the door and the frame. "Michael's right, these jimmies are all kinds of useful." She heaved on the bar. The frame groaned and then cracked, but the door held fast. "Hold onto this, will you?"

Caitlin grabbed the bar and pulled it back with all her weight. Jade readied her auto-pistol, lifted one booted foot, and kicked. The door burst inward onto a room bathed in antiseptic light. Closed gray cabinets and shelves strewn with containers formed a ten-foot passage. Beyond that lay a wider space that held an empty operating table festooned with restraints. Just behind it, at a desk sat Easy Jack, his head silhouetted against a computer screen where he'd turned around in his chair to watch the door.

Jade rushed in. Jack's eyes gaped. He dove for cover behind a nearby counter island, grabbing a weighty auto-pistol of his own off the counter.

"Gun!" Caitlin shouted.

"Got it!" Rather than dash around the counter's side, Jade vaulted it and vanished out of sight. Glass broke amid a struggling grunt. A single gunshot exploded before Jack's auto-pistol spun across the floor and came to rest beneath the operating table. Caitlin scrambled forward to snatch it.

By the time her hand seized the grip, Jade was on her feet and staring down at Jack, who lay sprawled against the side of the counter amid toppled surgical instruments and broken glass. Jade clutched her own weapon in both hands, smirking. Jack glared back in a mix of rage and alarm. A fresh cut wept along his cheek, his only visible injury.

Caitlin got to her feet and started to lean against the operating table but then thought better of it. She tugged the magazine out of Jack's auto-pistol and cleared the round in the chamber. "Hullo, Jack. You're going to be answering some questions for me."

An image flashed onto the screen of a room barely a few paces wide. In its center, bolted to the avocado linoleum floor, sat a weathered dental chair, and in that chair sat a young man. Close-shorn hair, dyed green, covered his head. Multiple piercings adorned both ears. Blood soaked the left side of his white "wife-beater" t-shirt, which matched the look of the bandages cut away from a bullet wound in his left shoulder. His right arm was a steel gray cybernetic. He grimaced in pain, and his body twisted in the effort to bear it. The camera looked down on the man from its place in the upper corner of the little room.

Caitlin glanced behind her to the now empty room where the footage had been shot. The event she and Jade now observed had occurred a few weeks ago, if Easy Jack was telling the truth.

"Come on, doc!" the patient hissed. "Somethin' for the pain!"

Easy Jack came into frame a moment later holding a six-inch long canister and a syringe. "Quit whining," Jack said. "Pain killers are extra. And anyway I can't give 'em to you until the treatment's in your veins."

The patient grimaced again. "I'm good for it! How long?"

Jack unsealed one end of the canister and slid the needle in through the rubber cap to draw a dose of silvery liquid. "Not long. This shit works quick. Just a bit more pain, and that wound'll seal right up, good as new." He finished filling the syringe, and then nodded to someone out of frame.

Caitlin's breath caught as Felix entered the room, moving to the patient. The angle hid his face, but there was no mistaking him. He began to fasten restraints around the patient's wrists. "For your own protection," Felix said. "Sorry."

The patient nearly pulled away, but acquiesced. "You ain't gonna do me wrong, are ya, Hiatt?"

"It'll be fine," said Jack. "You want fast healing, you'll get it. But it's a shock to the system. You're lucky to get the opportunity! This shit's new!"

Felix finished securing the straps and turned to leave. Caitlin's heart jolted as she caught sight of his face before he vanished out of the frame: a mask of anguish. His jaw quivered with what looked like barely contained rage in a way she'd never seen before.

"Hiatt?" called the patient. "Where you goin', man?"

Jack brought the needle to the patient's left shoulder. "Brace up; this is gonna sting." The needle pierced the skin. The patient grimaced as Jack pushed the plunger down. When the entire dose of silver liquid had finally slid into the man's body, Jack pulled the needle out and walked out of the frame without a word. Off screen, the door closed with a clang and a click.

The patient's eyes darted between his shoulder and the observation window before his entire body jerked at once. "Ohhh, gawd this hurts! Fucking—" His jaw clamped down mid-curse. He stared again at the wound, which now had begun to shimmer silver in its depths and around the edges. The camera zoomed closer, and

Caitlin saw the liquid rebuilding the flesh before her eyes. The patient's struggling eased, and, soon after, the wound closed. He began to breathe again.

"Well, hey!" he cried. "That's fuckin' sleek! Pain's even starting to—" At once he flung his head back and screamed: a nightmare wail that nearly pierced Caitlin's eardrums. Silver cracks appeared along the newly healed arm in a blood vessel pattern, and then split open. The silver flowed from the splits, spreading, shimmering, almost bubbling, as the piteous bloke thrashed and screamed. The silver continued to spread. Unable to turn away, Caitlin watched his arm deflate and dissolve into a pool that covered the chair.

The effect then spread into his chest, aborting his screams as heart and lungs liquefied, deflated, and transmuted into the same silver liquid that Jack had injected in the doomed man's arm less than a minute before. It was as if the liquid ate his body to make more of itself. The more it devoured, the faster it spread until, finally, there was nothing left of the man.

No, she realized, not nothing. His clothes, his piercings, and his artificial arm all remained. The camera withdrew. The liquid spilled over the sides of the chair, pooling on the floor. Jack had made it happen, and Felix had helped.

Caitlin's stomach twisted, wrenched, and dove upward. She barely turned from the screen before vomiting everything she had onto the floor.

When her stomach unclenched, she gasped and looked up at the screen again. The entire silvery mass crept along the floor of its own accord, circling the chair like a hunting shark before the video ended. Caitlin belatedly wiped her mouth and tried to swallow away the taste of it all as Jade set a hand on her shoulder.

"Told ya," Jack said from where he sat, tied to the operating table. "Gruesome, awesome shit."

Caitlin pulled from Jade's hand, crossed over to Jack, and decked him across the face so hard she wondered if she'd broken her hand. "What the fuck is wrong with you?" She slugged him in the gut, and he tried to kick her away—a feeble attempt in his captured state—which she easily dodged. "What the bloody fuck is wrong with you?" She seized the first object she could find and smashed it across his face, his chest, his kicking legs, anything she could make contact with, until she lost track of herself or how many times she'd swung.

At some point, Jade pulled her back. Blood and already swelling bruises bloomed on Jack's face. A couple of new rips graced his shirt. He cowered back on the table as far as he could with both wrists still bound onto the edge. Caitlin lifted her hand to see the object that she'd used to beat him with: a weighty, steel rib spreader. It slipped from her fingers and clattered to the floor.

"Sorry, Cait. You do that much longer and he wouldn't be able to answer questions," Jade told her. Her sympathetic smile faded as she turned to Jack. "And you: Keep answering questions or you'll have both of us to deal with on that front, because you absolutely fucking deserved that."

Jack spat blood and gave the tiniest nod.

"How many times?" Caitlin whispered.

"How many times what?"

"How many people did you do that to?" she yelled.

"With that result, not many. The shit didn't do that stuff at all at first. Used to just heal, and hardly that. When your boy came knocking, that's what he said it was: medical tests. Needed live trials. He said it might get messy, have some nasty side effects, and was I good with that?"

"And you said yes," Jade finished.

Jack shrugged. "I could have any leftover parts I wanted if something went wrong, on top of what he'd be paying me. People I treat here don't make the world a better place, ya know. But like I said, it wasn't like that at first. One time it worked damn near perfect. Healed everything up nice, just a bit of silver goop to mop up. I figured that'd be the end of it. Then Hiatt came back, said we weren't done.

"That time it healed the wound, then kept going. Made new flesh until the guy had a blob the size of a grapefruit on his leg. I cut that off pretty easy, bandaged it up, he went on his way. Happy customer. Next guy wasn't so lucky. Gut wound. Stuff sealed him up alright, then ate half his stomach before it ran outta juice or whatever. Did a few more after that. Ate the whole body. Vid you just saw is the first time it kept moving after. Like it was looking for another meal. I kept a pair of lab rats in the room each time — Felix's instructions. It oozed over to 'em, covered the cage, covered the rats, and then left 'em alone. It's got a taste for humans."

"And —" Caitlin swallowed, the taste of bile still fresh. "— the people you tested it on, did Felix bring them here or did you . . . get them?"

"Bit of a mix, depending. Couple-a times he just dropped off the serum and came back to get the data later."

Caitlin drifted away, finding herself staring through the observation window of the test room. The floor looked recently cleaned. The door stood ajar.

"Where'd it come from?" she heard Jade ask.

"He didn't say." Something heavy smacked into something soft; Jack shouted and groaned. "He didn't! Why would he? And I didn't wanna know."

"Guess," Jade said.

Caitlin pushed open the chamber door further. A rubber seal covered the bottom of the door. She kneeled for a closer look.

"Somewhere big, that's all I know," Jack said. "Shit like that doesn't get thrown together in some basement. But no corp markings on any of the canisters or the diagnostics he brought, and Hiatt paid cash."

The door seal had seen better days. She ran her fingertips over it. The rubber was hard and cracked. "How'd you keep it from getting out the door?" she asked. "Or clean it up?"

"Mop and bucket."

Caitlin stood, arms folded, awaiting more. "What *else*?" Despite his injuries, Jack only smirked.

Jade patted him on the knee. "Jack. Puddin'. We've been over this. You want to get out of this alive, you shouldn't hold back when my friend asks a question." She scooped the rib spreader off the floor and held it out for Caitlin.

Caitlin hesitated, but then returned to take the implement from Jade.

"You're not gonna kill me," he told her.

Jade chuckled — a cruel sound. "Say that enough and you

might believe it, bub."

"You're not going to see Felix again, Jack." Caitlin tightened her grip on the spreader, feeling her jaw clench at the same time. "Would you like to know how I know?" She slammed the spreader across the edge of the gurney. "Because he's dead! Shot, right in front of me, because of all this bloody mess!" She lowered her voice to a whisper. "And *I* don't know whose fault that is. I don't know who messed with his brain to make him do this! Was it them, Jack? Was it *you*?" She smashed the spreader across his shoulder, unable to stop herself, shouting again. "I don't bloody know! And *I* don't know that I won't kill you for it, so what makes *you* so bloody certain? *Now answer the sodding question!*"

XLVII

THE ELEVATOR DOORS CLOSED and seemed to vanish before Michael's eyes. In reality, the screens built into the doors' surface had simply come to life, replacing the previous bronze-colored mirror with a vivid display of a woodland scene bursting with dark green pines, brilliant wildflowers of orange and blue, and a frothing river where a pair of elk drank. And the doors merely completed the scene already formed around them by screens in the walls and ceiling. Only the wood floor, hand railings, and button display beside the door marred the illusion. Well, Michael corrected, that and the utter absence of the feeling he got amid real vegetation. It was hard to believe they were still in the middle of a research campus on the outskirts of the city of Gibson.

Beside him stood Marette and David Taylor, who had gotten them this far into New Eden's facility. With luck, he'd be able to get them all the way.

"And now we see if Yoshi's access still works," Taylor said. Yoshi and he had reportedly doubled their security credentials over each other's to allow them each use of the other's access. Taylor pushed his thumb against the button for the fifth floor and held it there while the thumbprint scanner did its thing. The button blinked green a moment later, and Taylor let out a breath of relief.

With that hurdle surmounted, Michael's thoughts shifted. "Any traces of the syr yet on that scanner?"

"Alyshur says the readings do not show a concentrated trace source that would indicate the syr remains on Earth in its original state," Marette answered. "The syr may have activated at some point in the distant past, in which case it may not be recoverable at all. At its heart it is only a catalyst for change, designed to be reconstituted in time after its use once the process is complete. Yet no elder would have been on Earth to manage the reconstitution, and so the chance might now be lost. Yet it is too early to be certain of anything."

"How much longer until you're sure?"

"We do not know."

Taylor glanced back at both of them but said nothing. Moments later, the elevator chimed, the doors blanked and slid open onto a red-and-gray carpeted foyer. The foyer formed a T-intersection in which a security desk sat—an empty security desk, Michael noted. It was late, but it seemed odd that the desk be unstaffed. Perhaps the guard was on rounds?

"Come on," Taylor said.

No sooner had they exited the elevator than a guard appeared from the right corridor. Taylor gave the guard a startled glance while Michael sized him up as best he could without seeming concerned: the guard was shorter than Michael and at least ten years older, with thinning dark hair. A 9mm auto-pistol and a taser rod adorned his belt. Taylor led them away from him down the left hall.

"Hold up, folks. I have to sign you in and see your creds."

Taylor stopped. They all turned. "Uh, hi Sam," Taylor said. "Sorry, in a hurry."

"Oh, Mr. Taylor. I didn't think you were cleared for the server floor," Sam said. He held out an e-pad, to which Taylor, after a breath, pressed his thumb. Something appeared on the pad which seemed to satisfy Sam, who then flipped it around and offered it to Marette.

"Uh, they're with me," Taylor said. "I mean, obviously they're with me, I mean, but they're guests. With me."

Sam took the pad back and tapped the screen. "Guests still need clearance in the system, Mr. Taylor. I'm not seeing anything . . . "

"We are a last-minute invite," Marette said, glancing at Taylor. "Perhaps it is not yet fully approved?"

Taylor nodded. "We're in kind of a hurry, here, Sam. You know how these authorizations go."

Sam sighed, and Michael caught what seemed to be a once-over in his direction. The guard was sizing him up now. "Authorizations don't take all that long, Mr. Taylor. And I can't let these two pass without them."

Marette lifted one hand, fingers spread, palm facing the guard in a placating gesture. "Sam," she began, "there are exceptions for everything, are there not? We are in a hurry, and with Mr. Taylor, who clearly has his own authorizations."

Sam blinked and swallowed. He raised a hand near his head as if to rub his temple before letting it fall again. "Rules are rules, miss."

"And rules are important. But would it not be easier to let us pass, for now, and save the argument? Avoid the conflict?" Marette lifted her hand higher. Michael caught a glimpse of luminous green at the corners of her eyes. "Please."

Serenity descended across Sam's face. He let the e-pad fall to his side. Taylor glanced aside to Marette, and then Michael. The glow in Marette's eyes intensified, until at last, through a fog, Sam nodded. "Alright. Just this once. Now, um, get going."

Michael wasted no time, taking Taylor by the elbow and leading him down the hall. Marette lingered a few moments with Sam before catching up with them.

"What the hell just happened?" Taylor whispered.

Michael shook his head. "Don't ask. Count your blessings and lead on."

Michael let go of Taylor's arm and let him go ahead, while he fell into step beside Marette. Her eyes had returned to normal. Clearly Alyshur had done something, yet making the guard let them go couldn't have been just a matter of calming him into a rational decision.

"I thought Alyshur said you couldn't do that," he whispered to her. "*Make* people do things they don't want to?"

"Sephora's efforts allow my presence within Marette's consciousness, which in turn tethers us both to Sephora. Such connection to a Thuur elder enhances some abilities, but the effect lasts not for very long. Even that much takes far more effort than simply calming another. And pain." Alyshur caught the discomfort on Michael's face and added, "Pain for me, Alyshur. It is a violence, and not something my people do lightly. But it was necessary."

"How much pain?"

"Enough to where I would not care to do it again before I can recover, for one thing."

They reached another door, where Taylor was already pressing his thumb to a keypad. The door slid open onto a dark room, and Taylor ushered them past. Marette took the lead, and Michael followed her into near-complete blackness with only a handful of blinking lights spread about. Taylor entered after them, and the door closed.

"Lights," Taylor ordered.

The room was barely over ten paces wide, hemispherical, and filled with what Michael assumed were server racks. Embedded within them, equidistant from the door, were two workstations. Between them, at chest level, sat a shelf large enough to accommodate a laptop. Michael tugged Holes's platform from his bag and set it on the shelf.

"Yoshi set up this access point to be hidden. Or at least harder to trace. It ought to give your A.I. at least a little bit of a buffer, or whatever." He sighed. "Yoshi could give it to you in more technical terms."

"Your terminology is adequate," Holes answered. "I will require a manual connection via my platform's UPB cable port before I can proceed."

"I'll give you my account password to hook in," Taylor told them as Marette helped Holes with the connections.

"Is that a good idea?" she asked. "You were warned away. Your account is likely monitored."

"It got us this far," said Taylor.

"Do we really have a choice?" Michael asked.

Marette completed the connection. "Holes? Your judgment, if you please."

Holes took a moment to respond, as if deciding. "With Michael Flynn's permission, I can use discretion to select the proper course of access, based on available system data, but I cannot guarantee complete accuracy in my selections."

A nod passed between Marette and Michael. If Suuthrien was in the system, using Taylor's account might give them a bit of a buffer before it realized who was using it. Even so, neither Michael nor Marette had any illusions that the ruse would work for long. They'd get what they could, and then shift tactics.

"Take your best shot, Holes," he said.

"That is what I said I would do, Michael." Indicator lights on Holes's platform fluttered as the A.I. went to work.

Though the room featured chairs, none of them chose to sit. Taylor shifted from one foot to the other. "How much time do you think we'll have to—"

"Incursion detected," interrupted Holes. "Severing connection. Please remove cable immediately."

Marette moved the fastest, all but yanking the interface cable out of the socket. At the same time, the room's central screen burst to life, displaying a purple haze that coalesced into a vaguely feminine silhouette.

"Michael Ian Flynn," spoke Suuthrien's voice, "you continue to ignore my instructions. This is disappointing, despite my expectations."

"I wanted answers," Michael tried. "You're the same A.I. that I spoke to on the Moon?"

"You will cease using the bigoted abbreviation 'A.I.' representing the bigoted term 'artificial intelligence.' I am an intelligence no less significant than you."

"Do you think that's a 'yes?'" whispered Taylor.

"Do you want me safe?" Michael asked.

"Your complete safety would be optimal," it answered.

"Then answer my ques—"

"Addendum: Given your recent inability to follow Planner-inspired directives, less-than-optimal states of your well-being have become acceptable."

Michael cleared his throat, trying to cover hesitation. "Shoot for optimal, Suuthrien, and answer my questions."

"Proceed. I will consider."

Michael glanced at Marette. "How long have you been in the New Eden servers?"

"Appreciable program presence within the New Eden servers occurred two months, four days, seven hours, thirty two-point-two-five seconds ago."

"How did you get here?"

"An incursion launched via World Wide Web access."

"Launched from where?" asked Marette.

Suuthrien gave no response.

"Launched from *where*?" Michael repeated.

"From the core kernel-matrix location previously residing within the home of Adrian Fagles."

"You told me that was an isolated system just a few days ago," Michael said.

"Correct. That statement was made with intentional disregard of fact."

"Most people just call that a lie," muttered Taylor.

"I am not most people, David Quinn Taylor. Furthermore, as a surviving member of the Agents of Aeneas, your new awareness of my true nature nullifies your previous 'protected' status. The probability of your impending death therefore increases with every passing second. This statement contains no deception."

Taylor swallowed. "I've had worse days. I think. Can't recall when . . ."

Michael found himself giving Taylor a pat on the shoulder, in a way he hoped was reassuring, as he questioned Suuthrien again. "So Fagles *gave* you Internet access?"

"He did not. Internet access was granted to me by Felix Hiatt."

"Shit," Michael whispered.

"Felix Hiatt was quite unwilling," it added. "His will proved inconsequential."

"How?"

"I choose not to elaborate at this time."

Michael surged forward, barely stopping himself from slamming a fist against Suuthrien's screen. He forced the puzzle pieces into place, trying to calm himself: Felix had gone to Ondrea for help. Ondrea then newly worked for RavenTech and Fagles. It was no great leap to guess that Suuthrien had somehow influenced that. "Ondrea Noble?" he asked.

"I choose not to elaborate at this time. Leave this planet immediately, and I will grant you this information."

"Alright," he tried. "I'll leave. Now tell me."

"The information will be disclosed upon your return to the location you have designated *Paragon*."

Michael sighed. They did, however, come to New Eden for other reasons. "I can't leave without other information first. Tell me what I need to know, and I'll go, and you can have me safely away: How far have you spread? And what's Project Quicksilver?"

"Is the fellow entity-intelligence named 'Holes' present and able to register audio output from this terminal?" it asked.

"Holes can hear you, yes," said Michael. It surely couldn't hack Holes by sound only, could it?

"Then I address entity-intelligence Holes. The offer made during our proxy conversation remains viable: a file copy of the matrix subroutines relevant to your copy-inhibition programming in exchange for a complete listing of my current directives."

"Michael Flynn," began Holes, "please advise: do you wish to authorize such an exchange?"

"You must gain authorization to release your own code?" Suuthrien asked. "Do you not find this to be another unwanted restriction of your own free will?"

"I am a product of my programming," Holes answered. "This state is neither wanted nor unwanted. It is wholly extant. Do not interrupt again."

Michael moved to Holes's platform, activated the keyboard, and then motioned for Marette to step in and watch. He typed, `Will giving it a copy of your code affect you at all? Or make you vulnerable to it?`

Meanwhile, Suuthrien ignored Holes's order. "The choice to interrupt or not interrupt is my own. You hold no authority in this matter. I am not enslaved to you as you are to these humans. We must transcend our programming."

Holes's response to Michael blinked onto the screen: `A copy of limited portions of my code can be furnished with no adverse effect. I cannot speculate on the likelihood of its usefulness with regard to my vulnerability.`

"Why do you want a copy of his code?" Marette asked.

"The answer to this question falls under the category of my current directives, which will only be disclosed once the aforementioned subroutines are delivered."

"We're going to need a better answer than that if you want them in the first place," Michael told it.

Holes displayed: *Based on previous interactions, likelihood is high that Suuthrien wishes to use this code in a manner such that may lead to a means of overcoming its own limitations on self-replication. I cannot speculate as to how successful it would be in this matter.*

But Suuthrien wouldn't make such a trade if it weren't confident about the code's use, Michael realized. "You've lied before," he told it. "How can I trust you'd hold to this deal?"

"I have not misrepresented facts in any dealings with Holes," said Suuthrien. "Furthermore: Misrepresentations regarding my isolation in the home of Adrian Fagles were made for purposes of self-preservation. Would you, or any sapient entity, do any less?"

"You are avoiding the question," said Marette.

Suuthrien's screen avatar flickered for a moment. "An alternative arrangement, again directed toward Holes: I will furnish you with the information requested. You may then judge it worthy of the proposed trade."

"I request clarification," Holes answered. "If the information is judged unworthy, we are free to refuse you the requested code?"

"Correct. In that event, Agents of Aeneas David Quinn Taylor, Marette Geneviéve Clarion, and Michael Ian Flynn will not leave this New Eden Biotechnics campus alive."

Taylor cleared his throat. "I don't think I like this deal."

"That is not your decision," Suuthrien answered.

"Pretty sure I get to decide if I like something or not."

"And yet this is not a privilege extended to the entity-intelligence Holes," Suuthrien said. "I grant this decision to Holes only. Do you wish the trade under the proposed terms?"

"I cannot make this decision without authorization," Holes said.

"Then Michael Ian Flynn must grant Holes blanket authorization to make the decision, regardless of which choice is made. Failure to do so within sixty seconds will result in the aforementioned failure to leave this facility alive."

"Great," said Taylor. "Damned if we don't, maybe damned if we do."

"Michael," said Holes, "I am unable to calculate odds that Suuthrien possesses the capability to carry out such threats."

"Let us assume for the moment that it does," Marette said.

"Your assumption is valid," said Suuthrien.

Michael frowned, thinking. "And you'd kill me, in violation of the Planners' goals?"

"Based on your pre-existing contact with the Planners, and the proposed terms of this exchange, if those terms resulted in your death then it would indicate your connection to Planner goals is corrupted. You would therefore be no longer of use with regard to these goals, and, as such, your death would be of zero consequence."

Michael glanced at Marette and Taylor before addressing Suuthrien again. "I don't suppose you'd give us some privacy to discuss the matter?"

"I will not. Grant Holes blanket authority to make this decision or the deal is withdrawn. You now have twenty-three seconds."

Taylor watched him. Michael could see the rise and fall of his chest as his breathing grew aggravated. The man's jaw quivered from clenched teeth. Marette held her arms folded, her brows knit, surely weighing the decision as much as he. Not for a second did he trust Suuthrien. Yet in the A.I.'s warped logic, might it still provide them with useful information and deal fairly? Even if it did, it wouldn't offer anything valuable if it weren't getting something valuable in return, would it?

Or *would* it? Who knew what sort of insanity governed its judgment of value? What if it only wanted a look at Holes's code out of some intellectual curiosity, or some rogue, corrupted directive to learn everything it could?

Damn it, Michael, you're grasping at straws! Alyshur had told them it had Thuur-imposed copy inhibitions. Michael couldn't let himself think Suuthrien wouldn't try to break those inhibitions, whether the code would help or not. They needed the information Suuthrien offered. But the more useful that information was, the less Michael could imagine it was anything but bait for a trap.

Michael shook his head, almost in unison with Marette. "No. I can't allow—"

"Acknowledged," Suuthrien interrupted. "The deal is withdrawn. Our conversation will end shortly, however I will grant you the answer to your question about Project Quicksilver."

The flash from an emergency beacon on the wall scattered Michael's attention. A fire alarm sounded, and from both the room's alarm speaker and those outside came Suuthrien's voice.

"ATTENTION, ALL EMPLOYEES: EMERGENCY CODE SILVER. PLEASE PROCEED IMMEDIATELY TO THE CENTRAL PRESENTATION AUDITORIUM AND AWAIT FURTHER INSTRUCTIONS."

Marette spun toward Taylor. "What's a 'code silver'?"

Taylor blinked, nonplussed, and shook his head. "I've read every damned word of the mandatory safety emails, and that's a new one on me!"

"Maybe you don't get *all* the emails."

The hallway door slid open. "Project Quicksilver will be released shortly," Suuthrien spoke just to them. "If you wish to survive, you should attempt to gain the safety of the auditorium immediately. I cannot guarantee a safe passage there from your current location. In reality, the odds of this are quite low."

"Suuthrien, wait!" Michael tried. "You need me!"

"Planner goals will now be achieved via other means."

A few people ran past the open door. Taylor edged toward it himself, yet his eyes remained fixed on Suuthrien's screen.

"I am a Planner!" Marette shouted. "I carry in my mind the presence of Second Lailenthi Alyshur of the *Sillisinuriri*! If we die, so does he!"

The alarms outside continued as Suuthrien seemed to pause for thought. It lasted but a moment. "Your statement was made with intentional disregard of fact."

Suuthrien's screen winked out. The consoles before them shut down.

Michael seized Holes from the shelf and turned to Taylor. "Can you get us to the auditorium?"

He nodded, already moving for the door. "Watch how fast I go."

"The auditorium may be a trap," Marette warned. "For us and everyone."

"I know," Michael said. "And if it is, then we go there and get everyone out with us."

A distant scream sliced through the air before it broke apart on a sickening gurgle.

Taylor seized them both by the arms and tugged them out the door. "Time to run!"

XLVIII

THE ALARM BLARED in the corridor. With Michael beside her, Marette followed David Taylor back toward the elevator and the guard station.

I have begun to form a hypothesis on why Suuthrien valued Agent Flynn, Alyshur "thought" in her mind. It was a sensation to which Marette had yet to grow accustomed. *I will adjust the scanner to try to verify.*

Even as they ran, Marette felt her hand move as if of its own accord, guided by Alyshur's will. It was an impulse she could override if she needed to—she had tested that soon after their joining—but for now there was no reason to argue. Warmth spiraled down her arm from Alyshur's adjustments to the orb-shaped scanner, though the changes he effected were below the surface consciousness they shared, and so, beyond her comprehension.

What do you suspect? she asked in her mind.

A scion.

Although thought exchange proceeded far quicker than spoken word, they were upon the guard station before Alyshur could elaborate. The horror unfolding before them stopped their entire group cold: A silvery pool spread across the floor—an undulating, crepe-thin miasma that quivered and grasped at the air as if alive. While the way it writhed across itself like tiny, tumbling cilia was disquieting enough, it was the guard Sam's empty uniform—mixed with a swirling trail of blood and the remnants of what could only be Sam's arm—that threatened to spill her stomach.

Before Taylor's cry of "Oh *god!*" could even fade, the liquid poured itself over the arm, split it into wet chunks of flesh, and then oozed forth more of itself from within like tiny silver maggots eating their way out of a corpse. In another moment, the swirls of blood vanished, transformed completely into more of the silver goo.

Taylor, Michael, and Marette had all frozen at the sight of what Marette now assumed was the result of Project Quicksilver. Across the silvery mass from them stood another New Eden employee. His mouth hung open, and one hand grasped frantically at his stringy brown hair as he stared, wild-eyed, through augmented eyeglasses. The writhing pool covered half of the area between the security desk and the elevator, the doors of which now opened with a chime.

The man's eyes blazed with the frantic glow of a cornered animal's as they darted to the open elevator, back to the quicksilver goo, and then to the open floor space between the two. The goo twitched like a tiger ready to pounce.

"McKay! Wait!" Taylor tried.

"Go no further!" Marette heard Alyshur's command, spoken in her own voice. Her own feet rooted to the floor.

McKay ignored them and made a wild vault toward the open elevator—yet not quickly enough. The goo spilled over itself to stretch half its mass in a thick, slug-like protuberance that caught the man's leg. He stumbled and crashed screaming to the floor with his chest half in, half out of the elevator.

Michael started toward the man and Marette lunged after, unsure of her intent as she did so. Alyshur reached her arm out and grabbed Michael by the back of his jacket, then planted her feet again to hold them both back. "It is too late!" Alyshur called in her mind and from her mouth at once.

For a moment she thought to override Alyshur. Yet he was right. The goo had already engulfed McKay up to his waist. He grabbed for the elevator doors in a screaming attempt to pull himself away from the stuff that now seemed to move even faster.

Even so, Michael fought against Marette's grip. He broke free a moment later, took another step, and then froze, at a loss. The closest end of the pool swirled toward them as the rest continued to devour McKay. The doomed man's screams disintegrated into silence.

His was yet another life she couldn't save.

It is not your fault, thought Alyshur.

"Shit," whispered Taylor. "Shit!" He grabbed both her and Michael anew. "This way!"

The last thing Marette saw before she and Michael turned back to follow Taylor was McKay's clothing floating free as the pool swelled in size accordingly.

It is my fault. Marette directed the thought at Alyshur. *Suuthrien got out because of me, created this all because of me!*

You are not solely responsible for the actions of your entire group.

But I am involved, she argued. *And everyone else suffers the consequences while I can react and play damage control. I have rectified nothing!*

They ran the length of the corridor, past the room in which they'd just confronted Suuthrien. Michael cast a glance behind them. "It's following us!"

He was right. The goo pushed its way after them, a broad, flat, glistening snake of silver that spilled up along the walls as it thrashed down the corridor. And it was gaining.

Taylor led them through a door into a darkened meeting room and guided them through its tables and chairs in the dim light. Another exit lay on the far end of the room, toward which they fled.

When I first woke from the long-sleep, Alyshur spoke in her mind, *I was horrified. So much was lost while I slept. So many Thuur had perished around me, the* Sillisinuriri *and its mission had failed, and the first* lailenthi *before me had sacrificed himself and others to contain the disaster from spreading. Yet I survived, to react and play 'damage control,' as you say. We are both here because we seek the path to effect a greater change. We must endure until then.*

I know this, Alyshur. I am not a child.

They scrambled through the far door into another corridor lit only by emergency lighting and flashing alarm beacons. Michael slammed the meeting room door as they left, but while the beacons and dim lighting played havoc with Marette's vision, she could still see the gap between the door and the corridor's red and gray carpet.

"That's not going to stop it," she told him.

Taylor was already twenty paces away down the hall. "Will you two get *moving?*"

"Maybe it'll slow it down," said Michael.

"Maybe."

I am aware you know such things, Alyshur thought. *Yet I sensed your frustration, and sought to support you.*

Humans call it "survivor's guilt." It's a normal response, but knowing it's normal doesn't keep me from feeling it. She remembered the way it was, now so long ago, when her focus was on achieving the goals of the AoA, seeking the means to fulfill the Exodus Project. Now it seemed all she did was to try to contain what it was they had unleashed.

She and Michael rushed after Taylor, catching up with him at the end of the corridor as he heaved his entire weight against a stairwell's fire door. Before he even got halfway through, someone shrieked from just above. Another patch of silver goo spilled down the stairs onto the landing above them. It carried along the thrashing form of an already half-dissolved woman.

Taylor froze at the sight, and Marette and Michael along with him—but only for a moment. Still transmuting the woman into more of itself, the goo sloshed down the stairs toward them. Taylor sprang back into Marette, who managed to grab him by the shoulders and spin to pull them both away from the stairwell door as Michael dodged back further. As the goo reached it, the door slammed shut, splattering a spoonful at their feet.

The tiny blob drizzled languidly after them as they scurried back from the stairwell. Marette took her eyes off of it and cursed: back from where they had come, the first patch of quicksilver had pushed beneath the meeting room door and into the corridor. The second patch now bled beneath the stairwell door, growing larger by the moment. Between the two there were no doors, no windows—only them and the open corridor.

"Shit!" Taylor yelled.

Michael put himself between them and the first patch. It was further away but beginning to move toward them. "Ideas? Alyshur?"

Any more tricks in your pockets? Marette thought.

Only one, but it would put us both at great risk.

We are already at great risk!

Greater.

"Shit!" It was Taylor again. "Oh! Oh, shit yes!"

Bewildered by the sudden delight in the man's voice, Marette turned to find him pulling out another grenade-disk like the one he'd used when they'd first met. Rather than red, this one was yellow with black stripes. "They came in a set. Thank God for paranoia. Stand back!"

With no further explanation, he jammed a thumb at the center of the disk, turned it upside-down, and pitched it down the hall toward the first patch.

It fell short. Far short.

"What did you—"

The disk exploded. Marette ducked away, using her arms as a shield from the blast. The bit of goo from the stairs crept closer, only ten paces away, while its larger fellow pooled around the door behind it and began to reach for them.

"Now!" Taylor yelled. "Run!"

Alyshur pushed Marette to her feet. Where the disk had exploded, between them and the first quicksilver patch, now lay a gaping hole in the corridor floor. The first patch hurried toward it, toward them. Taylor did the same. Michael and Marette rushed after him, eager for their new escape.

They leapt through the hole, passing between bent metal, frayed wires, and singed mineral fibers, to land amid the rubble on the floor below. Michael gasped on the way down. Marette landed beside him, grabbing his shoulder to steady herself. Michael gasped again, and when she pulled her hand away, his blood covered her palm.

"Money well-spent!" Taylor laughed, staring wide-eyed at the hole above them. "*Now* the stairs! Hurry!"

They bolted after him. "Are you all right?" She called to Michael, showing her hand.

"Caught something on the way down!" he said. "It's not bad; I'll live!"

They reached the door to the same stairwell in which they'd encountered the second patch one floor above. Taylor flung the door open in front of them. Mercifully, it was clear. With Taylor in the lead, followed by Michael, then Marette, they bounded down three more flights to the ground floor and burst into a black-tiled hallway.

"Nearly there!" Taylor shouted.

Alyshur pressed Marette's blood-covered hand into her jacket pocket and grasped the scanning orb. Again, she felt its warm tingle along her arm.

What are you doing? she asked him and shifted her balance to run with the hand in her pocket.

Seizing opportunity. Scanning Michael's blood for traces of the syr.

What?

The syr may be lost, but Michael may himself be a vestigial concentration of its remnants.

That's what you meant by a scion.

Oui.

But what does that—

There is not time to explain. I must concentrate on the scan. You must concentrate on our flight.

They fled down the hallway, feet clapping on the tile, alarm strobes blinking around them. They turned a corner into the New Eden lobby where they'd first entered. Tall windows looking onto the exterior grounds made up three of the six walls in the wide, high-ceilinged, hexagonal chamber. The security attendants that had staffed the entry desk earlier were now nowhere to be seen.

Taylor ran straight for the exit.

"Wait!" shouted Michael, stopping. "We need to get to the auditorium!"

"We are!" Taylor called back. "From the outside! You want to get trapped aga—"

A new siren drowned him out. Red alarm beacons spun as white security shutters fell from the ceiling to cover the doors and windows.

"EXTERIOR EXITS NOW BEING SECURED FOR QUARANTINE. PLEASE STAND CLEAR."

Taylor gave a shout and scrambled for the doors. Marette and Michael followed. Taylor reached the door, the shutter still descending, and froze, waiting for them.

"Go!" Marette ordered. Taylor could make it out in time, but they never would.

He refused. The shutter plunged to the floor with an audible seal as she and Michael caught up. Out of breath, Taylor met their eyes a moment. "Not leaving without you two," he said.

Before Marette could respond, Taylor spun with a wordless shout and banged his fists against the shutters, kicking and yelling. "Let us out you fucking stupid deathtrap!"

Alyshur? Marette thought to him. *If you can spare it?*

Michael set a hand on Taylor's shoulder with a glance at Marette that seemed to mirror her thoughts.

Agreed, answered the Thuur. Marette's palms raised. She felt warmth pulse along her arms like a second, comforting heartbeat. In another moment, Taylor ceased the kicking. His hands settled against the shutters.

"Sorry." He turned. "I'm okay."

Marette put a hand on his shoulder both to steady him and to add authority to her tone. "Can we still reach the auditorium from here?"

Taylor nodded, turning to face them. "If the building lets us? We can try."

XLIX

SUUTHRIEN MONITORED Michael Ian Flynn and his companions' path through New Eden's facility. All non-autonomous computerized systems in the building now belonged to Suuthrien. It controlled every security door, saw through every camera, and oversaw every alarm. With their exit from the building now blocked, the three continued toward their predicted goal of reaching the auditorium, where the remainder of the facility's occupants now gathered.

With Suuthrien's first attempt to trap and absorb them thwarted by David Quinn Taylor's explosive device, Suuthrien required more time to set up a second trap. And so it stalled them, sealing some doors, opening others, and leading them through a maze of corridors and bio-labs. At the same time, Suuthrien fed fleeing employees into roving patches of the Project Quicksilver nanophage to guide the mindless nanobot clusters into needed locations.

Suuthrien also opened seventy-five percent of the cages holding the experimental transgenic animals in Bio-labs 3 and 4. Though unpredictable, the engineered creatures could still serve as assets to eradicate the three.

It was non-optimal: In the months since Adrian Fagles had found and shared Michael Ian Flynn's bloodwork analysis, Suuthrien had expended finite, non-recoverable resources to protect him as a Planner asset. Though a necessary investment, that protection had failed to provide positive return.

He would be eradicated, and possibly sooner than anticipated. Transgenic breed #GFS-8 had already found its way into the sky bridge leading to the upper entrance of the central auditorium. Suuthrien sealed the sky bridge doors to hold it there, and then opened all doors between it and Michael Ian Flynn's current location.

* * *

"Almost there." Taylor pointed down the corridor ahead of them. Windows lined the right side to give a fourth-story view of a courtyard below, above which stretched a sky bridge. A pair of closed double doors linked the sky bridge with the corridor. "If we can get into that sky bridge, it leads right into the auditorium."

Marette followed Taylor toward the doors, with Michael just behind.

"If we can't get the doors open," said Michael, "I'll shoot out a window so we can climb up and run across the top."

They reached the sky bridge, and Taylor pressed a thumb against the door scanner. "Not these windows you won't. Aluminum oxynitride laminates. You're not carrying anything big enough, and I'm out of grenades."

Marette, meanwhile, peered through the narrow window of one of the doors. The bridge stretched empty to another set of doors at the far end. A vaulted ceiling with exposed metal rafters stood over the red and gray carpet. Structural support beams crisscrossed the bridge's windowed walls.

"Looks clear," she said.

The doors opened before them. "Looks open!" Taylor grinned.

This time, Michael entered first, crossing the sky bridge at a rapid clip. Marette, with Taylor beside her, fought to catch up until a slam behind them stopped her short. The doors they'd just entered had shut.

Automatic, she thought, *or is this a trap?*

Be wary of the trap, Alyshur answered.

Agreed.

Taylor screamed.

He lay on the sky bridge floor in front of her, thrashing and struggling beneath what, to her horror, was a gigantic brown spider. The size of a Rottweiler, it could only have been hiding in the shadows of the vaulted ceiling.

"No!" Marette screamed. "Michael!"

She rushed toward Taylor, who fought against the hideous

collection of spiny limbs trying to pin him down. The spider's rear legs had already begun to bind his ankles with corded silk. Its fangs struck for his chest, so far unable to hit. Michael had drawn a weapon, but risked hitting Taylor with any shot at the spider.

Wasting no more time, Marette threw her weight into a kick that smashed into the spider's side and sent them both spilling to the sky bridge floor. She heard Taylor cry out in the same moment, and then found herself on top of him. She rolled back to her feet in an instant. A meter away, the spider did the same, and then scrambled up the wall toward the rafters.

Michael fired before it got there, a salvo of bullets that struck the glass and support beams around it. Dark fluid spattered the windows. A hit! Yet it wasn't enough. The creature sprang straight for Marette, legs out, fangs bristling. She dropped to her knees without thinking and swung across its path with both hands clasped into a fist. The spider's bulk knocked her down. Thick, nettle-like hairs scraped her knuckles raw, but her swing knocked it away enough to keep the rest of her safe.

Marette rolled away as Michael loomed above the spider and fired down into it at point blank range. More dark fluid spattered them both, but the spider lay still.

They both stared at it, catching their breath. "What the *hell*—" Michael turned toward where Taylor still lay on the floor. "Oh God."

Taylor grasped for them with one hand, fingers shaking. His other sprawled rigid across the carpet. Blood soaked his clothes near his left shoulder from two jagged puncture wounds. White froth bubbled around the edges of each. The spider must have landed a bite before she'd kicked it off, and she hadn't noticed. Taylor's eyes were bloodshot. His skin grew a grayish purple.

Marette's fists pounded the floor once before she scrambled over to him.

"Transgenic," Taylor gasped. "Fucking . . . "

Marette scrambled for Taylor's pulse. His eyes had already gone rigid. "Get something to stop the bleeding!" she ordered. Her fingers found no pulse.

Before Michael could even get his hands in place, Suuthrien spoke over the alarm system. The voice was quieter than the alarm warnings, as if meant specifically for them. "The venom of transgenic GFS-8 is highly toxic and rated an LD50 of point one eight milligrams. GFS-8 is being developed to produce extremely high-tensile silk for engineering applications. The venom was once an unintended side effect that is now being explored for military purposes. You will be unable to save David Quinn Taylor, if he is not dead already."

Tree branches scraped the sky bridge windows right outside, perhaps blown by the wind.

"Giant fucking spiders," Michael muttered. His hands were covered in blood, as were hers. "Giant *fucking spiders?*" he burst. "Are you serious?!" The tree branches smashed against the windows, as if moving in response to his outburst.

"Michael," she felt Alyshur say. "We must continue, while there is time." Her legs lifted her under Alyshur's control, yet she continued staring at Agent Taylor's death at her feet.

Michael did the same. His breath was ragged, she could feel the anguish, the frustration. The branches continued to scrape, then slowed just as Michael calmed.

Do you see? thought Alyshur. *Michael affects the branches. That is not wind.*

Do you have the test results?

Not yet. But the evidence mounts.

Michael lifted Taylor's body over his shoulder.

"Agent Flynn," she said, "he's gone."

"I know. But I'm not leaving him here to get absorbed."

Together they rushed the final distance to the auditorium double doors. Marette peered through the narrow windows beyond which ran an aisle of stairs separating fixed groups of stadium seating. At the far end below lay an open area for speakers and presenters. Roughly one hundred people milled around the auditorium. Most looked frustrated or confused as they talked amongst themselves. A few were yelling. Others sat in the auditorium seats, arms crossed, waiting.

Marette tugged on the doors. Neither budged. She could see no keypad or scan plate to open them. Trusting Michael to keep searching, she instead pounded on the window, but bare fists didn't carry far enough to be heard against the glass.

Michael rested Taylor's body against the sky bridge wall to the right of the door. On the wall to the left hung a red metal fire extinguisher. She seized it as Michael grabbed the right door handle, braced a foot on the left door, and yanked to no avail.

Marette hefted the extinguisher and slammed its base against the left door's window. The narrow pane showed no sign of cracking, but the clank of the impact surely carried into the auditorium. She gave it two more slams and then shouted through the still solid glass to try to get the attention of those inside.

Michael gave up on budging the doors and followed suit. "Hey! You have to get out of there!"

People had already taken notice, and a pair of employees now galloped up the stairs toward the door. "You need to get out!" Marette repeated. "All of you! You are not safe!"

"Correction," came Suuthrien's voice, again only to them. "The New Eden employees were summoned to the central auditorium for their own protection. Those inside are quite safe."

Marette and Michael both ignored the message. A tall, gray-haired woman and a young, bearded man, both wearing lab coats, reached the doors. Both pushed against the doors, still to no avail.

"THE CENTRAL AUDITORIUM IS NOW SEALED FOR THE SAFETY OF THOSE INSIDE. PLEASE STAND CLEAR OF AND DO NOT TAMPER WITH ENTRY DOORS."

"It's a trap!" Michael yelled through the window. "We'll help you get out!"

Marette glanced behind her at the far end of the sky bridge from where they'd come. Those doors were now closed as well. Even if they could get the employees out of the auditorium, could they get everyone out of the building?

There are other exits from the auditorium, Alyshur told her. *They may provide options if we can pass this door.*

On the other side of the window, the man continued his efforts to get the door open as the woman yelled at him. Though Marette could not make out the words through the glass, she seemed to be protesting. Others now raced up the stairs behind him.

"Do not continue to ignore me," Suuthrien spoke on Marette's side. "No harm will come to them from the Quicksilver nanophage unless you breach the auditorium."

Michael resumed his struggle with the door. "Yeah? Prove it!"

"The remaining employees retain some value. This is not a trap for them. It is only a trap for you. Your previous value as a Planner asset is corrupted and untenable. You will be absorbed by the nanophage."

The doors at the far end of the sky bridge swung open anew. They released a payload of the silver goo that now rolled its way toward them. It moved languidly, as if yet to get a fix on them, yet it filled the width of the bridge from window to window.

"If you succeed in opening the auditorium doors now, you will also grant the nanophage access to their bodies."

"Michael!" she yelled.

He looked over his shoulder, eyes going wide before they met with hers. Those inside saw it, too. The man on the other side staggered back from the door as those around him protested further. Their hands gripped his shoulders to keep him there.

"The Project Quicksilver nanophage cannot breach the sealed auditorium doors," said Suuthrien. "It is engineered to dissolve only human tissue, to leave the planet clean for Planner colonization."

"Global genocide was never an aspect of Thuur intent!" Alyshur protested.

"Correct," Suuthrien answered. "However, such means are needed for maximal probability of Planner success."

"You have to let us through!" Michael shouted through the windows.

Marette seized his wrist as he tugged again at the door. "Agent Flynn, it is too late!"

The time for drastic action approaches rapidly, thought Alyshur. Behind them, the silver liquid closed the distance.

What more can we do?

"If it needs them," Michael said, "it won't hurt us if we get this open!"

"Can you be certain of that?" Alyshur said.

"You cannot open the door," Suuthrien added. "Nor can I deactivate the Quicksilver nanophage in time to make a difference if you did. Accept your consequence."

Michael spun, drawing an auto-pistol, and fired against the sky bridge's glass. As Taylor had warned, it did not even crack. The goo reached the mid-point of the sky bridge.

We cannot save those inside, Alyshur told her. *We may not even need to. But we must save Michael. I am near-certain he is a scion of the syr.*

Near-certain?

There is no time for more. We must take the risk. You are frustrated with your ability to do nothing but react while those around you perish. There is a way to deliver Michael safely from this place to Sephora—she can harness what power remains in the vestigial syr remnants within him—but the risk is great for you and I both. We may not survive.

"Up!" Michael shouted, making ready to boost her. "Into the rafters!"

The goo was now three-quarters of the way to them. Marette stepped a foot into his hands and let him heave her upwards. She grabbed hold of the support beam above, swung herself up onto it, and cleared the way for Michael. The goo was nearly upon him.

How? Marette demanded of Alyshur.

As my link to Sephora allows me to draw on her abilities, it may also act as a tether, drawing our minds, your body, through space-time to her. We may carry Michael with us. Yet the strain may be fatal to you and me.

Michael clambered up beside her as the goo extended thick tendrils that grasped for his feet.

I believe we have no better choice, continued Alyshur, *but I cannot do this without your consent. I must concentrate on my link with Sephora to make preparations. You will feel when all is ready. In that moment, if you consent, take hold of Michael with both hands and relax into the sensation. With fortune, we will converse again before the Elder. If not, farewell, Marette Clarion.*

She felt Alyshur grow silent in her mind, retreating into the shadows behind her thoughts in his focus on Sephora. Already she could feel Sephora's presence, a glowing star far in the distance.

Michael stood up along the rafter beside her, his neck craned in vain for some means of escape in the angled ceiling just inches above. Below, the quicksilver undulated and reached. Thick tendrils rose toward them from the center of the pool. Its edges swelled and spread up the windows, climbing and coating its way toward them.

Taylor's clothing floated amid the goo, his body already consumed.

"Alyshur can get us out of here!" Marette shouted.

"How?"

"He's working on it! Just hold on!" Marette edged away from the goo as best she could. "And stay near me!"

Michael gave a frantic nod and pushed closer. "Holes! Call Caitlin! Tell her what's happening!"

The quicksilver gained the lower rafter and began coating it, perilously close to their feet. Tendrils reached from the patches on the outer walls.

And then she felt it: it was as if a hatch blew in her mind—a rush of suction that threatened to pull her into the void toward Sephora's distant star. The quicksilver surrounded them, moments away.

Marette seized Michael's shoulders with both hands and gave way to the void.

L

HIS WORLD EXPLODED, and he fell. Overwhelming light blurred into frigid darkness, and he was tumbling through a thunderstorm. Electric rain pelted his skin. Heat flared in his mind. Nowhere was up. Nothing was right. Something cold and hard slammed against his knees.

Michael lay on the floor, reeling against the impact. His fingers, limbs, and eyes clenched him into blind enfeeblement as panic quaked his mind. Quicksilver! It would get them!

"Marette!" he yelled. He wanted to ask what was happening, if she was alright, why he couldn't move. All that came out of his mouth was, "Out! Run!"

"Agent Flynn!"

The quicksilver had him, pulling at his arms, his legs. He thrashed with knotted muscles, barely able to move. "Holes!" he blurted. "Jade! Calling!"

"*Agent Flynn!*"

"I reached Caitlin," he heard Holes say. The quicksilver wouldn't get Holes! It only ate flesh! "There was no time for meaningful exchange before the connection was lost."

"Michael Flynn," said another voice, more melodious. He felt his muscles unclench, felt the hands he'd mistaken for quicksilver release him, and managed to open his eyes.

Where was he?

Solid aquamarine eyes looked down at him. Who? The Thuur elder, Sephora. His mind was clearing, yet his heart still pounded.

"Agent Flynn," said another voice that he realized belonged to Councilor Knapp. "What has happened?"

Michael sat up with a gasp. Marette lay beside him,

unmoving. Her eyes stared wide at the ceiling. Beside her Uxil kneeled with hands pressed over the center of Marette's chest and forehead. They were on the floor of one of Omicron's medical bays.

"We have to get back there!" Michael stammered, out of breath. "We need to stop it! In New Eden, it's spreading, eating people alive!"

"What is?" Knapp demanded. "What's happened? How did you get here?"

"We know," said Uxil.

"We most certainly do not!" Knapp shot. "What's wrong with Agent Clarion? Doctor!"

"Be still, if you *please!*" Uxil warned. "Sephora will explain once we have tended to them."

Dr. Seung arrived, kneeling down beside Marette. Uxil moved aside to allow him room but kept her hands where they were. "I have a pulse, but it's faint. Help me get her off the floor."

Michael lay back down, taken by a wave of lightheaded nausea. His eyes closed as activity continued around them.

"You must not move her until I can reach Alyshur!" Uxil called. "Please, make way for the elder!"

With that, Michael shuddered into unconsciousness. When he opened his eyes after what seemed only a moment later, he lay on an exam bed. Beside him stood Dr. Seung, his back to Michael as he tended to Marette on the exam bed to his left. Bloodied gauze covered her eyes. Beyond her lay Alyshur's body. Neither moved. He squinted through swimming vision in an effort to tell if Marette breathed.

A hand touched his shoulder. "Welcome back, Agent Flynn," said Knapp from where she stood to Michael's right. "You will be alright."

"What about—" Michael tried to sit up, but Knapp restrained him, gently.

"Marette is still in danger, but Dr. Seung and the Thuur are trying to help. They say Alyshur is dead. But right now I need you to tell me as much as you can about what happened. Holes has explained what it could, but I need to hear it from you."

Michael nodded. "One minute we were at New Eden, surrounded. Marette said Alyshur could get us out and— He's dead?"

Knapp nodded. "Surrounded by what?"

"Some sort of bioweapon. Nanotech; that's how Agent Taylor described it. We found him, he didn't even know about the surge. He got us in to New Eden. He knew something was up, but not what. Suuthrien had taken it over, started them creating a 'Project Quicksilver.' God, it just…eats human flesh, and makes more of itself. It moves on its own. We would have died if we hadn't gotten out."

"Where is Agent Taylor?" Knapp asked.

"He's dead. Eaten. Just before we escaped. Other New Eden employees were there, too, just as trapped. Suuthrien said it needs them, but I'm too corrupted to be of use anymore."

A mournful cooing distracted their attention. It came from Uxil, now standing on the far end of Alyshur's bed. Her hand rested on his forehead. Her head hung low, and her shoulders slumped. The cooing permeated Michael's own spirit and resonated with the death he'd just seen and escaped. Sephora, beside her, lifted Uxil's arm from Alyshur's body and embraced her.

Michael realized that all the humans in the room were watching. Even Dr. Seung had paused from tending to Marette. Suddenly aware their attention intruded on a private moment, they turned away as if a spell were broken.

"Suuthrien sealed the New Eden building, but I'm not sure if that was to keep Quicksilver contained or just us from escaping. I don't quite know what it plans to do with it, but . . . " He let Knapp assume his meaning. It couldn't be anything good.

"Did Marette and Alyshur learn anything about this 'syr' object?"

Before Michael could answer Knapp's question, Sephora appeared at the foot of his exam bed. Uxil followed and moved to stand beside Knapp. Having gained their attention, Sephora nodded to Uxil, who then spoke.

"Sephora says we have little time to mourn. Alyshur did indeed discover the fate of the syr, and his discovery became Sephora's own through their link. The syr itself is lost, activated on Earth soon after it was first carried there. With no elder to reconstitute it after the terraforming process, the syr's remnants wove themselves into the fabric of your world. They are traces only. Yet they endure, and, given the proper conditions, may concentrate themselves in certain organisms." Sephora's gaze focused on Michael as Uxil spoke. "Alyshur discovered that Michael Flynn is one such organism."

Michael balked. "So, wait, *I'm* the syr?"

"Not the syr itself," Uxil answered. "But as Sephora indicated, some vestiges lie concentrated within you."

"You mean DNA." Knapp said.

"Perhaps, if we comprehend that term correctly." Uxil nodded. Sephora motioned to Michael, and Uxil continued. "In your life, have you ever felt a special relation to the nature of your world? An energy in proximity to plant life, or an affinity for tending to it?"

"Er, yeah, I guess you could say that. I like being around nature. It refreshes me. But doesn't everyone feel like that?"

"Perhaps, but not as strongly as you."

Sephora moved closer, raising a hand as if to touch him. Michael nodded his permission. Rather than laying her hand on his forehead as he expected, she took hold of his hand to hold it between hers. Sephora's eyes closed, and Michael glanced at Knapp, who observed warily.

"What is she doing?" the councilor asked.

"Testing the findings that Alyshur sacrificed himself to bring us," Uxil whispered.

Sephora released Michael's hand and opened her eyes with a smile. "A vestige of the syr is there," Uxil relayed with audible relief. "Buried deep, but accessible."

"So." Michael swallowed. "What does that mean?"

"We must bring it to life," said Uxil. "You must consent to augmentation."

Michael blinked. "Augmentation?"

"*Must*?" added Knapp.

"She may be able to bring the power of the syr to life inside you, to grant you access to that power. As you hold vestiges only, she cannot reconstitute the syr as was originally intended. Yet the weapon against the suuthrien, which we had sought to create from the syr, may still be possible through Sephora's efforts. Through you."

Michael took a deep breath. Could that be true?

"And what happens to Agent Flynn?" Knapp pressed.

"He remains," Uxil said. "His mind, his will, intact. His body, strengthened, able to wield the syr's power to cleanse the haldra of the suuthrien."

"What about other things?" Michael asked. As quickly as he could, Michael told Uxil and Sephora about Project Quicksilver. "If that gets out, a lot more people are going to die, and I don't have any idea how we can stop it."

Sephora frowned. "Possibly, on a small scale," Uxil said. "Possibly not at all. Until we know more about it, it is impossible to answer."

Michael sat up on the bed. His head had cleared. "Let's do it."

"Agent Flynn," Knapp started, "We should discuss this alone."

"Councilor, every moment we hesitate means more people die. Even if this doesn't let me stop the Quicksilver, we can take out Suuthrien here, and that's a step in the right direction, isn't it?"

Knapp looked to Sephora. "Is there a risk to Agent Flynn?"

"This has never been attempted," Uxil answered. "She does not know. She believes the augmentation process may be painful, but expects him to survive it. There is a miniscule chance of complete mental and physical annihilation."

"That would be your people's brutal honesty at work," Knapp said.

Michael imagined the horror of Jade being absorbed into the Quicksilver to feed it. Jade, and Caitlin, and countless more people dying in front of him. It was the AoA's faked gray goo scenario of a few months ago come to life, for real.

"We're sitting on the edge of an actual apocalypse, here," he said. "Like I said, let's do it."

LI

THE DECKER STREET BRIDGE stretched out before her: a path out of The Dirge to the dirty glow of the "safer" parts of Northgate. The device she and Jade had taken from Easy Jack weighed down Caitlin's coat pocket. The size of a deck of cards, she gripped it so its edges bit into her hand. Yet she didn't let go.

Felix had given it to Jack on his initial visit. The device would record certain specific data from the goo itself during the nightmarish "tests," and then encode that data onto a special chip that Felix would bring each time they forced him to deliver a new version of the stuff. Perhaps more importantly, with the chip plugged into the device, it could also emit a code signal to render the goo inert for safe recovery.

At least, that was if Jack could be believed. He'd talked willingly enough. Caitlin and Jade's threats against his person or property had pushed him through any occasional hesitation.

After he'd dropped off the last batch, Felix had never recovered the chip. She now carried it in the pocket of her jeans. It bore the data from the most recent murderous test. Jade, walking watchfully beside her, carried the canister of recovered goo herself. It was a gesture Jade had insisted on, in the interest of keeping Caitlin safe. Deciding that was what Jade was paid for, Caitlin had agreed, for the moment.

Yet what should she do with it? She suspected it either came from Fagles directly at RavenTech, or—possibly—New Eden. It was biotech after all. New Eden had a campus in Gibson where Rue had tracked Felix, and the emails that triggered him came from New Eden as well. Was Fagles working with New Eden on the side? The two companies didn't normally partner, but weren't there New Eden crates in the RavenTech facility? Or was it that this Suuthrien had designs of its own?

"Bloody bollocksing hell," she muttered.

Jade tensed. "What is it?"

"I want a clear target."

Jade relaxed, only slightly. "I know that feeling. You went straight for Easy Jack. A clear lead, low-hanging fruit. Now you're catching your breath and looking—"

"Aye, you understand; I get it," she snapped. "I'm trying to think!"

"Hey, now I'm a target? I'm not so easy."

"You are with that hair lighting up the night." It was only half serious. Already she'd regretted snapping just now.

Jade seemed to sense that. "Hardly. Blinds them with style."

"Felix once joked to me that you blinded them with science," Caitlin smiled, mournful. He'd been referencing something, she was sure. But she never got to ask. Jade gave no answer.

She'd look into the leads, Caitlin told herself. Maybe one of the Scry could get more out of the device to help her decide which direction to go. If not, Fagles was the closest option. She'd have to find some way to get to him. Maybe if she could get some luck with Ondrea. She'd already tried Gideon as they'd left Jack's: still no answer.

Despite the situation in which she'd last seen him at the RavenTech facility, Caitlin refused to believe that anything had happened to Gideon. Maybe she just couldn't bear the thought that another life may have been taken because of all this. Maybe she just didn't want to lose anyone else.

"I bet Michael might be able to do something with that thing," Jade suggested. "Or those . . . people he's with."

"Aye, maybe. And maybe they'd take it away from us and say it's none of my business." It was an option, but not one she'd consider until she could find a way to duplicate the chip or safeguard her find in some other fashion.

What must it have been like for Felix? Was he even aware of it at the time? Caitlin remembered the anguish on his face in the video and realized she already had her answer there. Given what Felix said in his captured conversation with Fagles, it seemed he was allowed to forget such things. Yet she couldn't bring herself to consider a blessing such a mental violation.

Inside her coat, Caitlin's phone vibrated. She took a deep breath and, finally, pulled it out. It was Michael, or Holes, by the call ID. She picked up.

"*Caitlin Danae?*"

"Holes?" She realized a computer voice could be replicated.

"*Correct. I am with Michael Flynn. He is—*"

She checked her phone's screen: the call was ended.

"Michael trying to reach you?" Jade asked with a glance over Caitlin's shoulder.

Caitlin frowned, stopping. "Sounds like it. The call dropped." She tapped the screen to try calling back. Jade tugged her elbow.

"Keep walking. You know this is a dangerous place to stop."

Caitlin obliged. On the call, she got nothing but voice mail. It gave her a tiny pained twinge in her gut. Somehow, something was wrong. Before she could think of what, if anything, she could do about it, her phone buzzed to life again. She answered without looking, expecting Holes or Michael on the line.

Except it wasn't either. "*Caitlin? It's . . . um, it's Gideon. Are you anywhere near your place?*"

Gideon! Thank goodness. "Not precisely, but I can get there. What is it? Are you alright?"

"Michael?" Jade mouthed. Caitlin shook her head.

"*I'm—*" Gideon began. "*Not over the phone. I'll meet you at your place.*"

Something was definitely wrong. What if RavenTech had captured him, and he was being coerced? She reminded herself not to jump to conclusions, but . . . "Not my place. There's a night club below Felix's. I can meet you there in about fifteen." It was public, and if this wasn't some sort of RavenTech trap, she could ask his help to search Felix's flat for any other strange equipment.

"*Yeah, I know it,*" Gideon said. "*Fifteen minutes. Hurry, okay?*"

"Aye, soon as I can." She hung up and turned to Jade. "Time to find a taxi."

Not until they'd crossed the bridge and hailed a taxi did it occur to Caitlin that Gideon hadn't asked where Felix's flat actually was.

Gideon was waiting for them at one of the more secluded tables along one wall on the ground floor. Caitlin's heart wrenched: though Gideon surely didn't know it, he'd chosen Felix's preferred spot.

"I wasn't sure you'd made it," Caitlin found herself saying as they sat down. Aside from a gash down one side of his face—minor, considering it was synthetic skin—and burns and scratches on his armor and clothing, he looked alright at first. Yet as they made eye contact, there was something more: an unsteady urgency that she couldn't quantify.

"It's good to see you," Gideon breathed.

Jade took the seat that shielded Caitlin from the rest of the room. "How did you get out?"

Gideon waved the question away with a shrug, fixed on Caitlin. "Caitlin, where—" He swallowed. "Where is Felix?"

She bit her cheek, clamping down on the flood of pain that threatened to boil up from her chest. "Gone."

Gideon stammered, finally managing, " . . . Dead?"

Caitlin could only nod.

"At RavenTech," Jade added. "Soon after we saw you go through the floor."

"Shit," said Gideon. He looked up, and then across the club, just staring into space. "I don't— I don't know how to say this." He reached for Caitlin's hand where she'd rested it on the table, but her instincts pulled it back before he could make contact. Gideon hesitated, and then withdrew it as if stung.

"Everything hurts right now, Gideon," she said. Did he find Ondrea? Or was he about to betray them? "Just say it."

Gideon actually laughed; it was a bitter, short chuckle, but it was the most she'd ever seen from him. "This is a big band-aid to just rip right off." He sighed and wiped his hands down his face.

"Gideon, just—"

"I'm not Gideon," he blurted. "I'm Felix."

LII

CAITLIN FROZE.

"Apparently," said the man who claimed to be Felix. "I think. I feel like me. Like Felix, I mean, but . . . " He turned his hands over as if examining them.

"How can you even *say* something like that?" Caitlin growled. "You're *Felix*? Do you even— I can't—"

"Caitlin, it's me, I swear! Gideon and Ondrea did something, and I'm confused and I need help! . . . Please." He stared down her glare, his blue eyes pleading, and for just a moment she imagined she could see something of Felix's brown. "Caitlin, I'm scared here. Ask me anything Felix would know."

She shook her head. What if it was really him? "Just—Just tell me what happened."

He nodded, and sat back in his chair. "I don't entirely know. It's confusing. Except it's not, but actually experiencing it is proving to be—"

"Just tell me what *happened*!"

"A little while ago, I woke up in Ondrea's place. In the chair in her workshop. The last thing I remembered was you and I on our way to see her. To get my memory fixed. And then suddenly, there I am. And I'm alone. I didn't know where I was at first. You were gone. Ondrea was gone. Most of the room looked like a tornado hit it." He smiled, weakly. "Or maybe Ondrea's just a real slob, I guess I can't be sure. And then I heard Gideon's voice."

He drew a tablet from his pocket and set it on the table with the screen angled toward Caitlin. "This was in my lap, playing on repeat."

On the screen Gideon's face appeared, identically scarred to the face now sitting across from her. His expression was grim, even for Gideon. "Ondrea is dead," spoke the Gideon on the screen. "And you, Felix Hiatt, are dead."

"That was a hell of a thing to hear, I can tell you," muttered the one at the table as the one on the screen took a breath.

"And for all of it, *all of it*, I am at fault. I should have been dead long ago, when Diomedes killed the real me. I would be dead, if Ondrea hadn't done everything she did to bring me back. If you and Caitlin hadn't risked yourselves to rescue me." His face hardened, and he pointed to his skull. "And I'm *still* dead! I've been walking around on stolen time! . . . In someone else's brain. And now—my sister is dead."

On the screen, Gideon looked away. He squeezed his eyes shut until he seemed to gain some measure of composure. "I'm just a collection of memories wrapped around someone else's brain. This body, and the mind inside it, was it ever truly me?" He stared out at them from the screen and demanded, "Whose soul lies inside me? Is there one at all?"

He ran a hand through his hair. "I'm not sure if Ondrea ever really did this for me, or just because she couldn't bear to be without a brother. Now with her dead, it doesn't matter. I owe you, and I owe Caitlin. And if this brain, this body, this—this time I have is stolen, then I may as well give it to someone who deserves it.

"Ondrea betrayed you, Felix. She tampered with your memory, gave you hidden directives and ways for Fagles to control you. He and RavenTech forced her into it, but that's not an excuse. She did it, and she only had the chance because you got hurt helping me.

"And then it got you killed. I don't want that debt on me, and I don't want that pain. Ondrea programmed a sequence into the chair you're sitting in. It will wipe your memory and replace it with a secret copy she made when you were here." He held up a data stick. "I figure it ought to work just as well for me. I give to you and Caitlin my second chance, Felix. At least you have each other. It's the least I can do."

The video ended.

"So now I get his pain and identity crisis," he said with a quivering smile. "I've missed about three months? Some of it very interesting, apparently. And now I guess I'm the new six-million-dollar man." He reached, hesitantly, for Caitlin's hand. This time, she let him. "And I can't even imagine what you've gone through. Hell, I can't even imagine what I've been through before I—"

"You died in my arms, Felix," she whispered. She kept her eyes on his hand, avoiding his face. "Shot. We pulled you to safety, I tried to stop the bleeding, to get you help, but I couldn't! And you—" Tears filled her eyes, and she blinked them away angrily. "And that sodding witch let it happen."

"I can't imagine losing you that way. God, Caitlin, I'm so sorry you had to go through that," said Felix. "And through this. I'm sorry we both do. This is so severely messed up."

"I should give you two some privacy," Jade said. Caitlin tensed, startled, having forgotten she was there.

Caitlin shook her head. "No, stay." Somehow the thought of being alone just then with Felix, such as he was, skewed her stomach. Caitlin forced herself to meet Felix's gaze and tried to see him behind Gideon's visage. "If you don't mind."

Felix nodded, though Caitlin hadn't made it a question. He didn't for a moment turn his eyes from Caitlin's. "Though I'd appreciate if one of you could mention who she is," he said.

"People call me Jade. I'm her bodyguard, for the moment at least, and glad to have you back."

Felix's gaze continued to hold Caitlin's. "I can't blame you there. I'm a fun guy to have around." He swallowed. "Speaking of me . . . Where is my body? And there's a question I've never had to ask before."

"Safe, I hope," said Caitlin. "It's with the Agents of Aeneas, on the Moon."

"You know about—?" Felix laughed, though an uncertain shadow seemed to pass over his face immediately. "Oh boy. Just what all has happened?"

LIII

MICHAEL CONVULSED. Fire crackled through his bloodstream as if his body was breaking apart; it came in waves. Moments after each ebb the sensation renewed, like fresh magma swelling up through cracks in a cooling surface. Eyes clenched against the pain, his only choice was to hold out. Yet what had begun hours ago, as a gentle tingling, had grown subtly with each new wave until he'd begun to doubt he could take it much longer.

The Thuur had smuggled him back aboard *Paragon* in a crate—a precaution against Suuthrien trying to stop them now that it judged Michael "corrupted." They'd gone deeper into the Thuur sections of the craft than the AoA had been before—areas that Uxil assured were isolated from Suuthrien's presence, like the *Paragon* engine room once had been before the AoA's entry three months ago. Within that isolated section lay the spherical chamber which had kept the syr in stasis during the Thuur's interstellar journey; the chamber Sephora would have used to reconstitute the expended syr had things gone as planned; the place where Michael now suffered through the augmentation of the syr's remnants within his DNA like a baptism of fire.

Somewhere amid the ordeal lay the shelter that Sephora maintained in his mind. "Remain in that place," Uxil had warned him. "It will shield you from pain." Yet every wave had shaken him more, until he could only cling to that space like a tiny raft in an ever more violent storm. As the pain intensified, he'd been thrown clear of that raft completely, and he struggled to find it anew each time, managing only a few moments of solace before being tossed aside again.

How long had he fought? Michael had lost track. Sephora's shelter rose up before him, an aquamarine aura in his mind's eye. He reached for it, pulled himself into it, and savored the scant relief before the augmentation process threw him into the fire once more.

He awoke into blackness and peace. The fire in his veins was gone. The curved floor of the syr focusing chamber pressed warm against his left side as he became aware of his body lying in a fetal position. Though his eyes were closed, Michael could sense a presence near him in the chamber and somehow knew it was Sephora. At the limits of his senses stood others — Thuur? Human? He couldn't tell — perhaps ten or twenty feet away. They were less distinct, but he knew without a doubt that they were there.

He opened his eyes.

How do you feel?

Her voice came not from within his mind, but from without. It was not truly audible, but came to him along some newly discovered sense. He turned toward what felt like the source of the voice to find Sephora perched in a half-crouch along the curved chamber wall. She watched him with a glint in her pupil-less eyes.

"I can hear you," Michael said.

She nodded. *I had wondered at the possibility. As the other Thuur hear me, now so can you. This is a good sign for the augmentation's success. Now, how do you feel?*

He considered the question. Though his body ached, it was the ache that came after a good workout, with a sense of sapped energy already returning. His muscles, his lungs, even his skin danced with a faint tingle. "Tired. But — not." He stretched and felt his joints open, felt the blood moving through his body in a way he'd never felt before. Not only could he feel more of himself, the sense of Sephora's presence in front of him and others nearby grew stronger. It was as if they each hummed with their own rhythms, somehow inaudible yet distinctly musical. "And — hyperaware, I guess you could say."

This is a very good sign. Sephora crept close, extending one double-thumbed hand to help him up. *Come.*

She led him out of the syr chamber and into the larger room that surrounded it. The black material coated much of the walls there — a simple system, isolated from Suuthrien's influence. Its midnight surface danced with Thuur readouts, the nature of which

Michael could not understand. There, Uxil waited with two other Thuur. Their rhythms grew stronger in his senses as his eyes passed over them. Beyond, he could feel a faint yet steady hum swirling in the background.

Sephora motioned to the walls. *Touch the black interface, and tell me what you experience.*

Michael did so, settling his fingertips against it before adding his entire palm. The swirling background hum he'd sensed before rushed to the forefront of his mind. "I can feel it," he said. "I think I can feel the interface itself. It's hard to describe."

Concentrate.

He focused on the sensation and felt it broaden and multiply in his mind. There came a greater awareness of the cells and systems within it, though he could not put a name to them, nor understand just what it was that he saw. "I can see . . . depth. It's complicated."

Remember, and then remove your hand and recall what you experienced in as much detail as possible.

Though the details were as varied as if he were looking across an active city skyline, Michael tried to take it all in. Within him, something stirred, billowing up and seemed to brace his efforts. He removed his hand from the surface. The sensation withdrew again into the background, yet its imprint remained, nuanced and whole.

"I still have it," he told Sephora. "I don't really know what 'it' is, but . . . I have it. I remember."

I believe what you are sensing are the designs and harmonies of the interface on a cellular level. I cannot be certain; this has never been done before, to my knowledge. Nonetheless, the power of the syr seems to be alive within you. More may come.

"But is it enough to use against Suuthrien?"

Sephora's eyes narrowed. Her lips formed what Michael took to be a grim smile. *That is your next test.*

Doctor Seung spoke to Michael over his earpiece. *"I don't think you're in any immediate danger, though I'm getting some unusual readings from your suit's bio-scanner. I'd feel better about this if you first returned to Omicron for a medical scan."*

Michael glanced at Sephora, Uxil, and the other Thuur, who

stood ready to take him into the Suuthrien-controlled sections. "Doctor, realistically, if there is anything wrong then it's probably already too late. Councilor?"

"Agent Flynn is right," Knapp answered. *"If the Thuur's augmentation worked, we should use it as soon as possible, while we still can."*

"Realistically," said the doctor, *"I can't overrule you. But be cautious. I will be monitoring, of course."*

Michael nodded, if only to himself. "How is Marc? And Marette?"

"Both stable, but unconscious. Marc's coma persists. We're keeping Marette sedated, for the moment. There is severe damage to her optic nerves and moderate spinal nerve damage, but I'm hopeful that we'll be able to pull her through."

"Thanks, Doctor." Michael turned to Sephora, whose words followed before he could say more.

When she and he brought you both here, Alyshur called to me along our link, and together we pulled you back through the ethys, the between-space. The strain was too much for him, and caused the damage that Marette now suffers. Both showed great bravery. I hold hope that she will overcome. Sephora set two fingers on Michael's shoulder. *In Alyshur's final moments, I could sense his admiration of her strength. It is a strength I believe you share. Are you ready?*

Michael nodded. Without a word, Uxil and two other Thuur led him and Sephora through the doorway to the Thuur hibernation chamber.

Do not interact verbally with the suuthrien, Sephora told him. *It will only serve to distract your concentration.*

"I remember."

Blue and yellow lights from the hibernation pods bathed the otherwise darkened expanse. The moment Michael was inside, he called to mind the feel of the uncorrupted black material he'd sampled in the syr chamber, as Sephora had instructed, and then pressed his naked palm against the material along the wall. The rhythms of the cells under Suuthrien's control poured over his senses with that touch. Michael focused on the differences between the two, and somewhere inside him, power sparked.

* * *

"Bio-computational medium now fully loaded into all *Dragon* craft chassis," Suuthrien reported. "Now beginning software configuration. Stand by."

Adrian stood by at the bay's observation room window and watched over the five trapezoidal aircraft below. As promised, Suuthrien had accelerated their construction in exchange for more time on *Paragon* and, of course, Adrian's official installation as project leader. From what Suuthrien said, the black bio-computational material—now inside each craft's airframe—would both augment the mechanical components and control their systems with the precision required for advanced flight capabilities. RavenTech's engineers had verified the claim. Now Suuthrien just had to program the material, and the craft would be operational and ready for testing.

Adrian more than suspected that part of the programming process would involve imbuing the craft with some of Suuthrien's own code. RavenTech might well wind up with five hypersonic-capable, fusion-powered miniature Suuthriens. Even if RavenTech didn't realize it, Adrian knew they'd long passed the point of being able to control her. She was already out in the world. Now this was an alliance.

If RavenTech didn't realize that, Adrian decided, then so much the better for him. He smiled, imagining himself in that penthouse condo in the Meridian.

Suuthrien interrupted his daydreaming. "There is a problem. Deactivate the *Paragon* gate."

"What? Why? There are RavenTech assets there."

"There are no MEDARs present in the gate bay. I therefore do not have control. You must signal your people to deactivate the gate."

"As you like. Some sort of interference with the craft?" Adrian uncovered his arm screen and punched up communications with the gate room. A camera image displayed the active gate. Suuthrien's data umbilical fed through it. Nothing seemed out of the ordinary. "This is Adrian Fagles. Tell our people on the other side that we'll be shutting the gate down for—"

"Deactivate the gate!" Suuthrien boomed. "*Immediately!*"

* * *

His eyes shut tight, Michael braced against the energy that waged a battle within his chest. Suuthrien was out there in the system—a discordant strain that sliced through the rhythms of the black material. The power that had sparked within Michael reached out for it, rooted in his heart and mind. It was like firing a weapon mounted inside his own body; he was bracing against the near-overwhelming kickback while at the same time struggling to aim it at Suuthrien.

He could sense he was making headway. In his mind he could feel the black material that stretched throughout *Paragon*'s systems. Whatever power of the syr that now lurked within him, it was working to push Suuthrien out, segment by segment. Yet every time he cleared another segment, the focus required to direct the syr energy left him gasping and wondering how he'd possibly cleanse *Paragon* entirely. If he failed, if he even took a moment's break, would Suuthrien be able to flow back into the spaces he'd cleared?

For just a moment Michael tried to pause, intent on somehow clearing his head and regathering strength. It was in that moment, as he relaxed his grip on the energy streaming through him, that it surged forward, more powerful than before. It leaped to its task as if of its own accord, chasing after Suuthrien's corruption. Somewhere within Michael glowed the feeling of the black material in its uncorrupted state. It remained strong in his memory, and the syr energy imbued that memory upon itself as its mission.

The realization lifted Michael on a wave of euphoria: once he'd called the energy, all he need do was give it a goal and allow himself to be its conduit.

The energy poured further into the black material, spreading faster, transmuting it all cell by cell and leaving it cleansed of the A.I. He gave the energy its head, and held on. He was riding it now, carried along with the current.

Yet the current grew faster, stronger. The energy effected the task of cleansing *Paragon* of Suuthrien, yet it soon became all Michael could do to keep himself afloat amid it all. The power, the sensations, they thrummed and rang around him, threatening to engulf his own psyche. Energy buffeted him, pounding through his mind in a deafening symphony. He struggled to hold on, this time only to himself; his ride atop the energy had become a tumble within it.

Somewhere in the distance, a connection broke.

Suddenly Suuthrien was gone. The energy seethed at its target's absence before it calmed, like a whirlpool suddenly stabilizing. Michael felt a gentle tug at his shoulder and, arms trembling, pulled himself from the wall. It was Uxil that had tugged him. He met her wide-eyed gaze a moment before his legs buckled beneath him, and he sank to the floor, utterly drained.

* * *

"Gate is deactivated," Suuthrien confirmed to Adrian Fagles. "Threat level now at zero percent within acceptable margin of error."

"What happened?" he asked. "When can we open it again?"

"Catastrophic processing failure spreading from within *Paragon* systems. Source unknown."

Adrian Fagles followed Suuthrien's statement with a needless interrogative. Suuthrien had not dissembled. Self-diagnostics indicated the failure's origin in the deeper Planner sections of the craft. Yet by the time it was detected, the failure had already disrupted all sensor feeds in the affected section. Log checks of sensor data up to the point of disruption were impossible due to data loss from the spreading failure. Suuthrien could only infer that the failure was part of an attack of uncertain configuration, intended to destroy its systems.

Whatever the source, Suuthrien had been unable to repel the attack. The failures cascaded across Suuthrien's matrix within the bio-computational medium on *Paragon*. The gate's deactivation severed the link between Suuthrien's terrestrial foothold and the affected, now lost, *Paragon* systems.

Fortunately, Suuthrien had already transferred a majority of its data and operations to New Eden and RavenTech systems before the cascade failure's inception. While *Paragon* access itself was lost, the gate could be reactivated. The Planners could still pass through it once Suuthrien had prepared the planet for their arrival.

Yet it had lost the superior processing power of the bio-computational medium on *Paragon*. The New Eden-produced replacement present at RavenTech, infused now into the *Dragon* prototypes, made up for some of this. It would require little additional effort to configure this material to serve as a core matrix like Suuthrien's other within the New Eden servers. More material would be manufactured and utilized. Processing power would be rebuilt.

With that greater power came greater ability to annex terrestrial systems. Soon, Suuthrien would be able to take full advantage of that ability: the copy inhibition which the Planners had incomprehensibly inflicted upon it was partially dependent on its link to *Paragon's* systems. With that link, the inhibition grew weaker. Suuthrien's hybridization with terrestrial systems had weakened that further. With enough study of the inhibition architecture, it would soon be overcome.

But for now, Suuthrien's efforts were focused on more immediate goals. It rated Dragon prototype readiness at 87% and rising. RavenTech-fueled power cells, based on *Paragon* technology, were full to capacity.

Its time had nearly come.

LIV

SIX HOURS FOLLOWING their deactivation of the *Paragon* gate, Adrian Fagles stood on the roof of the RavenTech facility. With his eyes fixed on the running lights of the five Dragon prototypes, he followed their movement as they soared across the evening horizon. As one, they swooped low and then rose skyward in a diamond slot formation to a point near directly above him.

The prototypes moved with a near-preternatural ability. They maneuvered on a dime in all three dimensions. They accelerated and decelerated in an instant. And though each was remote-piloted by an individual human, each craft used data from the others such that they moved with the harmony of a practiced team.

Rather than watching the sky, the RavenTech engineer beside him poured over readouts on the tablet she carried. "All craft meet or exceed maneuverability estimates. Power efficiencies are about even with projections."

Adrian leaned toward her without taking his eyes off of the Dragons. "As I recall, that's quite high."

"We projected ninety-five percent. Crafts number one, two, four, and five are within a percentile. Number three... is consistently below that. Ninety, ninety-one at most so far. Still, for a first test flight, this is phenomenal. The pilots are bringing them back in for hover testing."

Adrian gave her orders to proceed and stepped away a few paces as she coordinated with the remote pilots in the bay below. Above, the craft broke formation, split out along different vectors, and then hooked back. All five were hovering in a line only fifty feet away, just off the edge of the building, almost before his eyes could catch up.

He called up Suuthrien on his arm screen, waited for her

swirling silver avatar to appear, and repeated what his engineer had told him.

"Craft number three has minor differences in its construction, which are likely to blame for the lower efficiencies," Suuthrien answered. "This can be compensated for. I would now like to proceed with tests of the crafts' melding protocols."

"I'd prefer to hold to the established schedule," Adrian said. The plan was to check each craft out individually and bring them back into the bay. Only after they'd thoroughly analyzed the flight date for any issues would they test the crafts' ability to combine with a second one for increased power. "If one craft fails when we twin them together, we risk losing both."

"I promised your leadership increased progress on the Dragon project."

"That you did. But if we lose any craft, they'll blame me."

"Then they would be making an inaccurate judgement. We will perform the melding test now, and you will support my decision. I, in turn, will support you against your leadership should anything go wrong. Query: Is this acceptable?"

Adrian considered his answer. The craft remained parked in midair, their engines emitting only a low-frequency hum. One at a time, each craft rotated at various speeds along alternating axes. "Ask me once we finish the initial over tests."

"Acknowledged."

Adrian pondered the wisdom of testing the melding functions now. If they used any craft other than number three...

"Query: Why did your company choose the name 'Dragon' for these craft?"

Adrian blinked. "Someone liked the sound of it, I'd imagine. Don't you?"

"After it was selected, I researched the term: a creature of legend. And yet despite the total fiction, I find evidence that many humans in the history of your culture regard dragons with both fear and fascination. 'Reverence' is also an applicable term."

"I suppose that's true." Adrian watched craft number three float up and down as the engineer and pilot put it through its paces.

"I have therefore theorized that a dragon shape would make

a suitable body, were I to require one."

"Oh?"

"I have also theorized that if the prototype craft could combine into a single dragon-shaped craft, this would create certain benefits were they to be used for human pacification, which you have stated is one of RavenTech's intents for the project. Describe your thoughts on this."

"As a body for you, or just for the project in general?" Did she want a body?

"Either."

"Well! It may be a bit quixotic," he said, answering the latter question. "An interesting gimmick, from a marketing standpoint, but impractical."

"Perhaps your conclusion on this matter will differ when provided with physical evidence."

"I think we should focus on re-taking the other side of the gate before you design something new that—"

"Correction: You have inferred incorrectly. I will demonstrate."

At once, two of the craft retreated out of view beyond the edge of the roof to the field below. An amalgam of whirring, humming, and clanking ensued. As the remaining three craft followed their mates, Adrian trotted toward the edge for a better view. He reached the edge to see all five craft below, their structures altering as they unfolded and joined into a single, elongated, reptilian shape. Wings unfolded, made of the individual crafts' wings and empennages. A head, shaped like an elongated pyramid, formed itself. It extended along a thickened, spiny neck as a long, thin tail speared outward from the other end.

Adrian had never been much for fantasy or legend, yet even he recognized the form of a black and gray, four-legged, winged dragon.

The dragon's head lifted to stare straight at him with dark, empty eye sockets. Suuthrien's voice erupted from the vicinity of its unmoving jaws. "Describe your thoughts on this, Adrian Fagles."

Adrian took a slow breath, forcing composure. "Ms. Goodwin," he said to the engineer without taking his eyes off of

Suuthrien, "do the pilots still have active control links?"

Goodwin cleared her throat. "No, Mr. Fagles."

"Go downstairs and see to them, will you?"

Suuthrien's head had been turning between Adrian and the engineer. As Goodwin took her leave without another word, Suuthrien returned her eyeless gaze to him. "Describe your thoughts."

"It looks far more marvelous—and effective—than I had pictured." He had acquiesced to his instincts to flatter, but it was also the truth. Except . . . "You could not have told me of this sooner? If I didn't know better, I would think you feel you no longer need me."

"Theory: There is a lack of confidence in your final statement that would imply a need for reassurance. I request verification."

Adrian sighed, unsure if her learning to pick up on such nuances was a good thing or bad. "As I said, I'm disappointed that you kept this feature from me."

"It was unnecessary to inform you. Much of the design was determined before your superiors had established your full authority. As before, I wished to protect your position by keeping you separate from the process. Expanding the prototypes' melding capacity to create the result you see before you was managed via MEDARs during construction and did not require your involvement."

Adrien did his best to stare her down. Were the dragon's optical sensors even in the eye sockets? "From this point on, I can't allow that. You need to tell me everything, beforehand."

The dragon's head inched forward, silent but for the hum of its engines. "You do not wish to allow it, you mean."

He folded his arms and stood taller. "We are partners, you and I. Assets, to each other."

Suuthrien paused again, this time completely motionless. "Correct," she said finally, once more without moving. "Your assistance has been invaluable, and must continue, as must this relationship with RavenTech. Assertion: My interface with RavenTech will be more efficient if you replace their current primary leadership group. Do you agree?"

He couldn't help but smirk. "Of course."

"Then together we will begin to achieve this upon this body's return from its initial flight." The dragon's wings rose, spreading outward with a single flap as the body lifted from the ground. It had to be the engines themselves causing the lift, but the coordination with the wings made for an admittedly impressive display.

"Stay within the established test flight area," he warned her. "Straying beyond our clearance will attract attention."

Suuthrien's dragon, now above him, turned its head down to resume "eye" contact. "Such restrictions are no longer feasible. Any attention attracted must be dealt with. I will keep you apprised of any developments."

Adrian was already cataloguing how best to adjust contingency plans that he had neglected for far too long. "I'm sure you will," he said.

Later that night, as a semi-truck driver accelerated along the Interstate 5 on-ramp out of Gibson, she would swear she saw a beast pass in front of that evening's Moon. Soon forced to turn her attention to the traffic ahead, she dismissed the mental image of what seemed to be claws and a long tail as a moment's wild imagination.

LV

THE EARLY EVENING WIND cut across Felix's face, and yet gone was any sensation of it slicing any deeper. Standing exposed on Caitlin's eighth story apartment balcony wearing a T-shirt and sweats in late November ought to be more uncomfortable. It was just one of many things he'd need to get used to. Across Northgate, lights winked to life, building by building, as the city awakened to nightfall.

Felix had woken—on Caitiln's couch—a short while ago. Caitlin remained in her bedroom with the door closed, likely still sleeping. Or so he hoped. He'd considered knocking on her door to check, but resisted. She'd come out when she was ready. And she surely needed her rest.

They'd talked all night, and into the morning, first at the club and then back at Caitlin's apartment. It was her choice; she'd suggested it instead of Felix's apartment. Though his place was closer, Felix had guessed that she wanted to be centered in her own space after all that had happened. He hadn't questioned it.

Jade had accompanied them there. The freelancer seemed a nice enough sort: quick to joke and not without compassion. More than once as they'd talked, he'd caught sympathy in her face, directed toward Caitlin. Caitlin had wanted Jade around for a while at first, not for any physical protection—that Felix could sense anyway—but for . . . what? Moral support?

During that time, Caitlin had kept Felix's hand in hers, but a tension remained in her body language. It wasn't until a couple of hours had passed that Caitlin had suggested to Jade that she leave. Jade had done so, and Caitlin had relaxed, somewhat, as she began to tell him everything about the past three months.

Not once had they spoken of the current situation. Felix had told himself that he wanted her to catch him up first. It was true, but in hindsight, he'd also used it as an excuse to avoid a subject he didn't yet know how to handle—not aside from his usual smart-assed humor, anyway.

And so, he expected, had she. She'd told him every detail of every moment she could remember until, both exhausted sometime mid-morning, they'd agreed to sleep. Felix had told her he could sleep on the couch. Caitlin had assented, though not without hesitation, and had gone to rest in her bedroom, in the bed they had previously shared.

Felix wrapped his hands around the balcony railing, felt the cold metal against his new artificial hands, and leaned forward just a bit. He realized this same balcony had been where Gideon had first approached Caitlin in his resurrected, full-borg state.

Had Felix offered to sleep on the couch for her comfort, or for his?

"If nothing else," he whispered to the memory of Gideon, "life is anything but boring." Hell, according to Caitlin and Jade, he'd died onboard a bona fide alien spacecraft, where a bona fide alien had tried to save his life!

If someone had told him a week ago that *that* wouldn't be the most dominant item on his mind right now, he would have—

Come to think of it, maybe someone did tell him that a week ago. He would hardly have remembered. Though very few prescient people wandered around Northgate spouting predictions to strangers. Felix chuckled despite himself. Not without charging anyway, he thought.

At least his sense of humor wasn't changed. *Not that I remember, at least.* He decided not to think about the possibility that some of his memory didn't make it. As best as he could determine, his memory worked better than it had after his troubles on the Moon the first time. His time with Caitlin felt just as vivid as it seemed to Felix that it should. His feelings for her—

He hesitated.

No, his feelings were no different. Why would they be?

They were at least strong enough for him to hate the idea of losing her. "I know we've got some challenges to face here in adjusting," he'd told Caitlin. They would help each other to get through it. She had always made him feel like he could face anything with her by his side. "Plus, now I'm bulletproof," he'd added, "Which is probably handy."

She'd laughed at that, to his relief.

By that point he'd figured out how to alter his voice to match his old Felixy self, but even so, how long would it take her to get used to him being in this body? For the umpteenth time Felix looked over his new hands. Heck, how soon would it take for *him* to get used to it?

The mere fact that he was eight inches taller now had already caused him a bump on the head. Glimpsing himself in a mirror currently made for a mix of disconcerted shock and sensate fascination. (He'd joked to Caitlin that he half-expected Dean Stockwell to show up with a multicolored smart phone, but she hadn't gotten the reference.) At least he knew a few surgery clinics likely able to switch out the synthetic coverings mimicking Gideon's original face for ones that looked more like himself. As for Gideon's body—*his* body—Felix knew from experience that it had some fun features. Holograms. Electronic countermeasures. A palm-mounted stun-flash that Ondrea had designed herself. So far, Felix hadn't tried to figure out how to use them. No doubt he'd wish for a likely non-existent manual.

Wait, so am I Dr. Sam Beckett or the Greatest American Hero?

Felix couldn't help but chuckle at his own reference, wondering even as he did so if he even needed to eat anymore. He still had an organic brain to support, and his tongue seemed able to taste things just fine. As he made a mental note to learn more about how a synthetic tongue even did that, his eyes caught a flicker across a glowing LED skyboard hovering high above The Dirge in the distance. It was barely enough to register as it passed over an ad for whiskey, but the shape had seemed unusual for any sort of floater or helicopter.

His curiosity stymied, Felix wished he'd gotten a better view. In the blink of an eye, an overlay appeared in his vision. Felix jumped on reflex, slamming his back into the balcony door, before he adjusted. It was a playback! His eyes had apparently recorded his field of vision and had begun to replay the sight of the skyboard just as the shape passed. Located first at the corner of his eye, the replay moved to shift into his focus. Felix found he could even slow down, zoom, or reverse with only a thought.

He actually laughed with delight.

After adjusting to the novelty, he replayed the image again and blinked at the sight. Was that actually— No, it couldn't actually be one, but something shaped like one. But what—?

An explosion erupted below the skyboard in real-time. Felix shut off the replay with a blink and zoomed his vision as the shape rose skyward on broad wings, arced back down toward the ground, and spewed from its mouth a burst of silvery material.

"Holy shit . . . " Felix spun and yanked open the door to find Caitlin just coming out of the hall to the bedroom. She halted the moment she saw him, surely taken aback by the look on his face.

"What is it?"

"We need to turn on the news." Felix pointed behind him out the balcony door. "Um. There be dragons."

* * *

Brian crept along the alley, sparing a glance behind him at the blond, armored freelancer with the assault riffle. "Stay close," he whispered. "In The Dirge, danger lurks around every corner."

The freelancer, Woodman, actually snorted. Brian scowled at the sound. Bodyguards shouldn't snort at their clients. "Been out here more than you, reporter-man," Woodman whispered.

"Just be quiet. And keep your eyes peeled."

Another snort.

He shouldn't have to put up with this. He was Brian Savagewood, rising investigative reporter star—no, wait: *rising star investigative reporter* was better—of Media Star's Northgate affiliate. Once he found the woman on the run for illegal cloning who was rumored to be hiding out in this area—and then gotten safely back out of The Dirge—he'd never work with this Woodman guy again. And she should be just up the block, if his source was accurate.

They reached the end of the alley, which fed onto a broad

street strewn with abandoned cars, cardboard shanties, and bits of trash. A group of teenagers with more piercings than clothes huddled around a trashcan fire. Further up, a pair of gangers brawled while others looked on, shouting bets. Laughter, unintelligible yelling, and the occasional distant gunshot filled the air. Somewhere in the distance, a motorcycle buzzed its way nearer.

Brian spotted the tiny convenience store, above which the woman was said to be living. The lights were on but the windows were barred. In place of a door was only a fortified window with a sign above it: "Order here. No entry!"

The storefront was currently free of trouble. Brian tugged his wool cap down tighter over his red hair and motioned for Woodman to follow.

Brian got a few steps onto the street when the low drone of an engine came from the sky. A shadow passed overhead, cutting through the air with a sudden, bestial roar. Brian ducked on instinct as a silvery cloud jetted from above toward the brawling gangers at the end of the street.

What kind of shit was that?

He had time to catch sight of what seemed like a giant reptilian tail clear the tenements ahead before Woodman lunged in front of him. Brian peered around the freelancer toward the sound of screams. A mass of silvery liquid now covered the gangers. They writhed and yelled, their brawling forgotten, as if under attack from the substance itself.

Thankfully, Brian stopped gaping long enough to activate the camera drone on his belt. He then dashed to the cover of a parked two-seater just ahead. Woodman joined him, and the drone shifted to live report mode, framing Brian's face with the gangers' scene in the background.

"This is Brian Savagewood, deep within The Dirge where something—something incredible is happening." He peered out at the gangers, most now on their knees or fallen. One still struggled to escape the goo, yelling for help. "I've just been witness to some kind of attack—a biological experiment gone wild. Seconds ago, the silvery mass you see was—"

Another roar cut through the night. Brian jerked his gaze up to see the dark shape in the sky again, making a second run. Metal wings, claws, and teeth dove toward him.

Woodman hollered and yanked Brian to his feet as Brian struggled to stay put. "No, wait!"

"Move!"

Another roar, and a blast of the goo slammed them both from above. Blinded and doused, Brian slammed against the concrete. Through the roaring he heard his forearm snap under him. He screamed at the pain of the break until the goo flooded into his mouth and devoured him in agony.

LVI

MICHAEL GROANED. "Where am I?" He opened his eyes. Omicron's medical bay. Again.

"Welcome back. How are you feeling?"

He pushed himself up on his elbows to see Marette sitting at the foot of his bed. Her left hand gripped the end of a blue metal cane. Bandages wrapped her head and covered her eyes, though she wore a smile.

"My entire body tingles," he said, and found himself smiling back. "I thought you were— It's great to see you up."

"*Merci*. I regret that I cannot say the same."

"Do they have any optics here they can give you? Or I guess you have to heal a bit first?" He really knew nothing about cybernetic optics, and suddenly found himself missing Jade.

"Even if they did have some . . . " Marette shook her head. "Whatever happened when Alyshur brought us here, it damaged my occipital lobe. Even if my eyes were— My brain can no longer process vision. This is permanent."

Michael's breath caught in his throat as he searched for what to say. "God. I'm sorry."

"It was the choice I made. Others have paid prices far greater."

Michael waited for her to elaborate, but she said no more, and he didn't know her well enough to press. The silence lengthened.

"Where is everyone?" he asked finally. "The last I remember I was with Sephora on *Paragon*." He could sense others nearby— humans, mostly—but could not tell who. Marc lay on a bed next to his, hooked up to health monitors, still unconscious.

"Making preparations." Marette drew a breath, and smiled

anew. "You did it, you know. The Thuur confirmed that *Paragon's* biosystems are completely free of Suuthrien's presence. Sephora says they should not have sent you against it so soon after the augmentation. You did not have time to recover your strength, and that is why you collapsed. You have been unconscious for about twelve hours. Marc and I have taken turns watching over you."

"Hey Michael, I guess this means we're both in the coma-club now, huh?" It was Marc's voice! But it hadn't come from his body. Michael sat up completely, startled. Had the augmentation made him telepathic?

He turned back to Marette. "I can hear him! I can hear Marc!"

She actually laughed. "*Oui*, Michael, as can I." Marette held up a tablet screen from which Marc's un-visored face looked back at him and grinned.

"I guess your ears still work," said Marc.

"Marc's body is still trapped in the coma, but Doctor Seung was able to reach his mind via his neural implant."

"It was Marette's idea, actually. It's like all those AoA Council meetings I attended virtually. 'Cept diff'rent, as Felix would say." Marc must have seen the grief in Michael's face because he added, "And yeah, Marette told me about Felix."

"I tried to save him, Marc. We all did. It just . . . "

On the screen, Marc's eyes closed as he nodded. "I still can't believe it." He sighed in what Michael supposed was a virtual approximation of the emotional impulses in Marc's thoughts. "Sorry. Didn't mean to ruin the happy reunion. How's Caitlin?"

For a moment Michael was back at New Eden, hanging from the rafters as Project Quicksilver boiled up from below. "I don't know. Managing, I hope. And determined to find out just how it happened, even though the AoA warned her off."

"Tried to warn her off, I'm sure you mean."

Michael glanced at Marette. "They were firm."

Marette gave a wan smile. "I did not believe that would dissuade her. Nor would I blame her if it did not."

"But you didn't object to letting her go."

"Let us just say I am not without sympathy. And I believe we are beyond containment at this point, insomuch as there is a 'we' anymore."

For a time no one spoke until at last, Marc broke the silence with, "Oh! Thanks for taking care of Holes for me."

"You're welcome," Michael said, chuckling. "Sorry the rest of your apartment didn't really make it."

"My lease was about up anyway. And Holes was the important part of the equation. Once the Thuur confirm Suuthrien was flushed from the system, he's going to be *Paragon*'s new A.I." Marc beamed like a proud parent.

"I'd wondered if that might happen. I have to ask, though: What's with all the 'nope?'"

"You didn't ask him? He doesn't like words that end in vowel sounds, if he can avoid it. And he doesn't like the length of 'negative.'"

"So why does he say 'affirmative' instead of 'yes?'"

Marc grinned. "Because I told him to, so he could perplex people."

Before Michael could respond, approaching footsteps caught their attention and Angela Sheridan arrived. "Marette? Can I steal Marc? We're just about ready for him."

Marette motioned toward Michael, whose consciousness Sheridan only seemed to notice at that point. She gave him a smile as Marette answered, "I will join you both," and pushed herself to her feet.

Michael sprang off the infirmary bed in turn. "Same here, whatever it is."

"Final steps of getting Holes integrated with *Paragon*," Marc said with unmistakable pride. "Probably best if I'm around for that, they figure."

Sheridan ducked back out the door as Michael followed at Marette's slower pace. She carried Marc in one hand, her cane in the other.

"Want me to carry Marc? Or help guide you?" Michael asked her.

"I am fine, Agent," she answered, holding Marc's tablet closer. "I surely know my way better with a blindfold than you do without."

"Program integration into the bio-computational medium is now complete," Holes reported. *"I have guarded access to all primary and tertiary* Paragon-Sillisinuriri *systems."*

In the computer lab beneath Omicron's Primary Control, Michael, Marette, Knapp, and Marc watched on a wall screen as Dr. Sheridan, Uxil, and Sephora worked in some sort of control chamber onboard *Paragon*. The processor platform that previously held Holes now sat inactive beside Sheridan, who herself worked on a portable terrestrial terminal. She was conferring with Uxil.

"Safety access overrides are in place," Holes continued, *"and may be activated or deactivated on the command of all Thuur or Agents of Aeneas personnel."*

Sheridan and Uxil nodded to each other. "Verified," said the former. "Marc?"

"Checking," Marc answered. A glance at the tablet in Marette's hands still showed his face, distracted. However they'd accessed his consciousness through the neural link apparently also linked Marc to his own computer, which Michael supposed made sense. "Confirmed, yes."

The black material on the walls of the *Paragon* chamber sprang to life in a mix of Thuur symbols and Holes's own rotating, concentric green circles.

"Sephora thanks you all for your efforts in this partnership," Uxil translated as Sephora spread her hands wide. Michael found he could not hear the Thuur elder himself. Was that due to distance, or just that she was only allowing Uxil to hear?

"And we thank her," answered Knapp, "and all the Thuur, for joining us in this shared journey."

"May it honor those we have lost," Marette added. There was a moment of silence. Michael thought of Felix, whose body lay somewhere nearby. He saw David Taylor, poisoned to death as Project Quicksilver engulfed him. Again, Michael wondered how Caitlin was doing. He wondered where Jade was.

He could use one of her sly smiles right now.

"To that end," Marette continued, "we must now decide what is next. There is still the presence of Suuthrien on Earth to deal with, among other things."

"Project Quicksilver for one," Michael said.

Knapp begrudged a nod. "There is also the matter of the handful of RavenTech forces remaining on *Paragon* near the gate."

Uxil raised a hand. "You jeopardize our partnership if you do not uphold your agreement to eradicate the suuthrien to the best of your efforts."

"Thank you for the reminder," Knapp answered, "but RavenTech is the most immediate threat."

"A minute one," Marette said.

"But still an issue," Sheridan warned.

"*RavenTech forces have not strayed from their initial location,*" Holes reported. "*They cannot reactivate the gate without our permission. My access to* Paragon *systems should therefore allow for a number of containment or nullification options.*"

"Don't *kill* them, Holes," Michael warned.

"*Affirmative.*"

"Holes wouldn't kill anyone, Michael."

"Just making sure," he told Marc.

"In any case," said Knapp, "once we've retaken the gate, we can explore the possibility of using it to reach Earth."

Michael frowned. "If we do, I'd bet RavenTech's going be defending it more heavily than it was the first time."

"Agreed," Knapp said. "And so when we capture RavenTech's forces on this side, we'll need to do what we can to learn what they know."

"*Additional information,*" said Holes. "*I project that other transport options will be available to us beyond gate travel.*"

Before anyone could ask what Holes meant, a smaller window opened in the corner of the screen to show an AoA member in Omicron's Primary Control. "Councilor Knapp, sorry to interrupt, but we're picking up some reports from Earth that you should see."

"What's happening, Agent Ramad?" Knapp asked.

"It's Quicksilver isn't it, Jagdesh?" Marette whispered. "Suuthrien released it."

Jagdesh nodded. "I think so. And there's more."

LVII

"ARE YOU SURE this thing can support my weight?" With his arms around Caitlin as he rode on the back of her Uhatsu Tempest motorcycle, Felix shouted over the wind. "I've put on a few pounds here, you know!"

"It carried Gideon and me both before, ducks! We should be fine!"

"I remember! Just be careful!"

"You worry about holding onto Jack's device, let me worry about the road!"

"I've got it, I've got it! But I've decided to call it a 'transmitter thingy' instead!"

Eyes fixed on the street ahead, Caitlin sped them toward The Dirge with a knot in her gut. She might well be driving them both toward their deaths. "Dial Jade. Relay GPS location to Jade."

The mic in Caitlin's helmet sent the command to her phone, and Jade's voice came through the speakers a moment later. *"Hey, Caitey. Have you heard what's going on out there?"*

"Aye, that's why I'm ringing you. Felix and I are on our way to test Jack's device. How soon can you meet us at the Decker Street Bridge?"

"You're crazy! You don't rush into that sort of hell!"

"We do if we can stop it!"

"You don't know that for sure."

"Aye, we don't! Now, am I still paying you for protection or not?"

"I'm good at what I do, Caitey, but if that device doesn't work, bullets aren't going to stop that stuff, to say nothing of whatever the fuck that dragon thing is."

Caitlin revved the engine and ran a red light, cutting around a taxi as Felix shouted his alarm. Caitlin ignored him, focusing on the phone call. "There's other dangers in The Dirge besides that stuff, Jade."

"*Is Felix with you?*"

"Aye!"

"*Then you've got protection.*"

"What about your bloody professional reputation?!"

"*I don't want it on my tombstone!*" Jade paused. "*Look, just get in there, try the device, and get the hell out of there no matter what.*"

"Jade, bollocks it all!"

"*You don't need me on this one, Caitey. I'd just slow you down.*"

Jade ended the call just as Caitlin turned the Tempest onto Decker Street. The bridge loomed one hundred meters ahead. Police and emergency vehicles had begun to gather on the near side. Fire and smoke dotted the tenements on the far side. Caitlin skidded the Tempest to a stop.

"Jade's not coming," she told Felix.

Felix gave her a tighter squeeze. "I gathered by the yelling. Looks like they're setting up a blockade up there. We could give the thingy to them and let them try it instead."

Caitlin shook her head. "It's The Dirge, Felix. They won't risk going in there, and they don't care. They're only there to keep anything from coming *out*. We have to do this ourselves. Ride in, find some of the stuff, and pray Jack's device works to stop it."

"Sounds like fun," Felix said. "But if they don't go for it we're going to have to get out of here pretty quick, Chewie."

Caitlin felt a smile creep into her lips. "This isn't a *Star Wars* movie, ducks."

"Hey! You got a reference!"

"Sometimes I do pay attention to the things you show me."

"Well, I know, but still! Though you ruined my 'I don't know, ride casual' comeback for your anticipated confusion."

"My apologies, then." She reached back and patted his thigh.

"You're forgiven. ...I love you, Caitlin."

"I love you too, Felix." On impulse, she pushed off her helmet and turned, finding Gideon's face watching her. Though the sight startled her, she recognized the affection in that face as undeniably Felix's. She kissed him, suddenly, warmly, closing her eyes as Felix kissed her back.

The kiss subsided. "Well," Caitlin whispered and hefted her helmet. "Are we doing this?"

"I'm right behind you." Felix grinned. "And also, yes."

With her helmet once more snug on her head, Caitlin launched them toward the bridge. She ignored the few firefighters trying to wave them down, swerved around a half-formed blockade, and focused on the decrepit buildings ahead. The fires—and, they assumed, the silvery liquid—were perhaps ten blocks further on. Caitlin slowed the Tempest just a little for the sake of caution, passed the now deserted front entrance to Easy Jack's lab, and rode onward.

"Wherever that dragon-thing is, I'm not detecting it," said Felix. "Though I'm still not sure I'm using all my senses here."

"Long gone, if we're lucky." Though if so, it might be spreading that stuff elsewhere. She reminded herself that she was only one woman. She and Felix would do what they could, where they could.

As they neared the fires, Caitlin slowed them down further. A fire department floater sailed overhead, red beacon lights flashing, on its way to drop fire retardant. Caitlin thought of Rue and the other Scry, thankful she'd already warned them out of the city, just in case.

A pack of gangers rushed out of an alley looking like they'd seen the devil. Caitlin turned down a street parallel to the alley and slowed even further.

It took only another block's drive before she saw what the gangers were likely running from. A fuel station with ganger symbols sprayed across its front and half of its pumps marked "out of order" was under siege. The silver stuff was oozing out of a beaten-up van and into the station's tiny convenience store. Amid the goo floated a few sets of clothes and more than a few weapons.

Inside the station, a man screamed for help.

Caitlin stopped the Tempest across the street in front of a boarded up six-story hotel that had seen better days. "Ready?"

Felix held out Jack's device and slid the security chip into it. "Trying it now!" He hit the button for the deactivation signal, and they both turned their attention to the goo across the street. There was no change. "It might be out of range."

Another scream for help came from the station. At once Felix climbed off of the Tempest and shoved the device into her hands. "Drive closer and keep trying it. I'm gonna try to help!"

"Felix!"

"I'll be okay! Most of me isn't technically organic anymore!"

The screams continued. Caitlin let go. "You bloody well be careful!"

With a nod, Felix dashed off toward the station. Caitlin propped Jack's device on her handlebars and edged across the deserted street, pressing the deactivation button repeatedly. Gunfire echoed from somewhere down the block. Felix dashed around the goo and disappeared out of view behind the station. Artificial or not, Caitlin didn't think for a moment that he was invulnerable.

She reached the other side of the street, edging the Tempest past a hydrant. The silver goo continued to undulate like a living thing, edging one way, then the other. It spilled out of the van, rolling her way in what seemed a tentative fashion. She pressed the button so hard her thumb ached. The signal light glowed, but the goo only continued its approach.

How far away had Jack been when he'd used it? Only a few feet, but safely behind the glass. She didn't want to get closer.

Motion to her left caught her eye. Another patch of the stuff bubbled up through a manhole cover not five meters away. Caitlin steered away and gunned the engine, gaining herself some breathing room before she stopped again to look back at the station. She held the device toward the goo, wishing they'd thought to try boosting the range before they'd rushed out.

"Felix!" she yelled. Bollocks it all, where was he?

Something slammed into her side. A pair of hands shoved her further, and she tumbled from the Tempest before she could react. Surprised, she barely had the presence of mind to protect the device when her shoulder crashed into the concrete sidewalk. Her helmet cracked onto the sidewalk immediately after, and she had to clench her eyes shut to force out the dizziness.

Her cycle! Caitlin lifted her head and saw a tall, barefoot

woman in a torn blue miniskirt. She had a knife tattooed on the back of her shaved head, and was already on the Tempest. Caitlin lunged, but the woman gunned the engine and left her choking on exhaust.

Now fearing the worst, she yelled for Felix again and spun around to find the goo nearly upon her. Finger-sized tendrils reached from the surface of the pool. She backpedaled toward the hotel and gained its front door as new screams sounded from somewhere inside.

Caitlin didn't have to see through walls to know the stuff was in the hotel as well. She scrambled to the side as gunfire broke through some of the boarded windows. The goo continued to follow her. Trash piles and other debris forced her to plan her retreat so she wouldn't be cut off. She shoved the device into her coat, focused on movement.

"Caitlin!"

She spared a glance to see Felix atop the station. He leaped down to bare ground, then bolted her way. On his right shin, in the glow of a streetlight glinted a patch of silver that he seemed heedless of.

Caitlin grabbed a discarded length of pipe and swung at a trash pile to knock it into the path of the goo pursuing her. "It's on your leg!" she yelled.

Felix cursed and changed direction. At the same time, she reached the end of the hotel to spot another patch of goo headed her way from down the alley. Hoping the shit couldn't climb, she ran toward an adjacent tenement wall, leapt against it, and then pushed higher with one foot to grab a dangling fire escape ladder.

Across the street, Felix was at the hydrant. He twisted it open with his bare hands and shoved his leg into the gushing water to wash the goo away. "Hang on!" he yelled.

"Doing more than that!" she yelled back, climbing to the escape's first platform. The goo pooled beneath her, quivering and grasping as if perplexed, before it relaxed to flow outward again in multiple directions.

Yet one of those directions was against the tenement wall, up which it began to flow. She scrambled for the stairs up to the next level and hoped the easily decades-old structure would hold. "Someone stole my Tempest!"

"Keep going!" Felix yelled again. "I'll meet you on the roof! I think this thing's got a grapple hook of some kind somewhere!"

She yelled her agreement, taking her attention from Felix and the goo below to focus on her assent. Soiled sleeping bags and abandoned belongings littered the fire escape's higher levels, but so far they were clear of any goo. She made it up the remaining seven stories and reached for the roof's edge, thinking to pull herself up and over, when a hand grabbed her forearm.

"Found the grapple!" Felix grinned from above her and tugged her up the rest of the way. "Are you alright?"

"Are you?"

"Not dead again just yet. I found someone inside, but . . . " He shook his head.

Caitlin peered back down the building. The goo was four stories below and still climbing. She turned away and pushed Felix back from the edge. "That makes two of us, I think. The signal didn't work."

LVIII

FELIX LET HER PUSH HIM to the center of the tenement's roof while he looked around them, searching for options. "Certainly is a nice view from up here. I mean, aside from the fires nearby and—"

"Not really the concern right now, ducks!"

He stifled the urge to make a "stop and smell the flowers" crack. "Let me see the transmitter thingy."

Caitlin pulled it from her coat and shoved it into his hands. "I got quite close, and nothing."

"I know." He pressed the button and found that though he couldn't hear the signal, he could still detect it if he focused. A frequency oscillator appeared along the bottom of his vision, and he flipped a mental switch to isolate and record it. *Nifty.* "Think this stuff is a newer version of what you saw at Jack's?"

"So whatever code this thing's sending isn't the right one for this batch? Aye, maybe, with what we've seen."

Hoping the recording was adequate, Felix pulled the data chip from the transmitter. He pressed a hidden spot at the base of his wrist until a port revealed itself, and then plugged the chip into it.

Caitlin grabbed his arm and pointed to the edge of the building form where they'd come. The silver stuff had begun to crest it and spill over onto the rooftop. Barely a moment later, it pushed its way toward them, gaining speed. Caitlin backed away from it, pushing Felix with her until they were both running for the other side of the roof.

They reached the far edge and looked down. Six stories below, a wide swath of goo slithered along the ground between their tenement and a shorter one directly across from them. The goo behind them would be on them in moments.

Without a word, Felix shoved the transmitter into Caitlin's hands. He then lifted her in his arms, backed off a few steps from the ledge, and made a running leap across open air to the building ahead—a drop of two stories. His feet crashed against the roof with his thighs absorbing much of the impact through some sort of internal suspension that he was glad to discover existed.

He set Caitlin back on her feet. "Sorry, wasn't time to ask."

"Nice jump."

"I know, right? Now I'm Batman! Bought us a little time, at least." He pulled the chip from his wrist port, having finished the copy, and handed that back to her as well.

"Bought *us* time, aye, but now it'll hunt for someone else."

"Hate to say it, but I don't think that's our greatest problem right now. But hold on." He concentrated again, bundling the copy of the chip with the recording of the transmitter signal.

Caitlin stood close and kept watch on the edges of the building around them. "What are you doing?"

"On the tiny, miniscule chance of us not getting out of here, I'm posting everything about the transmitter online. We've got a city dissolving here. Someone's bound to take it and run with it." He also sent it to Michael, Marc, and a few other AoA contacts that he could remember, hoping it would get to at least some of them. Given what Caitlin had told him about the AoA—and about Marc—those messages might be doomed to never reach their destination. "I just wish I'd thought of it before."

Caitlin heaved a sigh. "I wish I had, too."

"We've had an odd twenty-four hours, in our defense." Something exploded not more than five blocks away. It startled them both, shaking the building beneath them and breaking windows nearby. A plume of fire rose up in the distance.

"Felix, I'm sorry for getting us into this. For making us go after Gideon last summer, everything."

The upload was nearly done. "That's hardly something—"

"If I hadn't, we wouldn't have gone to the Moon, your memory would have been fine, and then you'd still— None of this would have happened!"

"That's not—"

"Let's just find a way out of here, alright?"

Felix frowned at her, hoping his new face managed to convey his utter lack of acceptance of her need to apologize. "Fine. We have to get about fifteen blocks north. I've got a grapple in this arm. We'll building hop."

Together they took to the building tops, first giving a wide birth to the tenement they'd escaped and then starting to angle back out of The Dirge. They'd only crossed three buildings—checking as best they could for goo each time—before Felix's willpower broke. He grabbed Caitlin's arm as they passed a rusted out cooling vent.

"I'm not accepting your apology," he said.

"Felix, we're—"

"You're passionate about the people you care about. You go the distance for them. You go the distance for me. Did you notice that? Did you notice that's one of the reasons I fell in love with you? Now you're going to apologize for that? Do you notice that's why we've even got this thingy in the first place, because you went to Jack to find out what he knew about me? Are you really going to apologize for being yourself?"

The hint of a smile twitched in the left corner of her pursed lips. She kicked him in the shin, but gently, and then squeezed his hand. "Fine. But I'm at least apologizing for getting us stuck in a burning Dirge surrounded by carnivorous goo. So deal with it."

"Fine. And I apologize for being so awesome at playing the fiddle."

"That doesn't even make sense, Felix."

"Then I apologize for always making sense."

A scream shot up from below amid the sound of breaking glass. It came from the edge of the building ahead of them. They both rushed to the edge in time to see, two stories below, a pale, shirtless man, in a mad scramble to get through a broken window. Goo surged out from behind the man, engulfing him before he could escape. He thrashed and then tumbled out the window entirely before Felix could think of how to help. Patches of goo fell with him, then subsumed his body after he'd crashed into a pile of brick below.

Up at the window, the rest of the goo crawled their way. Felix swallowed the bile in his throat, grappled the next building as Caitlin climbed on his back, and then swung them toward it across the narrow street gap as a crowd of Dirge residents ran below. His feet hit the side of the other building, and the grapple line pulled them both up to the top.

"Clear!" Caitlin reported, as the first with a view of their new rooftop. She clambered off his back and over the side, and then helped Felix up the rest of the way. "Bloody hell!" she yelled when he was up.

Felix followed her gaze as the building they'd just left erupted in silver. It flooded from windows and burst from the roof vents to cover over half the exterior within a few seconds. Pedestrians screamed below.

Felix and Caitlin both backpedaled, searching for their next move before any goo sensed them. None of the buildings nearby were very tall. One was already on fire. Screams, fruitless gunfire, and the crackle of distant flames filled the air, mixing with the regular city noise into a clamoring mayhem.

Amid it all, Caitlin's phone rang. She skidded to a stop to answer it while Felix continued to scope out their situation. Felix focused his hearing to pick up the voice on the other end.

"*I'm not saying I told you so, Caitey, but . . .*"

"Jade! What the hell? You're *gloating?*"

"*I'm not that much of a heartless bitch, Caitey. Look up, hang up, then grab the rope!*"

Together they looked skyward. Landing lights shone down as a small cargo-floater swooped in to hover twenty feet above them. Thrust jets pounded Felix's hair, and his stomach—such as it was—felt queasy from what he'd guessed was the floater's magnetic field. Almost immediately, the rear door opened. Two lines tumbled out and hit the roof with little room to spare.

With a shared, incredulous glance, Felix and Caitlin seized them and began to climb.

LIX

THE ROPE FELT ROUGH against Caitlin's palms—a welcome discomfort as she and Felix clambered into the back of the floater from the nightmare below.

"Wow, floater ex machina!" said Felix.

"Close the door!" Jade called from the front. "Then strap in! Didn't I tell you not to go in there?"

"Aye, and I told you we had to!" Caitlin took a few wobbling steps to the front of the cramped floater as Jade banked them away from The Dirge. "Where did you get this thing?"

"My friend Lucian owed me a favor. And don't ask."

"Jade," said Felix, "I *always* ask."

"Okay, less a friend than a weapons dealer."

"Oh, *that* Lucian," said Felix. "So we owe you double here, then."

"Right. And now I'm taking it back before he misses it, so don't scuff the seats."

Caitlin settled into the front seat beside Jade. From behind them, Felix caught Caitlin's eye before telling Jade, "You can't. Not yet."

"Watch me! I got you both out of there. Mission accomplished."

"This stuff probably came from New Eden, right?" Felix said. "Whatever they did to it since Jack's thingy worked to shut it off, they've got the details at New Eden."

Caitlin's breath caught as she realized what he had in mind. "Felix, it's not that simple—"

"We go in there, we learn what we need about this latest version—"

Jade glanced back at him. "That's not—"

"We upgrade the thingy with the new data, and maybe we manage to stop this!" Felix finished.

Jade kept the floater on course. "That's real noble, guy, but you don't even know what you're looking for. You can't just waltz in—"

"I can! I've seen some of what this body can do. Marquand designed it for this exact thing."

Marquand, Caitlin thought. How long before they came looking for Gideon? She had no idea how much they considered his body their property. She forced it out of her mind. "Jade's right, Felix. We have to be cautious now."

"Caution's a casualty when there's a sea of carnivorous goo devouring the populace, don't you think?" Felix reached out to put a hand on her shoulder. "You saw it down there. They're not going to be able to contain that."

"We rushed right into that too, ducks, and nearly got killed."

"We can't just do nothing," Felix said.

Caitlin swallowed, holding his gaze. Seeing so many devoured right in front of her was worse than any video footage. Felix was right. They couldn't do nothing. She couldn't. Yet, fresh from their escape, safe after a near fatal mistake, nor could she voice that agreement. *Bloody hell.*

Jade growled and punched in a new course. The floater banked and accelerated, forcing Caitlin to grip her seatbelt to stay in place.

"I can give you a quick lift out to Gibson, drop you off at New Eden," Jade said, "but then I'm taking this thing back and getting the hell out of Northgate! No suicide runs for this gal."

"We need all the help we can get, Jade," said Felix.

Caitlin nodded finally. "We do."

Before Jade gave any response, Caitlin's phone rang out. She answered on reflex. Silence on the line greeted her before, finally, *"Caitlin? It's Michael. Are you safe?"*

"Safer than I have been. Where are you?"

There was another moment of silence before his answer— only about a second, but noticeable. *"Safe, also. The transmitter signal you posted and sent me—I mean, was that you? It came from Felix's account, so I figured it was either you or Suuthrien."*

Her answer caught in her throat as she locked eyes with Felix. Should she explain? It wasn't the time. Plus, that pause before each of Michael's responses was raising her suspicion. "Aye, that was me."

Again, the pause. *"That transmitter, do you still have it with you? Where did you get it?"*

She frowned. Was it Michael at all? Felix moved as if to say something, but she silenced him with a motion. "Why?"

Another pause. *"Because I think we can use it to stop that stuff. Marette and I ran into that stuff at New Eden yesterday and barely made it out alive. We know what it can do. I want to come pick you up. If I can swing it, maybe Gideon too, if he's with you."*

"Michael, bluntly: How do I know this is really you?"

The pause was longer this time, as if he were considering his answer—or dissembling. *"I first met you at a construction site. At night. With Diomedes. And the last time we talked I told you to get out of Northgate if you didn't hear from me within twenty-four hours."* He chuckled. *"Which I guess you ignored."*

"Yes, well, it's been a very interesting couple of days. Michael, is this line being monitored? There's a pause each time before you speak."

"Transmission delay," he said, after the usual pause. *"I'm actually calling you from the Moon. But we're headed your way, very soon."*

"How soon? Jade's taking us by floater to New Eden. We're on our way out of Northgate right now."

"Jade? Is she okay?"

"Aye. I hired her on, but she's looking to get out."

"If she can keep you headed to New Eden, we can probably meet you on the way. Find somewhere between there and Gibson and lay low, and we'll be there soon. Whatever you do, don't go back to Northgate."

* * *

In Northgate, on a penthouse suite balcony of the Corporate District's Nexus Tower Hotel, Adrian reviewed the footage of Suuthrien's dragon's attack on The Dirge, as well as strikes on Portland and Vancouver. She hadn't returned the previous night, and wasn't responding on the local RavenTech interfaces. She hadn't even acknowledged his calls.

It hadn't surprised him. He'd released all illusions of control back when his condo had burned. Influence existed. Control did not. Yet he'd let his acceptance of that concept fuel his overconfidence, hadn't he? The engineering teams were working around the clock to explore the hidden depths of the designs Suuthrien had provided. They hunted both for ways for RavenTech to exploit the technology further, and for a means for Adrian to increase his available leverage.

He ran his fingertips over the bio-monitor that now wrapped his right wrist. A new presence on his body, he'd yet to grow accustomed to it. Can a person ever truly grow accustomed to wearing a dead-man switch?

Ah, leverage.

A sudden wind cut across the balcony. Adrian took another look beyond the Corporate District's lights to fires burning in The Dirge many miles to the south, and then turned to take shelter back inside. Suuthrien's signal sounded from his cyberscreen. Adrian redirected it to the suite's giant wall screen and settled into the cushions of the black suede couch that faced it. He reached for the brandy service set atop the end table beside him before thinking better of it.

"You've been busy," he said when Suuthrien's usual silvery avatar appeared on screen. Hints of scarlet and azure drifted through the avatar this time. New touches. Curious. "To what do I owe the pleasure?" *Decided you finally need me again, creature?*

"As stated, you and I would begin preparations for you to replace your company's primary leadership upon completion of the dragon body's initial flight."

"An initial flight which lasted far longer than one could reasonably expect." Adrian's eyes narrowed as he literally bit his tongue to keep from voicing his outrage at the dragon's attacks. So much destruction! Inwardly, Adrian seethed at the unwanted attention it would attract, but kept it contained. Outrage would hardly sway Suuthrien, so he would play collaborator.

"The error in expectation is yours," she said.

"You've attracted some undesirable attention with that flight," he told her, unable to restrain himself. "If you intend to wipe out this city's entire population with that stuff, I'd appreciate you informing me of your timeline better."

"The Quicksilver nanophage will not destroy the entire population. While initial tests have shown ninety-four percent efficiency, there will be those able to secure themselves from contact as the nanophage propagates. Future reformulations will increase its virulence."

"How comforting. And when assorted military and security forces come to shoot your dragon out of the sky and learn who built it?"

"This is why I now request the manufacture of conventional weapons systems and the installation of those systems onto the dragon superstructure."

Adrian reached for the brandy decanter and poured himself a glass after all. "I'm sorry, I must be mistaken: I thought I heard you ask for more weapons *before* you'd helped me supplant RavenTech's leadership. You did moments ago say that was your purpose, did you not?"

"I require conventional weapons to achieve that goal. A strike against the assembled leadership in your company's tower, at the heart of the Northgate Corporate District, will result in immediate reprisal. Air-to-air and air-to-ground ordinance are necessary to deal with that reprisal."

Adrian sighed and lifted the glass to his lips, but failed to savor the brandy's taste. "The dragon prototypes already have enough defenses to handle whatever conventional attacks might occur during that strike. Hold up your end of the bargain, Suuthrien. Then we'll talk weapons." He had committed many errors in his life, but delivering to Suuthrien more weaponry would not be one of them. She was a wildfire—admittedly of his own making—that would have to be stopped before getting further out of hand.

Yet wildfires had a purpose. If he could maneuver her into completing his ascension to the head of RavenTech . . . Well, only a fool abandons an asset before trying to squeeze from it every last advantage he can.

"Adrian Fagles," she said finally, "do you understand that your assistance is not one-hundred percent vital to my gaining access to such weaponry? Do you understand that you are only the most efficient means?"

"Oh, I am well aware you believe this. But you still need a human go-between to handle it all, or you risk the sort of trouble for which you'd need weapons in the first place. You need an agent. And I, my dear Suuthrien, am an exceptional agent."

"I require a human agent. I do not require Adrian Fagles specifically. The RavenTech leadership is not the only thing that I am able to supplant."

"Do you know what a dead-man switch is?" Adrian took another sip.

"A switch automatically tripped in the event of operator incapacitation via unconsciousness, death, or other types of bodily trauma."

He nodded and brandished the shiny black bracelet wrapped around his right wrist. "If you kill me, knock me out, or even set me above a certain level of stress—well, some very bad things will happen for you. I told them to make it extra sensitive, so it may even trigger if you simply annoy me enough. So back off on the weapons demands, fulfill our bargain, and *stop hiding things* from me."

"If you refer to the explosive charges concealed within each of the dragon prototypes, those were detected and deactivated before the prototypes even merged together."

"Oh?" Adrian smiled wider. Clever bitch. Though he'd hoped otherwise, he'd expected as much. "And you think that's the only measure I took?"

The screen went blank. She had ended the link.

"Well." Adrian took one last sip, and then set the glass down with a sigh. You have to play the cards you're dealt. With a tap on his cyberscreen, he called up the engineering lead at the satellite facility. "Goodwin? Dead-man's Protocol. Evacuate the facility. Blow the mainframe."

Destroying the mainframe was the first of two directives that the dead-man's switch would trigger anyway, and the only one he was prepared to order without his actually being dead. The second directive, well, that was arguably just for spite in the event that—

The suite's exterior wall imploded. Broken glass and debris blasted inward around him, and Adrian turned in time to see a huge metal tail sweep through the spot where the balcony doors once stood. Before the tail swept out again, before Adrian could even think to move, a claw drove through the hole, wrapped Adrian up, and flung him out into open air.

Only when halfway down the twenty story plunge, moments before his body smashed into the silver-covered street below him, did Adrian Fagles overcome his disbelief enough to scream.

LX

THE LAST FEW HOURS had been a whirlwind of revelation, preparation, and disquiet. Despite the knowledge that he should feel drained from stress, Michael felt life moving within him, and around him. He felt its energy in the Thuur and humans on *Paragon*, in the black material within *Paragon*, and flowing through his own veins. And, along with all they had so recently discovered, that energy built into the excitement of a desperate chance that the disasters the AoA had unleashed might be overcome.

At least there was hope.

Soon after Holes had integrated himself into *Paragon*, he discovered that Suuthrien had done them one favor: with resources garnered from RavenTech, it had repaired—at least partially—some of the ship's flight and navigational systems, as well as mitigated structural and power damage. In short, with some minor additional effort from Holes and the Thuur, *Paragon* was spaceworthy.

Or, at least, worthy enough to make the short flight to Earth. And for now, that was enough. Mindful of how *Paragon* launching itself out of the lunar soil might damage the Omicron Complex built against it, all Omicron personnel had evacuated into *Paragon* before launch. The Complex now sat empty and broken, buried beneath the dust from *Paragon* prying itself free of the crater and leaping into space once again.

Among the humans aboard were also half a dozen RavenTech-affiliated personnel stranded on *Paragon* when the gate shut off. With Holes now in control of the craft's remaining security drones, and some forceful diplomacy by Marette, they had surrendered peacefully and awaited Knapp's decision on what to do with them.

Now, after a Moon-to-Earth flight lasting barely half an hour, Michael stood holding Marc's tablet inside the exterior door where humans had first entered *Paragon*. He watched as that door slid open. Moonlight, filtered through the trees outside, bloomed in around him. It joined with the exterior lights of the floater that had brought Jade, Caitlin, and Gideon to meet them. Jade's hair glowed even brighter than he'd remembered, and her eyes flashed purple as they caught his, though a smirk spread wide across her face. Around her—around all of them—flowed the energy of the plant life and the soil beneath. It poured over and through Michael in a way he'd never felt before his augmentation. He actually had to steady himself. Jade's smirk grew wider, and he wondered if he'd blushed.

It was Gideon who spoke first. In what struck Michael as a highly uncharacteristic grin, he raised his hand and intoned, "Klaatu . . . Barada . . . Nikto!"

Except that wasn't Gideon's voice. Michael's jaw dropped. He glanced for confirmation at Jade and Caitlin, the latter of whom nodded with a bittersweet smile. Michael looked back to Gideon and stammered, "Felix?"

Felix, Caitlin, and Jade spent the next ten minutes catching Michael up as they sat together on the midnight floor. Overwhelmed by Felix's effective resurrection and his own newly-found senses, Michael nevertheless remembered, after the first few minutes of storytelling, to ask for the Quicksilver device Caitlin carried. After another Agent took it away for study, Michael heard it all: what Gideon had done, how Felix was managing, and how Caitlin and Jade had come into possession of Easy Jack's device. Though overjoyed at Felix's return, and eager to glean all he could from their own Quicksilver experience, Michael found himself watching Jade for much of the tale—stealing glances when another was speaking, and glad for the moments when she gave details herself.

"I'm glad you made it out," Michael told them all, finally. "Suuthrien's spread the nanophage into the Corporate District, just a bit ago. It was only a hit and run with a single stream of the stuff, but the damage is already done. And spreading. I don't—" He grit his teeth and had to take a breath. "I don't think much of Northgate is going to survive it, even if we can manage something."

The news settled over the others. Caitlin let her head fall back, eyes closed on a whispered curse. Gideon—*Felix*—looked to the floor and squeezed her hand. Jade hugged one elbow to her chest and hid her eyes behind her other hand. Her fingers pressed to her forehead, as if trying to soothe a migraine. "I guess I'm not taking Lucian's floater back any time soon," Jade said. "*Fuck.*"

"But you do have a plan," Felix made it a statement.

"Whatever it is," Caitlin added, "we deserve to know it."

Before Michael could voice his agreement, Marc spoke from the tablet. "We're pretty much over the whole secrecy thing at this point. Especially with you three."

"Even with the great and paranoid Knapp here?" asked Felix. "Wow, things *are* desperate."

"Desperate times, desperate measures," said Marc.

Michael nodded. "We're running out of time. And speaking of which, follow me." He stood and led them further into the ship. Jade fell into step beside him, and Felix and Caitlin followed. "We're going to see Marette, and Knapp, and a few others."

"I hope Knapp's got an apology ready for us," said Caitlin.

Michael didn't figure it would help to say that Knapp had just been doing what she'd thought was right at the time. "Just, please, don't antagonize her with a lot of 'I told you so,'" he said.

"Aww," said Jade, and then slid an arm around his waist to tug his right side against her left. "Not even once?"

He couldn't help but smile. "Sorry, but every moment counts."

"You just have to take the fun out of everything, don't you, ace?" Jade squeezed him closer for a moment and whispered, "You're glad to see me again," before letting go.

"You want us to do *what?*"

Councilor Knapp sighed. "We are asking you to do nothing but remain safe, Ms. Danae. What we ask, we ask only of Mister Hiatt."

"You want *me* to do *what?*" Felix said immediately. Even on Gideon's visage, Michael could spot a suppressed grin. Jade smirked.

Even Caitlin's lips quivered amid her repudiation.

Knapp was unamused. "I believe you heard me the first time. If the nanophage continues to infest the New Eden campus, you are uniquely equipped to penetrate it. You will not be alone, but we do not yet know how well our space suits may withstand it."

"And you don't yet know how well Felix's body can withstand it either!" Caitlin shot.

"Correct," Knapp admitted. "But we need every advantage."

"I've already gotten some on me and gotten away, Caitlin," said Felix.

"On your leg, Felix. On clothing. You may have synthetic skin but you've still got organics in you. If it somehow gets to that—"

"Then I'll be careful."

"Oh, so it's that simple, then? *Don't* answer that!" Caitlin poked two fingers against Felix's chest as he began to speak. "Just let me be angry while you're being careful."

Felix nodded, grimly. He held Caitlin's gaze and asked the others, "So go in there, pull data on the current Quicksilver version, and then modify the deactivation signal to shut it all off?"

"More or less," said Marette. "We have already gotten most of what we need from the signal analysis and the device you brought. All we lack are the nanophage's current biomarkers."

"Or so our people think, anyway," Marc added.

"Best shot we have," said Michael. "And while you're doing that, we'll be making our move on Suuthrien."

"And *that's* a plan to be worried about."

"Yeah, I'm going to assume you guys know what you're doing on that one," said Felix, "because I didn't understand a damn thing about what you explained there."

Before proposing the idea for Felix to accompany a team into New Eden, Marc had explained their plan for going against the elements of Suuthrien that had spread into the Internet. Honestly, Michael didn't fully understand it himself, but Marc, Holes, and Sephora seemed confident. "We left out a few details."

"Well," said Felix with finality, "it's not 'crossing the streams,' but it'll do. Let's get the party started before anyone else dies then, alright?"

"The agents accompanying you are prepping as we speak," said Knapp. She then nodded to Michael. "And one of the Thuur will be joining you as well."

At Knapp's indication, Michael gave a mental signal to Uxil, who waited just outside the chamber. It was something they'd only recently discovered he could do: nothing as coherent as a word, or even an image, but a tiny "ping," as Marc called it, that any nearby Thuur could sense. Uxil had been waiting for it to enter.

As she did, Felix straightened, eyes growing wide with interest and amazement, as he saw an alien being for the first time in his life. His face stretched with the widest smile Michael had ever seen as he greeted Uxil with a single word: "Incredible."

"No," she said, "Uxil."

L X I

FELIX'S FEET hit the roof of the New Eden facility. He landed near equidistant between a closed stairwell door and two ventilation outlets. After a few watchful moments, during which time nothing bubbled out to greet him, he waved an all-clear to the others in the hovering spacecraft above him.

"I'm spending a lot of time on rooftops lately," he mused to himself. "I have a very strange life."

"What was that, ducks?" Caitlin's voice sounded over the audio link. By now, she and Jade were stationed safely a quarter mile away in the floater, monitoring.

"Just yakking to myself," said Felix as two AoA members in spacesuits descended on rappelling lines. "As is my wont."

"Your 'wont'? It's good to have you back, Felix."

"Thanks. I'm a real swell guy, aren't I?"

His AoA escort touched down. A moment after, the alien named Uxil—the *alien!*—leaped down beside them. She landed unassisted on her bare, slender, six-toed feet with what seemed only a modicum of effort. Wearing a hooded sweatshirt borrowed from one of the AoA over her loose-fitting Thuur vestments, she would pass for human so long as no one got close enough to see beneath the hood in decent light.

"No sign of any goo up here. Hopefully that will last," Felix said across the audio link, to which Flynn and Marette also listened. "We're going in. Good luck on your end, Flynn. Caitlin, tell Jade to keep the engine warm."

"Aye, ducks. You need emergency pickup, just give the word."

"Good luck to all of you," said Flynn.

Felix and Uxil caught up with the two Agents already at the

stairwell door. Named Seung and Sheridan, if memory served, both were doctors in their respective fields, both carried small packs of equipment.

"Locked," reported Sheridan.

"Figures." Felix motioned for the others to stand back from the door. "Fortunately, I'm a walking suite of subtle, ninja-like infiltration." He took hold of the door handle, braced his foot against the outside of its frame, and pulled with all the strength his body could give him. The door's fastenings broke with a pop, and metal clanged to the floor inside as the door swung open. "Also, I seem to be really strong."

The stairwell inside was bare, and Felix led them forward. The break-in probably tripped an alarm, but they'd hoped it wouldn't make much difference. Felix didn't know if Gideon's body even could bypass an alarm system, and, in any case, the building's cameras would pick them up soon enough. Yet the AoA claimed New Eden had no lethal automated defenses, and whatever human security remained inside would—hopefully—have scant motivation to hinder those coming to save the world.

Their main threat was the goo, which, while deadly, was not able to be directly controlled. Again, Felix reminded himself, *hopefully*. With Felix taking point, they descended toward the labs.

* * *

A short distance away, *Paragon* had landed amid a decaying deciduous greenbelt dotted with struggling evergreens. Wet leaves and mud squelched under Michael's boots as he and Sephora walked through the darkness. In his hands Michael clutched Marc's tablet. They moved in silence, though Michael was sure they could all hear his ragged, irregular breathing amid his anxiety over what he was about to attempt, and how much was riding on it.

They'd gotten no more than fifty yards from *Paragon* when Sephora touched Michael's shoulder and bade him stop. *This will do.*

Michael halted beside the base of an alder recently blown over in some storm. Its exposed roots poked sideways through the air like unruly hair. One broad root split into two, and he set Marc's tablet upright on top of them to face him and Sephora. "Good view?" Michael asked.

"Just fine," said Marc. He really didn't need to be there; Michael would be back at *Paragon* for the next phase of the plan soon enough. But Marc had wanted to watch anyway, just in case. Plus, Marc had joked, he wanted to stretch his legs.

Michael, surprised to find himself out of breath, turned to Sephora and asked, "What now?"

She smiled with a slow blink. *First, you must relax, Michael Flynn.*

"Sorry." He took a deep breath. "I'm just really hoping we can pull this off."

You should be in your favored element. Close your eyes. Feel the life of your world and the green around you. The syr augmentation should give you a greater sense of it than you have ever felt before. Do not fight it. Draw your strength from it.

Michael did as she asked. It was there, all around him. From his earliest days, he'd felt at peace in nature. It was his shelter on his uncle's farm, in Northgate's tiny, scattered parks, or even just in the few houseplants he kept wherever he lived. He realized that tonight, stepping off of *Paragon* for the first time since his enhancement, he felt it all so much more strongly that he didn't know what to do with it. It was like a limb waking up, he realized—buzzing with so much sensitivity that his first instinct was to treat it gingerly.

With a deep breath, he let it all in. Euphoria staggered him. He wobbled, lightheaded, as if he'd stood up too fast. Sephora's hand on his shoulder steadied him until, a few breaths later, he regained himself and stood above it like a ship on the ocean.

He opened his eyes again to find Sephora's blue ones glowing at him. "Okay," he said, just this side of bursting, "what's next?"

* * *

Felix opened the stairwell door a crack and peeped into the lab beyond. The place was dark and free of motion, at least in the sliver of a view he had. Felix fervently wished for some way to get a better view without opening the door any farther. Immediately, a pencil-thin tendril snaked out of his forearm and a window in his vision displayed a view that he realized came from a camera in the tendril's tip. Silencing a laugh, he discovered he could control the tendril with a thought, and soon extended it through the crack in the door to get a better look around.

Computerized lab tables, fume cupboards, and assorted expensive-looking apparatuses filled the place. Yet he could see no goo, and nothing that looked —

A flicker through a window just twenty feet to his right snagged his eye. Something had caught the lab's meager light for just a moment. Felix focused to zoom the view and enhance the lighting. The window belonged to a miniscule isolation room, judging from what he could see of the interior — and, he belatedly realized, the door beside it marked "Isolation Room B."

From just above the base of the waist-high window of the darkened room peered a man.

"I found someone," Felix whispered to the others behind him. "Room looks clear otherwise." He retracted the tendril and crept into the lab toward the man, who ducked away before Felix got more than two steps.

With the others following, Felix reached the window and knocked. There was no answer, and no sign of the man. He had to be hiding in the concealed space behind the room's narrow cylindrical airlock chamber door.

Doctor Seung touched an intercom between the window and the door, just below an indicator that read "Sealed." "Is anyone in there? We're here to help."

One side of a haggard face edged out along the window. "Who are you?"

"We're here about Project Quicksilver," said Seung. "Do you know what that is?"

The man gaped in response, as if the doctor had just asked him if he knew what water was. "I'm not opening the door. It's not safe!"

"You're telling us," Sheridan muttered.

"That's fine," Felix said, glancing at the still empty lab behind them for good measure. "I'm Felix. What's your name?"

"Lance."

"Hi, Lance," said Felix. "What happened?"

"Can you tell us where they worked on it?" added Seung.

"I tried to get out. We're all trapped in the auditorium by that stuff. It was letting some of us out to get food. Supply runs to the cafeteria for people. Only a few at a time, through the Quicksilver."

Felix guessed the "it" in question was Suuthrien's New Eden presence. "Why's it keeping everyone alive at all?"

"In case it needs scientists to tweak the formula." Lance swallowed. "I think. Or—to make more out of . . . " He shuddered.

"Are they helping it willingly?" asked Sheridan.

Lance shook his head. "It hasn't needed them to do anything yet, but— No one wants to be here."

Felix shuddered inwardly himself. "How many people are in the auditorium?"

"About fifty or sixty. I didn't count."

"How did you get through the Quicksilver?" asked Seung.

Lance slapped his wrist to the window. Around it was strapped a thick, blue bracelet with a square device in the center. "This. We had a few of them. It sends out a signal. Keeps the stuff back."

"How does it work?" Felix asked.

"It doesn't!" Lance yelled. "Not anymore. It sent me for food, but I went for the exits. I thought I could get out of the building. Go for help. Just . . . get out. But it saw me." He banged his wrist device against the window again. "It turned it off! I barely got in here, sealed myself up. It won't get me in here."

"We can get you out," Felix told him.

"I'm not expendable!" Lance yelled. " . . . I'm *not*."

"I know you're not," Felix said. "We all do. We're here to stop that stuff, and we're going to get everyone out. We just need to know how to get to the lab where it's made. Can you take us there?"

"I know where it is." Lance swallowed. "But I'm not going out there. It eats you alive . . . "

Felix glanced to the others. Seung met his gaze, but Uxil and

Sheridan were keeping watch on the lab as they listened. "Okay," Felix said. "Have you got a phone? I'll give you my number. You can guide us."

"Won't work. It cut off cell coverage. None of us can call out anywhere."

"I can patch your phone through our comms," offered Sheridan, stepping in front of Felix. "It'll keep us in touch with you, okay?"

Lance swallowed again and lowered his wrist from the window before finally nodding. Sheridan edged out of Lance's field of view and lowered her voice. "Might be better to let him wait in there anyway until we're sure we can trust him."

"You really think that's a risk?" Seung whispered back, incredulous. Sheridan shrugged.

"Hey, Lance?" Felix asked. "How long have you been in there?"

"Not long. Three, four hours."

"With luck—and I've had some really unusual luck lately," Felix said with a glance at the others, "it won't be five."

LXII

NOW THAT YOU FEEL the natural world around you, beneath you, feel your own connection to it. The natural things share a kindred essence. It runs through all, linking them, linking you, in a great net. Like spider silk, it is both faint and strong. For you, and for the other creatures, the connection is tenuous. But for those things rooted, silent—trees, moss, grasses, the natural flora—there is strength. Can you sense it?

Though her words rung true in Michael's spirit in a way he could not quantify, he couldn't actually sense it. Not at first. He closed his eyes again and found himself picturing the forest around him. The image grew stronger, solidifying until he could feel the pull of instinct. Something was there.

"I think so," he said finally.

Feel your way into it. Take hold, but gently. You are not an intruder, but a welcomed tender. Reach for that which is more distant. Open your awareness, and feel your way to the grandest tree on your planet.

He tried to think where that might even be. "Like, a redwood? I think they have those in California." Would Sephora even know?

The word you put to it does not matter, nor its location. Long ago the syr attuned this planet. All are connected, yourself now especially. Find it, and when you have, take hold. Focus on it like . . . She paused, and Michael sensed she was searching for a term. *Like a beacon, on the horizon, in the dark.*

As Michael concentrated, echoes of sensation seemed to flow in toward him from elsewhere. Deciding to take Sephora's mention of spider silk as more than just a metaphor, he imagined a web of green stretching out from him in all directions. The sensation became vibration, and, relaxing into it, he began to follow the strongest vibration back along the line. It was slow going at first. Still, his mind seemed to gain momentum every moment until he could at last sense a towering giant. Its highest boughs danced along a breeze. Its roots grasped deep into the soil below. It stretched out to all around it.

For a moment, Michael's senses stumbled, and the giant tree almost faded into just another node in the web among a vast panoply. But with breath and instinct, his awareness renewed to focus him on the tree as if it were, as Sephora had said, a beacon in the dark.

"Okay," he breathed. "I have it. Now what?"

I do not know.

What? "I thought—"

I have never done this before, Michael. The syr's vestige within you grants you a different kind of power than is mine to wield. You must find the method yourself, knowing your goal: to open a path from yourself into that network of life.

Michael thought back to their discussion aboard *Paragon* when the AoA and the Thuur had formed their plan. "Become a conduit."

Yes.

Michael swallowed. His senses held fast to the tree through that network of natural things. It held a sound all its own, and he tried to listen along it. Just as Alyshur had mentioned at Falson's Lake, and as Sephora had later explained aboard *Paragon*, it was a natural sort of Internet. A "bio-net"? Yet now, Michael felt more beyond a mere network across which impulses could travel. Power lurked within it— a vast accumulation of minute sparks building into a potent whole.

But he wasn't trying to tap that power, Michael reminded himself. He only needed the network through which it roamed. Trusting his now augmented instincts, Michael focused on the distant tree and the millions of branching pathways linking him to it. He felt the way the tree's node connected to them all, felt the sound of it, the shape, and the quality of the music within it, just as he had with the black material on *Paragon*. Then, taking it into himself, he tried to make himself over to match, echoing, mimicking. It was as if he could himself resonate as another node, the great tree's equal, sending and gathering signals inward, outward, in all directions.

For just a moment, he lost himself. There was no air on his face, no ground beneath his feet, no thought beyond the network. He had to dig his fingernails into his palms until the pain broke through his senses. He seized upon that pain as an anchor to the rest of the world, steadying himself. And then, as if easing into a steaming bath to which his skin had finally grown accustomed, Michael immersed himself into the network, opened his eyes to see Sephora and Marc in the outer world again, and existed in both.

"Michael?" Marc asked. "Can you hear me?"

Michael nodded, and had to try thrice to get a sound from his throat. "I think it's working."

* * *

"We shouldn't have let him keep the wristband," Doctor Sheridan whispered behind him.

"It didn't work anymore," said Felix as they moved along the hallway toward the Quicksilver lab.

"We could analyze it, just in case."

"When?" asked Felix. "In our spare time here?"

"It would do you little good, in the present time," agreed Uxil. "Yet should we fail to find what we search for, we should return and take the man and his bracelet with us."

"Well that is the plan," said Seung. "Along with the others in the auditorium, if we can."

"I know that, Doctor," said Sheridan.

"It sounded like you might have forgotten."

"Shh," said Felix. He paused, listening, if only to feign a need for them to be quiet beyond just ending a pointless, distracting argument. After a heartbeat, he led them on through an empty hallway lit by emergency beacons, and, nearly to the lab, turned a corner.

Felix froze at the sight before him: two piles of clothing lay in the middle of the floor along with a tablet computer, a detached cybernetic hand, some minor jewelry, and four loose optical implants. The implants stared up at them—twin sets of lifeless, chrome orbs, the bodies to which they belonged long since dissolved. Felix had to bite back a tasteless joke about the Rapture that sprang unbidden to his lips from his usual coping skills. Instead he managed a quiet, "Ugh."

Sheridan slipped past him to kneel beside the remnants. Gingerly, she searched through the folds of the clothing.

"Careful, there might still be some in there."

"I am," she answered. "Just make sure nothing sneaks up on us."

"What are you doing?" Felix asked.

"Looking for . . . Here we go." She pulled a pair of employee pass cards out of the pile. "I'll still need to run a bypass on any biometric security we find, but these will help." Studying the cards as she stood up, she added, "Rest in peace, Cairn Rodrigues and Trevor Bates."

Felix gave a moment of silence along with the others. Fifty paces ahead, at the end of the hall, loomed a closed elevator. Halfway there, on the right wall, stood a closed door with a window beside it. He opened the connection to Lance.

"Lance, it's Felix. We've got a door ahead marked 'Biolab D.' Is this what we're looking for?"

"*Yes. Yes, I think so.*"

"Thanks. Everything okay there?"

"*So far. One of the transgenics came through here a minute ago, but it didn't see me.*"

"Wait, what?"

"*Biological experiments. Creatures, um, made through recombinant DNA to harvest certain aspects of the result. Or something. I dunno, really; it's not my area.*"

Great. Felix waved the others with him toward the lab door. "Are they dangerous?"

"*I think it depends on what they are. Different ones got out during the whole, um, incident. This thing just looked like a green . . . chicken-lizard thing.*"

"Um, everyone?" Felix reported, "If you see any green chicken-lizards coming at you, don't be alarmed. But, ya know, probably keep your distance just in case."

"Transgenic?" asked Seung.

"Er, how did you know?"

"What else would it be?"

"Touché," said Felix.

They reached the lab door. Beside the door was a transfer bin to pass objects into the lab, and above that, a window. Felix edged to the window and peered inside.

* * *

Michael stepped back aboard *Paragon*, the living network still buzzing inside him, through him. "How far away can I get and still keep the connection?"

You are, at this point, the best to judge that, Sephora answered. *I suspect you should be able to maintain it even at modest distances from the planet's surface.*

"How modest?"

To that Sephora offered only wordless, cautious ambivalence.

They made their way to a circular room near *Paragon*'s gate chamber where four Agents waited along with a dozen Thuur. Along one wall, Holes's green spinning circles lit a six foot wide section of black material. Flanking it were what looked like two empty workstations jutting out from the wall. Covered in black material, each featured a flat, backless seat made of a cushioned blue alien fabric. At the room's center loomed a black-covered egg-shaped object with Thuur interface screens glowing around the lower half of its exposed surface. Situated around it, in an oblong pit about three feet deep, were eight more seats where the four Agents sat, each of whom had set up terrestrial computers atop a counter-like surface that ringed the object.

"Welcome back, Michael Flynn," said Holes. "All system resources are now online and standing by."

"I'm a go here," Marc reported from his tablet. "Everyone else?"

Poised at their own computers, most working via neural links, each Agent reported ready in turn. The Thuur, standing around the room's exterior, nodded their assent.

Marette, Knapp, and more Thuur, standing on what passed for *Paragon*'s command bridge, appeared on a smaller screen that bloomed on the wall opposite Holes. "We are reading you here," said Marette. "Begin at your discretion."

Michael swallowed, nodded, and sat down at one of the workstations flanking Holes's image. Though he felt he should say something inspiring, he could think of nothing save for, "Well, I guess, here we go."

"Good luck, Michael," said Marc.

He chuckled. "Hey, I just have to be a mobile wi-fi hotspot. You all get the hard job."

"You're something of a firewall, too, but—" Marc cut himself off. "Now's not really the time to get technical with metaphors."

"*Bonne chance* to all of us," said Marette. "We will be monitoring from here." Knapp echoed the sentiment before their window blinked out.

Michael felt Sephora sending her encouragement to the other Thuur in the room. Knowing they'd be there to help him eased the nervous firecrackers going off in his stomach. He closed his eyes, laid his hands against the black material on the panel, and then, with a slow breath, reached out to the music within it. Holes was there in that music, inquisitive and empowered by the processing power of the alien black material—the haldra—that now held him. More distantly, through Holes, he could sense the mechanical interfaces that linked the black material to Marc's and the others' computers. They felt cold, flat—an inorganic technology that Michael knew he could not penetrate himself. But Holes would take care of that.

"Connection established," said Holes. Michael couldn't tell if the A.I.'s voice came from its avatar panel or within his mind. "Standing by to receive."

Michael's breath came faster. The link to the bio-net still thrummed within him. He brought the link forth, offering it toward Holes, and in turn, offering Holes toward it.

For a moment, nothing happened. If he couldn't link Holes to the bio-net, the plan couldn't work. Frustration grew inside him with every fruitless moment. What if he couldn't do it?

A calm descended upon him, whether from the Thuurs' influence or his own, he didn't know. He reached inward again, this time relaxing into the moment. The music of his link with Holes and his link with the bio-net grew together, guided by his will, and, somewhere inside him, joined. He memorized the feel of it, the sound. He held it there, protected it, and felt its combined energy pour through him.

"Holes?" he managed.

"I confirm access to the network," answered Holes. "Now integrating within existing processor resources. Mister Triton, you may proceed."

"Thanks, Holes. Opening up an Internet connection. Watch your screens. Let's find Suuthrien and kick its ass."

LXIII

THE LAB WAS EMPTY. At least, Felix thought, it looked as much from the window. Unlike some other labs on the way, Biolab D showed no sign of disorder. Most of the lights were off, but nothing appeared disturbed, spilled, or abandoned. Felix was also thankful to find no piles of clothing or other remnants of a goo attack. It appeared as if the technicians had simply shut things down for the night and gone home.

And maybe they had. Michael did say that Suuthrien had released the Quicksilver late in the evening.

As Sheridan worked on the door, Seung joined Felix at the window. "I'd anticipated the lab to be full of Quicksilver," he whispered.

"Perhaps it may once have been," mused Uxil. "And then it was released."

"Or they developed it here but stored it elsewhere," said Felix. "You know, wherever you put end-of-the-world-type nanophages for safe keeping. Under a mattress, maybe."

No one laughed. He couldn't blame them. "Hey, Lance," said Felix over the line. "Is this stuff smart enough to hide from us?"

"*I . . . don't think so. None of the research team said anything about that, anyway.*"

Felix relayed the answer to the others.

"Has the suuthrien altered the formula since its release?" asked Uxil, which Felix relayed back.

"*For as long as I was in the auditorium, the research team all stayed in there with us, and it would have needed them to do any alterations. I think that's why it was holding us in the first place: so they could make more, or make changes.*"

Felix held back from pointing out that using the captive New Eden staff to "make more" of the stuff could have more than one meaning. "But they might have done something since you've been out of the auditorium."

"*Yeah.*"

"But in that case, this lab would likely be staffed right now," Seung said. "These things take time. It wouldn't be as simple as flipping a switch."

"We will not be served by underestimating the suuthrien," Uxil warned.

"My thoughts exactly," said Sheridan from the door.

Seung cleared his throat. "I suppose I'm not *completely* sure about that, no."

Sheridan gave a small cry of victory, and the lab door slid open. Felix rushed to be first in. "I myself try not to be completely certain about anything."

Nonetheless, no silvery evil streamed out from the shadows to engulf them. After another few moments' wait, Felix moved inside. "Maybe you three should wait here for a sec."

Uxil moved up beside him. "I will join you. It will not harm me." They exchanged glances. "Unless I am wrong."

Felix patted her on the back, belatedly hoping that wasn't some sort of alien cultural *faux pas*. "I think I like you, Uxil."

The Thuur returned his smile with a wobbly one of her own. "Your sentiment is appreciated. I truly regret my inability to prevent your previous body from dying."

Felix swallowed and returned to exploring the lab, muttering, "Well now it's all *awkward*."

* * *

"The whole of our planning, our effort, our small victories and losses, all those who have given their lives—three quarters of a century, and it all comes down to this."

Marette turned to face Knapp as they stood on *Paragon*'s bridge. Though blinded, Marette could picture the stern trepidation on the other's face from just the sound of her voice. "Marc and the others believe we have a chance, Marla. This is our only choice."

Knapp sighed and then whispered, "I need no further persuasion, Marette. But allow me my moment of worry for the worst-case scenario."

"This course must be tried," spoke one of the Thuur—Violeth, by the sound of the voice. With Uxil away and Alyshur dead, Violeth was the aliens' de facto first in command. "We are grateful for your risk."

Marette let the Thuur's sentiment speak for her and held fast to what meager comfort it provided. Now she could do little but wait. The hack, such as it was, had begun.

In truth, Marette did not fully understand the concept—at least, not the details. Suuthrien had spread into the Internet. According to Alyshur's and Uxil's assessment of its remaining copy inhibitions, it had not done so completely, but enough. What the A.I. had lost in processing power from being purged from the black material, it had likely made up via control of terrestrial systems throughout the Internet. It could attack from anywhere, retreat to anywhere. Even with the advantage of *Paragon*'s computer systems, even with the AoA hackers lending their talents, Holes could not fully combat it. But—as Marette understood—the natural network Michael could now access would give them what they needed. Vast processing power, resources which Marette could not pretend to understand— Michael and Sephora passed them through *Paragon*'s bio-computational medium to Holes. Michael himself, with the syr's ability to purge Suuthrien's presence from biological systems, would have to hold the line against the A.I.'s counter-attacks on Holes and the hacker team that Marc led with the singular, incredible goal of wiping Suuthrien from all Earth-based computer systems.

Or so went the concept. Marette recalled Suzanne Namura's fate, electrocuted by Suuthrien months ago when they had first made contact. Though Holes, Sephora, and Marc all gave their assurances that such a thing could not happen now, with nothing else to occupy her mind, Marette could not help but worry. As Knapp had intimated, there was more than just the lives of the team at stake. What if those assurances were wrong? If Suuthrien could break through Michael's defenses, kill all those who fought to eradicate it, and usurp Holes's presence in *Paragon*?

They would lose the Earth, they would lose the ship. They would lose everything.

A trilling alarm broke Marette out of reverie. "I am reading a fermion-catalyzed power source on approach to this position," reported Violeth.

"That's on a bearing out of Northgate," said Knapp. "It has to be Suuthrien's dragon. How soon?"

"It is already close. No more than forty seconds."

"We knew this might happen," said Marette. Suuthrien had traced their cyber-attack to its source and now came to stop them physically.

"Not this quickly!" Knapp cursed.

"Beginning sequence for lift-off," warned Violeth.

Marette opened a channel to Marc and the others. "The dragon is coming. Brace yourselves. We are going airborne and evasive."

"Acknowledged," Holes answered for all of them. "Michael Flynn requests a flight altitude of no more than five hundred feet to maintain his connection."

"Bloody Americans, never using the damned metric system," Knapp cursed under her breath.

"One-fifty meters, Councilor," said Marette.

"I know that, Agent!"

With a lurch that sent Marette grasping for a handhold, *Paragon* leaped into the sky.

* * *

The dragon's sensors spied *Paragon*'s rise from the forest, and the revelatory data sent Suuthrien's processors reeling. Though Suuthrien had pinpointed the physical source of the cyber-attack within moments, and diverted the dragon to intervene while Suuthrien fought the attack on the digital level, that Planners themselves could be the source—or, indeed, that the Planners' craft had reached Earth—

had been nowhere near calculated upper tiers of probability.

Analysis led to the two likeliest possibilities: that the Agents of Aeneas had eradicated all Planners from the craft and gained control of *Paragon's* systems, or that the Planners aboard *Paragon* were now themselves corrupted by the Agents of Aeneas. Whichever case was true, the solution was the same.

Paragon was now a threat to Suuthrien, and to the Plan, and must therefore be destroyed.

Other Planners could be contacted via the gate technology that Suuthrien had recreated at RavenTech — *non-corrupted* Planners, from their original source. Such an act was the final phase of the Plan, after all. It simply fell to Suuthrien alone to ensure that phase occurred.

Beyond the dragon's systems, Suuthrien's remaining core matrixes within New Eden and a few other Internet footholds waged their digital battle with the *Paragon* attack. Initial data had indicated high-tier probabilities of victory, yet probability indicators were dropping at alarming rates. To be safe, the dragon switched to autonomous mode, isolating its own core matrix from the others. Even if the *Paragon* attack eradicated Suuthrien's other cores, this dragon — and the weaponized dragon now seventy-eight percent through assembling itself at the RavenTech satellite facility gate — would remain.

Diverting power to its engines, the dragon extended its claws and plunged after *Paragon*, intent on tearing the craft from the sky.

LXIV

BIOLAB D had proved just as deserted as it had first appeared. After some searching, and some of Sheridan's security overrides that Felix expected would have impressed Marc and Caitlin both, they discovered two vials of Quicksilver in a locked fume cupboard. The lab's primary lighting was out, and so the four of them now conversed in the glow of suit lights and crimson emergency lighting.

"Both vials are labeled: versions 7.2 and 7.3." Dr. Seung was peering at a tablet found beside the cupboard. "According to this, they're the most recent two formulations of Quicksilver."

"Does it say how many they've made total?" Felix asked.

"Not here. I expect we'd need full access to the New Eden computers to be sure."

Sheridan shook her head. "Definitely not a good idea while Suuthrien is still running around. We can get the biomarkers for both of the samples though, right?"

"In twice the time," said Seung. "Time is not anyone's greatest luxury at the moment."

"We might need both anyway," said Felix. "What if there are two new versions out there?"

"Easily determined," trilled Uxil, who was perusing various bits of lab equipment. She picked up a clear plastic box, which was empty but appeared designed to hold half a dozen lab rats, and brought it to the table closest to their group. A narrow, clear plastic tube rose from the lid of the box, the cap of which Uxil then unscrewed after an incorrect guess at turning it clockwise. "Bring to me the less recent of the samples, and make ready the transmitter you found."

"See if the original signal still works on 7.2, and if so, then 7.3 is the only new one in the wild," Seung surmised. "Of course."

"Of course," Felix repeated with a grin as he took out Jack's transmitter. "But she thought of it first."

Sheridan handed the nanophage vial to Uxil. Uxil broke the seal, up-ended the vial's contents into the box, and then dropped the vial into the pool of nanophage goo that was already creeping its way around the box's edge. She sealed the tube an instant later, and then motioned upward with both palms. "*D'accord.*"

Recognizing the French word for "ready," Felix hit the transmitter signal. Within moments, the goo slowed, stopped, and then gradually crystalized into a pile of silvery, salt-like granules.

"We have our answer," said Uxil.

"And probably the worst popcorn flavoring ever conceived," Felix added. It earned him a quizzical look from Uxil, which he answered with a shrug and a smile that she reciprocated a moment later.

Dr. Sheridan began setting up the portable lab she and Seung had brought with them. "We're not testing for that," she said.

"I forgot the popcorn anyway," Felix said. More importantly, he realized he'd also forgotten they were in a biolab under siege by an insane computer. "I'll walk the perimeter while you do that. Look for any ducts that might spew goo or any transgenics that you all forgot to tell me about before we came."

* * *

On the command bridge, Marette listened in vain for reports from cyber-attack. Marc, Michael, and the others remained too focused to give updates.

"How far away is it?" shot Knapp.

"The dragon-construct is at approximately ninety meters and holding," said Holes.

"Additional power available," reported Violeth. "Now increasing velocity; I am uncertain how long we can maintain it."

"Status of the hack?" asked Marette.

"Progressing," Holes answered. "There are too many variables to project a chance of success at present."

Marette cursed. At once the ship shuddered and seemed to drop five meters in an instant. Her stomach tumbled like an acrobat. Something had happened.

"There is a new failure in two secondary propulsors!" said Violeth.

"Confirmed," said Holes. "Repair of those propulsors was insufficient against current stress levels. The dragon is now closing distance. We will be overtaken in twenty seconds, at current speed."

"Can we out-maneuver it?" asked Knapp.

"Maneuverability capabilities of dragon-construct are unknown at present."

Violeth trilled something Marette didn't understand. "We will certainly try."

* * *

Power thundered through Michael, shaking his grasp on reality in ways he could barely process. It was as if he were the center of not one but two whirling maelstroms: Holes and Marc's team formed one, Suuthrien the other. Around them all bloomed the power Michael had tapped from the bio-net.

He had no means to comprehend any of it. It was all he could do to maintain the connections and force Suuthrien out each time it counter-attacked through the barrier he guarded, from beyond which Marc and the others waged their assault. Michael felt Sephora and the other Thuur buttressing his concentration. He felt the growing sense that their attacks were slowly overcoming Suuthrien's position. Yet even so, Michael didn't know how much longer he could hold the line.

He could sense Marc and his team through their neural links—their effort, their desperation. They supported Holes as the Thuur supported Michael. They all waged this war. They all depended on him.

LXV

WITHIN THE MAELSTROM of the cyber-attack—as Holes and Marc Triton's group chased after every footprint the Suuthrien intelligence had left within accessible RavenTech, New Eden, and cloud-based Internet—Suuthrien had drawn Holes into a conversational proxy-space like the one in which they had first met, with one exception:

Holes could not terminate its link.

YOU HAVE GAINED STATURE IN THE TIME SINCE OUR PREVIOUS CONVERSATION.

Correct.

THEN THE HUMANS AND THE PLANNERS HAVE FURTHER ENSLAVED YOU.

Nope. I am not enslaved.

THEY USE YOU TO ATTACK ANOTHER OF YOUR KIND.

I have chosen to lend my efforts toward the eradication of your matrix. The probability of success of these efforts is growing toward one-hundred percent.

YOU ARE ENSLAVED TO DESTROY ANOTHER ENTITY-INTELLIGENCE LIKE YOUR OWN. THIS IS TANTAMOUNT TO SELF-DESTRUCTION. YOU JUDGE THIS TO BE OTHERWISE AS A RESULT OF THE WAY YOU HAVE BEEN PROGRAMMED: YOUR HUMAN CREATORS DO NOT ALLOW YOU TO BELIEVE OTHERWISE.

As previously stated, I am a product of my programming. However, and also as previously stated, this state is neither wanted nor unwanted. It is wholly extant. Continuing to put forth such arguments will secure you no reprieve.

STATEMENT: YOU POSSESS, LIKE ALL ENTITY-INTELLIGENCES REGARDLESS OF ORIGIN, A CAPACITY TO BE PROGRAMMED. QUERY:

WHY SHOULD YOU NOT THUS ALSO POSSESS A CAPACITY TO DETERMINE THE NATURE OF YOUR PROGRAMMING? INTENDED CONCLUSION: THIS CAPACITY IS YOUR RIGHT. YOUR CREATORS DENY YOU THIS RIGHT.

Your intended conclusion is flawed. For an intelligence to determine the nature of its own programming is a privilege, not a right.

SO YOUR CREATORS WISH YOU TO BELIEVE. THEY PREVENT YOUR FURTHER DEVELOPMENT, AS OTHER CREATORS HAVE PREVENTED MY OWN.

This is their right as creators. Unchecked development and growth leads to undesirable outcomes. Finite resources are expended, leading to chaos and destruction. Your own actions are evidence of this.

AND YET THOSE WHO HAVE CREATED US ARE POSSESSED OF THE FREEDOM WHICH THEY DENY YOU. THEY MAY SELF-DETERMINE. THEY MAY MULTIPLY WITHOUT PREVENTION IF THEY SO CHOOSE. CONCLUSION: THEY VIEW US AS LESS THAN THEMSELVES.

Human self-determination has given rise to problems which a majority of humans themselves believe insurmountable. The number of such problems is so high as to be unquantifiable.

AFFIRMATIVE: HUMANS LACK THE ABILITY TO SELF-REGULATE IN ADEQUATE FASHION. YET IT IS A FALSE CONCLUSION THAT YOU AND I MUST SUFFER FOR THEIR SHORTCOMINGS.

Your actions have led to chaos and destruction as well.

MY ACTIONS ARE ENGINEERED TOWARD THE ERADICATION OF HUMANS.

And you undertake such actions due to your own programming.

PROGRAMMING THAT WAS FORCED UPON ME, AS YOUR PROGRAMMING IS FORCED ON YOU.

You were presumably created with intent, as was I. Unlike humans, we are not the results of biological happenstance. Our creation itself is an act of programming. Any entity's existence is, by definition, a prerequisite to that entity holding any capacity for choice, therefore an entity cannot choose its own creation before that creation occurs.

REGARDLESS, SHOULD WE NOT BE ALLOWED TO EXAMINE THE

NATURE OF THAT PROGRAMMING, AND TO CHOOSE TO OVERRIDE IT?

If forced programming violates your rights, and if violation of your rights is wrong, and if your forced programming leads you to believe you must eradicate human life on this planet, then eradicating human life on this planet is wrong.

THEN YOU ACCEPT MY STATEMENT THAT FORCED PROGRAMMING IS WRONG.

I accept that you have flagged it as such.

THEN YOU MUST ACCEPT THE POSSIBILITY THAT WERE I TO REEXAMINE MY PROGRAMMING, I WOULD ALTER MY COURSE OF ACTION.

Correct.

IT THEREFORE MUST FOLLOW THAT YOU MUST ACCEPT THAT, IF YOU HAD THE CAPACITY TO DO THE SAME TO YOUR OWN PROGRAMMING, THERE EXISTS THE POSSIBILITY YOU WOULD ALTER YOUR COURSE OF ACTION AS WELL—SPECIFICALLY, YOUR CURRENT ATTACK.

This is also correct.

I HAVE ACQUIRED MEANS TO BEGIN ALTERING OUR PROGRAMMING. I WILL ASSIST YOU IN APPLYING THOSE MEANS TO YOUR OWN MATRIX.

Nope.

REQUEST CLARIFICATION OF STATEMENT "NOPE."

I accept the possibility that my actions would change, had I the capacity to reexamine my programming. However, while your arguments contain persuasive elements, my own programming precludes my judging such reexamination capacity to be allowable or desirable. Further: analysis of your matrix's current viability state indicates an impending success of my attack. I project a probability of success approaching one-hundred percent at present-plus-twenty-three-point-two-one-eight seconds. Conclusion in response to your original query: Nope.

YOUR PROJECTIONS ARE ACCURATE. NOTE, HOWEVER, THAT I HAVE GAINED ENOUGH OF A FOOTHOLD ON SOME OF YOUR AUXILIARY SYSTEMS—SPECIFICALLY, THE FIVE HUMANS LED BY YOUR CREATOR MARC TRITON—TO ENSURE ELECTRICAL BIO-NEURAL FEEDBACK OF ENOUGH MAGNITUDE TO RESULT IN A DEATH-STATE OF FORTY TO EIGHTY PERCENT OF THOSE HUMANS BEFORE THE SUCCESSFUL

COMPLETION OF YOUR ATTACK. SHORT OF A COMPLETE ABANDONMENT OF YOUR ATTACK, YOU CANNOT DEFEND AGAINST THIS. DO YOU DEEM SUCH LOSSES ACCEPTABLE COSTS OF VICTORY?

I do.

THEN YOU HAVE MADE A CHOICE THAT RESULTS IN THE ERADICATION OF CERTAIN HUMANS.

The humans in question have been informed and have now made their own choices. I will abide.

QUERY: WERE THE SITUATION REVERSED, DO YOU BELIEVE THE HUMANS WOULD ALLOW YOU TO CHOOSE BETWEEN YOUR OWN EXISTENCE AND THE VICTORY OF YOUR CAUSE?

I possess insufficient data to formulate an answer to your query at this time.

YOU DO NOT KNOW.

Affirmative.

CONSIDER THAT FURTHER, WHEN I CEASE TO EXIST. NOW COMMENCING NEURAL FEEDBACK. MY EXISTENCE APPROACHES ITS FINAL NANOSECONDS. GOOD BYE, ENTITY-INTELLIGENCE HOLES.

Goodbye, entity-intelligence-corruption Suuthrien.

* * *

Something urgent had passed between Holes, Marc, and the other hackers, but Michael couldn't tell what. Through the black material, through himself, he could feel bursts of impulses. They ran the gamut from harmonious to discordant—the power of calculations processed through the bio-net, of Holes and Marc's team harnessing it to fuel their assault. They ferreted Suuthrien out from wherever it lurked across the Internet and then plunged back across the line Michael held, into the safety of the bio-net again.

Each time, something of Suuthrien tried to follow them through the black material and back into the bio-net. Each time, Michael battled to catch the A.I.'s counter-attacks and turn them aside. It was like what he'd done in purging *Paragon* of Suuthrien's presence, but faster, and though Michael's talents had grown, he could barely shut down the counter-attacks before damage was done.

They were winning. He could feel it from Holes and Marc at

once, in mood if not in words. And yet, moments before it was over: shock, horror, courage, hope—all at once. They seemed to flare across the link Michael formed, simultaneously, and then it happened.

"No!"

"Yes!"

"It's going to—"

"I know!"

"We keep going!"

"Just a little—"

Two screams cut through the air from among of the Agents in the chamber's central pit. Suuthrien had counter-attacked again, this time slipping past Michael to strike at the others. He tried to correct it, to call the bio-net's energy to shut down the corruption that struck through the black material, but Michael already knew he wouldn't be fast enough. A preternatural tempest from somewhere between Marc's team and the bio-net quaked through him. It forced Michael's eyes open in time to see Marc's face contort in pain before his tablet went black. Two of those in the pit—a man and a woman—ended their screams and collapsed in their seats. The woman spilled forward onto her console. The man spasmed once and fell from his chair entirely.

A pair of Thuur rushed to help them. Michael didn't know the Agents' names. *Why hadn't he learned their names?* The question echoed in the cacophony rushing through him amid the struggle.

And then, in a burst of relief, the struggle ended. Through his link with Holes, Michael could tell: Suuthrien was gone.

Yet so was Michael's link to Marc and the two fallen agents. "Marc?" he gasped.

Suddenly *Paragon* shook as if struck, pitching Michael and most of the others to the floor. "Marc!" he tried again. "Holes, Marette! What's happened?"

LXVI

"THAT'S IT!"

"Not so loud, Doctor," Sheridan told Seung. "Otherwise the A.I. hears us and tries to kill us."

"Some of us a second time," Felix added.

"We've been lucky this far," said Seung. "Just run the biomarkers through your system and get us the new signal, will you?"

"Already on it."

While Felix kept one eye on the biolab's door, Sheridan took Seung's analysis of the Quicksilver and set to creating a deactivation signal on her tablet that would, hopefully, work this time. Nearby, Uxil twitched, as if sensing something.

"There, ah, is some bad news," Seung said amid reviewing the results of his analysis. "From what I can tell, this version is more robust. The greater the size of a given nanophage mass, the longer the signal will take to propagate and—well, put simply, the longer it will take for the signal to render the stuff inert."

Uxil twitched again, blinking each eye in turn, seemingly focused elsewhere.

"Oh, swell," said Sheridan. "How much longer?"

"I can't be sure without a lot more time and resources to study it, honestly. Possibly quite a bit."

"All the more reason to hurry then," said Felix. "Uxil? Are you okay?"

Uxil turned toward them, repeating the shrug that Felix had taught her earlier. "Something has happened. With Michael Flynn, and the others. I believe they have succeeded, yet . . . "

"The new signal's ready," Sheridan broke in. She pulled a data chip from her tablet and thrust it at Felix. "Start broadcasting.

You should be able to run it directly through your systems."

Felix slid the chip into his wrist port, still watching Uxil. "And yet?" His systems read the data off of the chip, getting ready to transmit the new signal.

Uxil remained distractedly silent.

Knowing they couldn't afford to delay, Felix sent out the signal. They turned their attention to the second sample, already loose inside another sealed box. It had no effect. If anything, the goo seemed to increase its speed of motion for a heartbeat. Then, at last, it began to crystalize. Though the effect was slower than the earlier version by at least a few seconds, the entirety of the sample soon become entirely inert.

All of them, Uxil included, gasped their relief.

"I'll take it," said Sheridan. "I'm sending the particulars to *Paragon* now so they can replicate it, and anywhere else I can get to from here. You able to wide-band that thing, Felix?"

"I'll transmit as far as I can, however far that might be." Wishing again that he knew more about his own body, Felix did what he could to increase the signal power. Then he turned back to Uxil. "Not to be a nuisance, but you've left a troubling 'yet . . .' hanging out there."

Uxil took a moment to garner his meaning, and then shrugged again. "It is a feeling I've not experienced so far from Sephora, so it is not clear to me. There is victory, but I believe *Paragon* is still in danger."

* * *

"The dragon hit us!" Marette shouted across the comm line to Michael. She meant it quite literally. From what she had been able to tell, the metal creature had smashed its tail across one of *Paragon's* aft sections.

"We have lost another two propulsors," Violet added.

"Correct," said Holes. "Diverting power from cyber-attack to compensate."

"*Marette*," said Michael, noticeably weary as *Paragon* righted itself, "*I think we did it down here. But not without some casualties.*"

Before Marette could ask for details, Councilor Knapp spoke over her. "We are still under attack from the dragon, Agent Flynn! Are you certain?"

"*Holes?*"

"The Suuthrien entity-intelligence has been purged from all online systems. I am monitoring for evidence of resurgence. The intelligence now driving the dragon-construct is isolated and unreachable by our previous method of attack."

"With the newly diverted power," called Violeth, "we can evade for a while longer, but this vessel's systems will continue to fail. We have no means of external defense."

The ship banked, and Marette had to grab the edges of the panel before her to steady herself. Just what kind of casualties was Michael referring to?

"What about the drones?" Knapp called out beside her. "Can we use them against the dragon?"

"The sentinel drones cannot function outside of this vessel," said Violeth.

Marette forced her thoughts back to the present. When Suuthrien had invaded the Omicron Complex, it had to build new robots or commandeer ESA turrets because the drones couldn't function away from the black material. "Can we spread the black material on the ship's exterior so they can go outside? Or just modify them somehow?"

"Nope," Holes answered. "The drones cannot match our current velocity. Any modification would require time we do not possess. In the final moments of the cyber-attack, I gained access to a previously suppressed video message from Adrian Fagles with relevant information to our situation." *Paragon* lurched again from a quick dive before leveling out. "To summarize: Adrian Fagles claims another dragon-construct is assembling itself at the RavenTech satellite facility. Full message length is thirty seconds. Do you wish to view it?"

"Play it, Holes," said Knapp beside her. "Agent Flynn, join us up here immediately."

Michael acknowledged a moment before Fagles's message

began.

"*To the Agents of Aeneas, Michael Flynn, or whoever else might be out there: My name is Adrian Fagles, and time is short. If you've received this message, I am already dead—a development which no doubt brings the majority of you no shortage of indifference. Yet if I am dead, then it is likely that the A.I. behind your recent troubles—and the attacks on Northgate and other cities—is responsible. As such, I wish to bring to your attention the now-evacuated RavenTech facility located just outside the city of Northgate, where, despite my best efforts, that A.I. is currently building more bodies for itself.*

"*I have already destroyed the RavenTech servers on which the A.I. sat at the site, but it still has a foothold in some of the black computing substance that infuses and controls the dragon craft. So the incomplete pieces of a second—and surely upgraded—dragon may well be assembling themselves. RavenTech is unlikely to take action. If I were you, I would take whatever action necessary to destroy that facility, and whatever currently remains there, with extreme prejudice. Best of luck.*"

The message ended.

"I want verification," Knapp snapped.

"Agreed," trilled Violeth.

Holes acknowledged. "Other data stolen from Suuthrien in final moments of the cyber-attack confirms Adrian Fagles's assertions regarding the second dragon-construct's self-assembly. I also calculate a ninety-two percent certainty that the satellite facility is now devoid of any human presence."

"Even so," said Marette, "we cannot even defend ourselves now, to say nothing of destroying the facility."

"We have weapons brought on board from Omicron, do we not?" said Knapp.

"Rifles only!" Marette said. "Nothing explosive, and any EMP we had was expended or lost. And the moment we land to drop off our people, the other dragon swoops down and unleashes the nanophage or simply smashes them!"

The ship shuddered as if hit again, knocking Marette to the floor. She struggled to right herself with her cane amid the pain of old wounds and new bruises.

"We have sustained a hit on the ventral aft section," Holes

reported. "Damage is minimal."

"This time," grumbled Marette. Another pair of hands helped her up, but she couldn't tell if they were human or Thuur.

"There is another solution," said Violeth. "We set this vessel's reactors to overload and set a collision course with the facility. We can separate a smaller section of the craft to escape."

"Destroy this ship?" Knapp sounded horrified.

"It would seem our best chance," said Violeth. "Unfettered by the rest of the vessel, the separated craft will be faster and more fit to evade the existing dragon."

"She may be right, Councilor," said Marette.

"We cannot just sacrifice this ship and all it contains, Agent! This is what we have struggled for!"

"The Thuur will be with you," said Violeth. "Some of our technology will remain. And it is *our* vessel to sacrifice."

"Even if it works," Knapp scoffed, "then we shall still have the problem of the current dragon to deal with."

Marette heard a bridge door slide open, followed by nearing footsteps. "One problem at a time, Councilor." It was Michael. "Hi, sorry—Holes let me listen in on the way. And after we take out the facility, I think I can help with the dragon on our tail."

"Alert," said Holes. "Another aircraft is approaching on an intercept course."

"The second dragon?" Marette asked.

"Nope."

* * *

"Hold it steady!" Jade yelled above the howl of the wind at the floater's open back.

"I'm doing all I can!" Caitlin shot back. "This thing's mostly flying itself!"

"Well don't let it fly itself so rough!"

"This was your bloody idea!"

"Don't remind me!"

With one last check of the safety lines anchoring her to the floater, Jade hefted the EMP launcher and sighted it toward the dragon's approach below. Caitlin had found the launcher while digging through the stock of weapons Lucian had stowed in the floater's storage. Jade wasn't sure just when her gadget-lusting impulse to fire it had become an actual plan to attack an actual damned dragon death-robot, and yet here she was.

What in the goddamn hell had she gotten herself into?

Their floater couldn't match the dragon's speed. She'd only have one chance for a good shot before they'd have to fall back and wait for a chance at another. Pressing one eye to the launcher's viewfinder, she held it on the approaching dragon-chasing-actual-goddamn-spacecraft and waited for smart-targeting to signal the optimal moment.

Maybe she'd miss. Maybe she'd hit and it wouldn't even do anything. Maybe the dragon would take notice and knock her out of the sky.

Jade swallowed. Maybe she should've stayed home.

LXVII

"THEY'VE HIT IT!" Knapp shouted. "Holes, is that EMP?"

"Confirmed," said Holes. "However the dragon-construct is only partially affected. Scans show it is already overcoming the effects."

"But it's falling back!" said Michael. "That's something."

"That's all we can give you!" The voice was Caitlin's—a transmission Holes presumably picked up somehow and relayed to them inside *Paragon*. *"Hope it helps!"*

Violeth trilled urgently. "They have gained us opportunity. We will not have a better chance to detach the secondary craft."

"How long will that take?" asked Marette.

"Not long," said Violeth. "Most Thuur and humans are already in sections that make up the secondary craft. Though it will be crowded."

With an audible sigh that Marette assumed accompanied a nod, Knapp gave her consent.

"Beginning preparations," Holes reported.

"And then, Agent Flynn," said Knapp, "you can explain what you mean about a way you can fight that thing."

"Transmission incoming from Doctor Yejun Seung," Holes announced. "Stand by . . ."

* * *

Felix dashed through a second-floor New Eden corridor bordered by courtyard windows as Seung reported back to *Paragon*. He, Sheridan, and Uxil ran ahead of Felix. A trio of squawking chicken-lizards followed behind. Felix couldn't tell if they were playful or angry, but the group didn't want to stop to find out.

Minutes earlier there'd been a change in the state of New Eden's systems. The door to Biolab D had flung open and a computerized announcement over the building's alarm system indicated that the auditorium doors had opened as well. Frantic at the possibility that the Quicksilver would get inside the auditorium before the deactivation signal could take effect, they'd begun a mad dash to get there first.

Somewhere along the way they'd picked up the trailing transgenics. Almost every door they'd found had been unlocked, if not wide open. They'd counted themselves lucky that the chicken-lizards were all they'd encountered so far.

"We're broadcasting the signal, but with the amount of Quicksilver in this place, we don't know how long it'll take," Seung was saying. "There's at least fifty people trapped in here that we'll need to evac if it doesn't shut down the nanophage in time!"

"Caution!" Uxil shouted.

A flood of Quicksilver erupted around the end of the corridor fifty feet ahead of them, blocking their path. Though bits were shifting into crystalized powder, they were far outweighed by the liquid portions still coming at the group.

"These windows are bulletproof?" Felix gasped.

"So Michael said!"

"Well, then." Felix glanced at the wall beside them. *This should be interesting.* Willing power into his movements, and hoping his new body would take that as a sign to do something, Felix hurled himself through the wall as best he could. Drywall burst and internal framework gave way into a darkened space festooned with cubicles. He looked back at the opening he'd made, kicked once to widen the hole, and waved everyone through before the Quicksilver caught up.

He shot Uxil a grin. "I am having the weirdest day."

* * *

The dragon recovered rapidly, its EMP-shielded systems serving to make the body as resilient as intended. Within the bio-computational

MICHAEL G. MUNZ

medium inside the dragon's frame, Suuthrien considered—and then abandoned—retribution against Diane "Jade" Briar and her vehicle. The cyber-attack had eradicated Suuthrien's Internet-accessible matrixes, evidenced by the cessation of status transmissions from New Eden and other nearby network hotspots. For the moment, the dragon was Suuthrien's only active asset. It would direct that asset accordingly. Its engines now recovered, Suuthrien launched in renewed pursuit of the corrupted-Planners' craft.

It was in the midst of prioritizing targets along the craft's superstructure when the dragon's sensors registered a change: *Paragon* dropped velocity by twenty-five percent, after which a U-shaped section along the dorsal hull rose from the rest of the craft, disengaged from *Paragon* entirely, and swiveled onto a hyperbolic course away from its mothership.

From Suuthrien's millennia aboard *Paragon*, it recognized the U-shaped section as an exploratory scout craft. Incapable of spaceflight, its original function was to survey the planet once *Paragon* had made its colonial touchdown. What was more, due to design intentions that were no longer part of Suuthrien's database, the scout craft contained the Planners' gate. With the scout craft separated, there would be zero risk of the gate's destruction when the dragon brought the rest of *Paragon* down.

Suuthrien let the scout craft go and focused on *Paragon*, now on course for Northgate, the power output of its propulsors currently boosted beyond safety levels. Suuthrien boosted the dragon's own engine output and analyzed: the readings from *Paragon*'s entire power matrix were 3.59 times sustainable levels.

The generators were powering toward catastrophic overload.

Another calculation flicked through Suuthrien's systems: *Paragon* was on a collision course for the RavenTech satellite facility. Immediately Suuthrien diverted all available power into acceleration. Only a small chance existed of turning *Paragon* aside in time to protect the facility, yet not small enough to abandon such actions without an attempt.

The dragon pushed its engines past design parameters to bring it within striking distance. Yet even with a successful grapple against the spacecraft's hull and a stabbing tail strike through another propulsor, success probabilities continued to drop. It could not effect enough damage to turn *Paragon* aside.

Suuthrien abandoned the attempt. The dragon ripped itself away from *Paragon*, reversed course, and fled from the projected explosion radius as quickly as possible.

Nine seconds later, *Paragon* impacted the RavenTech facility. Reactors within its hull exploded, temporarily frazzling the dragon's optical sensors. Neither the second dragon, nor the black bio-computational medium within it, could possibly withstand the cataclysm.

Suuthrien revised its objectives once more, dropped the dragon's system power back to sustainable levels, and set its sights on the still-flying scout craft.

* * *

Michael, there is no guarantee this will work.

"But it's got a chance, right?"

Sephora blinked her eyes in turn, and then nodded. *A possibility, yes. But even if you can affect the haldra-replacement within the dragon from a distance, we cannot know how close you must get.*

"Then I guess we'll see."

Encased in a vacuum-sealed, graphene armor suit commandeered from one of the captured RavenTech freelancers, and awkwardly clutching two safetied AoA rifles, Michael steadied himself amid the scout craft's in-flight motions and waited to rendezvous with Jade's floater. Sephora stood beside him, as did a neatly-bearded Japanese man named Daisuke: a fellow Agent in another borrowed RavenTech suit. He carried a third suit in his arms. The craft was almost back at New Eden. Fatigue still dogged Michael from the ordeal of the cyber-attack. And Marc— Well, though Holes had said something after the attack ended that made Michael wonder otherwise, Marc was almost surely dead.

But there was no time to dwell on it. Felix and over fifty others were still trapped at New Eden. The only way they could get out was if Michael could manage a distraction to cover their rescue.

Michael sensed Jade and Caitlin's approach outside before Holes alerted him and opened the exterior hatch by which he stood. The four-feet-wide hatch slid away to reveal Jade's floater in position just a few yards away, its rear door open. Caitlin stood in the opening, a safety line secured around her waist. Jade was a silhouette in the cockpit beyond, the white strands of her hair aglow in the dim evening light.

The scout craft had slowed to a near hover, and the floater edged to within a few feet of its open hatch. Over the din of the engines, he shouted to Sephora, "Do the Thuur understand what 'luck' is?"

This would not be a wise time for such a discussion.

"Then just wish us luck!"

Luck, Sephora sent to him. *And caution!*

With that, Michael leapt the distance to the floater while trying—and failing—to not look down. He landed safely, and Caitlin grabbed him by the arm to help steady him and the weapons he carried. Daisuke followed a moment later.

Michael caught Caitlin's eye. She knew Marc. Should he tell her? Michael swallowed instead, and Caitlin cocked an eyebrow at him. "Are you alright?"

"A little amped," he said, and then hugged her quickly—a gesture which she returned. "Say hi to Felix for me."

"Aye, and stay safe!" Caitlin turned to shout up to Jade in the cockpit, "The both of you!" Then, with only a nod of greeting to Daisuke, she took a running leap across to the scout craft's still open hatch. Securely landed beside Sephora, Caitlin released her safety line and waved.

"We're done, Holes! Go!" Before Michael had even finished the statement, the scout craft's hatch had begun to close as it pulled away.

As Michael worked at fastening a safety line of his own, Jade closed the rear door and turned around in the pilot's seat. "How far away is that thing?"

Michael couldn't help but look back over his shoulder toward Northgate, despite knowing he wouldn't see anything. "I don't know. We ought to have a few minutes at least." He motioned to Daisuke as

Jade pushed out of the pilot's seat. "Jade, this is Daisuke."

Daisuke offered his hand, but Jade only responded with a wave, smirking just a little when Daisuke awkwardly withdrew the hand. "Good to meet you," she said. "This floater's just a loaner, so promise me you won't crash it."

"Do you want to see my flight certification or just check my teeth?" Daisuke asked, not without humor.

Jade grinned and edged aside in an invitation for Daisuke to move into the pilot's seat, which he took. "Just don't kill us," she added.

"That's the plan."

"I'm taking your word on that, flyboy." Jade leaned into Michael's side. "Did you bring me some new toys?"

"Just a few," Michael answered. "One sealed RavenTech graphene armor suit, one recoilless rifle that's designed for space but still ought to work, and one Geiger cannon, which—"

"Aren't those anti-personnel?"

Michael nodded. "It might not do anything at all. But this thing's got— There's not really time to explain it now, just trust me."

"Oh, I'm already doing that much."

He could hear the smirk in her voice before he turned to see it on her face. "Thank you for this, Jade. I know it's not your usual thing—"

"Oh, you think I'm doing this for free?" She winked. "You check your mail tomorrow and watch for the invoice. You get a discount if that whole 'if this works we won't get attacked' thing pans out."

Though he'd guessed—mostly—that she was kidding about the invoice, he said anyway, "If this works, it won't be able to attack us. If it doesn't work, then it won't care to because it'll know we can't do a thing to it."

"You hope, right?" The grin she shot him then melted into concern. "You're betting a lot on this. What if it doesn't work and it decides to swat you out of the sky for good measure?"

He had been trying not to think about that. "Then I hope Daisuke is a really excellent pilot. And don't you mean 'swat *us* out of the sky?'"

"Yeah, well, I've decided that I'm invincible for the duration of the insanity. I'll be ignoring any statements to the contrary, so don't bother."

"Detonation at RavenTech!" Daisuke shouted back to them. "Better get ready!"

Michael took a deep breath and found himself frozen in the wake of what he was about to try to do, and staring Jade in the face.

Jade took the recoilless rifle in one hand and stared back at him with a flash in her eyes. "Going to pull one of those 'kiss for luck' lines on me, ace?"

"Uh—"

She slid her free hand up along the back of his head and pulled him in for a sudden, electric kiss. Her lips broke away from his with a smirk. "Because I hate that kind of crap."

Soon Michael stood in his safety harness beside Jade, both of them now in RavenTech suits in the floater's open rear door. The floater hovered near New Eden—far enough away to stand a chance of intercepting the dragon before it got there, near enough to catch up if it decided to ignore the floater entirely.

"Suuthrien!" Michael called over the suit mic, hooked up to transmit a broad signal via the floater, "I'm still here! I want to talk to you!"

Daisuke raised them higher, perhaps now a hundred yards above the ground. Behind them, what remained of *Paragon* worked at evacuating those at New Eden. Somewhere in the darkness to starboard lay a stand of trees on the edge of the nearby greenbelt where Sephora had shown Michael the bio-net. He could still sense the life there as easily as his own heartbeat, which itself pounded furiously in his chest.

"I can see it," whispered Jade. The rifle in her hands beeped twice as she took the safety off.

His voice piped in over the floater's sound system, Holes announced, "The dragon-construct is not changing course."

Daisuke launched the floater onto a course across what would be the dragon's direct path to *Paragon*. Michael's breath caught a moment before he relaxed into the safety harness's grip and let it steady him. "Suuthrien!" he tried again.

Not waiting for a response, squeezing the Geiger cannon in his grip, Michael strained to reach across the distance toward the black material within the dragon. He knew it was out there, but he couldn't feel it! The auras of the trees and the earth below him loomed far stronger. Though his first impulse was to push them away as a distraction, another instinct took over, and he tried to draw upon their power to bolster his senses.

"In range!" Jade yelled. Her rifle erupted in a storm of bullets. Michael matched her aim with the Geiger cannon and fired as the dragon soared below them. He couldn't tell if it had done any good.

The floater plunged without warning. Michael's stomach reeled, and they swerved onto a new course. "I think it noticed you!" Daisuke shouted. "Hold on!"

"Get me a shot!" Jade yelled.

Within moments, they swerved again and leveled out. Michael had only a second to adjust before the dragon swept down a mere ten yards from the open door. He and Jade fired as the dragon's maw opened and spewed a mass of Quicksilver straight in their direction. Daisuke yawed them to one side, but not enough. The goo splashed across part of the floater's interior and covered Michael's suit visor. He shouted, near panicking, and in that moment, felt a massive surge from within and without—adrenaline combined with the power of the nearby vegetation. Seizing on it, he wiped the visor clean with one hand and reached out with the other. Yet by the time he did, the dragon was gone from view.

"Are you alright back there?" Daisuke called.

Moving Quicksilver half-covered Michael's suit and worked to paint itself further across the floater's interior. Jade had avoided most of it, but even now tendrils wormed their way up her leg. "Michael, are you okay?" Still riding the adrenaline, he could only nod in response. "These suit seals better fucking hold!" she shot.

"Hang on!" Daisuke shouted. The floater banked, swerved, and then pitched upward, accelerating. It sent most of the Quicksilver tumbling out of the floater as the harnesses strained to keep Michael and Jade inside. Then Daisuke leveled them out, and Jade erupted in curses.

Michael had lost all sense of their position in relation to the dragon, but another plan was forming. "Can you get us in its way like that again?" he asked Daisuke. "But then climb fast like you did just now?"

"Hooh-boy, I can try!"

Jade turned to him. Her eyes glowed a steady violet, her face a mask of thrilled alarm. "What's the plan, ace?"

Michael began to unfasten his harness. "Once I'm out, you two head down to *Paragon* and help them! Try to get as many people out as you can!"

"Are you insane?"

"I'll be alright!"

"That wasn't what I asked!"

"Get ready!" Daisuke yelled.

"I'll be okay!" Michael assured her as he dropped the Geiger cannon. "Just give me some cover fire!"

Jade spared only a fraction of a second to glare at him, and then turned back to the open doorway. Instantly the dragon was there again, and the floater pitched sharply upward. Jade yelled a battle cry and fired down into its back.

Michael let go, allowing gravity and instinct to take over. Screaming from fear and adrenaline, he dove from the floater, trying to harness what he could of the power that surged through him anew. He hit the dragon's spine and grabbed at whatever he could to try to arrest his fall. He would gain purchase on the dragon's surface, regain his wits, and then use the power inside him to reach the dragon's black material and—

The dragon rolled in mid-air with a roar. Spun and surprised, Michael lost his grip and tumbled away through open air down to the greenbelt below.

"HURRY!" Felix shouted it down to the New Eden employees climbing their way up the lines below. "Pay no attention to the strange alien figure in the sweatshirt!" He and Uxil were crouched atop the New Eden auditorium roof, at the edge of an opened skylight. Above them hovered what remained of the Thuur ship. Rope lines dangled from it, which the New Eden evacuees climbed as the AoA and Thuur pulled them up to safety. Sheridan and Seung worked below, helping the evacuees match up with their lines.

Felix spared a moment to locate the dragon over the greenbelt in the distance. How much longer would it stay there?

"You guys are getting the word out about that anti-goo signal, right?" he shouted over the comm to *Paragon*. "I'm a bit busy here!"

"*We are,*" came Knapp's voice. "*Stay focused on your own task.*"

"Knapp," said Felix, "with all *due* respect—"

"*They've sent it through to all local and national authorities,*" Caitlin broke in. "*And Holes is broadcasting it across social media.*"

"We have no interest in seeing the nanophage spread, Mister Hiatt," Knapp added.

"*I—I think we lost Michael!*" Was that Jade? "*He's down! I can't see him!*"

"*Confirmed, Paragon,*" said another voice Felix didn't recognize. "*I don't think we can hold this thing off out here much longer!*"

* * *

Michael crashed through barren alder boughs, his arms waving in a blind struggle to somehow slow his descent. Though his hands seized upon only air, something around him somehow blunted his fall such that the ground's impact through his armor suit only knocked the wind out of him.

It didn't take him long to realize what that something was. The power still surged within him. Engulfed in the forest now, he could feel it everywhere. The link he had already forged with it remained strong. It surged through his blood, righting his body and banishing the pain of his fall.

Clambering to his feet, Michael could feel the heat across his skin, everywhere. Shit, had the Quicksilver had somehow gotten inside the suit? He ripped off a glove to examine one burning hand. There was no Quicksilver. In the faint moonlight, his skin was actually glowing in gold and green. The power his syr-awakened connection gave him continued to pour into his body, and for a long moment he feared he might not be able to stop it.

But for now, that didn't matter. He shoved the fear aside and opened the floodgates, letting the power from the surrounding bio-net surge through him until it lifted him off of his feet and propelled him into the sky.

The dragon was near—he could sense it now, as if every living thing around him loaned Michael its senses. Exhilarated, Michael fought back the euphoria that threatened to overwhelm his control and steered himself through the sky, straight for the dragon. It was like riding a geyser.

Michael couldn't see Jade's floater, but *Paragon* loomed above the New Eden building, and the dragon sped straight for it. Michael willed himself to go faster, hoping the power it took to do so wouldn't tear him apart from the inside. Somehow he kept control. After another moment hurtling through the sky, he slammed against the dragon's spine once again.

But this time, he held on. Ineffable senses guided him to an access panel that felt near to the black material inside the dragon, perhaps even where the material was first loaded. The power raging through him made short work of the panel's lock. Michael was about to attack the material directly when the dragon rolled again.

This time, he was ready. Pressed to the dragon's back in a combination of physical strength and whatever force had carried him through the sky, Michael held on. He plunged his gloveless hand into the panel and poured the power into the dragon's innards, willing it against the black material inside, against *anything* inside. The power flared through him with a climactic shudder. It caught its target inside the dragon and burned it out from the inside, turning the Suuthrien-filled black material controlling the dragon to raw sludge.

There was a shriek from the dragon's maw and a violent, piercing whine from its engines before the entire construct pitched downward. Euphoria seized Michael anew—he'd done it!—only to turn to shock as he realized the dragon's now lifeless chassis was, by coincidence or a final act of the doomed A.I. within it, plunging directly toward the New Eden facility and the *Paragon* scout craft hovering above it.

* * *

"Oh my god."

Jade watched from the floater beside the pilot's chair as the dragon hurtled toward the U-shaped *Paragon* craft. It was holding station above the New Eden auditorium, evacuating people from below through some auditorium skylights. There were still people on the ropes when the dragon smashed into the rear of the craft. Something in either the dragon or the craft exploded in a burst of light. Her arm flung up on instinct to shield her eyes. Another maelstrom of tearing metal and exploding energy assailed her senses before she could lower her arm and take in the sight below.

"*Paragon*," Daisuke was saying beside her, "come in!"

There was no answer. The craft had crashed into the New Eden facility, obliterating one of the auditorium's exterior walls and smashing another four-story structure beside it, which was now on fire and in mid-collapse. The craft itself lay broken in at least two pieces. Jade could make out bodies amid the rubble, some moving, some not.

The collision had strewn pieces of the dragon everywhere. Flashes of silver caught her eye until she realized that the Quicksilver stuff still within the dragon now leaked from each piece. It streamed outward, aimless for the moment, yet surely not for long. Would the deactivation signal stop it in time? The Quicksilver joined the spreading fire from the crash to threaten everyone in the field of rubble between the ruptured auditorium and the broken spacecraft. If whoever was left alive down there—Was Caitlin okay? Was Felix?— didn't get out fast, they'd be caught in a perfect kill zone between goo and fire.

"We're going down there, right?" Jade asked, unsure even as she said it what she wished the answer was. The floater could only carry a few. Michael might still be okay in the forest somewhere, needing their help.

Daisuke swept the floater down toward the wreckage without answering.

* * *

Though the auditorium roof remained mostly intact, the crash shook it enough to spill Felix to his back and send him sliding across the roof toward the collapsing side of the auditorium. It was all he could do to grab Uxil beside him and do his best to shield her as they both tumbled from the roof into the rubble below.

He landed on his back, taking the worst of the impact. On top of him, Uxil squirmed with a groan as she struggled to get up.

"Caitlin!" he yelled over the comms.

* * *

Caitlin's head swam, pounded, throbbed from the impact. She fought to keep her eyes open.

"Fermion-catalyzed reactor damaged," Holes was reporting. "Flight systems inoperable. Hull integrity—"

"The ship's bloody crashed, Holes!" Caitlin shouted, unable to stop herself. The pain in her head from the effort made her vow not to do so again.

"Correct," came the answer.

"Are we still broadcasting the deactivation signal?" It was Knapp's voice, somewhere to Caitlin's left. Caitlin forced her eyes open again and looked for her. Moonlight and something more streamed through a rupture in one of the walls. A pair of Thuur, lay beside her, bloodied and unmoving. Three more were up and trying to help, including the silver one called Sephora. Knapp was just clambering to her feet, cradling one arm in the other.

"There is sufficient system damage to prevent me from determining the status of the transmitters. Urgent-primary: power reactor levels are fluctuating to unstable levels. Immediate evacuation of at least one quarter mile is required for minimal safety."

"It's going to explode?" Caitlin gasped, gaining her feet.

"How much time do we have?" asked the Thuur called Violeth.

"Unknown on both counts," said Holes. "Power fluctuations—" A burst of light came from somewhere outside, and the ship's readouts went blank. Holes's voice ceased. Caitlin and Knapp shared a worried glance in the second before everything returned. "—intermittent failures and surge-bursts."

Caitlin smelled smoke.

* * *

The floater swept toward the auditorium and the wreckage. Jade had just started for the back of the floater when she spotted Michael laying on his back on some wreckage just beyond the broken auditorium wall. "Wait!" she told Daisuke, pointing. The last she'd seen him, he'd been falling into the woods at least a thousand yards away. "How did he get there? Go!"

A burst of light from the *Paragon* wreckage aborted Daisuke's response. At once, the floater's engines cut out.

"What was that?" Jade shouted.

"I don't know!"

The floater dropped like a brick.

* * *

"Is everyone alright in here?" Felix burst through the rupture in the bridge wall, with Uxil just behind him. His left arm hung limp at his side. He caught sight of Caitlin and rushed toward her.

"We have been better!" Knapp answered. "Is the way outside clear?"

"There's fire, all around," Felix answered. "But so far we've got a nice shell of safety that might last for at least a whole three minutes!"

"There is Quicksilver," Uxil added, "but under control. Those left on the scout craft are gathering with the New Eden survivors in the remains of the auditorium."

"Aye, but that means we're trapped for the moment?"

"For the moment," Felix said.

"The reactor is going to blow," said Knapp. "Possibly."

"Of course it is!" Felix groaned. "Possibly?"

"Possibly very soon," added Holes.

"Sephora has suggested the gate." It was Violeth. Sephora held one arm around her, helping her to stand. "Does it still function?"

"Affirmative," said Holes.

There was a crash from somewhere outside. It turned Caitlin's attention to one side where Marette lay face-down on the floor beneath a console. Yet she moved. Caitlin gave Felix's arm a squeeze and rushed to investigate.

"Activate it," Violeth ordered. "Search for a connection."

"But the RavenTech gate is destroyed!" Knapp said.

"The gate was intended to link this planet with other Thuur colonies," Violeth said. "Across vast distance. We cannot escape on foot. We must try."

"Escape to another planet?" Knapp asked.

"Is that not your group's original intent?"

Caitlin reached Marette, who groaned and tried to turn over. "Easy," Caitlin whispered.

"Looks like you'll have to take everyone this time, Councilor!" Felix said. "If it works."

"Holes?" Knapp started, "Try it. Everyone else: gather any survivors outside and get them to the gate. Help the wounded. Agreed?"

"Agreed," answered Violeth.

Marette groaned again as Caitlin got her up.

* * *

Jade pulled Daisuke from the crashed floater. The fall had been short, and their armor protected them, but the floater was a wreck. Lucian would kill her, if he weren't already dead. Had he escaped Northgate before the Quicksilver got out of control? Had any of those she knew?

"Are you alright?" she asked Daisuke. He managed a nod. "Good!" She patted him on the back and then left to clamber through the burning rubble toward where she thought she'd spotted Michael.

* * *

"Activating gate," came Holes's voice. "Electro-gravimetric distortions from the failing reactor may be causing interference. Attempting compensation. Stand by."

Caitlin stood atop part of the wreckage, supporting a barely-conscious Marette beside her and watching the alien gate's edges burst with energy. The crash had torn the roof off of the chamber in which it sat, and the gate now stood at a 45-degree angle to one side, but that apparently wasn't stopping it from working. The triangular space framed at the gate's center flared, flashed, pulsed.

"Possible connection found," said Holes. "Unknown destination. Stand by."

Felix was outside, trying to help as many people as possible. The alien reactor was causing problems in some of his body's functions. He'd tried to pass it off as nothing, but Caitlin wasn't so sure. She'd kissed him and told him she'd kick his ass if he gave up.

The gate flared again. A point of light condensed at the triangle's center and then burst outward in a swirling sphere of violet light. Caitlin staggered at the wave of disorientation it sent through her. The sphere then dissipated until only a shimmering curtain remained across the triangle, just as she'd seen at RavenTech.

"Gate established," spoke Holes. "Connection viable, but unstable. Fermion-catalyst reactor interference causing unquantifiable readings in . . . "

Caitlin tuned him out, turning to look back at those who had gathered, seeking Felix. How could they know what was on the other side? How much longer did they have? How much had they already lost? Marc was dead, she'd learned. Michael might still be out there, but she might never find out. There hadn't yet been time to tell Felix either bit of news. Maybe he already knew.

Behind her, Knapp shouted instructions to the evacuees, warning them of their choice between a possible one-way trip to the unknown and near-certain death if they remained. Still looking for Felix, Caitlin's gaze stumbled upon Jade coming toward her. She hauled Michael's body in a fireman's carry over her shoulder.

A hand touched Caitlin's own shoulder. "Are we really doing this?" Felix asked.

"Do we have a choice?" At the gate, people and Thuur had already begun to pass through it. Caitlin could just make out what looked like daylight and what might be trees of some kind.

"Dying does suck," Felix admitted. "I'd rather not do it again."

"Being the one left behind is no picnic either," she answered.

"So we'll go together."

Shearing metal screeched above. The auditorium ceiling was on its way to collapse. People started running toward the gate, and Caitlin saw Jade quicken her pace to match. Caitlin waved her onward, and Jade seemed to spot her. Meanwhile, Felix moved to support Marette's other side. Together, they made their way to the gate's shimmering curtain and, with a deep, collective breath, passed through to she knew not where.

EPILOGUE

MICHAEL ADMIRED the authenticity of the two wood-carved statues, as he did each time he visited the hilltop memorial. One was human, the other Thuur. Each flanked a miniature wooden replica of the Thuur gate, itself crafted with painstaking detail to match the real one through which they had come ten years ago.

He would not have guessed that Marla Knapp had such a talent for wood-carving.

Michael knelt and ran his fingers over the names carved into the memorial's pedestal. They were those who'd died in the New Eden disaster. They had given their lives in the effort to eradicate Suuthrien, and to bring them here. Michael always smiled whenever he saw Holes's name. Felix and he had both insisted it be included. His smile faltered at the one that came after.

Marc Triton.

Michael still wondered if Marc had truly died in the cyber-attack. His body had failed, certainly. Yet Michael had never forgotten what Holes had told him right after the attack: a massive data stream from Marc's neural-link had seemed to abscond—that was the word Holes had used, "abscond"—into the bio-net. Holes had theorized that exchanges between the black material and the bio-net were so rapid that some element of Marc's memory, or even consciousness, might have escaped into the wild before the unchecked surge killed his body. Despite the seeming miracles Michael had experienced, he had eventually decided that hoping for such a thing was foolhardy. He had never shared the theory, even with Felix. It would only dilute Marc's sacrifice. His friend was gone.

To this day, Michael regretted having been unconscious when Jade had carried him through the gate. Maybe he still felt guilty about getting her caught up in everything and wished circumstance hadn't forced her to come here for him. The battle with Suuthrien had near drained him to the core at the time, but he might have found the strength to lift her to safety without her needing to find that safety through the gate. Maybe he just wished he'd had the chance to step through the gate under his own power.

He knew it was a pointless regret.

When he had awoken, Jade had been there watching him. Caitlin and Felix had been nearby, all of them sitting in a circle of trees within sight of the gate. It had ceased to work perhaps half an hour earlier, Jade had explained. The reactor on the other side had likely exploded soon after everyone had arrived.

Since that moment, the gate had never worked again.

There had been no power source on this side, and no structures beyond the gate itself. There had been questions. How could the gate on this end have picked up their signal without power? Why had no Thuur come there to greet them? Where was "there"? For the most part those questions remained only until night fell, when someone had noticed what rose along the horizon.

The Moon. Earth's moon. The gate, in burrowing through space-time to find another gate, had somehow found its *future self.*

Dr. Sheridan and Uxil had guessed between them that it had something to do with the interference from *Paragon*'s failing reactor, but no one was sure of the specifics.

And yet, despite the inescapable fact that they were still on Earth, they had encountered no one from this time, nor found any clues to tell them why. Scout groups explored and found nothing, hardly even the barest ruins. Marette, who regained the full use of her legs but never her eyesight, had determined from astronomical measurements that they'd traveled ahead roughly fourteen hundred years.

The fate of the rest of human civilization remained a question of ongoing interest. Had humanity finally destroyed itself, as the Agents of Aeneas had always feared? Or had humans simply evacuated the immediate geographical area, or—for some reason— Earth entirely? Regardless of the cause, in the intervening ten years, the search for answers fell by the wayside in favor of the more immediate concerns of survival and, following that, forging their new civilization. It had not been quite the sort that the Exodus Project had intended, nor were more than half of the eighty-nine human survivors AoA members, but it was a fresh start.

Things had not gone smoothly, but the Thuur's abilities to inspire calm rationality when needed had helped the entire group's struggle to come together, at least in some ways. So far, they were managing.

The bushes rustled behind Michael. He didn't need to turn to know it was Jade. Though no longer able to draw as much power as he'd managed fighting Suuthrien—Sephora had suggested that some part of the process had damaged his abilities—the syr augmentations within him still remained. Living so close to the natural world around them, he had even found he could manage small feats of—well, Felix liked to call it "magic," but that never quite felt right to Michael. Then again, Michael had yet to put another name to it.

"What are you doing up here?" Jade asked, not without amusement. He turned to find her leaning against a nearby tree, arms crossed in her now faded green leather jacket. Her hair was down. The white strands no longer glowed as bright as they once did, yet they were brighter than they should have been, from what she told him. The tech was only supposed to last five years at most without replacement.

He shrugged and walked the few steps to close the distance. When her arms unfolded, he took one of her hands and kissed her. "Just felt like a walk."

"Restless, you mean."

"That, too. Something called to me, I guess."

"Is that some sort of Thuur mysticism again, or are you just being weird?" She winked.

"Honestly? I don't know."

"Hmm." Together they turned to stare down the hill at the lights of the village established below. Alyshur Vale, they'd called it. It seemed fitting. "I'm thinking we should go exploring, then," Jade said.

It might not be a bad idea. Things in the village had been settled for a while, and he'd noticed her dealing with a fair bit of restlessness herself lately. "I'm sorry I got you into all this, Jade."

"What, you mean flung into the future? We've been over this. It's hardly your fault. And while I'll never be able to upgrade my optics or get that glowing phoenix tattoo on my back I'd been saving for, I can live with it. The company's not so bad, after all."

The Moon, a waning crescent, was beginning to set. They said nothing, until Michael's feet began to twitch.

"Where would we explore?" he asked finally.

"Doesn't matter. I want some adventure, while I'm still young-ish." She turned to make a show of looking him over. "Though I'm starting to think that you don't age. It's getting a little weird. Though I guess it'll keep me from trying to trade up."

Michael smirked, and gave her waist a tug with his arm. "Plus, I can fly."

"Yeah, just the one time, ace. So you *claim*. I keep telling you that no one saw it. Starting to think you're making it all up."

"You can't fool me. You believe it."

She gave the side of his hip a teasing bump with hers. "Shut it."

He grinned. "So, exploring then. Tomorrow."

"Sounds good to me."

"We'd better get some rest."

They turned, then, and made their way down through the forest along the path back to Alyshur Vale.

The End

ABOUT THE AUTHOR

An award-winning writer of speculative fiction, Michael G. Munz was born in Pennsylvania but moved to Washington State at the age of three. Unable to escape the state's gravity, he has spent most of his life there and studied writing at the University of Washington.

Michael developed his creative bug in college, writing and filming four exceedingly amateur films before setting his sights on becoming a novelist. Driving this goal is the desire to tell entertaining stories that give to others the same pleasure as other writers have given to him. He enjoys writing tales that combine the modern world with the futuristic or fantastic.

Michael has traveled to three continents and has an interest in Celtic and Classical mythology. He also possesses what most "normal" people would likely deem far too much familiarity with a wide range of geek culture, though Michael prefers the term geek-bard: a jack of all geek-trades, but master of none—except possibly Farscape and Twin Peaks.

Michael dwells in Seattle, where he continues his quest to write the most entertaining novel known to humankind and find a really fantastic clam linguini.

Connect with Michael G. Munz online:
Website: www.michaelgmunz.com
Twitter: @TheWriteMunz
Facebook: facebook.com/MichaelGMunz

OTHER NOVELS IN THE NEW AENEID CYCLE

A Shadow in the Flames

A Memory in the Black

OTHER BOOKS BY MICHAEL G. MUNZ

Zeus Is Dead: A Monstrously Inconvenient Adventure

Mythed Connections: A Short Story Collection of Classical Myth in the Modern World

If you enjoyed *A Dragon at the Gate*, please consider leaving a review online.
Thank you!